OF
THE

She approached, her white night rail flowing around her bare feet, her black hair spilling in wanton disarray.

He found no peace, no serenity in her now. Only the need of a man for a woman, for the surcease of passion shared. But she was still innocent. What would she think of the hot, desirous thoughts that set him to tossing through the night?

"Do not take me too lightly, Tabitha," he said. "I do not consider denial a path to heaven."

"What have I denied thee?" she asked breathlessly.

"What have you not?" His voice was as rough as the storm of unfettered emotion that whipped through his chest.

He claimed her mouth, punishingly, possessively, passionately. Her slight frame surged against him and he dove like a swimmer into a red-hot delirium, a drunken joy. Lost, and he didn't care . . .

Avon Books are available at special quantity discounts for bulk pur-
chases for sales promotions, premiums, fund raising or educational
use. Special books, or book excerpts, can also be created to fit
specific needs.

For details write or telephone the office of the Director of Special
Markets, Avon Books, Dept. FP, 105 Madison Avenue, New York,
New York 10016, 212-481-5653.

HEART OF THE FALCON

DIANE WICKER DAVIS

AVON BOOKS  NEW YORK

HEART OF THE FALCON is an original publication of Avon Books. This work has never before appeared in book form. This work is a novel. Any similarity to actual persons or events is purely coincidental.

AVON BOOKS
A division of
The Hearst Corporation
105 Madison Avenue
New York, New York 10016

Copyright © 1990 by Diane Wicker Davis
Inside cover author photograph by Terry Atwood
Published by arrangement with the author
Library of Congress Catalog Card Number: 90-92992
ISBN: 0-380-75711-7

First Avon Books Printing: September 1990

AVON TRADEMARK REG. U.S. PAT. OFF. AND IN OTHER COUNTRIES, MARCA REGISTRADA, HECHO EN U.S.A.

Printed in the U.S.A.

RA 10 9 8 7 6 5 4 3 2 1

To
Pam Hart
and
Ginny McBlain

There is no treasure greater than a faithful friend.
Thank you

Chapter 1

April 1825

Black horses were out of favor among the Nobs of Society, so Robert Bragg Ransome, Viscount Langley, rode the blackest of black Arabians. With a playfully wicked gleam in his violet eyes, he had named it Sin.

Proper riding attire was *de rigueur*, so he galloped over the sandy heath *sans* frock coat, cravat, and topper. His long, muscular legs were sheathed in leather breeches. The tapered vee of his upper body was draped in a ruffled and frilled cambric shirt. His lustrous blue-black hair, its cherubic curls tangling with the balmy breeze, framed an angular face whose skin was burnt the color of toast by the searing sun of the foreign climes from which he had recently returned.

All of Society had rushed to London for the advent of the Season, so he rushed to the Surrey countryside just outside the environs of the City to escape the onerous duties and obligations his father considered "the divine rites of the gentleman"—among them, the duty to take a wife and sire an heir to the earldom of Darenth. Robbie would rather have been hung, drawn, and quartered.

The thought of a wife was not unappealing; the pleasure of a son was not one he wished to forgo. But they would put an end to his footloose wandering—and that

1

was one of the few things that could make him shudder in his highly polished Wellingtons.

His father, John Ransome, the Earl of Darenth, had never understood the son who was so different from him. Where he was a man of few words, Robbie was a man of many. Where he looked before he leapt, Robbie leapt before he looked. Where he found his strength in the roots of time and place, Robbie found his in incessant, unremitting, and preferably dangerous change.

Even now he looked forward to his imminent departure from England. The Turks had landed Egyptians in Greek Morea, and if he didn't hurry, the war would be over before he arrived.

Of course he had not told his father his intention. They had arguments aplenty without adding that faggot to the fire. He had, however, informed the earl that he would not be responsible for his actions were he introduced to one more simpering miss whose impeccable lineage was matched only by her dearth of wits.

Leaving a furor behind in London, Robbie had created another in the square and graceless Georgian manor of his country seat, Langleyholm, where he had arrived unexpectedly. The slumbering staff had been galvanized into action, a flurry of chambermaids scurrying about to whisk holland covers from the furniture and raise clouds of dust.

Robbie, sneezing, escaped that scene of domestic mayhem, collected his falconer, and set out to hunt . . .

Langley Heath was a desolate two-hundred-acre expanse of sand broken by thickets of gorse, clumps of heather, and patches of furze. It was shaped, Robbie said, like a woman with an hourglass figure, the narrow waist being a passageway for the heronry to the south.

"Leave it to ye to see a woman in a stretch o' good earth, milord," said the falconer, Simon Crumpp, a chuckle taking the dour note from his voice.

"Surely you can see it, Simon," Robbie persisted,

his violet eyes alight with laughter. "The bosom there in the hills to the west, the hips in the spread—"

"Aye, and it's enough of that we'll have, milord," said Simon, with a fine inattention to Robbie's consequence. "It's my grandson acting as cadger for ye"— he cast a glance at the attentive youth holding the cadge of hooded falcons—"and he's of an age to be as randy as a goat."

Robbie looked at the boy, who blushed to the roots of his straw-colored hair. "Sym, I shall expect you to lead your grandfather as merry a chase as I led him."

Sym grinned, until his grandfather grunted, "Humph! He's not above getting a hiding with a willow switch."

"Nor was I at his age." Robbie propped his gauntleted hand on his thigh, lush ebony lashes narrowing his eyes against the sun's glare. "But I never understood whether I got that hiding for being caught in the hayloft with the milkmaid or for forgetting to wash down the mews."

"Both, milord," said Simon comfortably. "There's naught like a willow switch to impress a lesson."

"Well, it's true enough that I never forgot to wash down the mews again. As for the other—"

"Aye, ye were a rackety lad, milord, and ye've made a rackety man. 'Tis wondering I am when we'll have us another lad of the manor to train to the mews."

"The devil take you, Simon!" said Robbie good-naturedly. "Are you in league with my father to see me leg-shackled and producing a string of mealy-mouthed brats?"

"Mealymouthed, with you as sire?" Simon's weathered face shone with amazement. "Humph! They'd be a string of rackety rascals that would set England on her ear once they were of age."

"Not," Robbie said grimly, "if you'd seen the tasteless morsels my father has served up for my choosing."

"Ah, well, milord. Ye'll need a woman like no other,

and that's a truth as any who know ye would swear to."

A woman like no other. Aye, that he would. Robbie stared across the landscape that was as thorny and prickly as he felt. In the distance a wood lark began to sing with clear, fluting notes. He was a man of light and dark, of sunshine and shadow. Could he ask any woman to endure the latter?

As if he had sensed that unspoken question, Simon Crumpp shifted in his saddle and settled a penetrating gaze on Robbie. "To my way of thinking, milord, the woman as can nail yer boots to the floor 'ull be doing the asking."

"You think so, Simon?" Laughter threaded Robbie's voice. "And what will I be doing while she's doing the asking?"

A glint of amusement starring his faded blue eyes, Simon Crumpp turned to his grandson. " 'Tis time to hunt. Hand up"—his glinting gaze turned to Robbie— "Samson and Delilah."

At dusk the weary cavalcade of three returned to Langleyholm. The cooling wind brought the faint soot-smoke smell of nearby London's chimney pots to infiltrate the vast park with its dainty-limbed deer nosing among the ferns and grottoes. The smell lingered far into the night, as if, Robbie thought, his father were summoning him back to a choice on the Marriage Mart.

After twelve years of restless, rootless wandering, he was unaccustomed to listening to any voice save his own. Home scarce a month, and he chafed at the strictures of fashion and Society and family. He'd have been away before now, but he waited to see his sister, Anne, who was due to arrive from the Continent at any moment with her family. Robbie could scarce believe that the hoyden of Darenth Hall was now a mother thrice over, a blissfully happy wife, and a princess—the Princess of . . . Schattenburg.

Like the relentless falcons diving on the graceful herons, memories swooped through Robbie's mind and spread a film of sweat across his brow. In the small library, he sprawled in a leather wing chair with his feet propped atop a stool. The ornate design cut deep into a crystal tumbler of Irish whiskey etched itself into the tips of his clenching fingers. Ruthlessly, he slammed the door on those memories, trembling at the dim, wordless screeching echoing through the corridors of the past that he dared not search.

He tossed back the whiskey, welcoming the fiery pool of heat that spread through his belly and scudded through his veins.

Lud! Would Anne never arrive? Neither she nor his parents would ever forgive him if he left without seeing her, but it was bitterly hard to abide the wait with any degree of patience.

A knock at the door came as a welcome intrusion on his thoughts. "Come," he said quickly.

"This was just delivered by a footman from Darenth House, milord," said his long-nosed butler, Thistlewood, proffering a billet on a silver salver.

Robbie eyed the creamy vellum topped by the family crest with some misgivings. If it was a demand for his return to the bosom of the Season, he might be tempted beyond resistance to take ship and escape.

Come at once, commanded his father's imperious script. *Anne has arrived.*

While Robbie urged Sin through the spring night, a stir brewed in the nursery of Darenth House. It was watched with bright-eyed interest by the raven roosting atop the tester overhead. The legendary guardian of the House of Schattenburg, the bird was never far from the prince she protected with her beating wings, sharp beak and needle-like claws. But this was merely a family squabble, and she leapt atop the pineapple finial to engage a better viewing point for the budding mill.

Prince Karl had lost his temper, a rare thing for so contented a man. Princess Anne had collapsed in a fit of giggles, utterly wrecking what little authority her

husband had established over their sons, two minia-
ture rapscallions. She was rewarded with a warning
glance from eyes the heady blue of cornflowers. He
obviously saw nothing humorous about a battle royal
waged with sweet biscuits as cannonballs, accompanied by appropriate sound effects.

The culprits stood at attention, their eyes as round
as coins and their silky black hair standing on end. The
youngest, five-year-old Franz, shot his mother a triumphant look that summoned a bittersweet memory
of her brother, Robbie, at his devilish worst.

"Did you see, Mama? Did you see? I got Karl right
between his peepers!"

Eight-year-old Karl swelled up in flush-faced wrath
and let fly with a fist. Franz, never willing to rest on
his laurels, eagerly accepted the invitation to brawl.

A moment later the combatants dangled from the
collars of their gowns, firmly grasped in their father's
hands. "Anne, you will excuse us, I am sure," the
elder Karl said in his most forbidding tones. "Your sons
and I wish to discuss the finer points of discipline."

Under the beseeching force of two pairs of eyes the
same silver-gray of her own, Anne lost all urge to gig-
gle. "And why, may I ask, are they *my* sons only when
they misbehave?"

"Because, sweet Anne," he said with a betraying
tremor of laughter, "that is when they are most like
you."

"Wretch," she said softly. "I trust you will not be
too harsh with them."

He flung her a speaking look that propelled her
through the door, tears of suppressed laughter shining
in her eyes and her small white teeth firmly clamped
over her lower lip. She stumbled to a chair standing in
the golden glow of the fire that warmed the Nursery
Parlor and collapsed with a squeaky arpeggio of giggles.

"Oh, Tabby, Tabby—" She gasped for breath and
turned a watery gaze on the Quakeress Tabitha Fell,

her distant kinswoman, her sons' governess, and her trusted friend. "What will we do with that man?"

Tabitha, comfortably ensconced in the adjacent chair, raised a peaceful, misty gray gaze from the neat stitches that mended a rip in a small trouser leg. "Friend Karl will never be a disciplinarian. Thee has long known that."

"He tries so hard." Anne heaved an unsteady sigh.

"And fails so often," came the soft pronouncement, rich with gentle humor and understanding.

Anne sobered. "He wants them to have the happy childhood he never had, one like that which Robbie and I shared."

"Thou art worried about him?"

"My brother, Robbie? Yes." Anne moved to the fire to warm her hands. "Father is convinced he is still the perennial boy in search of adventure."

"Some men remain so," Tabitha said gently.

"Mother believes he will be off on his travels again very soon. She says he grows more restless by the day."

"Perhaps she sees only what she fears."

"And perhaps she is right." Anne paced up and down, rubbing her arms and frowning. "He cannot be allowed to leave again."

"Thee wants him safe, but is that what he wants?"

Anne swiveled around, her eyes wide. "You've read his letters! He speaks of fighting Barbary pirates and fending off brigands in the Albanian mountains and being in the midst of an insurrection in Spain and a revolution in Portugal—all as if they were a good day's sport! The provoking man! He hasn't wit enough to keep himself safe."

"So thee will try to do it for him?"

Anne rubbed her arms, trying to chase away a chill. "He should stay in England, surrounded by the people who love him."

Tabitha laid her stitching in her lap. "Some men can be held close only by letting them go."

Anne, sighing, touched her shoulder. "Who will give

me such good advice after you leave us to wed at summer's end?''

"Listen to thy heart, Anne. It will never lead thee astray.''

And her own heart? Tabitha wondered an hour later. What was it trying to say?

The boys had settled down for the night. Anne and her beloved Karl were abed. The mending was done, and tea steeped on the hob. Tabitha took a cup from the cupboard, pausing for a moment to study the fragile bone china. One small finger with a neatly pared nail traced the exquisitely painted rose design. It was sinful to take such pleasure in beauty, for beauty was fleeting and sin everlasting, but somehow she could not believe that God would mind her weakness. He had created too much beauty in His world to frown on those who enjoyed it as He must.

If it was a sin, it was one she had shared with her father, who had taught her to accept all that life offered, the good and the bad, the pleasant and the painful. The only thing she could not accept was his loss.

Friend Ephraim Fell had been the best of men, one who daily practiced the Golden Rule by doing unto others as he would have them do unto him. No widow lost her lodgings and no child went ragged in the environs of the village of Lamberhurst. All knew that Friend Ephraim had a purse as ready as his laugh and a hand as open as his heart. Tabitha's earliest memory was of a bitter-cold winter day when a beggar, fed and clothed and warmed by the fire, repaid that kindness with the theft of her father's purse. She had never before seen a sign of dejection wrinkle his brow. She had never since forgotten the gentle hand her mother laid to her father's cheek or the soft bracing words she spoke: ''Thou art the best of men, Ephraim Fell. Do not be downcast. Mayhap he had more need of the coin than thee, for thou art rich beyond worldly treasures.''

He was, as they all had been, Ephraim Fell, his wife,

and fifteen children. Rich in love for one another. Rich in the love and respect of all who knew them. Rich in all but the modest prosperity that had been siphoned away by the depression of 1819 and the needy that came begging, never to be turned away. In the heat of that summer her father had lost his shop. In the heat of the fall he had lost his health, though he lingered for four more years. Four hard years of struggling to put food on the table, yet he never lost faith, nor did any of his family.

Tabitha carried the cup to the small table before the hearth and sank onto a child's stool, a rare frown wrinkling her brow.

Her oldest dream was to be joined to a man as good and kind as her father, to have a family as loving as her own. The man she was to wed, Friend Abraham Leeds, was just such a man, strong in his faith, a frequent speaker at Meeting, humble and righteous. Self-righteous? she had wondered when he obliquely blamed her father's openhandedness for the destitution of his family. If so, it was the only flaw in a man who was, otherwise, perfect for her.

She would lead the life she had always known and wanted. A life of simplicity and worship and good works, with children and gardens to nurture and love, with a hearth to sweep and chairs to polish and curtains to sew . . . and a man who never smiled.

Goodness and piety were more important than humor, but she could not forget her father's easy laughter. Though some, like Friend Abraham, frowned on levity, it had made the good times better and the bad times bearable. She could not imagine a life where every moment must be borne in solemnity.

The unease that grew ever stronger with the swift approach of her marriage shamed Tabitha. There was no reason to delay. The difficult times following her father's death were over. Her family was now comfortably settled at Darenth Hall, where her brothers worked on the home farm. They no longer needed the stipend she received as governess. Friend Abraham,

having patiently awaited her freedom from familial ob-
ligation, had now firmly set the last day of the Eighth
Month as the day for them to *testify*—to wed. Implying,
Tabitha thought, that he would brook no further delay.
She was eager for husband, for home, for children,
and yet . . . the unease persisted.

Had she been tainted by worldly longings? Riches
held no appeal, for they could not buy peace of spirit.
While she admired Anne's exquisite gowns, intricate
laces, and beautiful jewels, she had no desire to adorn
herself with them.

She was the same woman who had, after her father's
death, written to her cousin, the Countess of Darenth,
asking—not begging, for, in spite of her strong faith
and her family's need, she suffered the sin of pride—
if Friend Agatha knew of any in need of a governess.
She had explained that she was clean and neat and
quiet, and well used to children. She had further explained that she had received her education at the
Croyden School for the Society of Friends' daughters.
She could cipher and read, knew her geography and
her stitches. At the end she had appended the news
that Ephraim Fell had died as he had lived, in God's
love.

The countess, fearing that her distant cousin had left
his family destitute, came flying with her husband,
Friend John, in his spanking new curricle, with a cart
trailing and burdened with hams and jams and prov-
ender. Flushed and pretty, decked in laces and ribbons, she had greeted the austerely garbed family Fell
with assurances that all would be well, and, smiling,
noted the striking resemblance between Tabitha and
her daughter, Anne.

Soon, the family Fell had been removed to Darenth
Hall, and Tabitha had left for Schattenburg to act as
governess to Anne's two small sons. In the tiny German principate in the Neckar Valley south of the Rhine,
she found a worldly, princely family with as much love
as she had known at her own poorer hearth and a welcome she had never expected to find outside the Soci-

ety of Friends. Anne had become more friend than employer, confiding her concern for her brother. And Tabitha, with the sympathy that was born and bred in her for all who suffered, thought often of Robert Ransome, Viscount Langley. Too often.

She had become inexplicably fascinated by a man she had never met. Like his nephews, she listened by the hour to Anne's stories of her brother. While the boys wanted endless repetitions of the time Uncle Robbie served the Archbishop a grass snake on a platter, Tabitha's favorite was the time he broke his arm while returning a baby robin to its nest. Through every story ran a common thread: Robbie Ransome was greedy for life, brimming with eagerness and courage and laughter, yet exposed to every harm by the passions he could not control.

Who would have thought that his youthful desire to be in the thick of battle against Napoleon's army would have had such far-reaching consequences? He had been captured and imprisoned by his father's deadliest enemy, Prince Friedrich of Schattenburg. Anne, trying to save Robbie's life, had been forced into a treacherous game of treason and double cross by Friedrich's minion, Heinrich von Fersen. The Earl of Darenth, his father, had nearly been killed.

Yet all had ended happily. Robbie had been saved. Anne's beloved Karl had regained his rightful place as Prince von Schattenburg and joined his new monarch, the King of Württemberg, in repairing the ravages of the Napoleonic Wars on the German states. After twelve years, Anne's fear that von Fersen would reenter her life to wreak havoc once again had died.

But what of Robbie's fears?

At the ancient castle of Schattenburg, Tabitha had explored the tiny crypt where he had been imprisoned. The cold stone walls, slippery with mold, seemed to have absorbed his torment and reflected it back to her. No man could have lived in that darkness and damp for more than a year without carrying the scars on his heart and soul forever after. Especially not a man like

Robert Ransome, who had, as his father complained, tolerated no restraint since he took his first unsteady step.

Was that why he had taken such a hold on her thoughts? Because he gave vent to the passions she struggled so hard to suppress?

While Tabitha wondered about Robert Ransome, he was stabling his horse behind his bachelor lodgings in Ryder Street, racing across the dew-laden back garden, and taking the stairs two at a time, his violet eyes burning with passion. The passionate desire to escape England and its attendant ties to his family, his duties, and his obligations. That flaw in his character resided in his heart, uneasily yoked to his equally passionate love of his family. He sometimes thought his imprisonment in Schattenburg had changed him beyond recognition. More often he knew the change had been one of degree. Once, he had been made uneasy by the thought of being irrevocably bound to his duties as Viscount Langley and to the wife who would share his life. Now it made him wild, as furiously fearful as a newly captured falcon desperately fighting the shackles of jess and leash.

Not daring to appear before his father dusty and disheveled from the road, he flew into the parlor of his bachelor lodgings like a whirlwind, shedding his coat and calling for his valet. A furiously active few minutes later, Cheddar wailed that he had died a thousand deaths of mortification since he had been in milord's employ. Robbie had resisted a temptingly offered *Irlandaise* stock on the grounds that he had no wish to be throttled and wore instead a soft, unstarched silk bow *à la Byron*. Cheddar, considering it the last word in slovenly attire, puffed up like a sulky toad. The familiar skirmish left Robbie with a smile that departed abruptly when he climbed into a claustrophobic hackney coach.

He could have walked, but that would have meant yielding to his fear. So he sat with his back ramrod straight, disdaining to raise the leather window flaps, though a cold sweat filmed his brow and his breath deepened in a gasping search for air. He filled his mind with memories of sunny climes and wide open spaces, but still the walls closed in on him. Just when he thought he must tear open the door and plunge into the street beneath the expanse of the starry sky, the hackney rocked to a stop before the door of Darenth House.

His peremptory knock summoned the sleepy-eyed porter, an ancient family retainer who informed him that the earl was abed.

"But I was summoned to come at once."

"Aye, and no doubt ye were, milord." The man nodded, the pointed tail of his nightcap flapping against his sunken cheeks. "But ye see, the footman, he were sent wi' the billet nigh to noon—and, no doubt, he's had a devilish time trottin' after ye for the day—and here's the watchman callin' midnight and the bells ringin' fit to wake the dead. His lordship's abed, and her ladyship wi' him. But there was a ruckus in the nursery a bit ago what brung to mind many a time when ye was a rackety lad."

"My nephews?" He cast a curious glance up the stairs. Were they as much like him as Anne's letters had proclaimed?

"And two more like ye will never be born."

Robbie grinned. "A sight not to be missed."

The light of the porter's lamp falling across his handsome face, Robbie moved rapidly, taking the stairs two at a time. He expected to find a scene of disorder and mayhem. Instead, an aura of serenity pervaded the Nursery Parlor.

He paused in the doorway, captivated by the quietude radiating from the slip of a woman sitting in the fire's glow. A stark white cap neatly cupped her head, its narrow ribbons tied sensibly beneath her chin. A simple gray gown hugged the generous swell of her breasts, snugged about her slender waist, and draped the floor in deep folds around the small child's stool

on which she sat. She could be no other than Tabitha
Fell, that paragon of virtue Anne had praised in the
infrequent letters that had found him on his travels. A
woman whom his father, who had no respect for humanity at large, seemed to think was above any vice.
She was, the earl had commented cryptically, utterly
unique in the experience of his long life. Which Robbie,
with youth's scorn for the wisdom of age, interpreted
to mean she could not be matched for insipidity and
excruciatingly tedious saintliness.

He shifted impatiently, preparing to ask after Anne.

Tabitha Fell's head turned slowly, her profile briefly
etched against the fire's glow with its tip-tilted nose
and small, determined chin. There was a remarkable
family resemblance to Anne in the heart shape of her
face and the delicate arch of her black brows. But where
Anne's gray eyes were as bright as silver, these were
as soft as mist. Where Anne was ivory and rose, this
girl was peaches and cream. Where Anne was the scin-
tillating brilliance of sunlight, Tabitha Fell was the
muted glow of moonlight, bathing all she surveyed in
peace. A peace Robbie felt stealing over him with a
promise that all would be well.

Wry humor tugged at his mouth. Five-and-thirty was
yet too young to be developing the fancies of old age.

"Why do I think that thou art still capable of serving
the Archbishop a grass snake on a platter?" she asked,
her voice softly musical, each word measured and slow,
as if she thought carefully before she spoke.

The illusion of insipidity crumbled before her artless
smile. One Robbie answered with a smile of his own,
wide and reckless, sparkling in his violet eyes and crinkling the sun-burnished corners. "I see my reputation
precedes me."

"Anne speaks of thee often." She rose without
haste, a small, lissome figure that moved with the innate grace of unself-consciousness. "I am Friend Tabitha—"

"Fell. I know." At her approach, the sensation of

peace grew stronger. "My father speaks highly of you."

"So thee must think lowly of me?" she asked gently.

Robbie paused. He didn't like being so quickly—and accurately—assessed. "Isn't that the way of fathers and sons?"

"Some move shoulder to shoulder through life, leaving pride to trail behind, a shadow in the dust."

"For some of us pride is not the shadow but the substance," he said soberly. "I've known what it is to lose pride, hope, and faith. I should not like to be without them again."

"And have you rediscovered hope and faith? Or only pride?"

"A man is nothing without it," he said, frowning.

"If it is all that sustains him, he is nothing with it."

"Are we discussing theology or philosophy?" he asked sharply, stung to the quick.

"I would not presume to do either," she said with unfeigned simplicity, "since I am woefully ignorant of both."

Robbie was both cursed and blessed by a ticklish sense of humor. Even on so short an acquaintance, he could not imagine her failing to "presume." A smile spun slowly across his mouth, curling the corners, the startling white of his teeth contrasting with his sun-darkened skin. "Since it is beneath my dignity to come to cuffs with a woman, I recommend that you summon Anne to act the mediator."

"I pray thee will forgive me," she said softly. "I fear I have a hasty tongue."

"A formidable weapon, indeed." He laughed. "I shall come full armored to our next engagement."

She gave him an odd look that set his heart to tumbling. As if she could see through the mask of humor to the pain beneath.

"Anne is abed, but I will—"

'Don't wake her. She will be weary after the Channel crossing, and I can as easily see her on the morrow when she is refreshed.'' He paused. ''I assume my nephews are asleep.''

''When it is quiet, they are asleep,'' she said, smiling. ''Would thee like to look in on them?''

''I shouldn't like to wake them,'' he said. ''Besides, I can see them on the morrow.''

''Only if thee returns before dawn. I am taking the boys to Darenth Hall for the summer, leaving Anne and Friend Karl to enjoy the Season here.''

''Then perhaps I should—''

''Of course.'' She took up a candle, gliding toward the bedchamber.

Robbie slipped in, his curious gaze probing the dark shadows draping the bed. The circle of candlelight crept across the covers, finding a small hand curled into a loose fist, a tiny face burrowing into a pillow.

''Franz,'' Tabitha whispered, shifting the light to the far side of the bed. ''Karl.''

Robbie stared at his nephew, seeing the cloud of silky black hair, the snub nose and pink cheeks and long, girlish lashes. ''They look like angels,'' he murmured.

''Looks, Friend Robert,'' she said, smiling, ''can be deceiving, as thee will see soon enough.''

''I fear I will not have that opportunity.'' He suffered a twinge of regret that he would have no time to spend in Kent with Anne's sons, no time to learn more of the disturbingly tranquil Tabitha Fell. ''I am to sail for Greece five days hence.''

''They will be greatly disappointed,'' she said. ''They have talked of nothing but their uncle Robbie since they learned that thee would be here.''

He could have sworn he heard disappointment in her voice, that he saw a regret akin to his in her eyes before she turned to lead him into the Nursery Parlor. She set the candle atop the small child's table, and his appreciative gaze slid over the gentle bell of her hips, the innocently seductive sway of her skirts. ''Perhaps I can get down to Darenth Hall for a day before I leave.''

''Then thee should be prepared to be peppered with

demands for bloodthirsty tales of fighting Barbary pirates and Albanian brigands.''

He grinned. ''Henry below said they were much like me.''

''Rascals cut from thy cloth, so thy father says.''

''I strongly suspect he did not smile when he said it.''

''Indeed, Friend Robert, thou art wrong, for Friend John spoke with fond recollection of thee as a boy.''

''I am too much the gentleman to suggest that you err, dear girl, but my father and I have been at odds since my first memory.''

''Perhaps he is willing to put the past behind him.''

Once, Robbie had wanted nothing more than his father's love and respect. Now a rapprochement would bind him, if only emotionally. Though he carried the past with him like an unhealed wound, he could not tolerate any ties that threatened his independence.

He flashed the smile that had won him many a feminine heart. ''I fear I must make a hasty farewell. Much more of your presence, and I shall find myself reformed beyond recognition.''

He raised her hand to his lips for Society's customary kiss of parting . . .

''I pray thee, do not.''

''Though I know I will regret it, I am compelled to inquire—why not?''

She left her hand quiescent in his, while her translucent gray eyes gazed directly into his with none of the coy flirtation he was accustomed to seeing in the women of his acquaintance. Unease crawled through him. He wanted to drop his gaze, to shield himself, but that would be as revealing as an outright confession of secrets and darkness and doubt. So he forced himself to gaze deep into her eyes, to see the purity and peace that both attracted and repelled him.

'' 'Tis a vain and idle custom, Friend Robert,'' she explained.

''But a pleasurable one, Friend Tabitha.''

''One that fosters perverse passion and vanity in the

giver and receiver, one that leads to excess pride and—''

''You fear adding the dram that sends me to perdition?''

A twinkle starred her eyes. ''Thy father says thou art an arrogant young pup.''

''He should know I come by that quality honestly.''

''Anne says thou art a devil with the ladies.''

''Modesty prevents my comment.'' He grinned broadly, his violet gaze dancing. ''And now that you have met me, Friend Tabitha, what do you say?''

Her twinkle died slowly. Robbie had been so amused, he was unprepared for the serious expression in her searching gaze. The unease returned full force, tightening his throat, shuttering the unruly emotions he kept so carefully hidden away.

Her hand turned in his, grasping it lightly before she released it. Her gaze fell, a delicate blush suffusing her cheeks. ''I think, Friend Robert,'' she said softly, ''that thee might be the best of men.''

An odd sensation fluttered in Robbie's chest, a lightness that he firmly tamped down. ''And I think, Friend Tabitha, that your heart might be too tender for your own good.''

Robert Ransome's disturbing presence lingered long after he had taken his abrupt leave. The air seemed to be charged with energy, like the sharp taste of an approaching storm on the wind. Tabitha Fell, a lover of quiet, peace, and spiritual order, was incapable of achieving any of them. Her thoughts led the way, impulsively trampling quiet and peace in a helter-skelter rush.

She had planned to meditate upon the fire, awaiting the divine presence of the Inner Light in the hope that it might rid her of the unease that assailed her. But her thoughts became insistently frivolous and light-minded, dwelling on the glint of mischief in Friend Robert's eyes, on the blue-black sheen of his hair, on the wayward smile that creased his cheeks and made her heart stutter-step before it settled into its steady, resolute beat. And those thoughts were followed by a sorrow that dwelt on the pain behind his smile and on the dark regions of his eyes where humor did not reach.

Surely in the light of a new day she would recover her equanimity. But, after a sleepless night, the predawn light found her thoughts still rattling like dried peas in a pod . . .

The chaise-and-four with the earl's crest emblazoned on the doors headed for Darenth Hall in Kent at a spanking pace. Tabitha would have suggested to Anne that the boys remain in London for a few days, but that would have meant breaking the news that her brother was leaving shortly. And that news should come from him. Far better to leave Anne and her mother in a flurry of anticipation and preparation for the ball planned at his family's London town house—on the night before Friend Robert was to leave. Far better that Tabitha hurry to her family, to the man she was to wed, to the life she had always wanted.

Yet the unease would not leave her.

Did she suffer nothing more than the normal uncertainty of a woman planning to join herself for life to a man? The same uncertainty her mother had confessed she, too, had suffered? And look what a joyful and fruitful union her parents had created.

Moving steadily closer to a decision, Tabitha felt her unease dissipating like the clouds of dust boiling up from the carriage wheels. Friend Abraham might not be a man of smiles and laughter, but he was dedicated to worship, good works, home, and family. They shared all that was important for the life she wanted. On some future day, with her husband praying at table and her children gathered around, she would not remember that she had once feared that something—something vital—was missing from her dream. At last beginning to anticipate her future, Tabitha focused her gaze on her charges with a loving light.

Karl, a smudge of dirt on his cheek and rips at his elbows and knees, bounced on the azure-blue squabs in an excess of high spirits, looking more like an urchin than the heir to a princedom. Franz, Tabitha's fingers curled into the waistband of his trousers, leaned through the window, hallooing at the postilion riding the rumble—the latest in a series of heroic figures he had found to idolize. How she could be related to these lively imps—though so distantly it was hardly worthy of note—was a source of constant wonder to her.

It was a blissful day. Lemony sunshine played over the green hills of Highgate and Hampstead. The air sparkled in the thickets of masts winding in and out of the trees that lined the Thames. The breeze turning the windmills on the Isle of Dogs carried the redolent green scents of England, of home. How much she had missed it: the songbirds trilling above the clattering coach wheels; the countrymen dressed in the colors of the earth they tilled; the hedgerows, bright with color and seething with life; rabbits peeking from beneath brier rose and bees humming around the hawthorns and hummingbirds sipping the nectar of honeysuckle.

"I'm going to be a postilion when I grow up." Franz flung himself back on the squabs, his black hair speckled with the dust of the road and his eyes shining with excitement.

Tabitha didn't remind him that in the space of a week he had decided to be a ship's captain, a soldier, and a king, for a small boy's dreams were as real as a woman's and just as capricious. "And honest work it will be."

"Tabby," said Karl, "will we catch salmon in the Darent like Uncle Robbie used to?"

"And fly his falcons, Tabby?" added Franz.

"And ride his gelding, Sin?"

"And climb from the schoolroom by the ivy?"

"And—"

"Enough!" She laughed, ruffling Franz's curls, reaching over to tap Karl's bouncing foot. "Thee will give me gray hair before the summer is over."

"When will we see Uncle Robbie?" asked Karl.

Before Tabby could form an answer that would not promise too much, the crack of a pistol shot shattered the peace of the day. The postilion screamed. The coachman shouted. The chaise-and-four lurched ahead. Impetuous Franz scrambled across Tabitha's lap and poked his head through the window.

"Highwaymen, Karl! Highwaymen!" he shrilled.

A musket ball whined by. Tabitha yanked him inside, pitching him to the floor and dragging Karl down with him. She threw herself over them. Highwaymen! But Blackheath had been free of them for years!

Karl squirmed beneath her. "Tabby, I want to see!"

"Thee will stay down," she said, her tone so calm it amazed her. She looked up and saw a villainous face keeping pace at the window, his musket pointed at the coachman's back.

"Stop!" His shout revealed the stubs of blackened teeth. "Stop, or I'll blow yer liver out!"

The coach began to slow, the huffing of the winded horses carrying clearly back to Tabitha.

"If I had Papa's dueling pistol—" began Franz vengefully.

"And I had his sword—" added Karl.

"Shh." Tabitha pressed their heads to her breast. "Fighting would gain thee nothing."

The coach rolled to a stop. The door flew open, admitting a cloud of dust ripened by the odor of stale sweat and the acrid smell of gunpowder. A feisty bantam of a man with greasy strings of hair poking out from under his hat grinned wickedly.

"We have nothing of value," Tabitha began.

The man's pale, cold gaze raced over her face, as if searching out every feature. At length, he nodded and laughed. "Oh, but ye do, and that's a fact."

Chapter 2

Bond Street came alive during the rush of afternoon shoppers. A street fiddler scraped a toe-tapping tune. The iron-rimmed wheels of a high-perch phaeton screeched around a lumbering dray. A tiny boy with a huge basket perched on his thin shoulders cried, "Hot muffins! Muffins all hot!" In the bow-fronted shops lining the footway, hatters, tailors, and bootmakers, hairdressers, perfumers, and jewelers prepared to cater to the gentleman's exquisite taste.

A taste only partially shared by Robbie, who rejected the starched formality of his elders and the affectations of the *ton's* youthful Pinks. His topper was cocked at a rakish angle, the brim tipping toward a lively eye. His frock coat rode his shoulders too loosely to conform to the latest mode. His soft cravat in the Mail Coach style—one that his valet, Cheddar, considered even more vulgar than the soft silk bow, *à la Byron*—blazoned his refusal to bend a knee to the current fashion.

He walked off his restless energy, for it was only at night, with the darkness reminding him of the crypt, that he must prove to himself that he could tolerate an enclosed carriage. Fortunately, he would not be tested by the uncanny Tabitha Fell. She'd be at Darenth Hall with his nephews by now. He would, he determined, get down to Kent for a day to show the boys the secret places that he and Anne had discovered, the fascinating nooks and crannies of the manor. And for a short while, he would enjoy the peace he found in Tabitha's presence. She was, after all, a cousin. However infinitely removed, that kinship made her safe as a nun.

He pursed his lips and whistled, twirling his amethyst-topped ebony cane, his signet ring of an unjessed falcon winking in the sunlight. He must contrive a moment alone with Anne. She could smooth the path of his departure with his parents, who would bitterly oppose it.

Anne had always been the island of calm in the stormy sea of the Ransome family, protecting him from his father's wrath and his own reckless lust for adventure. The lust that beckoned now with a curl of a seductive finger. A twinge of guilt gave rise to a fleeting frown.

At Darenth House he expected to find quiet preparation for a typical afternoon of receiving *cartes de visite,* of shopping, of riding in Hyde Park. What he found instead was an uproar.

Henry, the porter, gabbled of disaster while the few strands of grizzled hair topping his bald pate stood at electrified attention. Rumford, the minuscule butler, uttered a heartfelt "Thank God you've come, milord" and propelled him willy-nilly into the drawing room. His mother was slumped on the settee, her snow-white head bowed over a sodden handkerchief. His father paced before the hearth, a missive gripped in his hand as if it were a throat he longed to strangle. Anne and Karl stood by like a pagan warrior and his Valkyrie preparing to do battle.

Before Robbie could greet them, his father spun around, his blue eyes like ice as he raised a crackling paper in his hard fist. "Will we never have an end to the suffering caused by your thirst for adventure?"

"Father!" cried Anne. "Robbie had nothing to do with—"

"Didn't he? If he hadn't insisted on going to the Russian front, he would not have been captured. If he had not been captured, you would not have been forced to—"

"Ancient history, Father," she said firmly.

"Is it? I should say," he added in a cold fury, "that it is as current as the front page of today's *Times*."

"Father, I pray you, don't—"

"Enough, Anne," said Robbie, his throat tight and dry. How quickly they had fallen into the familiar and painful pattern of his youth: his father attacking; his sister defending; and he, no doubt, guilty as ever. "What has happened, my lord?"

"This is a ransom demand!" The earl raised the missive. "Von Fersen, thinking he had Anne, has kidnapped Tabitha Fell."

Tabitha Fell, of the misty gray eyes, of the peace and serenity. Robbie clenched his cane, while rage came flooding out of the secret places of his heart, glittering from his eyes with an unholy light.

"Then he has made the last mistake of his miserable life."

The fashionables moving in the sunlight of their own consequence were unaware that London sprawled over an underground world. Burrowing through the earth, sealed off from above, were egg-shaped tunnels and ancient cellars of crumbling medieval brickwork, stone aqueducts and bathhouses from Roman times.

Bathhouses, like the one that entombed Tabitha Fell as surely as the crypt had once entombed Robert Ransome. Its only exit was the low door opening onto a slick-walled tunnel knee-deep in filthy water. Buried beneath the earth, it was a large chamber with a raised bath filled with the muck and mire of centuries, mosaic walls speckled with mold and damp, broad stone benches crusted with rat droppings, and corners that swallowed the light of the torch, vanishing into an infinity of darkness. The gaseous effluvia of the sewer thickened the air, stealing the breath from Tabitha's lungs as effectively as her two captors' hissing argument was stealing the strength from her knees.

She had been tossed onto the back of a horse, transferred to a rickety coach, driven into the City, and forced into the yawning mouth of a culvert that poured its sludgy contents directly into the Thames. Through the twists and turns of the sewer tunnels, she had been brought to this chamber. Not a single question had been answered. Not a word had been spoken by her captors until they reached their destination.

She still did not know what they wanted, and a riot of possibilities stormed through her mind. Even in her tiny village far from wicked London she had heard tales of innocent maidens stolen for sale to brothels or transported over the sea and sold into harems. Yet it made no sense. For that purpose she would not have been brought here. This was a hidden place for deeds that could not bear the light of day. For rapine and murder? she wondered.

Tabitha trembled like the droplets that gathered on the curved roof of the tunnel and dripped steadily, monotonously into the sluggish current. If Anne's father searched for her, as he surely would, he would never find her here. And she, hopelessly lost in the maze of passageways, would never find her way out alone. It was no wonder they had not bothered to bind her with ropes. She was as helpless as a child. And like a child, she blinked back tears and tamped down a longing for her mother.

The two men, small and wiry, with long faces seamed by hard—and evil?—lives, stared at her with kindred expressions of cupidity. One fingered the knife at his waist, and the other smacked his gums, as if he anticipated a tasty meal.

For one wild moment, Tabitha's terrified gaze searched the chamber for a weapon. For one wild moment, she forgot the teachings of her faith: acceptance, peace, and pacifism. The moment fled on a rush of shame. She could not take another life to save her own. It was against all she believed. Yet everything that was mortal in her screamed that she would use a weapon if one came to hand. Never had she realized how weak she was, how fragile her untested faith.

'' 'Tis a coker, Bert, fer sure,'' said the first man,

nodding his scraggly cap of ginger-colored hair and eyeing her up and down.

"And if hit ain't?" asked the second, scratching at his groin.

"Then we'll 'ave our sport and send 'er to roost and none the wiser."

"Shive!" shrilled the gum smacker in a whisper. "Yer daft as a March hare! If 'e thinks we slumguzzled 'im, 'e'll put us to bed wi' a shovel."

Shive, fingering his knife, scowled at Tabitha, the angry lines of his face demonic in the flickering torch-light. "Gi' us yer name again."

"T-Tabitha Fell," she answered, her teeth chattering. "Why hast thou t-taken me?"

"Shive"—Bert sidled up, plucking nervously at his companion's ragged fustian sleeve—"she sounds like one o' them Quakin' ladies. Blest if we ain't chalked it."

"Why hast th-thou taken me?" Tabitha asked again, desperately wishing they spoke a language she could understand.

"What were ye doin' in Darenth's rattler?" asked Shive.

"R-rattler?"

"Carriage! What were ye doin' in it?"

"I—I'm governess to the Prince—"

"Governess, Shive!" said Bert, dancing up and down in angry frustration. "We done snabbled—"

"Stubble it! Stretch yer neck through the door and see if 'e's come yet."

Bert approached the door on the scuffed toes of his ragged boots, bending over, tail up, like a rooster in search of a worm. He returned at a run, his face pasty white. "Shadwell, Shive! Milling-Jemmy Shadwell, like death's head on a mopstick!"

"Aye, 'e said 'e'd come cry beef in need. I'm blest if I'll stand blum. Let's hook it!"

They fled to the door, scrambling through and splashing away, leaving Tabitha ignorant of their intentions. But she did know that Shadwell's arrival had frightened them as much as it had frightened her, for Milling-Jemmy Shadwell had been Heinrich von Fersen's henchman when the German was forcing Anne to spy against her own country in order to save her brother's life.

If Shadwell was a part of this, then was von Fersen also? Had she been taken by mistake? If they had wanted Anne instead, what would they do to her when they learned they had the wrong woman?

She had to escape!

Tears of terror stinging her eyes, her heart throbbing wildly, and the sodden hem of her skirt dragging, Tabitha flew to the low door and stumbled onto the first of a trio of steps leading down to the water.

Echoing back from the direction in which her two captors had turned came the splash and splatter of their fleeing steps. In the opposite direction, in the distance before a bend in the tunnel, a torch flared with an oily yellow flame. Beneath it, a silhouette behind the mist curling up from the viscous black water, stood a man with a massive frame. Though Tabitha could not see them, she could feel his eyes on her. Those eyes Anne, shuddering, had described as "utterly without soul or humanity."

There would be no escape.

Slowly Tabitha slipped to her knees on the step. From dust she had come and to dust she would return—but not yet, she prayed fervently. She wanted to live.

How desperately she wanted to live. As desperately as Friend Robert while he had been walled into the dank crypt at Schattenburg? Had he, too, suffered this fear that gorged itself on hope and faith and humanity, leaving a quivering shell behind?

She closed her eyes, summoning a vision of him. Wanton black curls agleam in the candlelight, looking as soft and touchable as a babe's. Violet eyes luxuriantly fringed with ebony lashes and glinting with a surface humor that never reached soul-deep. A wide, generous mouth that had known both pain and laughter. But it was not his appearance she needed. It was his strength. The strength that had sustained him through the darkness and fear of more than a year.

He had survived; so could she. She needed only to cling to hope and faith, to believe as she had always believed that there was goodness in every man, no matter how depraved he seemed.

Her speculative gaze lifted to Milling-Jemmy Shadwell. Was there any goodness to him to which she might appeal?

His massive body quiescent and his thoughts as dark as the far reaches of the tunnel, Shadwell stared at the woman. In the netherworld of London's rookeries, he was a king because he felt no hope, no pity, no fear, no remorse. When men looked into his black eyes they saw an emptiness, an absence of humanity that forced either flight or submission. He'd learned his hard lessons early on: love no one; trust no one; look neither forward nor back.

"Why am I here, Friend? Why was I taken?"

Her gentle voice bounced from the sweating walls like the echo of long-forgotten thoughts. It was not familiar, and it should have been. Twelve years, yet he still remembered the authority in Lady Anne's voice, even when she was terrified, as she had been when they met on von Fersen's business. Shadwell's coal-black eyes squinted in the round moon of his face.

'Ad those cutthroat culls snabbled the wrong pullet?

Von Fersen would be in a rare taking. He was that desperate to revenge himself on Lady Anne. Not satisfied with a ransom, the German was as determined to murder her as Shadwell was to stop him. It wouldn't be good for business. Every Bow Street Runner, every magistrate on the bench, and every man jack of the Nobs would howl for blood. Profitable murder aside, her death would see his rookeries invaded, his network of thieves and cutthroats riddled down to nothing, and his comfortable living upset.

"Who art thou, Friend?" the woman asked.

WHO ART THOU, FRIEND? Who art thou, Friend? who art thou, friend . . .

The echoes whispered away, hissing as they fled. The coarse black hair on the back of Shadwell's neck stirred in a warning of danger. His eyes narrowed to cunning slits. She stood on the lowest step, the scummy water lapping at the riser inches beneath her feet. He could see the glimmer of her neat white cap, the pale smudge of her hand at her throat, but all else was obscured by the mist rising like steam from a cauldron. The sensation of imminent danger grew stronger.

Aye, ye're dicked i' the nob, Jemmy-boy. Ye could snap 'er like a rib bone.

"I pray thee, why am I here, what will thee do with me?"

Thee. The prickling at his nape became more insistent, as if tiny spades were at work on his brain, digging up a carefully buried memory like sack-'em-up-men unearthing a corpse. He shifted uneasily, his belly aquiver. Look neither forward nor back. Never back. Yet the memory seemed to be drawing strength, to be sliding out of its coffin, like a ghost come to haunt him.

"I pray thee," she began more insistently.

"Dub yer mummer!" he said low and hard, his voice pitched in a deep breathy rumble.

Robbie had exchanged his Bond Street best for a beggar's rags. In the dark of that night, he sat on the lowest platform beneath the sleeping giant of London Bridge, scratching at his ribs where the unwelcome tenants of his coarse linen shirt feasted on his flesh. The stench of nearby Billingsgate Fish Market was leavened by the coal-and-hay dust swept from river barges, by a driftwood fire and roasting potatoes and unwashed men. The refuse of humanity, they shivered in tattered rags, seeking shelter from the cutting wind. In the adjacent river, the tide foamed through the narrow arches, seething around the sturdy stone supports like Robbie's thoughts.

In moments the earl, following the detailed directions contained in the ransom note, would arrive carrying a small casket containing the money. The thought of his elegant father in this milieu would have amused Robbie if he could have rid himself of the vision of Tabitha Fell terrified and cowering, her eyes spangled with tears and her serenity shattered. Another dragged into danger because of him, but she, he swore, would be the last. Von Fersen's death would end it.

It was the perfect spot for the exchange of a ransom demand. Perfect for von Fersen, who might even now be among the men tumbling in restless sleep or gathered around the fire—and Robbie would not know it. He had never seen the man, nor had he been seen by him. A definite advantage if he was to succeed in stalking the German to his lair and rescuing Tabitha.

The plan was well laid. His boon companions, Audley and Lethbridge, more familiarly known as the Spaniard and Old Nick, waited on the stairs above, assuredly scratching in their borrowed rags as he was. Karl, too easily recognizable to their quarry, waited in a coach at the turning of Lower Thames Street, surely cursing the thoroughfares uprooted for the imminent construction of the new London Bridge. Darenth House footmen had scattered as lookouts. Not a mousehole was left to sneak through, yet Robbie was uneasy. Von Fersen had an uncanny knack for squirming out of traps.

Moonlight poured across the scarred toes of his stout boots, casting Robbie in deep shadow where he leaned against the wall in a counterfeit pose of relaxation. Quiveringly alert, he scanned the dark cavern of the platform with a fierce intensity that held equal parts of rage and anticipation.

Men slept against the back wall, lying in ranks like soldiers in a misbegotten camp. All wore the dun-colored uniform of the poor: heavy brogans, corduroy trousers, and fustian coats. None fit Karl's description of von Fersen: a small and dandified man with a cruel slash of a mouth and a wedge-shaped face. Nor did any of the quartet ranged around the fire. One was too young, another too old. A third was too large, and the fourth, though the right age and size, had a ghastly, pockmarked face.

Robbie studied him. The pox left smooth ovoid indentations. These were deep gouges, the kind a raven's sharp beak would leave—like the guardian of the House of Schattenburg, the raven that had savaged Prince Friedrich and von Fersen when they attacked Karl. While Friedrich had not escaped, his henchman had, but—if this viciously scarred man was him—he had not escaped unscathed.

Caw! Caw! Caw! came a cry out of the night.

The pockmarked man trembled violently, his fearful gaze rolling over the open expanses between the columns fronting the river and adjoining the sloping bank, searching for the raven.

Robbie's suspicion coalesced into certainty. His every muscle ached for action, but any move would be a deadly mistake. He contented himself with squeezing his fingers around the smooth handle of his cudgel and pressing his arm against the knife sheathed at his belt.

In the starlight John Ransome, the Earl of Darenth, came striding down the flight of steps, his top hat as firmly set as if he were strolling the Mall with his wife on his arm. He paused on the bottom tread, the small casket grasped beneath his arm and his mouth rigid with tension. Their eyes met, the earl's arctic blue and Robbie's the dark pansy purple of violent emotion. Whatever personal differences kept them at odds, they were united in this matter.

Robbie's hard gaze moved to the man at the fire. Did he know he had taken the wrong woman? Neither highwayman described by John Coachman had fit the German's description. It was very possible, Karl had said, that the cowardly von Fersen would hire men to do the deed and never see his captive. It gave them scant hope that Tabitha would not be killed before her rescue.

The German rose slowly, his rags fluttering in a gust of wind. Firelight played over his ravaged face and

emaciated frame, revealing the bulge of pistol butts beneath his coat.

Recognition and disgust darkened the earl's face.
"We meet again, *Graf* von Fersen," he said with the
aristocratic chill of centuries of breeding.

The man's head snapped back. His pocked face
flushed beneath his ragged hat brim. His pale eyes
bulging with a malignant hate, he swept the russet flap
of his coat aside and pulled a steel-barreled percussion
pistol from his belt.

Robbie jolted upright. Damn! He should have
known! Karl had warned that von Fersen could not be
trusted, but even he had thought the ransom demand
would be sufficient.

Robbie's cudgel thudded dully against the flagstone
floor, a sharp contrast to the heavy pounding of his
heart. His fingers closing around the smooth hilt of his
knife, he heard the ominous click of the pistol's hammer and the shot that sent his father sprawling over
the step with blood splattered across the stark white of
his shirt.

Robbie's rage exploded in the hard, rapid pulse at
his throat, in the throbbing pressure at the back of his
eyes, and in the clouding of his mind. He drew back
the knife and threw it with every ounce of his fury and
strength, following after it in a lunge over the fire.

The blade dug deep into von Fersen's shoulder. He
arched back, his mouth gaping, his face twisted with
pain. Then Robbie was on him, a brutal fist digging
beneath his ribs and snapping him forward with a
"Whoof!"

Men fled into the darkness, leaving Robbie alone
with his foe and his wounded father. He was oblivious
to everything except the vicious blows he inflicted. The
thud of flesh on flesh, the crack of bone against bone,
the rip of skin, and the spurt of blood; he was lost in
the need for violence, the only cure for the rage that
had been born in the six-by-six-foot hell of his prison
cell, in the suffocating darkness and the seeping damp
and the ever-present guilt and fear. It had risen out of

him then as it rose out of him now, an ancient atavistic darkness that was mindless, relentless, and pitiless.

"Langley! Leave him be!" Old Nick sped down the stairs, elegant even in his beggar's rags. "We need him alive!"

"Lethbridge," the earl whispered, "stop him."

Robbie was caught from behind, his arms pinioned. He struggled to escape, his breath coming in gasps, his mind a frenzy of blood-lust. "Let me go," he snarled.

Lethbridge had the slight-framed look of a boy and the habitual expression of a man trapped in the enervating depths of ennui, but when he chose to act, it was with a single-minded purpose that never met with failure. "Enough!" he hissed. "Get hold of yourself, man!"

Slowly Robbie's rage drained away, leaving behind the old horror. But there was no time to wonder if he would always be subject to passions he could not control. Von Fersen was lying at his feet, bleeding from his knife wound and staring up as if he beheld the Devil himself. He appeared as helpless as the earl, who was sprawled across the stairs, his hand at his chest and his face as white as wax.

"Get Audley! We'll need his help."

Lethbridge raced up the stairs while Robbie fell to his knees, regretting the many ways he had been a disappointment to his father.

The earl's lashes fluttered up. His face was taut with pain, but his gaze held the same stunned horror it had worn in Schattenburg when he had found Robbie in the crypt, a feral animal snarling in his cage. His hand closed feebly around his son's arm. "Your anger. You cannot control it," he whispered. "This is why you have stayed away for so many years?"

"We must get help for you." Robbie anxiously watched the blood trickle over his father's hand.

"I will have an answer, and now! What happened to you in Schattenburg . . . it was so long ago."

"Not long enough," Robbie said, his gaze locking with his father's. A knot of apprehension clenched like a fist beneath his breastbone. "A beast was born in that hellhole, Father."

"A man could tame him."

Robbie flinched, the color fleeing his face. He'd never been man enough for his father, never steady enough, never—

"God, even now I say the wrong thing. My son, my son," the earl whispered, his hand trembling against Robbie's arm, "there is a beast in every man. He cannot be escaped, only tamed."

He had tried, but the beast was always there, awaiting the chance to spring to life. The beast, the darkness, the shadow on his soul that he could neither escape nor accept.

He heard the slap of running feet on the turning of the stairs overhead. Audley and Lethbridge. Between them they could carry his father up—

"I wouldn't move, if I were you," said von Fersen in a voice as cold as the thrill of danger that sped the length of Robbie's spine.

From the corner of his eye he saw the pistol—the second pistol that he had forgotten, damn!—trembling in the German's hand as he struggled to rise, his breathing labored and his blood dripping steadily from the tips of his fingers. By all rights von Fersen should have been too weak to escape, but he seemed to have as many lives as a cat. Robbie, speculating on whether he dared jump the German, didn't waste his time on useless self-recrimination.

"It's never wise to turn your back on a snake, especially one you think harmless," he said.

"A lesson learned too late," boasted von Fersen, coughing and wavering on his feet. "The casket."

Robbie passed it over, his eyes meeting the German's.

"Don't try it. I couldn't miss at this distance." Von Fersen hooked the casket beneath his arm, bracing it against his ribs. Backing toward the archway opening onto the riverbank, he warned, "I'll shoot the man that follows me."

"You'll have but one chance," Robbie taunted, fighting the futile anger that bubbled inside him. "And if you miss—"

"I won't."

While Lethbridge and Audley came pounding down the stairs, von Fersen vanished into the darkness.

"See to my father," Robbie ordered, grabbing the cudgel and slipping into the shadows to follow the trail of blood.

Minutes later, he lost it.

Robbie crouched on the sloping bank, cursing the creaking of the masts and the slap of water against the hulls below. He could not hear the pant of breath or the pad of footsteps. He searched the darkness, studying the distorted shapes carved by moonlight and shadow. Above, Karl waited in the carriage. Secreted along the length of Lower Thames Street were the Darenth House footmen. If they'd sighted their quarry, Karl would have removed the shutter from the coach lamp in a prearranged signal.

Von Fersen headed downriver. What did he expect to find?

In the distance a torch flared, then vanished, as if it had been swallowed up by the earth.

Robbie roused from his crouch, moving quickly with the cudgel in his hand and murder in his heart. The German would never again hurt his family. Nothing would stop him now.

But something could indeed stop him.

Robbie stood before the yawning black mouth of a sewer culvert.

It was the only place von Fersen could have gone to.

The only place he himself could not.

His head swam with memories of the six-by-six-foot crypt of his prison, windowless and doorless, save for a single stone's opening. He remembered the terror of watching the mason mortar the stones one by one, raising the wall that sealed him in while he had been trussed up like a fair-day goose and helpless to save himself. And when his bonds had been cut, what a travesty of freedom it had been. He couldn't stand upright or stretch out full length or move at more than a crabbed pace. And the dark, thick as axle grease, he could touch it and feel it, a smothering pressure on his chest that crowded out the air. Soon came the madness growing day by day, week by week, month by month, slowly stealing from him a man's capacity for compassion and reason.

Beads of sweat swelled like drops of blood on Robbie's brow, rolling in thick rivulets down his taut face. He could not risk the claustrophobic darkness, the debilitating fear . . .

Neither could he let von Fersen escape.

What man worthy of the name would let his father's attacker escape unpunished? And Tabitha Fell, sweetly serene, what of . . .

A thought rocked him back on his heels, turning his gaze to the mouth of the opening. Was she in there, alone in the dark, learning to fear it as he had, learning that neither prayer nor plea could protect her from herself?

He took a hesitant step, bending down to the moss-rimmed opening, inhaling the gaseous exhalation of the sewer. His knees quivering, he crawled in with a last whiff of the clean night wind teasing his nostrils. The egg-shaped tunnel of crumbling brick stretched out before him, dimly backlit by a stray shaft of moonlight. In the far distance von Fersen's torch beckoned through the humid mist.

Robbie stood hunched over, his boots buried in muck, his hair brushing the sweating ceiling. The walls seemed to press against him, as if they sought to crush him. The terror came in a rush, stealing the strength from his knees. A hoarse cry scrabbled at the back of his throat. He clenched his teeth. This time . . . this time he would defeat the darkness, the madness.

His heart thudding painfully against his ribs, he moved forward, deeper and deeper into the bowels of the earth, deeper and deeper into the nightmare that had driven him through the years of his manhood in a fruitless quest for peace.

He was deaf to the squeaking of rats, blind to the red gleam of their eyes. There was only the torch—until it disappeared, leaving behind a dull glow that picked out the geometric lines of the bricks.

His heart sank, slithering like the eels in the cold water that had risen above his boots to his knees. Everything in him screamed to turn around, to find the opening, to plunge into the night and savor the spacious sky and silvery moonlight and fresh air. But he couldn't fail himself now.

He lunged forward, the cudgel in his hand, sweat seeping through his shirt to dampen his coarse coat. Every step became an agony of effort, his stooping crouch pulling at the muscles of his neck and burning between his shoulder blades.

At last he reached the joining of the new tunnel. In the distance von Fersen's torch winked like a firefly on a moonless night. Robbie stumbled on endlessly through a maze of twists and turns, into tunnels so small he had to crawl. And always the terror was there, burrowing into his soul and stealing stretches of time, while he doggedly followed the light, wondering if this new hell would ever end.

Von Fersen vanished once again, but there was another torch affixed to the wall far ahead. Robbie paused and stared, his every muscle screaming with the strain of stooping beneath the low ceiling. Was it imagination, or was there another man? Bigger, thicker, a ghostly shadow looming out of the mist. He blinked. The shadow was gone.

A man's voice echoed down the tunnel, and following it, echo for echo, a woman's voice as gently melodious as the songs of the wood larks on Langley Heath: Tabitha Fell, buried alive in the stench and filth of this rat-infested sewer. And this was where the German would have brought Anne. Loving Anne, who had endured more for Robbie's sake than any sister should have to endure for a brother.

The rage came with its familiar pounding of blood and churning of belly and mindless resolve. Robbie gritted his teeth over a roar of outrage and plunged ahead, his cudgel slamming into the wall and sending a torrent of crumbling brickwork cascading into the water behind him.

"Who are you?" The high-pitched echo of von Fersen's voice rippled down the passage, trailed by the softer feminine response. "Damn them!" screamed the German. "Damn them! The wrong woman!"

Robbie scaled the trio of steps and lunged into the chamber to find Tabitha backed against a column, her wide eyes focused on the bore of the pistol. The metallic click of the hammer seemed to come from inside Robbie's head, so loud did it sound in the hushed quiet that was undisturbed by the rippling water behind him. He'd never reach the German in time to stop him.

"Von Fersen!" he roared, drawing back the cudgel and throwing it across the chamber, then following after it in a manic charge.

The German spun around, his face haggard and gray, one arm limp at his side, blood dripping steadily from the tips of his fingers. The cudgel dealt him a glancing blow that tipped him off balance. The pistol discharged, leaving the air reeking of gunpowder.

Pain exploded in Robbie's side. The force of the shot lifted him up, suspending him in air for the moment it took to suck air into his empty lungs. The rage pushed him on for one step, two, three, before he leapt on his quarry, locking his fingers around von Fersen's scrawny neck.

The German arched back, pulling Robbie down. Eye to murderous eye, they tumbled and rolled, leaving the slick trail of their blood intermingled on the ancient mosaic floor. Beneath Robbie, the German bucked and squirmed, desperately trying to escape the vise of his fingers.

"Not . . . this . . . time," Robbie warned breathlessly. "This . . . is . . . for . . . Anne."

Von Fersen hooked a knee into Robbie's wounded

side. Agony shot through him, weakening his hold, curling his body around the pain, stealing consciousness with a gathering darkness lit by blood-red starbursts. Von Fersen pulled away from his nerveless fingers. Robbie struggled to hold him, but the bony knee came again, jamming into his side and setting it afire. Rolling away, he heard a scream and wondered dimly if it was his own.

Tabitha clung to a column, her raw throat aching, like her heart, like her soul. She had never seen such violent rage. It frightened and sickened her, but no more than watching von Fersen struggle upright, draw back his booted foot, and kick Friend Robert in the back. "No!" she cried helplessly. "No!"

He angled his head around, his eyes narrow slits of evil intent, the thin arc of a cruel smile pulling at his lips.

An icy chill shuddered through Tabitha, freezing her heart, numbing her mind. He would kill Friend Robert, and she, a woman of peace, could not stop him by forceful means. She could only plead and pray, and neither would sway him.

He turned to Friend Robert and drew back his foot.

Heedlessly, thoughtlessly, against every tenet of her religion, Tabitha lifted her skirts and ran. Ran, not away from von Fersen, but toward him. Ran, tucking her shoulder, aiming for the vulnerable middle of his back. She crashed into him, sending him flying, his arms outflung, and herself tumbling after him. She fetched up against the wall, his scream ringing in her ears. Dazed and horrified, she watched him crawl away.

Friend Robert's hand snaked out and clamped around von Fersen's ankle. "The cudgel," he gritted breathlessly.

Her eyes locking with his, she shook her head slowly. She couldn't take that last sinful step of putting a murder weapon in his hand. And he had not the strength to hold his enemy.

Von Fersen kicked back, his heel breaking Robbie's

grip on his ankle. *"Shadwell!"* he screamed, crawling to the door.

A shadow darkened the tunnel. A man hovered beyond the light.

Shadwell was uncertain, a condition foreign to him. He should kill them all and let them molder to bones here, where they would never be found. Von Fersen was mad and dangerous to him. The Nob—not even rags could hide that air of authority—now knew his name and would have the Runners after him. The woman . . .

Von Fersen crawled slowly, painfully toward the door. The Nob inched toward the cudgel. Shadwell studied the woman sprawled on the floor. Not her face, not her breast, not the slender ankles exposed by the wet hem of her skirt, but the plain gray gown and the neat white cap, now crumpled and dirty. The ghost of a memory skipped beyond his grasp, but it left behind the faint impression of a feeling he thought he had never known—a feeling of well-being, of tenderness and care as if once long ago he'd known what it was to be loved and protected.

Von Fersen reached the steps at his feet, saying, "Kill them! Kill them!"

Shadwell reached out, one hamlike hand piercing the wedge of light, gathering the German's shirtfront, and dragging him into the shadows to hold him up, feet dangling, as easily as if he were a babe. Von Fersen would not stop until he had Lady Anne; he would always be a danger.

Shadwell's free hand captured the German's narrow jaw and twisted. The bones in von Fersen's neck crackled. His head sagged on his shoulders at an impossible angle. Shadwell negligently tossed him into the sluggish current, and turned his attention to the Nob and the woman.

He had survived in his cruel world because he did whatever was necessary. Now it was necessary to kill the Nob and the woman—but he found that he could not. For a man of his ilk, weakness was the beginning of the end. Though he flayed himself with that, he still could not do it.

Cursing foully, he flung himself down the tunnel, chased by the feeling—real or imaginary?—of well-being, of tenderness and care.

Chapter 3

Shadwell was gone. Von Fersen was dead. Robbie was alive, and for the first time in twelve years, he was glad. Even with knives of pain stabbing his side and fetid air filling his lungs, he could smell, taste, feel how precious life was. Anne need never again fear von Fersen. Robbie need never again wake in the night with guilt gnawing at him like a rat with a meaty bone.

Tabitha huddled against the wall, her face in her hands, her shoulders shaking in soundless sobs. She looked like a lost child against the massive stone bench, her pristine white cap crumpled and dirty.

Robbie crawled to her, hitching up against the wall. He wanted to comfort her, but the exertion had set fire to his side. Sweat poured from his brow, while his rasping breath slowed and the agony gradually eased to a sharp, intermittent throb.

"Tabby," he said softly, using Anne's familiar name for her.

Her head lifted slowly. Her small face was bloodless, her eyes reflecting the torchlight like shattered mirrors.

"You are safe," he soothed.

"Am I?" She drew her knees up, locking her arms around them and rocking like a child who was beyond any comfort.

"Soon this will seem like a bad dream. You will forget—"

"Never!" she cried. "Could I forget that Shadwell

murdered von Fersen? That I heard the bones in his neck snap? That I saw thee locked in mortal, murderous combat with him? Thee!''

Tears welled in her eyes, spilling over, racing down her cheeks, and dripping from her chin. He longed to gather her to him, to take her pain as his own. It would be easier for him, since his disillusionment was old and hers was new and yet raw.

''Anne told me so much of thee,'' she said mournfully. ''I thought I knew thee, but . . .''

She tentatively touched his hand, her fingers trembling against it. A harrowing reminder of the touch that had brought him such peace in the Nursery Parlor of Darenth House, a peace that was not to be found in her now.

''How could the hand that once returned a baby robin to its nest now try to choke the life from a man?''

Her gaze rose, meeting his with a question he could not answer. How could he explain to her what he could not understand himself? ''He would have killed you,'' he said, offering his only explanation.

''I would rather have died than imperiled thy soul.''

''And I would rather have imperiled my soul than been the cause of your death.''

''No man deserves to be murdered.''

''If ever a man did, von Fersen was that man. You don't know how many lives he has twisted and ruined and taken.''

Tabitha laid her hand palm to palm with his, pressing lightly, as if that pressure could instill in him her belief. The belief reflected in her eyes, slowly restructuring the bastion of peace that Robbie yearned to find for himself. Had he not been so glad to see it, he would have envied her ability to shrug off cruel circumstances and find the core of herself again.

''No man is so black-hearted that there is no goodness in him,'' she said with such fervor it seemed to have some deeper, stronger meaning for her. ''It is that goodness we must reach.''

She was wrong, of course. There were men beyond

redemption. Robbie had been intimately, painfully acquainted with them. He was one of them. Even so, he could not destroy her illusions.

He shifted. Pain flooded through him, wave after wave crashing through the barrier of proud stoicism and forcing a groan from his lips. Unconsciously, his fingers threaded with hers. "We must escape," he gritted through clenched teeth.

Tabitha felt the grinding pressure of his pain in the bones of her hand. She felt the strength and determination that might be betrayed by the weakness of his wounded body, and she was racked with shame that she had considered only herself. However much he had frightened and disenchanted her with his vicious rage against von Fersen, he had also ignored his own pain in order to comfort her.

Disenchanted. What a strange word to use. Yet a true one. She had been enchanted by Anne's tales of her brother; enchanted by the boy he had been, so greedy for life, brimming with eagerness and courage and laughter. Now she had met the man. She had seen him at his worst. With his hand gripping hers, she was no longer frightened, no longer . . . enchanted. But she was something more, something deeper. She wanted to look away from the eyes that watched her with an expression that was both tender and wary, but her gaze locked with his.

"I must try to stop your bleeding," she said.

He nodded and eased away from the wall to begin the slow, agonizing process of removing his coat and shirt. Clothed, he had the lean elegance of the aristocrat with no hint of his hard, honed frame. Muscles strapped his shoulders, undulating beneath the pelt of black hair that spanned his chest. Below his ribs and down his belly, the muscles linked like chain mail, vanishing into the waistband of his trousers. Tabitha was beset by a shameful interest and an even more shameful warmth that blossomed in her cheeks and flowed through her like warm honey—until she leaned down to examine the wound.

The shot had ripped through his side, deflected by a rib. A white fragment of bone gleamed in the pooling blood. Honeyed warmth was replaced by the chill that settled low in her belly like frost on fertile earth.

"I must remove the splinter of bone." Even as she was wondering whether she could, Tabitha was fumbling in the small reticule attached at her waist. She withdrew a shiny coin, a roll of thread, a paper of needles.

He leaned back on his hands, his arms bunching with tension as he braced himself for the pain she would inflict.

Her fingers closed over the tiny sharp scissors, her very soul shrinking from the thought of using them on him. "I—I don't know if I can."

His violet eyes turned so dark they looked black in the pale, masculine frame of his face, the grimace of his lips arced into a bracing smile. "Courage, Tabby," he said. "Courage."

In his smile she saw not the man of violence, but the boy he had been. In that moment her heart seemed to float free, as if it had been tethered by some unwanted bond and was now released. She shrugged out of her pelisse, rolling the dry top to staunch the flow of his blood and leaving the filthy wet shirt to trail on the floor. She stripped his shirt into lengths to use for padding. Thoughtlessly, she hefted her plain gray skirt and struggled with the ribbons of her underslip, dropping it around her ankles, exposing the slender length of her legs.

"So it's true. There *is* a silver lining in every cloud," Friend Robert said breathlessly.

Her head whipped up. His meaningful gaze climbed from her ankles to her knees, sliding up to meet her eyes with the merest suggestion of a twinkle. Her skirt fell; her color rose. Flustered, she stepped out of her slip, turning away to strip it into lengths for bandaging.

She knelt beside him, settling her hand on the hard,

muscled ridge of his ribs, her gaze meeting his with an unspoken apology.

"It must come out," he said. "We both know it."

She nodded, her throat too tight for speech, sweat forming on her brow and oozing down her face. She drew the back of her hand across her eyes and bent to her unpleasant task, sliding the sharp point of the scissors into his torn flesh, feeling the warmth of his life's blood sliding slippery and warm over her fingers. Grasping the splinter of bone, she yanked it free and heard his gasp and felt the rapid rise and fall of his chest beneath her hand. The padding pressed to the wound, she waited until the blood came in a sluggish trickle. Then she wrapped the strips of makeshift bandaging around him, drawing them as tight as her strength would allow. Only when that was done and the knot tied tight did she allow herself to shudder.

When she began she couldn't stop. It was as if all of the horror from the moment of her abduction till now had taken hold of her. She knelt beside him, her teeth chattering, her body shaking until it seemed her bones must begin to rattle.

"I—I'm sorry," she whispered.

"Don't be."

He shifted back, bracing against the wall, and reached for Tabitha, pulling her to him. She rested on the broad width of his chest, weakly glad to lie there and tremble against him. Slowly she became aware of his manly scent, of his strong arms, of his warm lips at her brow. It felt so right, yet was so wrong. She was to *testify* at summer's end, to become the wife of another man. She should not now be lying in Friend Robert's embrace.

Her gaze met his, meshing with it and holding it for an eternity, while a powerful current flowed from him to her. A current that heightened her senses, making each painfully acute. She could hear his soft breath. She could feel the pulse of his blood and the shift of muscle beneath the fingers curling into the hard plane of his chest. She could see into his heart, see the suffering and self-doubt, the need for peace.

Slowly, his head lowered and his lips touched hers. Gently, so gently, they moved over hers, possessing them fully.

A tingling sensation sped through her lips. She could feel the tremors racing through the muscles beneath her hands, the heat of his skin, the raging need in his questing mouth—a need to fill the emptiness, to banish the loneliness, to rid himself of the fear.

This was not like the swift pecks on the cheek she had received from her father and brothers, or like the single hard, purse-lipped kiss of Abraham Leeds, who had flushed afterward, as if shamed by it. This was a kiss that demanded everything a woman had to give.

She was horrified to discover that she wanted to yield herself up to him, to follow wherever he led. But another man waited for her, as he had waited patiently for years. One who offered not the dubious exhilaration of the senses, but a lifetime of sharing and good works.

Tabitha jerked back, her hands pressing against his chest, the crisp hair curling around her fingers as if he would not let her go. Shamefully, it would have taken so little to make her stay. "I pray thee, don't."

His chin climbed, his violet eyes blinking in the torchlight, his tongue sliding over his lips as if he gathered the last nectar of her kiss. Slowly, his hand climbed to cup her cheek, his thumb gliding over her mouth.

Her traitorous mouth that longed to feel the pressure of his again. Tabitha turned her face, and his thumb trailed over her cheek, delicately foraging beneath her cap and finding the tender spot beneath her ear. "Thee must not. I must not," she said breathlessly. "I—I am to *testify* at summer's end."

"Testify?"

"Wed. I am to wed Friend Abraham Leeds of the village of Darenth."

Leeds! Robbie frowned, remembering the man as a

boy, humorless, pious, and unctuous. The idea of gentle Tabitha yoked to that dry stick filled him with revulsion. She would wither in the arid landscape of marriage to Leeds.

Not that it was any of Robbie's concern. With the sweet taste of her lingering on his lips, he carefully removed his wandering finger from the hollow beneath her ear as he carefully quelled the desire she aroused in him. Not the physical desire that came so easily, but something new and heretofore unexperienced. The desire to protect her, to take her away to some private place and shield her from every disappointment, every disillusionment life would surely offer her. But how could he do that for her when he could not do it for himself?

"He is a good man," she began, as if Robbie had denied it. "Strong in his faith, a frequent speaker at Meeting, humble and righteous."

Self-righteous, Robbie could have said. He contented himself with intoning dryly, "A paragon."

Her gaze gently rebuked him. "Thee should not be unkind to one who lacks thy . . . thy . . ."

She looked away, and he, curious, questioned, "My?"

"He is a good man," she repeated.

How that nettled his pride. "And I, assuredly, am not."

Her gaze rose, her expression tender. "Thee knows I did not mean it that way."

And Robbie felt the peace stealing through him, smoothing the raised hackles of his pride. He felt a stirring deep in his heart, a tenuous awakening, like the first glimmering green announcing the birth of spring. For a moment he wondered what it would be like to have her always at his side, to bring her his disappointments and disillusionments, to have them banished by her serenity. But only for one weak moment. He was not a man to have and to hold, and she was a woman who deserved nothing less.

"We must leave here," he said, desperate to escape

the feelings she roused. They could bring nothing but anguish if they were allowed to grow, which they would not be. He would be leaving soon, sailing for Greece and war.

"Art thou strong enough?" Tabitha asked, intruding on his thoughts.

"I will have to be."

She helped him to rise, her slight shoulder beneath his arm. Pain exploded in his side and blood seeped through the bandage. He turned away, snatching up his coat and shrugging it on. A foolhardy bit of business. What stupidities a man's pride could drive him to. He sagged against the wall, the blood draining from his head, leaving him dizzy and weak. Weak as a babe, he thought in roiling disgust.

"We can wait," she said softly.

His knees trembling, Robbie began to turn away but staggered against Tabitha, nearly overturning them both. Her small hands splayed against him, branding his back and chest, a damning reminder of his weakness.

"I pray thee," she pleaded, "wait until thou art stronger."

"We both know that time won't come soon," he said sharply. "The wound is likely to fester. We'd best not wait for that."

"And the casket?" she asked. "Von Fersen said it was—"

"Leave it. It's a small price to pay for our lives."

Fortunately, the torch was set low on the wall. Robbie hefted it and descended the steps unsteadily. The tunnel seemed smaller when he was knee-deep in sludgy water, his back bowed beneath the low, arching bricks. He tried to breathe, but the air seemed to solidify before it reached his lungs. He tried to think, but all he could do was feel . . . the walls hemming him in . . . the ponderous burden of the earth pressing down on the arch overhead . . . the shroud of mist wrapping him tightly.

When he thought his heart would burst from the

strain of holding back a shameful groan of fear, Tabitha's hand touched his forearm and glided down to his wrist—an offer of comfort that quickly turned into something else. Her fingers dug into his flesh like talons, and her hand began to tremble uncontrollably. He turned and saw stark and dark horror in her eyes. Eyes that stared behind them. He followed her gaze and saw von Fersen's body bobbing on the current, snagged by an unseen obstacle and a writhing mass of rats baring his back to the bone.

Robbie caught Tabitha around the waist and pulled her to him. "Don't look."

A useless command. She could not turn away.

"Tabitha!" He shook her. "Tabitha! Look at me!"

Her pasty-white face tilted up. Her gaze rose to his face, revealing the full horror of violence and murder. A horror visited only on innocents. He wanted to comfort her, but what comfort was there to offer? He wanted to hold her until her shaking stopped, until she rediscovered her serenity of mind and soul, but there was no time. The blood was running warm down his hip.

"We must go now," he said. "Do you understand me?"

She nodded like a child. "I . . . I won't hold thee back."

His thumb trailed a tender path along her cheek. "I know you won't. Follow me closely."

He stumbled forward, daring to look ahead. But where he expected to see the narrowing black maw of the tunnel, he saw the dim glow of torchlight and the indistinct form of a massive man. Shadwell. Before Robbie could react, the man beckoned with his torch and began to move away, a huge shadow floating ghoulishly above the glistening water—leading them to safety or leading them to their deaths?

Shadwell could have killed them earlier, so he must be leading them to safety. But why? There had to be a reason, but what it might be escaped Robbie.

"Don't be afraid," he murmured, fearing he was

saying it to himself even as his pride insisted he was reassuring Tabitha.

Pride, she thought. It was in every rigid line of Friend Robert's body, his refusal to yield to the exhaustion that slowed his steps, to the weakness that sent ripples down the forearm holding the torch aloft. It was sinful to have so much pride he would rather break than bend. So why, Tabitha wondered, did she admire that sinful pride?

She was blind to the pairs of eyes peering out from chinks in the walls, deaf to the squealing chorus, oblivious to the deepening water, now sloshing around her thighs and dragging at her skirt. There was only Friend Robert moving steadily ahead, the light gleaming in his black hair.

If the mud that pulled at her feet like quicksand and the current that pushed against her every forward step were draining her strength, what were they doing to his? His breath gusted like the wind, magnified by the walls that echoed every sound. A grunt of pain greeted his every misstep. More frightening, blood was seeping through the bandage, running down his hip, and spreading in a dark red stain like oil over the water around his thigh.

"Thee must rest." She touched his arm, feeling the muscles quiver with strain.

"If I stop, I won't make it." He trudged on.

A rat swam toward her, his head sleek and wet, his tail wriggling like a snake. She choked back a cry and flung herself away, splattering and splashing.

Friend Robert spun around. "Tabitha?"

"It's nothing. A rat. Nothing."

"Did . . . did he bite you?"

"No, only frightened me." Embarrassed by her foolish fear, she reluctantly raised her gaze to him. He was ghastly pale, his face drenched in sweat that pooled in the hollow of his throat and ran in rivulets down his bare chest. He wavered on his feet, obviously at the end of his strength.

"Let me help thee!" She splashed toward him,

grasping him around the waist and settling her shoulder beneath his arm.

He leaned heavily on her, his lashes drooping over his eyes, his head hanging as if it were a weight too heavy to carry. "If I . . . I can't make it, I want you to leave me. You can send someone back—"

"No," she said, horrified at the suggestion. He must know what would happen to him, unconscious, in the darkness. The rats would gnaw the flesh from his bones. She swallowed a surge of nausea. "Together," she said, more boldly than she felt. "We will escape together or not at all."

His gaze, glittering in the light, shifted to her face. The suggestion of a smile pulled at the corner of his mouth. "Together," he whispered, as if the word were new and strange to him, as if it held an appeal that somehow he regretted.

She began moving forward, and she saw the torchlight in the distance, the massive man wreathed in mist.

"Shadwell," Friend Robert said softly.

"Why is he helping us?"

He shook his head, and she knew that his strength was waning, for the torch was hanging low in his hand. Yet she could not both support him and carry it. On she moved, Friend Robert at her side, struggling against the current, moving through the darkness, following Shadwell until he stopped and the groan and squeak of a rusty grate began traveling back through the tunnel.

Ahead, a fat beam of sunlight pierced the darkness, like the Lord's Inner Light piercing the darkness of the human soul. Just as all doubt and grief and human frailty vanished with that Light, so did Shadwell.

The grate was beyond Tabitha's reach, at the top of a round brick wall that rose from the roof of the tunnel to ground level above. Robbie, despairing, leaned against the slick wall, the sweat scudding down his face. He had to reach up, pull himself out, and haul Tabitha up by brute strength. Failure—he listened to the squealing of unseen rats—would mean an unthinkable alternative. He shrugged out of his coat and tossed it into the current.

"Thee cannot—"

"I must." He rose on tiptoe, grasping the lip of the opening. At his side, the flesh tore and blood soaked into the bandage.

"God give thee strength," Tabitha whispered fervently.

Robbie pulled himself up, the muscles of his back knotting, the tendons of his arms straining. Slowly, his head crested the rim of the opening and a cool, clean breeze washed over his face. With a last burst of effort, he fell over the side, rolling down the dusty incline into the filth of an alleyway. For a moment he lay gasping with the morning sun on his face and the fragrant air scouring his lungs. Church bells tolled, as if chiming in joyous celebration of their escape. But it wasn't *their* escape yet. It was only his.

His side feeling as though a hot poker had been thrust into it, his arms aching, he crawled back to the opening, hanging over and reaching for Tabitha. Sunlight flooded her uptilted face, her dirty, smudged cheeks. Her cap was canted back, revealing lustrous black waves and a widow's peak at her brow. She wore an expression suspiciously akin to Anne's at her mulish worst.

"Thee must find help," she said. "Thee cannot lift me out."

And he, with his side afire and his strength waning, felt an enlivening burst of rage. "The devil I can't! And here I had begun to think you a woman of excellent understanding!"

"I am," she said, obviously unruffled. "That is why I insist that thee—"

"Insist!" He scowled down at her. "Unless you want me joining you down there, you will reach up and grasp my wrists!"

"And here I had begun to think of thee as a man of excellent sensibilities," she said. "Surely too enlightened to be stung to the raw by any suggestion that thee, wounded as thou art, might be too weak—"

"Tabitha," he growled a warning. "My patience wears thin."

"Dost thou feel thy strength returning?" she asked.

He stared down into her sparkling gray eyes, a suspicion growing. "Minx. Let me assure you that you've twitted me into a lather that has left me remarkably refreshed."

"Good." She reached up, and he wrapped his long fingers around her delicate wrists. "I should not like to be dropped."

Chapter 4

Sunlight poured into the alleyway, where Tabitha and Robbie sat in utter exhaustion on the hard-packed earth littered with refuse.

"The Lord moves in mysterious ways," she said.

Robbie, struggling to ease the pain in his side, slanted an inquiring gaze at her.

"Using His servant Shadwell to save us," she explained.

Robbie blinked. Shadwell as the Lord's servant was beyond his comprehension. Shadwell saving them for some purpose of his own was not. He frowned.

"I must get thee help." She was up and away before he could protest.

She ran as fleet as a deer, her soggy skirts slapping audibly against her legs, her dirty cap sliding back on her head to reveal the thick black braid looped and bound at her nape. She had learned nothing from her experience in the tunnel, he thought. She was like a child that met no strangers, expected no harm, gave of herself too freely—and children needed to be protected.

But was Shadwell a threat? If only Robbie knew why the man had rescued them . . .

But he didn't. Until Shadwell was safely jailed by the authorities, Robbie would have to keep Tabitha nearby. And that posed a danger to him, for he was finding it difficult to think of her as a distant cousin.

Even as he watched her with a warming gaze, he caught a whiff of the sea rising from the Thames, a scent of spices and exotic woods seeping from the warehouses flanking its banks. Both beckoned him irresistibly to the dangerous unknown, to those uncivilized corners of the world where he could test himself anew.

He thrust away the yearning to shed this new responsibility. His father had, on receipt of the ransom demand—nearly a day ago, though it seemed like a lifetime—sent word to Fell Cottage on the manor lands of Darenth Hall. It was likely that one or more of Tabitha's brothers would have arrived, planning either to help in the search for her or to escort her home. That he had to stop at any cost. The only problem was, how?

They arrived in high-toned St. James's Square before the elegant Adam's exterior of Darenth House in a dustman's cart drawn by a moth-eaten mule wearing a tattered straw hat.

A furor rudely awakened Robbie, whose face was cushioned against Tabitha's breast, her small, comforting hand resting in the center of his chest. He vaguely remembered the painful climb into the cart and the jolting journey over the cobbled streets, while the babble of voices rose around him.

"Fear not. He is alive," came Tabitha's soft, sweet murmur.

"Henry, summon Dr. Kennon from Father's chambers!" It was Anne's frightened shriek.

Robbie tried to open his eyes, but his lashes lay like lead against his cheeks. His fingers curled up away from his belly, and his hand was grasped in a hard, masculine grip.

"We'll have you abovestairs in a trice," Karl said softly.

"Father?" Robbie asked.

"Alive," said Karl, his deep melodic voice soothing and reassuring. "Your mother is with him."

A hot prickling began at the back of Robbie's eyes.

To cover that soft emotion, he tried to smile, but feared it was more of a grimace. "When did Anne start . . ." He paused to catch his breath, waiting for a knifing pain to subside. "Start screaming like a . . . like a fish-wife?"

"You rag-mannered wretch!" said Anne with a catch in her breath, as if she struggled to suppress a sob.

"Friend Tabitha!"

The voice was one Robbie knew well and liked little. Deepened by the years, it still held an oily note of unc-tuousness, but it was more than his dislike of Abraham Leeds that carved a scowl into Robbie's brow. Leeds would expect Tabitha's immediate return to Fell Cot-tage, and that he must prevent.

"Friend Abraham," Tabitha said gently, but her hand curled against Robbie's chest into a tight fist.

"I—I scarce know what to think of thee!" said Abra-ham Leeds, as if he considered her responsible for all that had befallen her.

"Thee might think," she began a trifle sharply, "that I have been delivered from evil by the grace of God and with the help of Friend Robert."

But it was no heavenly being that compelled Rob-bie's heavy eyes to open and gaze with spurious in-nocence into Abraham Leeds' round brown eyes. "Don't believe her," he whispered, wishing he had the strength to laugh. "Had she not swooped on von Fersen like a falcon with a threatened nestling, neither of us would be here now."

Leeds' eyes, nearly starting from his head, rose slowly. "Force, Friend Tabitha? Thee used an animal's brute force?"

She looked not at him but at Robbie, her misty gray gaze rich with understanding and—did he mistake it?— a gentle dance of amusement. "Thou art a devil, Friend Robert."

"Thy speech is unseemly, Friend Tabitha," began Leeds.

"But true, I should think." A short, dark man ap-peared at the cart wheel. His weathered and sun-browned face had a suggestion of Tabitha around the peaceful eyes and smiling mouth. "Adam Fell," he said, "Tabitha's brother and first mate of the *North Star*. I thank thee for returning her safely to us."

Adam Fell's gaze shifted to Tabitha, the smile lingering about his mouth. "Tabby," he said lovingly, "had I the courage to dare thy foul odor, I should give thee a hug."

"Coward," she responded with an equally loving laugh.

The doctor approached, his bag in hand, his bluff, ruddy countenance wearing its perpetual smile. "What have we here? Gad! The smell!"

"We've toured the London sewers, Sir Kennon," Robbie said.

"No doubt." He hung over the cart.

"He was shot, Friend Kennon," said Tabitha. "The bullet passed through without lodging within him."

"Ahh." He nodded sagely. "We'll take him above, clean the wound, and bleed him to rid him of the foul humors—"

Tabitha jerked as if stung. "Bleed him! Can thee not see that he has bled enough?"

Dr. Kennon's ruddy face darkened. "Madam, I think that I would know better—"

"So I, too, should think," she said with a flame of ire. "However, it does not seem so! Bleed him! I shan't allow it!"

"You . . . you shan't allow it?" He gaped, obviously stunned by this unexpected opposition.

"Friend Tabitha!" said Leeds, aghast. "Thee forgets thyself!"

Robbie, seeing the way to keep her near—but more strongly niggled by the devil—announced in a fainting voice, "Tabby shall be charged with my sickroom. All decisions will be hers."

Tabitha leaned over him, her palm cradling his cheek, her expression so deeply concerned he nearly, but not quite, regretted that mischievous pronouncement. "I shall take the very best care of thee, Friend

Robert," she said earnestly. "I shall not leave thy side until thou art hale and whole again."

"Friend Tabitha," began Leeds, in a quivering effort to maintain the moderate speech and emotion that were a part of the Friends' creed, but foreign, Robbie suspected, to his deepest nature, "dost thou forget that this . . . this person is not of thy kin? What of thy maidenly modesty? What of thy—"

"My boy," interrupted Dr. Kennon, at no pains to contain his fury, "you cannot mean that you will place yourself in this chit's hands, ignoring the advice of a trained physician? One who, I might add, was deemed of sufficient skill to attend the Dowager Queen in her last days."

Robbie, slyly, heaved a tremendous sigh. "I fear I must. Tabby has proven herself to give the most tender of care."

"Robbie," came a warning from Anne, low-voiced and lighter noted, assured that he would live after all.

"Friend Robert," sounded another warning from Tabitha, this holding an undercurrent of laughter that recognized his irresistible urge to roast Friend Abraham.

Before she could say more, a quartet of footmen trooped down the steps carrying a hastily unbolted door as a makeshift stretcher. A few pain-racked minutes later, Robbie was being carried up the stairs, while Tabitha trailed in her wet skirts, issuing orders.

To a footman: "Bring up the bathing tub and fill it with water as hot as Friend Robert can stand."

To Dr. Kennon: "Bring a healing ointment to his chamber."

To Karl: "See that Friend Robert is scrubbed clean, taking care not to disturb the wound further."

To Anne: "Have the cook send up a strengthening broth."

Robbie, countermanding, said, "Meats and bread and cheese."

"Broth," said that stern taskmaster with the sweet face of an angel.

And Robbie, lying prone on the door, smiled to himself. He would be in good hands, and she would be safe.

His smile was quickly wiped away by the ham-handed footman who aided him in his bath with Cheddar hovering anxiously.

Ham-handed. Robbie looked to Karl, who sat nearby. "It was not I who saved us, but Shadwell."

"Shadwell!" Karl straightened, a lock of butter-yellow hair falling over his frowning brow. He shot out of his chair, in that instant transformed from the contented husband and father, the diplomat and musical composer *extraordinaire*, to the hard and suspicious spy whom Anne had first met. The man who had met and conquered every danger in his service to England. The man who had saved Anne's life and Robbie's. The man who had brought von Fersen's London-based spy ring crashing down around his ears. He paced the chamber like a tawny lion seeking the limits of his cage, a cage whose bars he would set asunder with the angry fists clenched at his sides.

"Why?" Karl demanded, his melodic voice flat and dangerous, his cornflower-blue eyes narrowed and wary. "He was in league with von Fersen during the late war, his second-in-command, terrifying Anne. Why would he now—"

"Murder the German?" Robbie offered.

"Murder!" Karl spun around, his handsome features taut with shock. "Shadwell killed von Fersen?"

Robbie nodded.

"To save you and Tabitha?"

"It would seem so."

"I don't like it," said Karl.

"Nor do I. There is no reason—"

"There is always a reason." Karl moved to the window, fingering the curtain and staring down into the garden below. "The trick is to find it. What happened to the money?"

"We left it in the sewer—"

"Where Shadwell can find it. Good," Karl said

crisply, turning about with a militant stance. "What we learned of Shadwell in '13 may still hold true. He is, above all, a man after the main chance. He does whatever he must, but he doesn't look back. We can hope it was simply a falling-out among thieves with the money as the object."

"But can we believe it?" Robbie asked.

"No," said Karl with an approving, hard-lipped smile. "Had you not been so hell-bent on acting the soldier at the Battle of Borodino, you would have made a damn fine addition to Castlereagh's silent corps of spies. Suspicion, as Anne can tell you, is the key to survival."

"So you, too, think there is something havey-cavey about this?"

"It smells of a dead rat." Karl sank into the chair, his long, muscular legs stretched out before him, his fingers steepled at his nose. "Was this the reason for that little scene below? To keep Tabitha with you until you've solved this puzzle?"

"I think it might be wise."

"Infinitely so." Karl leaned forward, his gaze intent. "I'll head off to Bow Street. We'll have a peace warrant issued for Shadwell's arrest. Do you have any clue to why he helped you?"

"Only a hunch. Tabitha."

"You think he might—"

"I don't know."

"I don't know," Tabitha whispered. She didn't know if she *should* stay to nurse Friend Robert, she only knew she would.

Though Anne obviously bubbled with curiosity, she had left Tabitha alone in the Nursery Parlor with the steaming bathing tub. The boys and baby Magda, with the nursery maid and an armed escort, had been sent to the safety of Darenth Hall. How empty these chambers were without them.

Tabitha should have been glad to see Abraham Leeds, but she had been . . . irritated by his intrusion and afraid he would insist that she go to Fell Cottage. She should have felt lighter of heart, soothed and protected by the presence of the man she was to wed. Instead, she had felt threatened.

Now he awaited her below with her brother Adam. He would, she determined, have to wait longer. Friend Robert needed her.

Will thee now begin to lie to thyself, Tabitha Fell? prodded the severe voice of her conscience. *Friend Robert would be cared for by his sister and his mother and his manservant. Thee will be lost if thee refuses to seek the Truth.*

And the Truth was . . . what? For the first time in her life she closed her eyes to the inner voice of warning, to the Truth.

She knew only the remembered feel of Friend Robert's lips on hers, the yearning that was new and strange to her. He had found a virginal region of her heart and claimed it as his own. And she, foolishly, did not seek to escape him.

She told herself that, when recovered, he would return to his world as she would return to hers. Their two worlds might touch, they might collide disastrously, but they could never unite in the peace and harmony that was so necessary to her.

In spite of that wisdom, she was possessed of a feverish impatience to reach his side.

Friend Robert's eyes turned to Tabitha eagerly, as if he had been anxiously awaiting her arrival. Her trembling haste had been worthwhile. What a strange thing the human heart was that it could soar out of despair's depths to elation's heights, that it could insist that all was right when all was wrong. Yet she gave no thought to wrong as she hurried across the exquisite carpet, her small feet seeming to float above it. She gave no thought to wrong as she reached for the hand he held out to her.

He lay abed, his hair clean and damp and curling. Spots of hectic color stained his cheeks, a sign of fever that was affirmed by the unnatural brightness of his eyes.

"Thee should not have chafed Friend Abraham," she said, more commonsensically than she felt.

A twinkle lit his eyes. "He brings out the worst in me."

Just as Friend Robert brought out the worst in her. How had he transformed her from a woman of abundant sense to a flighty changeling? She shouldn't be amused by him, but she was. She shouldn't be nursing him, but she was. She should be considering the consequences, but she wasn't. Instead, she was smiling at him, her cheeks dimpling.

"I fear 'tis the devil he brings out in thee," she said.

"No doubt."

He drew her down to his side, where she perched on the edge of the bed. A man's bed, and she an unwed maiden. What, she wondered, would he have her doing next?

"You look tired."

His finger gently coasted down her cheek, and she wanted to stay there forever with her heart at flood tide. "Next thee will say I am positively hagged," she said softly, rising, escaping his touch. "I must ask Anne how thee gained thy reputation for charming the ladies."

His lips twitched and spread in a grin. "Lud! Don't tell me I'm losing my touch."

"Do not take the Lord's name in vain," she said with as much dignity as she could muster around a growing smile.

"Thee did not answer me, Friend Tabby."

The sparkle in his eyes brought a hot flood of color to her cheeks, while she admitted—if only to herself—that he was charming her out of all sensibility.

"I must change thy bandage. Friend Abraham awaits me below," she said gently.

The sparkle died, leaving his eyes flat and blank above his slowly dwindling smile. "You won't leave with him," he said, more a command than a statement.

"No," she said. "I will stay with thee until . . ." How painful the thought was. "Until thee needs me no longer."

Until thee needs me no longer. But how would she explain that to her brother and to Friend Abraham?

Leaving Robbie bandaged and resting and fighting sleep as if he were afraid of it, she descended to the drawing room. She went to Adam first, her hands outstretched.

"How glad I am that thee was in port," she said as he gathered her into his strong arms and hugged her tightly. A whiff of the sea lingered about him, a salt-sea smell that hinted of foreign climes and the restless men who sought them. Unwillingly, her thoughts returned to Friend Robert. Restless Friend Robert, who would be leaving soon. How easy it had been to caution Anne against trying to keep him safe when her own heart had not been engaged. How easy it had been to say that some men can be held close only by letting them go.

"Friend Tabitha," intruded Abraham Leeds, "it is beyond my comprehension that thee would choose to attend the sickbed of—"

"Friend Robert saved my life," she said, wondering at the irritation that scraped her raw. "How can I do less for him?"

"He has his sister, his mother, his servants."

"And his father, wounded and ill unto death. I stay because I will be needed." Or because her wayward heart willed it?

"Dost thou think this wise?" Impatience sharpened his tone. "Friend Robert's reputation is the very poorest."

She should not have smiled, but she did. His reputation was undoubtedly poor and deservedly so. Hadn't he already tilted the balance of her safe, secure world, leaving her to feel that she might slip off into the dark unknown of her heart?

Friend Abraham stiffened, his lips thinning, and Tabitha hastened to speak. Before she could do so, Adam coughed lightly, folding his thick arms across his chest.

"Art thou suggesting that our Tabby might succumb to any improper advance made by Friend Robert?"

The hard warning note in his voice was not lost on Abraham. A dull flush darkened his cheeks. "Of course not," he blustered, and Adam's gaze met Tabitha's, his brow tilting in a skeptical question. "I merely wonder how this will look to others."

"I should not think we need concern ourselves with that," said Adam repressively. "Any who know our Tabby know that she is of the sternest moral fiber. They know, too, that Friend Robert is no fool. He will recognize her worth and honor it."

The two men turned to look at her, and it seemed they should be able to see the imprint of Friend Robert's mouth on her lips, of his smile on her heart.

"I hoped thee would honor thy decision to testify at summer's end," said Friend Abraham, "that thee would honor my wishes. If thee does not . . ."

The implication was clear. Should Tabitha not do as he wished, he might choose to back out of the marriage. Her unease heightened. Though she longed for the home and family he promised, for the worship and good works that marriage would bring, she could not turn her back on Friend Robert.

"Perhaps, when I arrive at Fell Cottage, we should discuss what we wish to do," she said.

"Very well." He marched stiffly to the door.

Adam came to her, his dark face somber. "Whatever happens, Tabby, thee must listen to thy heart."

And an unruly heart it was. Had she, by refusing Friend Abraham's demands, lost the chance to wed? Already five-and-twenty, she might have no second opportunity. While that thought grieved her, she could not grieve the loss of Friend Abraham. The unease had become an assurance that he and she would not do well together. Perhaps, in her years of working as governess, she had become too accustomed to going her own way. Whatever the reason, she could not deny the dictates of her mind and heart.

Robbie dared not close his eyes. If he did, he would sleep. If he slept, he would dream. If he dreamed, it would be of Schattenburg and the fear that had unmanned him.

His eyes were hot, and his tongue parched. But worst of all was the strange weak need to have Tabitha return, to feel her cool hand on his brow, to experience again her unassailable serenity.

Even now she was talking to Leeds. Saying what? Planning the wedding? Robbie scowled across the room, bringing Cheddar upright in his straight-backed chair.

"Are you in pain, milord?"

Robbie shook his head, shifting his hot, dry gaze to the window where a breeze belled the lace undercurtains. Tabitha's brother had looked a good sort, too sensible to allow his sister to wed where she should not. And she definitely should not wed Abraham Leeds. He was the worst possible choice for her. Perhaps, Robbie thought, he could talk to Adam Fell, explain to him . . .

Lud! Before he knew it he would be a worse busybody than Cousin Knox. And all of London Society knew none could touch the Dowager Duchess of Worth on that head.

If Tabitha was to *testify* with Leeds, it was none of his affair. After all, he would be leaving soon, taking ship for Greece and war. Leaving only—his heart sank—if his father recovered. Which, if the worry dwelling in Anne's and Karl's eyes was any measure, was in some doubt. Soon the fever would be taking him away. He would be too weak to see his father should anything . . . happen.

He rose on an elbow. "Cheddar, my dressing gown."

The valet stood abruptly, his pear-shaped body swaying. "Milord, you cannot mean to rise!"

"I must."

" 'Tis madness! I shan't be a part of it!"

His eyes narrowed in menace. "Get my dressing gown!"

"Robbie!" Anne sailed in, trailed by a panting chambermaid with a tray of steaming broth. "Don't badger your man. You haven't the strength to rise."

"I must see Father."

Her wary gaze revealed the war between her fears for their father and for him. "Wait until you are stronger."

"That may be too late, and we both know it."

"Push yourself further, and it may be too late for *you.*"

Into the stalemate Tabitha brought an aura of calm. She paused in the door. "Friend Robert?"

"I must see my father," he said, hating the need to explain, hating the weakness that made him waver.

She crossed the chamber, gazing deep into his eyes. "Yes, thee must," she said gently.

"But he's too weak to climb the stairs!" protested Anne.

"He was strong enough to save us both. He will be strong enough for this." She lifted a curl from his brow, sliding her hand across it, the faintest of smiles etching her mouth. "He is too stubborn to fail."

It seemed to Robbie that his heart was bared before her penetrating gaze. None of his need, none of his fear, could he keep from her. Oddly, he was bereft of the desire to shield himself. How long had it been since he had trusted anyone with the secrets of his heart?

"Anne, would thee summon two sturdy footmen to help him?" Tabitha asked.

Robbie stood in the door of his father's chamber staring at his mother, accustoming himself anew to her glistening white hair and the lines creping her fashionably pale skin. Memory insisted that she was yet a youthful beauty, her hair as black as Anne's and her skin untouched by age. But grief had stolen her youthful beauty during his imprisonment at Schattenburg. It was another bit of floss to color the tapestry of his guilt.

She turned and smiled, her silvery-gray eyes lighting. "You should be abed."

"I had to come." He took her hand and felt her fragile bones quaking against his palm. He had a swift vision of that hand firmly swatting his rump for a youthful indiscretion. How quickly the time had passed for both of them. "You are tired."

"There will be plenty of time to rest when your father is recovered."

"And he will flay us all if we allow you to—"

"I am not yet in my dotage," she said acerbically.

"Assuredly not." He kissed her papery-dry cheek, breathing her favorite orris root fragrance. It had drifted through his nursery chambers, lingered at table through his childhood, and summoned him out of the depths of despair at Schattenburg. In the intervening years he had on occasion caught a whiff of it in foreign ports and been filled with longing for the lush and fertile green of England, for the home and family he had left behind. Now it filled him with regret for the parting that must come.

"Robbie."

His father's thready voice summoned him to the bed. The earl's face was as white as the linens, his steel-gray hair as rumpled as the embroidered silk coverlet. He looked so old and frail, and his skin was so thin that blue veins mapped it like rivers flowing through a snowy landscape. He who had once been so tall and strong, so immortal, it had seemed to the son who had always worshiped him, now looked small and weak.

"Father?" Robbie caught his hand, feeling it move feebly against his.

The earl's lashes fluttered, his once clear ice-blue eyes now cloudy. "Tabitha?" he whispered.

"Safe," Robbie said.

"Good," he whispered, and closed his eyes. He appeared to have gone to sleep, but he stirred once more, grasping Robbie's hand. "I must speak with you, alone."

"I will be outside should you need me," said his wife.

The earl's face twisted with pain. "Swear that you will not leave your mother alone. Should anything happen to me—"

"It won't!" Robbie said fiercely.

Through the pain came the hint of his father's old smile. "Perhaps I will be too stubborn to die, but if . . ." He paused, breathing in shallow, rapid pants. "I will have your word on it."

The shores of England, the ties of family took a stranglehold on Robbie's throat. He wanted to plead with his father not to lay this burden on him, not to trust him when he could not trust himself. But for the first time, his father needed him.

"My word, Father. I will not leave her alone."

Chapter 5

Tabitha knew something was wrong the moment Friend Robert appeared in the door, shrugging off the footmen, his gaze searching the chamber until he found her standing beside the window. The barest hint of a smile softened his mouth, even as a haunted desperation glittered in his eyes. She had been right to stay. For this little while he needed her.

"Thy father?" she asked.

Pain clouded his face. bringing her across the lushly carpeted floor. "For the first time, he looks old, Tabby."

She knew how he felt, how sad and frightening it was to see a sturdy and robust father wither so quickly into old age. She had watched her own father grow thin before her eyes, his smiling face lined and creased, his broad, capable shoulders sagging.

"Anne is hopeful," she said encouragingly.

"And he is stubborn."

"Like his son," she said softly, afraid but not sure why.

The ghost of a smile that slipped across his mouth was not echoed in his eyes. "Let us hope too stubborn to die."

"I will pray that he lives a long, fruitful life," she said, searching for the reason he wore the expression of a poacher caught in a mantrap and frantic to escape.

"Do that, Tabby. Perhaps He will listen to you." He

tucked a finger beneath her chin, tilting her face up to his. "I have no doubt that your prayers rise on angels' wings, while mine dissipate in clouds of soot."

"Thou art troubled."

He stared through the window, focusing on the far distance, his head cocked as if listening to a beckoning voice. "My father has asked me to stay with my mother should . . . anything happen to him."

"And . . . and thee does not wish to."

"I gave my word that I would."

"But thee fears that thee cannot."

"I gave my word." His face hardened.

"And if thy father lives?"

"I will leave as planned."

How painful it was to hear that. "Do not despair. Friend John is strong. He will live, and thee will be free to seek . . ."

She paused, unsure what he sought. Surcease? But from what? The angular lines of his face and the rigid set of his mouth betrayed nothing new. He was deeply, frighteningly unhappy, and there was nothing she could do to ease him.

She turned away, assuming a brisk air as she moved toward the bed. "Thou art weary. Thee should rest."

But rest seemed far from his thoughts when he settled in the mahogany four-poster in the soft shadows of the yellow silk curtains. He insisted she perch on the bed beside him, then cradled her hand in his, one finger idling over her palm. "Have I caused you much trouble with your Abraham Leeds?"

She should have been angry, but the glint of mischief that had returned to his gaze summoned an unwilling smile. "Thee has convinced him that I am not the woman he thought I was."

"You've got bottom, as my father would say. Too much spine for a man like Leeds."

A strange light entered his eyes. A look of admiration that a man might give to an equal. How odd. In that moment she wanted only the look a man gave to a woman. Another sign that her heart was more deeply engaged than was good for her.

"You are a worthy companion for adversity, Tabitha Fell."

Higher praise she had never been given. How easy it would be to forget the moderation in thought, action, and speech that was so necessary to the Friends. "Do not spend thy strength on foolishness," she said, gently tugging at the crisp wedge of side-whiskers framing his cheek.

He brought her hand to his lips, the kiss he pressed in her palm settling like a benediction in her heart. But no true blessing could it be, for they were out of unity. He, an Anglican; she, a Quaker. He, a man of violence; she, a woman of peace. Yet with only the two of them in the silence of his chamber, it seemed that nothing mattered, that all was possible.

She shook herself from wishful reverie with a new awareness of how easy it was to slip down the greased slope of temptation.

"Thee must feel the bite of hunger."

His eyes shone with suppressed laughter. "If it's broth you intend to—"

"It is," she said, as firmly as she could when his growing smile was shattering her every good intention.

"You're a hard woman, Tabitha Fell."

"Thee will not charm me into giving thee a crust of bread and a haunch of meat, Friend Robert."

"You are sure of that?" His glossy black brow climbed into an inverted vee that lent a diabolic cast to his features.

Minutes later, as if she had no will of her own, she was yanking the bellpull and ordering meats and bread and cheese. A wheedling Robert Ransome, claiming himself to be on the verge of starvation, was not to be resisted.

By nightfall her suspicion that he would be a difficult patient had been confirmed. He refused to sleep. His tender humor metamorphosed into irritability that combined with the rising fever to sharpen his tongue and temper.

He wanted to read, but nothing suited him. He wanted to play chess, but he couldn't concentrate. He wanted Tabitha to talk; she did until she was hoarse. Twilight began spreading its shadows, and he wanted candles and more candles set about his chamber. Light flickered over a pair of delicate china candlesticks set atop the bedside cupboard. A silver candelabra blazed atop the mahogany bureau; in its delicately painted lozenges of sea battles, the tiny figures seemed to move, to stab with their swords, to swing from the shrouds—as restless as the fretful man scowling into the canopy of his bed.

Branches of candles were reflected in the cheval mirror. It was a shameful waste, yet she could not regret it. Not when his gaze turned again and again to the window and the gathering shadows of night with a look so akin to fear she seemed to feel the eerie chill of the crypt in Schattenburg settling around her shoulders.

"Come and sit by me, Tabby." The words slurred with the weariness that had etched lines of tension around his mouth.

She wrung out a linen cloth and laid it across his brow. Her thumbs massaged his temples, and his lashes began to droop over his eyes. "Thee should rest," she crooned like a mother with a babe.

He relaxed, his bare chest rising and falling in the even rhythm of sleep. Slowly she moved her hands, waiting for a deeper sleep to claim him before she began to inch from the bed.

He woke abruptly, his body jerking, his eyes wide and unfocused. "Tabby?"

"I'm here."

His gaze slowly focused on her, his eyes dark and impenetrable. "How . . . how long was I asleep?"

"Moments. No more."

He caught her wrist, his grip painful. "Did I . . . I do anything, say anything?"

"Thee slept as peacefully as a babe." But what did he expect to do, to say? she wondered.

A sigh eased between his lips, as soft as the night breeze whispering round the eaves. "As peacefully as a babe," he murmured, the taut line of his mouth softening. "Have you given me that peace, Tabby?"

"And why should thee not have it thyself?"

He looked away, his eyes closing, a muscle rippling in his clenched jaw.

Tabitha heard the church bells ring the hour of midnight. Cheddar arrived, to watch through the night, freeing her to rest on the trundle bed. Friend Robert had succumbed to sleep, but no sooner had his valet strutted into the bedchamber than he began tossing and turning and muttering.

"It has begun," said Cheddar gloomily.

Tabitha cast an anxious glance at her nursling's face, now twisted as if tortured by dreams. "What has begun?"

"Perhaps it would be best if you went above to the nursery chamber, Madam—"

"Friend Tabitha, I pray thee."

"Friend Tabitha," he said tightly, an expression of exquisite pain wrinkling his brow. "His lordship will be greatly agitated through the night. I should not think he would wish you to see him as he will be."

"And how will he be?"

Cheddar folded his small, delicate hands over the jut of his belly, eyeing Tabitha as if she were a peculiarly unfavorable species of bedbug he had found trundling across his lordship's linens. "Agitated, mad—Friend Tabitha, agitated."

He obviously gave his loyalty to bloodlines. Just as obviously, he was inordinately devoted to his master. For that she could easily forgive his distaste of her. "Thee has been with him long."

"I entered his service when he was yet a boy."

"And I have come to him of late, but together we might give him the tenderest of care. Tell me, why will he be . . . agitated?"

He studied her with a curious, impassioned gaze, as if he would see into her heart, scouring its corners to find how true she would be. "You know of . . . Schattenburg?"

It came to her with swift dread, the reason he needed the light, why he feared to sleep. She turned to study Friend Robert's face, burnished by the candlelight, his features contorted. "He relives it," she whispered, her hands curling into fists at her waist, her heart atremble.

"Always when a fever is on him."

She groped blindly for Cheddar's arm. "Is there nothing we can do?"

Hesitating, he covered her hand with his, sealing an unspoken pact. She was but a lowly governess and, worse, of a dissenting faith, but she would be—just barely—good enough to see his lordship through the dangers and trials ahead.

"It will run its course, no matter what is done," he said. "I have tried in the past—"

"Tabby," came Friend Robert's voice, as hard and harsh as his eyes, a fathomless black in the candlelight. Yet it seemed to her he lingered in the throes of the nightmare, pulling himself by sheer strength of will to the portal between dream and reality. "You must leave now," he commanded. "Cheddar will—"

"No!" She flung herself to her knees at his bedside, taking his hand between hers and trembling at its dry heat. "I will stay as long as thee needs me."

The nightmare tugged at him, a shimmer of horror lighting the glassy surface of his eyes. His fingers curled around hers, gripping tightly, as if she were an anchor to hold him fast.

"Why, Tabby? Why?"

Why? Surely she was too sensible for the answer that would never bring her peace, harmony, or happiness. She was in love with Robert Ransome, Viscount Langley, a man with whom she could share nothing that was important to her. She was immoderately, passionately in love, and she had never been more deeply grieved.

"Thee saved my life," she said, echoing what she had told Friend Abraham. "How could I do less for thee?"

"Cheddar can—"

"I pray thee, Friend Robert, let me stay."

He slipped away, vanishing across the portal of reality and taking the first steps of his nightmare journey. "Dark. So dark," he moaned. "Where is the light?"

She hastened to draw a candle closer, and though he looked directly into the flame, he did not seem to see it.

"Anne, Anne, what have I done to you?" he cried out, his voice thick with grief and guilt.

He sat up, the coverlet falling away from the flushed expanse of his chest. Tabitha pressed him back down, but he sent her flying with a casual sweep of his arm. She landed against a mahogany tallboy, a tangle of arms and legs and skirt. Cheddar set her aright, his expression saying he had warned her. Rubbing a bruised elbow, she hurried to the bedside.

"I'm afraid. So afraid," Friend Robert whispered. "Can't let them see me like this. God! God, why? Why has this happened to Anne, to me?"

He peered into space, and Tabitha thought of the single stone's opening in the mortared wall of the crypt. He had lived for more than a year expecting that opening to be sealed at any time. He had then watched it being mortared into place, and found himself alone in his tomb, and suffocating.

Her trembling hand rested on his heated brow, her heart in a ferment of pity and admiration. He had braved the dark enclosure of the tunnel in order to save her life. Only now could she understand the courage that act had required.

"Friend Robert," she said, but he did not hear.

"Robbie, Robbie," she whispered, and he turned to her.

"Anne? Anne! I'm so sorry! God, I'm so sorry!"

"There is no need to be," she said, joining in his delusion. "I am safe. I am well."

"But treason, Anne! They'll hang you if they catch you!"

"They won't catch me. I'll hide beneath Granny Goody's bed. Remember the game we played?" Anne had often told her of the trick she had played on him and how, instead of being angry, he had laughed until he cried. Tabitha remembered how she had smiled over her stitching, knowing she would like this man who could laugh at himself. Had the seed of love been planted then?

"Granny Goody's," he murmured, his strength fading.

"I am safe now," she sang in the cadence of a lullaby, while she gently urged him back against the pillows. "Rest, Robbie. Rest."

His eyes closed like an obedient child's, and hers rose to meet Cheddar's uncertain gaze.

"He has never been so easy to soothe, Friend Tabitha."

Only because his fever was climbing to frightening heights, she thought. She forced barley water down him, drop by drop, rubbing his throat, insisting that he swallow. With Cheddar's aid, she stripped him bare and bathed him with cooling water throughout the waning hours of the night.

No man had ever been so finely formed. His skin was dark and honey-tinted with the texture of satin tautly stretched over the sleek muscle beneath. His body was long and lean and powerful, tempting her to touch the curve of his shoulder, the sweep of his rib cage, the bulge of his upper arm. Her foolishness took her so far, she thought the first man wrought by God's hands must have looked just so in the innocence of the Garden of Eden.

His blue-black hair sharply contrasted with the stark

white of his boldly masculine face, with its lean, well-defined lines softened by his sensuously generous mouth. Tabitha touched his hot cheek, the small square of her palm caressed by the crisp wedge of whiskers neatly squared at his jaw.

"It's morning," said Cheddar with amazement.

Her gaze rose to the window. The first rays of sunlight turned the clouds to rose pink. As if summoned by that light, Anne hurried through the door. "Robbie?"

"The same," she said wearily. "Thy father?"

"The same." Anne hooked an arm around Tabitha's waist. "You look exhausted."

She was. There had been no time to think about the aching of her back, the trembling of her hands, the bone-deep exhaustion that slurred her words.

"Go above and rest," Anne said.

"But he needs broth and—"

"Cheddar and I will see to it," Anne said in a tone that brooked no opposition.

Tabitha jerked awake with a guilty start, her eyes wide in the heavy gloom of twilight. Her first coherent thought: Did Anne know of Robbie's fear of the dark? His need for candles and light?

With more haste than sense—how quickly she had abandoned the required moderation of her creed—she performed her ablutions and skimmed down the stairs, flying through the door of Friend Robert's chamber. Every candle was lit, their flames dancing gently in the whisper of a breeze that slipped through the window. Anne was nowhere to be seen. Cheddar dozed in a chair, his triple row of chins chucked beneath his pouting lips.

Tabitha hastened to the bed to assure herself that Friend Robert was alive. His breath was so shallow she leaned down, her hand cupped beneath his nose. A slight stirring of air brought a fierce surge of gladness to thicken her throat. Her hand turned over his lips and her finger glided gently down the seam of his mouth to the corner with its slight upward tilt promising a smile, and after tarrying there, coasted along the soft arc of his lower lip with a tender touch, a lover's touch. A soft breath hissed through her throat, and her hand curled into a fist, drawing back from temptation.

Listen to thy heart, Anne, she had said with such easy assurance before she had met Robbie. *It will never lead thee astray.*

But hers had. It had set her reluctant feet on the road of a love that was doomed never to be returned, never to be fulfilled. Yet she could not regret it. How pale the emotions she had previously experienced. How . . . moderate they had been. For the first time she knew why a woman would risk everything for the man who claimed her heart.

"Tabby," said Anne, coming all a-hurry, her face bleached of color and her eyes ringed by sleeplessness, "how is he?"

She shrugged helplessly. "And thy father?"

Anne drew a shuddering breath, tears trickling down her cheeks. "I'm so afraid," she whispered. "So afraid he will die. So afraid Robbie will blame himself. If only they had come to a better understanding of one another."

"Perhaps they have. Perhaps . . ."

Anne shook her head. "Mother says they had been arguing since Robbie's arrival. Father insisted that he settle down, take a wife, sire an heir, but he—"

"Refused," Tabitha finished sadly.

"If Father were not so ill, I would give him a good scold!" Anne laughed through her tears. "He has paraded every eligible miss on the Marriage Mart beneath Robbie's indifferent nose. Mother says a more insipid and witless lot has not been seen since Cousin Knox's come-out; and Father has always insisted that was the only way, to use his words, 'that wretched woman managed to leg-shackle the Duke of Worth.' Of course, Cousin Knox and Father have always"—she paused, a reminiscent smile curling her mouth—"rubbed together like pumice stones."

"It doesn't seem to be the way to engage Friend Robert's interest," Tabitha said cautiously.

"I should say not! How Father could be so henwitted I shall never understand! But then, he has always approached Robbie with all guns firing. He has never learned that getting Robbie to do what you want him to do requires . . . subtlety."

In spite of the acute discomfort aroused by thoughts of Friend Robert seeking, choosing, wedding another, Tabitha smiled. "Doesn't thee mean . . . dishonesty?"

"Sometimes," Anne said staunchly, "a man doesn't know what he really wants."

"And always it is better to let him learn for himself."

"Unless he is stubborn."

"Especially if he is stubborn," Tabitha said gently.

Anne shook her head, smiling. "Tabby, do you never tire of being wise?"

"But I am not always wise." Her gaze shifted to Friend Robert. If she were, she would not have allowed her heart to slip from her grasp.

Tabitha pondered the tangled skeins of wisdom and foolishness in the wee hours of the night. Anne was abed, taking a much-needed rest. Cheddar, having protested vehemently, now snored on his narrow cot in the adjacent servant's closet.

Though Friend Robert's wound was clean and crusting as it should, his fever continued to rise. Endlessly, Tabitha bathed him in cooling water. Endlessly, he shifted and tossed and muttered unintelligibly, until he went rigid and opened his eyes and stared with the blind gaze of madness.

"A knife," he said in a conspiratorial whisper. "If I am dead, he won't have a hold on Anne. A knife . . ."

She jerked alert, a chill coursing through her. "No," she said softly. "That is never the way."

She touched his arm, her fingers sliding down toward his hand, stopping abruptly at the raised scar an-

gling across his inner wrist. Another chill settled
around her heart, encasing it in ice, sending her swirling down in the deep sea of his despair.

"A knife." He rolled away, tried to rise.

"No!" She threw herself after him, wrapping her
arms around his chest.

Weak as he was, he shrugged her off, diving for the
satinwood writing table where the scissors gleamed
atop fresh linen bandages. She scrambled after him,
grabbing the thick, muscular fist wound around the
ring handles.

"I pray thee, don't! Don't, Robbie! Listen to me!"

But he was deaf to her pleas, blind to all save the
blade glinting in the light. The blade he pulled inexo-
rably, not to his wrist, but to his heart.

"Help!" she screamed. "Friend Cheddar, help me!
Help me!"

She wrapped both hands around Friend Robert's
wrist, braced her feet against his, and pulled back.
Strain corded her neck and bowed her back. Terror
stole her breath, leaving sharp, shallow pants scraping
through her throat.

The tip of the scissors bit into his flesh. A thin trickle
of blood skidded down to the edge of the wide bandaging and spread along its rim, the pulsating red of
life.

Her horrified gaze swept up to his eyes, pansy purple, dark with despair and resolve. What he had once
failed to do he would do now. And she did not have
the strength to stop him.

"Friend Cheddar!" she screamed.

The valet came in a tumbling, fumbling rush, his
footsteps pounding. His delicate hand, surprisingly
strong, hooked around Tabitha's shoulder and
wrenched her away. She fell back with a lost cry,
watching that hand ball into a dainty fist and tap Friend
Robert's jaw, gently, it seemed. But he went flying, his
arms spreading, the scissors sailing through the air and
landing with a clatter on the marble hearth.

She scrambled after him, her fingers racing over his

face, touching the knot swelling on his jaw, racing down his chest to the shallow wound. His breath was thin but steady. She sighed with relief, bowing her head and trembling. She was so tired and so afraid, for him, for herself.

She lifted his hand, lightly rubbing the raised scar, raising it to her cheek and holding it there. Her eyes closed over the hot tears that welled up from her grieving heart. "Where did he find a knife in that . . . that place?"

"He sharpened the handle of a wooden spoon, but they stopped him before . . ."

Cheddar did not finish. He did not need to. She lifted her eyes, awash in tears. "I am so glad."

"But he is not, Friend Tabitha."

The wee hours of the night passed peacefully for Friend Robert and wretchedly for Tabitha. She insisted that Cheddar return to his rest, and she sat alone in a splat-back chair beside the bed.

But he is not, Friend Tabitha. He was not glad that he had lived. It was a heretical notion, for she found intense pleasure in life. Yet, knowing him as she did now, she had a glimmer of understanding. It was his pride, his rigid, stiff-necked pride.

He could tolerate neither failure nor fear, and that intolerance gnawed at him as the commission of a sin would gnaw at her. He was sustained by neither faith nor hope nor her belief that every life was guided by an ordained Plan. If he could accept that, he would know that everything had happened for a reason, though he might never know what that reason was.

But she could see the good that had grown from the bad. Anne and her beloved Karl were blissfully wed, bearing fruits of their union in the boys and baby Magda. Anne had changed *die Engländerin* from a curse to a prayer, showing the Schattenburgians the kindness and love of a people they had feared. Out of the horrors of the Napoleonic Wars had grown a newer, more stable Europe, modeled on Lord Castlereagh's theory of a balance of power. Europe was no longer carved into a multitude of tiny principalities that were incapable of defending themselves. Many, like the Principality of Schattenburg, had been grafted onto larger states, making them stronger and less vulnerable to conquest. Karl, after his initial disappointment that he would not continue the rule of his ancestors, had become a wise and benevolent counselor to his king and was bringing peace and prosperity to his country.

Every Plan had its time of suffering and self-doubt, and Friend Robert still stumbled through his, just as she had been propelled into hers. She had always been certain she knew the Plan for her life. Now she feared it would take her far from everything she knew and loved, far from everything she wanted.

She was deep in unhappy thought when Friend Robert began breathing in the short, rapid pants of panic. He jerked up, his eyes wide and terrified. "They're mortaring the stone! The dark. The air. Can't breathe!"

"Robbie!" Tabitha said sharply. "Robbie!"

He clawed at his throat, gasping. "Can't breathe!"

"Robbie, listen to me," she whispered, her own throat thick with tears. She touched his bare shoulder and he flinched, freezing, his breath rasping through his throat. Her palm smoothed up and down, feeling him quiver with tension. "It's over," she soothed. "Thou art safe. Safe at home in Darenth House."

He blinked, his gaze rising to meet hers. A blind gaze that saw, yet did not see. He caught her, spinning her down onto his lap, holding her in a crushing grip, while his body trembled against hers and his breath blew hot against the tender flesh beneath her ear. "Am I dreaming?" he asked hoarsely.

"Yes," she said simply, her small hands moving in comforting circles over the hard ridges of his back. He had been so alone and afraid. Like she was now, afraid for him, for herself, for the uncertain future.

"Then I must make the most of it," he said, his lips coasting from the curve of her collar to her earlobe.

Desperately ignoring the thrill that scampered beneath the touch of his warm mouth, Tabitha tried to lean back. "Friend Robert, no—"

"Yes," he said in a voice like velvet, while his lips moved along her jaw, captured her willing mouth, and possessed it fully.

Possessed her lips, her heart. Possessed her body and soul. For one tumultuous moment she lay quiescent in his arms, ravished by his tender quest for the softness of her lower lip, the arch of her upper lip, the moist secret corners, enchanted by the supple meeting and mating of his mouth to hers, of her heart—

She must not yield to him or to herself. Tabitha pulled away, her hands pressed against the hard plane of his chest. "Friend Robert, I pray thee, do not."

He released her reluctantly, leaning back against the pillows, his spurt of strength obviously waning. But the look in the violet eyes that restlessly roamed her features was one of both puzzlement and yearning.

Her fingers lightly curled around his wrist, finding the raised scar that angled across it. "Rest, Friend Robert. Thee must rest," she coaxed.

"What a sweet dream you are," he whispered, holding her hand while he drifted back into the nightmare world of his dreams.

He looked like the small Franz with his black hair tumbling across his brow and his face as innocent as a child's. But that innocence was deceptive. He had learned more of inhumanity, of his own limitations, than any man should. Yet it had not destroyed the core that was as true as gold, the capacity for tenderness and love and laughter.

Her knuckles skimmed down his cheek. She wanted to do so much for him, for Anne's beloved brother, for this man she had come to know through Anne's memories of him, for this man who had dared his greatest fear to save her, though she was nothing to him.

He had stolen her heart bit by bit, taking the peace and harmony that were so necessary to her. Knowing she should not, knowing she would never again be the same, she leaned down and kissed his lips, lingering over them as he had so recently lingered over hers, cherishing them as she wished he might cherish hers.

Rising up, her heart aching, breaking, she studied the dark planes of his cheeks, the noble reach of his brow . . . his brow, damp with sweat. The clean healthy sweat of a breaking fever. Relief and melancholy warred for supremacy. Soon he would be well . . . and no longer need her.

She heard a step and surreptitiously wiped the tears from her cheeks, turning to find Anne in the door.

"Father has passed the crisis. Dr. Kennon says he will recover if we can keep him still until he regains his strength."

"How glad I am for thee." Her gaze shifted to Friend Robert's face. Now there was nothing to keep him in England, nothing and no one to keep him safe from himself.

Chapter 6

His ship sailed for the Aegean with the tide, but Robbie was not on it. Instead of heading for the rigors of a campaign in Greece, he was being cosseted like a babe. Which of the three women in his life irritated him more, he could not have said. His mother incessantly plied him with bland possets better suited for a toothless antiquarian. Anne sharpened her tongue on the whetstone of his foul mood, as if she had forgotten that he had no patience with languishing abed. And Tabitha . . .

Something was wrong with Tabitha.

She attended him assiduously, but she was . . . distant. She shied from his touch. She spoke little and said less. She seemed fascinated by his mouth, but if he caught her staring, she would look away, her cheeks shading to dusky rose. Each time he was swept by a feeling too insubstantial to be called a memory, too real not to be one. Somehow, he knew how her mouth felt as it flowered beneath his, how her body felt as he molded it to his. His tongue slicked across lips that were indelibly impressed with the satin-soft texture, the erotic innocence, of her mouth.

He remembered kissing her in the shadowy depths of the Roman bath, but this feeling—this memory?—did not arise from that. It was more powerful, more tauntingly seductive.

What had happened during his fever? Had he kissed

her? Done something more? Was that why she had become so distant?

Each time he tried to ask her, his courage failed him. Each day it seemed more imperative that he have an answer.

The noonday sun slanted through the bedroom windows, prying Robbie's eyes open. His hair was fragrantly scented of Castille soap; his bed was eiderdown soft; his mood was savage.

He should be, if not happy, at least satisfied. His father's fever had passed, and while the earl's recovery promised to be slow, it was assured—if his overly solicitous wife and daughter didn't twit him into another bout of fever.

Robbie would have been free to leave England, but . . . the casket had been left on the steps of Darenth House with the money untouched, and only Shadwell could have brought it. What should have been a blessing was instead a curse and an alarming mystery that neither Robbie nor Karl could fathom. The man was a low denizen of the rookeries who would not cavil at thievery. So why would he return the money . . . unless he had another reason for murdering von Fersen and saving them.

Robbie could not forget those last moments with Shadwell appearing, a shadow in the door, his attention palpably focused on Tabitha. Years of travel in dangerous foreign lands, of living with one eye to his back and the other to his purse, had honed Robbie's instincts to a razor-edge. Those instincts now said that Tabitha was the key. If there was a danger for any of them, it would be for her.

He heaped the pillows against the marquetry headboard and slumped against them, scowling at the embroidered coverlet tented across his toes, casting angry glances at the brilliant noon light, casting angrier glances at the empty splat-back chair.

Where was Tabitha? For three days he had waked to find her sitting in that chair, her head bowed over her mending, her sweet smile his first greeting of the morn. A thought came. He thrust it away. She wouldn't leave without telling him goodbye, would she? He flung back the linens, bellowing for Cheddar, who came at a huffing, puffing run.

"Milord," he said, his dignity ruffled, "there is no need to shout like a costermonger hawking his wares."

Robbie resisted the overpowering urge to throttle him. "Where is Tabitha?"

"I haven't seen her, milord."

There was no reason for the fear that spread through him. She was safe. She was well. But he leapt from the bed, heedless of the sharp ache in his side.

A short time later, he hurried from his chamber with the despairing Cheddar shaking his head over the leather breeches belted at Robbie's waist and the full, flowing white cambric shirt. He took the stairs two at a time.

Tabitha was not in the Nursery Parlor or in the governess's bedchamber. The disappointment that knifed through him took his breath away. He raced down the stairs.

Sunlight pierced the dining room windows in wide swaths of lemon yellow that lent a rich color to the mahogany sideboard *en suite* and the brass-strung lyre-back chairs that marched down the long linen-covered table. At its head, in the fragrant spring breeze belling the lace curtains, sat Karl and Anne—but no Tabitha.

Karl had pushed his empty plate aside and reclined in his chair, a tawny lion whose sparkling gaze was riveted on Anne's face. A smile of lazy amusement and pleasure softened his mouth as she waved a forkful of roast lamb and laughed. "You'll put me out of temper, should you again suggest that I—"

Robbie paused in the archway, his arms akimbo and his feet spread. "Where is Tabitha?"

Anne exchanged a curious look with her husband before laying her fork aside. "She rose with the sun, as is her habit, and requested that she be allowed to leave immediately for Fell Cottage. She feared her family would be—''

''And you let her go?'' he asked hotly, substituting anger for the emptiness that filled him.

''Is there some reason I should have kept her here?''

''You cannot be that bird-witted, Anne! Did she tell you—''

''Everything,'' she said.

As taut as a bowstring, he leaned forward. ''And you do not find it strange that Shadwell rescued us, then returned the money? You have not wondered what was more important to a thief than his ill-gotten gains?''

Anne straightened, her face blanching. ''You cannot mean—''

''Think about it. If he had a grudge to settle with you or Father, he's had twelve years to do it. If he wanted to kill von Fersen, why did he choose that particular time and place? The only piece that fits the puzzle is—''

''Tabitha,'' she whispered, stricken.

''Yes,'' he said sarcastically, ''Tabi—''

''That's enough.'' Karl rose from his chair, pulling Anne into the circle of his arms while he frowned at Robbie. ''She's had enough worry and fear for a lifetime. I wanted to keep this from her for as long as possible.''

''You knew?'' questioned Anne, her gaze searching his face.

''Yes, he knew,'' said Robbie coldly, ''and he let her—''

''Don't forget that we are as yet without proof. It may be that Tabitha is safe, and we will never hear of Shadwell again.''

''And it may be that we are right, and you have let her leave here unprotected.''

''Since I know how I would feel were Anne in danger, I will not take offense at that accusation,'' said Karl with a thread of steel. ''I ordered four armed outriders to accompany Tabitha's carriage.''

Robbie nodded stiffly, his emotions too raw for a verbal apology. Outriders or no, he wouldn't rest until he knew she was safe. He spun around.

How long could one youthful mistake hound a man and all those he loved? Not, he hastily assured himself, that he loved the saintly Tabitha Fell. It was simply that he owed her his life, and he was a man who paid his debts.

"Where are you going?" Anne called out, running after him, as fleet and light as the hoyden she had been in her youth.

Robbie was caught by a swift, nostalgic yearning for those innocent days before he had learned the true meaning of despair, the emptiness that could scar a man's soul.

"Darenth Hall," he bit out.

"We will go with you," she said quickly. "I want to see the boys, to assure them—"

"I suggest you hurry. I'm taking time only to see Father, and I'll wait for no woman dithering over her wardrobe."

"Perhaps," she shouted after him as he scaled the stairs at a run, "I should join you as Lady Godiva!"

Trailing after came the deep vibrato of Karl's chuckle. "I think not, sweet Anne—though, perhaps, tonight?"

Robbie began the trip on Sin. Weaker than he realized, his side began to ache, to burn. He was forced to join Anne and Karl in the carriage. Like a limp-kneed dandy, he thought with acid disgust.

As the miles sped by, he found himself the object of a careful, almost cautious scrutiny. Anne's gaze dropped, and she absently toyed with the Brussels lace at her wrist.

"It hasn't been much of a homecoming, has it?" he asked.

"Hardly what I expected." She looked through the window, biting her lip. "Is . . . is von Fersen really dead?"

"Yes. It's over for you." But was it over for Tabitha? he wondered. Damn!

"And you, Robbie?" She studied his face. "Will it ever be over for you?"

Could it ever be over for a man who had journeyed deep into his own soul and found a primordial beast that could be neither tamed nor killed? Could he ever feel whole or secure when that beast might be loosed to wreak death and destruction?

As it had been loosed when he was accosted by thieves on a dark Westminster street shortly after his return from Schattenburg. Sickened and shamed by the broken remains of what had once been two men, he had fled England, vowing never to return. He should have stayed away, for he would have done the same to von Fersen in the shadow of London Bridge had Old Nick and his father not stopped him. And what would have happened to Tabitha then?

Tabitha. What had he done during his fever? Revealed his weaknesses, fears, ungovernable rages? Was that why she—

"Robbie?"

He focused on Anne's face, on the glossy black hair peeping from the brim of her sassy straw bonnet, on her silver-gray eyes, darkening with concern. Had he ever deserved her loyalty and love? Always he had gone his own way, leaping from daring to danger, leaving Anne to take the brunt of their father's anger.

"Yes," he said softly. "It's over."

"Liar," she whispered.

His gaze shifted to the window. The carriage rattled down Dartford's Highstreet, passing the Bull Inn where Wat Tyler had fomented his rebellion against Richard II. The tale had fascinated Robbie as a boy, but it had been only a tale, as unconnected to the present as Granny Goody Peabody's stories of fairies sunning themselves on daisy petals. Robbie had not then lived long enough to see the rippling effect of a single event spreading over the smooth, glassy sea of time. He had not seen his father beaten and shackled or his sister nearly wed to a madman or, twelve years later, an innocent woman abducted, all because he could not quench his thirst for adventure.

"You plan to leave us again," Anne said, her voice thin with strain.

He stared through the window. Reckless and feckless, he was a threat to all who loved him—his father had been right. Though he longed to order the carriage to Gravesend, where he could leap aboard the first sailing ship and leave behind the curiously disturbing Tabitha Fell, he couldn't. He owed her too much.

"When I have made sure that Tabitha is safe from Shadwell."

"There is something else she may need to be protected from," Anne said, so casually Robbie shot her a penetrating look. "Scandalmongers," she said.

"Scandal—"

"Robbie," she said urgently, leaning forward, "you must know that the village will seethe with speculation about Tabitha's abduction and particularly about her nursing of you."

"Ridiculous! Anyone who knows her—"

"Knows that she is of the sternest moral fiber, just as they know that you are the rakehell son of the manor, famed for your exploits in the boudoir since you were caught with a milkmaid in the hayloft before you sprouted a beard. Which do you think will weigh heavier with those who wish to believe the worst?"

The thought of foul tongues slavering over Tabitha's misfortune brought a quick spurt of anger. She shouldn't have to suffer for his every adventure and misadventure, and she wouldn't have to, though he would not be the one to save her. In spite of his relief, his mouth puckered as if he had bitten into a lemon.

"I assure you the scandal will be quickly laid to rest. Tabitha is, after all, to wed *Friend*"—he stressed the word with a touch of sarcasm—"Abraham Leeds in the village, who, I am told by her, encompasses all of the virtues."

Anne stared at him, a glint in her eyes looking suspiciously like laughter. "Implying that you encompass all of the vices?" she asked. "If I did not know you so well I would think she had tweaked you where it hurt."

One black brow arched high over a steely gaze. "I can hardly quake before the truth."

"And the truth is that we have known *Friend* Abraham since he was a boy. Do you really believe he will have her now?"

Robbie's gaze shifted back to the window, to the greening hills rolling away to the beckoning horizon. "I suspect he would not. His wife would need to be as above reproach as Caesar's wife."

"Well?" Anne prodded ungently.

Robbie folded his arms over his chest, his violet eyes flashing dangerously. She could not be asking if he would do the honorable and marry Tabitha. Honorable . . . and disastrous.

"The answer," he said flatly, "is no."

He settled in a corner, tipped his hat over his eyes, and ignored the furious whispering on the seat opposite: Anne determined to engage in battle, Karl equally determined to stop her. It ended with a woman's typical, quelling word: "Men!"

Anne flounced on the seat and subsided, leaving Robbie to brood in peace.

Why had Tabitha run away from him? She could have waited a few hours to leave for Kent. Worse, why was he so irritated by it? He himself planned to run away as soon as he had seen that his father was fully recovered and she was protected.

If not by Abraham Leeds or by him, then by whom? He frowned in the shadow of his hat brim and caught a glimpse of the avenue of chestnuts leading to Darenth Hall. Bolting upright, he bellowed through the window at the coachman, "Stop here!"

The coach slewed to a stop. Anne, clutching at the leather strap, frowned. "Why?"

"If Leeds refuses to do his duty by Tabitha, then her

brothers must be warned. I'm riding over to Fell Cottage—''

''Now?''

''The matter cannot wait.''

She stared at him blankly for a moment before a smile began to form. ''Why don't you admit that you cannot wait to assure yourself that Tabitha is safe?''

''I should not impress my actions with too much significance, were I you,'' he said stiffly. ''Do not forget, I owe her my life.''

''Of course!'' Anne responded, her gaze wide and spuriously innocent. ''Did I imply anything else?''

Robbie darted Karl a can't-you-control-your-wife look and found him smiling indulgently at her. Another reason to avoid the married state, he thought in disgust. It honed a man's finer sensibilities to a dull edge.

While Robbie informed Anne to expect him when she saw him, Tabitha reveled in her first moment of privacy since her arrival at Fell Cottage. She would mourn neither what might have been nor what she wished might be. She would not abandon all she was, all she wanted, simply because she fancied herself in love with Friend Robert. She could not trust a love that sprouted from danger and circumstance without regard to differences in beliefs and dreams. And it was that lack of trust in her feelings and in herself that had driven her from bed before dawn and sent her pleading to Anne to send her home. Only here could she find the peace and harmony she needed and escape the urgings of her unruly heart.

She leaned against the fence. Chickens strutted around the hayricks. Beyond, in the paddock, a mule lipped a lush red bloom from the rose climbing the gatepost. Behind, in the yard, an apple tree was in full blossom, a pink-and-white cloud that trembled in the breeze, sending out a sweet, heady fragrance.

''Tabby?'' Adam approached. He wore the farm laborer's garb of leather breeches, stout doublet, and smock-frock, but he had the sailor's wide step and rolling gait, the jack-tar's tough bronzed hands, half-opened, as if he were preparing to grasp a rope. "Do I intrude on thee?"

"No," she said, smiling. "I am wickedly idle."

"Even God rested on the seventh day."

"And surveyed His handiwork." She folded her arms over the top of the rail fence and swayed against it, her gaze lifting to the sun-splashed sky. "I shall never take this for granted again: the sun, the flowers, the scent of spring. How wonderful it all is."

He settled his thick shoulder against the rail beside her and filled his clay pipe with slow, sure movement. When he had it drawing to his satisfaction, he narrowed his blue eyes and studied her for a long, uncomfortable moment. "Would thee like to tell me what thee did not choose to share with our mother?"

"Thee knows me too well."

He smiled, the same slow smile of his youth, his eyes sparkling with humor. "Aye, I know that thee changes the subject when thee wants to avoid answering a question. Tell me about . . . Friend Robert."

"Thee would like him."

"Not, I suspect, as well as thee."

"Have I always been so easy for thee to read?"

"Always." He puffed contentedly on the pipe, sending clouds of blue smoke shredding on the breeze.

She had feared that the life of a seaman would change Adam beyond recognition, his God forgotten, his speech coarse, his ways not those of the Friends. But the differences were only on the surface. His voice was deeper, his shoulders broader, but his heart and soul were the same. He was still the older brother who knew her better than she knew herself.

"I . . . I am so confused," she said softly.

"Thee has prayed on it?"

"I have tried, but . . ." She looked away, watching the swallows dart overhead, as restless as her thoughts. "Nothing happens. I get no answer, no peace."

"Perhaps the answer comes, but it is not the one thee wants."

"I was to testify with Friend Abraham Leeds," she said, her chin climbing as if to meet a blow, "and I should."

"Should thee?"

"It would be a marriage in unity," she added.

"Aye." He nodded sagely, squinting against the smoke curling around his face. "In unity with the Friends, but . . . would it be in unity with your heart?"

"It would be what I want."

"And what of God's Plan for thee?"

"I betray it with my foolish desire—"

"Or follow it," he said gently. "How can thee know which?"

"Thee doesn't understand."

"Then tell me."

She turned around, leaning back against the fence, digging at a clump of clover with the toe of her shoe. "This . . . feeling I have is not shared by Friend Robert, and even if it were . . ."

She paused, listening to hoofbeats galloping up the country lane winding between tall hedgerows. Her brothers never rode so fast. And Friend Abraham had a new cabriolet, bought, so he had written, in anticipation of their joining.

A glossy black Arabian came flying into the brilliant sunlight at the foot of the yard, but it was the man on his back who pulled Tabitha's hands to the throbbing pulse at her throat. Friend Robert! But why was he here? Had something happened . . . ?

She lifted her skirts and raced toward him, her neat white cap slipping back to dangle on its strings, her heavy hair pulling from its pins and cascading down her back in a lustrous sweep of waves that ended around her hips in a froth of ebony curls. Friend Robert leapt from the saddle in a single lithe movement, his mirror-shined boots hitting the ground running. In spite of her fear, Tabitha's heart soared like the liquid notes of the skylarks sailing over the hop fields. It seemed she had not seen him for days, rather than hours.

She reached him in a breathless rush, her hands sliding up his arms and grasping him tightly, his hands settling at her waist and drawing her to him.

"Has something happened?" she asked. "Is thy father—"

"Well when I left him," Robbie said in a rush, impatient of a sudden to have an answer to his questions.

"The Lord's blessing upon thee, Friend Robert," said Adam Fell, approaching at a leisurely pace. "I am glad to see thee strong enough for travel."

Tabitha's fingers convulsed around his arms, and she moved away quickly, leaving his hands curling into fists, his nails scratching his palms where the vibrant feel of her lingered.

"I have your sister's—" he began.

Tabitha blushed hotly, her hands climbing to her nape and rapidly gathering the luxuriant tresses rippling down her back. Robbie had watched practiced courtesans perform the same task without any effect, while Tabitha, with trembling haste and no artifice, was stealing his breath. He tore his gaze away.

"I have your sister's—" he began once more.

His gaze slid back to Tabitha, who was rolling her hip-length curls around her hand and tucking them beneath her cap. How disappointing to see her glory hidden beneath the linen. Almost as disappointing as the fact that he dared not reach out and capture the escaping tendril dangling at her temple, to rub it gently beneath his fingers, seeking its silken texture, to raise it to his nose and breathe deep of her womanly fragrance.

"Thee has my sister's?" prodded Adam Fell, a suspicious disturbance in the smooth basso of his voice.

Robbie straightened with a snap, his face burning. "I . . . I have your sister's tender care to thank for my recovery."

" 'Twas the Lord's will," began Tabitha.

"And your hands," he insisted, his gaze falling to the small, fragile, yet so capable hands, now folded neatly at her waist. How gentle those hands were. He could still feel them touching his face, so cool with the fever on him.

" 'Tis a lovely day," said Adam, studying the fluffy white clouds sailing overhead. "Aye, a lovely day, but a touch warm to my way of thinking. Perhaps a stroll down to the river . . ."

He eyed Robbie with a speculative gaze, as if to say, *Well, mate. There's the rope. Can thee tie the knot?*

Robbie, befuddled but not completely witless, hastily turned to Tabitha, but found himself bereft of speech. Practiced in the arts of seduction and unfailingly successful, he was suddenly afraid she would refuse.

Her solemn, searching gaze met his, a glimmer of fear in her eyes. Robbie's throat tightened, choking off the air. Had he kissed her? Had he revealed the raging beast? Was that the source of the fear he saw?

"Dost thou think it wise—"

"Wise?" He forced a smile. "I leave wisdom to saints and prophets and old men. Come and walk with me, Tabby."

He stretched out his hand, and she hesitated for a moment that seemed eternal before putting her hand in his.

Together in silence, they walked between the hedgerows that vibrated with birdsong, through the sunspeckled, flower-deckled wood, and down the mossy bank to the River Darent.

Robbie stared at the crystal-clear current, thinking of the rough and muddy Thames, of the whitecapped sea. Soon he would be sailing away. For the first time he dreaded that leaving, hated the restlessness that goaded him, a restlessness that seemed to have been banished by the tranquility of Tabitha's presence.

He was beset by a painful yearning to settle into the domestic adventures of a country squire with calving and lambing and harvest and stripling sons tumbling milkmaids in the hayloft. Yet that yearning also roused the familiar sensation of suffocation. His gaze lifted to the blue sky, the far distance, and its promise of untrammeled freedom—of the loneliness and emptiness that already had begun echoing through him.

"Why did thee come?"

She stood at the damp water's edge with silver-white lady's-smocks springing up around her skirt. He would never forget this scene, Robbie thought. Tabitha in her plain, unadorned gray framed in the green of the willows and her eyes shining brighter than any jewel that lent luster to a crown.

"Why, Tabby? Why did you leave?" *Me*, he wanted to add.

Her gaze searched his, her expression solemn. "Thee had no more need of me."

But he did. He needed the serenity of her presence, the gentle caress of her hands, the hope and faith that were an integral part of her. All things that he must turn his back on, as he turned his back on her now, staring toward the thin bank of woods climbing the low hill.

"Did I . . ." He swallowed hard. He wasn't sure he wanted to know. "Did I kiss you?"

Tabitha knew immediately which kiss he meant, the kiss taken and given in his fevered state. A lie rose quickly to her lips, startling her into silence. Had she fallen so far from grace that she would sink to the dishonesty that was anathema to the Friends? Yet she could not form the answer his question demanded. It was too personal, too powerfully moving. Even now she could feel the hard, possessive demand of his lips, and her own weak desire to yield her all.

Robbie waited for her answer in slowly growing horror. Though he tried, he could not dredge up any fragment of a memory that might tell him what he had done. When he realized she would not answer, he turned to face her.

"Answer me, Tabby. I must know."

Her gaze drifted away to the thick woodland on the opposite bank where a blackbird whistled in the shadows. "Yes," she said, so softly Robbie had to lean closer to hear.

"And?" he asked urgently.

The color in her face fled, leaving her eyes luminous. "I pray thee, do not ask me."

Robbie's chest tightened in a vise of dread. Had he been so lost to reason that he had ravished her against her will? Nothing else adequately explained her reluctance to tell him what had happened. "I must know," he said raggedly.

Tabitha's long, spiky lashes fell over her eyes, casting shadows on her cheeks. While human perfection was impossible, one way to strive for it was with absolute honesty. There could be no white lie to save face or feelings.

"It was a wondrous fair kiss," she temporized, hoping that would be enough. A glance askance found his taut expression demanding more. Heat stole up her cheeks and burned to the widow's peak cresting her brow. "It was uncommonly pleasant."

Robbie studied her fiery blush and her hands clasped together with white-knuckled strength. It didn't sound as though she had objected to whatever he had done, but then she wasn't telling him everything. "Is that all that happened?"

Her gaze swept up, colliding with his, skittering away. "If thee must know the last of it," she said, her soft voice sharp and defensive, "I kissed thee."

Robbie blinked. "You . . . you kissed me?"

" 'Twas shameful," she said in obvious and acute misery, adding, "And unmaidenly."

The beginnings of a smile softening his mouth, Robbie stepped closer and skimmed his forefinger down the tender length of her neck. "Have you never been kissed before, Tabitha?"

"Of course I have," she said quickly. "My father, my brothers, and once . . ."

"Once," he prompted.

"Friend Abraham Leeds."

Robbie frowned. Leeds, again! "That dry stick. I shouldn't imagine it was"—he paused, a suppressed smile winking at the corners of his mouth—'' 'uncommonly pleasant.' ''

"He does not have thy . . . thy . . ."

"Experience?" he added helpfully.

She flashed him a look with a spark of fire. " 'Tis not a thing thee should boast of, Friend Robert."

Which thoroughly quenched his incipient amusement, bringing a scowl. Not because she had said it, but because she was right. He had lived his adult life, his amorous adventures, like a drunken bee buzzing from flower to flower. Why was it only now that the thought filled him with revulsion?

"Forgive my hasty tongue," she said gently, her hand rising to touch his cheek.

Robbie shied away, feeling unclean.

Her hand paused in midair, curled into a fist, and dropped to her side. "I pray thee will . . ." She drew a shuddering breath. "I have become so accustomed to touching thee . . ."

She blushed furiously, hot tears welling in her eyes. Was she lost to all maidenly modesty, to all pride, however sinful it might be?

"Tabitha . . ." Robbie captured her small hand, hooking a finger into the curl of her palm and raising it to his lips. "I should have died without your help. It should be I who prays forgiveness for my . . . my churlishness."

His lips touched her knuckles, his breath wafting warmly over them. Tabitha attempted a smile. " 'Tis a vain custom, Friend Robert," she said softly, echoing their first meeting.

And he, smiling, pressed another kiss to her knuckles. "But a pleasurable one, Friend Tabitha."

All remembrance of pleasure vanished when Robbie strode into Darenth Hall and found Anne waiting for him—like a spider with a fly, he thought, folding his arms over his chest and frowning.

"You told them?" she asked impatiently.

"Told who what?"

She sank back on her heels and stared as if he had sprouted a cyclopean eye. "Told Tabitha's brothers about Shadwell, of course."

Of course.

Only he had forgotten.

Forgotten everything except Tabitha.

Chapter 7

Abraham Leeds' shiny new cabriolet careened into the yard while Tabitha was hanging over the fence and dreamily watching the setting sun. Friend Robert was long gone, and she was sinfully, deliciously, wickedly idle. He was—she smiled at the knuckles he had kissed—a terrible influence.

"Ah—choo! Ah-choo! Ah—whoa, Gabriel!—choo!"

The cabriolet scraped her mother's cherished sloe hedge, tearing a blizzard of white blossoms from the shiny black branches. The walleyed hack dragged the carriage through the bed of narcissus and daffodils and came to an abrupt halt beneath the apple tree. From the shaking branches, raining pink-and-white blossoms, came Friend Abraham's despairing cry: "Lord, give me patience with this son of Satan. Back, Gabriel! Back!"

Gabriel dropped his muzzle to the wild candytuft sprouting beneath the tree, neatly severed the crown of starch-white flowers from the stem, and began to chew.

Mimicking that motion, Tabitha's small white teeth gnawed on her lower lip. It would be unkind to laugh.

The branches rattled. Friend Abraham's plain, square face appeared, ringed with blossoms. "Friend Tabitha," he began, his voice carefully modulated and his expression benign, as if any visitor might be expected to swing out of the apple tree. No sooner had he said

103

her name than his mouth yawned wide, his nose wrinkled, and he folded up over a violent "AH-CHOO!"

She hurried to him, parting the branches.

"De vlowers! De vlowers!" He stuffed his handkerchief to his reddening nose, glaring around the yard as if he would like to personally uproot every "vlower" he saw. "Of course," she soothed, with guilty mortification for her amusement. He was obviously miserable, his eyes watering and his nose running. "Come into the parlor for a cup of chamomile—"

"Chamomile!" He jumped to the ground, looking as ruffled as a cat whose fur had been rubbed the wrong way. "Chamomile does not agree with me. Water will do."

He reached for his broad-brimmed hat, settled it on his head, tugged at his drab coat, and marched off with a nosegay of apple blossoms bouncing on his shoulder.

Tabitha lost all urge to smile. She must tell him she would not wed him. Whatever she had said to Adam, she could not promise her heart when it was already given. Was that what had been missing from her neat, orderly plans for the future?

She admired Friend Abraham's rectitude, his painful honesty, and his determination to live his life according to the ways of the Friends. Only now had she begun to recognize how difficult that was, for he had as much pride as Friend Robert and no ability to laugh at himself. How hard it must be for him to practice the humility required by his faith.

Yet she did not love him, never had loved him. She loved only what he represented, and what comfort would that be in the intimate setting of a marriage? She knew herself too well to think that admiration would blind her to his faults. Even love would not do that, but it would make her more accepting. As accepting as she was of Friend Robert, who skirted the ideal of human perfection by a breathlessly wide margin.

Her gaze turned to the north, staring beyond the hop fields, beyond the home wood to the twin chimneys of Darenth Hall pointing above the treetops like cautioning fingers. There was no future for her there, just as there was no future with Abraham Leeds.

She was sad, not despairing. With the example of her father and the teaching of her faith that a woman's duty was to relieve the wants of the poor, her life would not be empty. Her pilgrimage through life might be taken alone, but it would never be lonely.

She followed Friend Abraham into the parlor, where her family congregated to exchange quiet greetings with him. Something else to reaccustom herself to after the noisy, boisterous years as governess to Anne's sons—the silence, the soft laughter. She longed to see her two charges bounding into the room, excitedly exclaiming over the latest treasure they had found, and tugging at her skirt until she knelt to marvel with them.

"I would ask thee, Friend Fells"—Abraham Leeds' gaze encompassed them all, from her mother to her wide-eyed baby sister—"that thee will pray for the decision about to be made." His gaze lifted to the plastered ceiling. "Lord, thee sees the sinners among us. We ask thy forgiveness . . ."

It was, Tabitha thought, a beautiful prayer delivered in the sonorous singsong of the speakers at Meeting.

"And, Lord," he ended, "deliver these thy servants from the wiles of wayward women. Keep us ever faithful, ever true to thy holy light. Let us not be led astray. Amen."

"Amen." Tabitha's gaze met Adam's, which seemed to ask, with a sparkle, if she was the wayward woman from whose wiles Friend Abraham prayed deliverance. Adam, like her father, like her, had often had an inappropriate, but keen, sense of the ridiculous.

Her family filed out, one by one, Adam at the last, casting her a glance that warned her to listen to her heart.

Friend Abraham sniffed mightily, swiped at his nose with his handkerchief, and sat squarely in a Windsor chair, his hat on his head, his hands on his knees.

"I trust thee left Friend Robert recovered from his wound."

She sat in the chair opposite, rigidly erect. "The Lord's will was done," she said softly.

"And it is the Lord's will that we must do here this day."

"Yes, Friend Abraham, that is why I . . ."

His raised hand effectively stopped her. "It is our belief, the Friends' belief, that a godly union comes only when man and maid are in a sanctified state. If one has not achieved a victory over worldly temptation, then they marry in their own wills and affection, which leads to certain doom and care. We must first love the Lord, for His love forms the bond of unity between man and wife. Has thee sought the Inner Light, Tabitha Fell?"

"Yes, but—"

"As have I, as is proper. But I remain unglorified and reminded that Eve, leading Adam into sin, begat trial and travail for their posterity. As punishment for her disobedience, woman remained the weaker vessel, subordinated to man, the stronger. Yet thee willfully refused to heed my request. Thee willfully nursed Friend Robert, a man known for his sinful, wicked ways."

"Much exaggerated, I would like to—"

"Like Eve, thee must live with thy punishment for thy willful ways."

"Punishment!" Tabitha's color rose intemperately.

"There is in the village a hissing over thy name, a cackling of gossips—may God forgive them. None believe that so godless a man as Robert Ransome would leave a maid untouched. I am not among those believers. Not because I expect more from Friend Robert—may God grant him the glory of His holy Light—but because I expect the highest of thee. Thy sin, I am sure, is naught but willfulness."

What could she say? She had chided herself for that sin.

"This is the only reason I believe we would not be in unity. Thou hast not yet lost thy desire for the world,

Tabitha Fell. The Lord has warned me by withholding the Inner Light.''

As He withheld it from her. She could not fault Friend Abraham for his honesty or for the truth he saw as clearly as she did. She hadn't lost her desire for the world, for one piece of the world in the form of Robert Ransome.

She stood. "Will thee pray for me, Friend Abraham?''

He approached her slowly, taking her hand between his. For a moment his mask of rigid rectitude cracked, and he gazed down at her sadly. "Thee will always be in my prayers, Friend Tabitha. Thee will always be in my heart.''

She searched his plain face, seeing that in his way he loved her as much as she loved Friend Robert. "I am so sorry, Abraham,'' she said softly.

"Thee has nothing to be sorry for, Friend Tabitha.''

"I pray thee will forgive me for—''

"The Lord's will be done.''

Moments later she stood in the parlor listening to the rattling of the apple tree, the rolling of the carriage, the last ''ah-choo'' fading into the distance. What was the Lord's will?

If He had chosen Anne as His messenger, Tabitha thought the following day, He had chosen well.

They strolled down the country lane, Anne leading her horse between the hedgerows humming with life. Butterflies, bees, and the occasional early dragonfly flitted among the hawthorn.

"It's the boys,'' she said.

"Thee said they were well.'' Tabitha's voice rose with alarm.

"And they are, only . . . it's really two things. They miss you, as we knew they would, but even more than that, they are terrified that you will be abducted again. I've tried to explain, but I'm afraid there is no reasoning with their fear.''

"Thee knows that I will come to them if they need me."

"Could you come today, now?" Anne asked. "I must return to London to help Mother attend to Father. And Karl must meet with his publisher about his latest musical compositions. The man refuses to brook another delay." She paused, her face betraying a strange expression, poised midway between laughter and fury. "I'm afraid the other reason has to do with Robbie. That sapskull! That . . . that addlepate! No sooner did he meet the boys than he led them out of the house like the Pied Piper and taught them to climb the ivy to the schoolroom in the attic!"

"He didn't!" Tabitha paled at the vision of her adored charges clinging to wispy stems of ivy far above the earth.

"He did!" Anne cried. "I dare not leave the boys alone with him. What mischief might he lead them into—as if they could not find enough! And he refuses to leave the manor—"

She stopped abruptly, her eyes widening, but Tabitha had no time to wonder why. Trampling the heels of her worry about the boys was fear for Friend Robert. "His wound?" she asked quickly.

"He favored his side at dinner, but—"

"Then I must come immediately to ensure that he does not lead our lambs astray or injure himself again."

"If you only would," Anne burst out. "I know you wanted to spend a few days with your family and . . . and Abraham Leeds will be sure to object, but—"

"Friend Abraham's objections are no longer my concern. If—"

"Tabby! Have you broken your engagement?"

She smiled ruefully. "In honesty, it was he who—"

"Thank God!" burst out Anne. "You would never have suited!"

"He is a good man," Tabitha said gently.

"And you are too charitable." Anne heaved a sigh of relief. "I don't know when I've had such good news!"

Tabitha bit back a smile. "I should not have expected thee to take such pleasure in my misfortune."

Anne, instantly contrite, hugged her fiercely. "Forgive me, but I cannot believe your release from a lifetime with Abraham Leeds is a misfortune."

"Nor can I," said Tabitha. "I fear I would not have made him a good wife."

"Not have made him—" Anne's jaw snapped shut. "You value yourself too little, Tabitha Fell! He should have kissed your feet and sung your praises! It was he who was the fortunate one—"

"Enough." Tabitha laughed. "Thee will have me puffed up with sinful vanity."

But it was not vanity that puffed Tabitha up when she and Anne arrived at Darenth Hall to find Robbie, Karl, and the boys sliding down the steep railing of the stairway and howling like banshees.

She was not surprised to see Friend Robert at the bottom, hauling his leg over the endpost, his eyes dancing with merriment. It was exactly the sort of thing one would expect of him. But Friend Karl? The pianist-composer whose music seemed like angels' songs? The advisor to the King of Württemberg who could be so stiffly proper in his tailored uniforms dripping with awards and decorations? But he was also, she admitted, the loving husband and the tender father for whom the necessary disciplining of his sons was an almost impossible task. He was the man who had had an unhappy childhood—which he seemed to be making up for now.

When Tabitha entered, he was halfway down the railing, sliding at a breathtaking pace that whipped his butter-yellow hair back from his brow, his broad shoulders reared back and his hands over his head.

"Karl!" Anne said staunchly.

Had Tabitha not been so appalled, she would have laughed at his expression of guilty chagrin, his quick and failed scramble to stop himself before he slammed into the frozen Friend Robert with an audible "Ooof!" and a breathless "Now, Anne, I can explain."

"Explain?" she responded, her toe tapping on the oak flooring. "I can see quite clearly—"

"Tabby, Mama, watch me! Watch me!" Franz was at the top, his tiny rump butted up against the turn-post, his small fingers grasping the rail, while he awaited his turn. He released the railing, and Anne stifled a scream. He careened down, wobbling from side to side, gathering speed, until he slammed into his father's back with a thud.

Tabitha flinched. Anne sank onto a nearby bench, as though her knees would no longer support her.

Franz's small face peeped around his father's arm with an ear-to-ear grin. "Want to see me do it again?"

Friend Karl slipped off the rail and scooped Franz up, tossing him in the air. "I think your mother has seen enough for today."

"I've seen the outside of enough!" said Anne, surging up from the bench with a militant expression.

"Have you, my love?" he said with a mellow and intimate tone, striding to her side to loop his arm around her waist and gaze deeply into her eyes. "I'm sorry if we frightened you."

"Karl," she said, obviously struggling to stoke the fires of her anger.

It wouldn't last above a moment longer, Tabitha knew from long experience. He had but to run his finger down Anne's cheek and to cradle her close, as he did now, and she would melt like hot wax.

Tabitha, turning to Friend Robert, determined that she would not so easily relent. "I must change the dressing on thy wound."

He straightened, startled. "But I had it done this—"

"Not, I am sure, to my satisfaction," she interrupted, her level gaze meeting his.

His eyes widened with comprehension, and a quick smile flitted across his mouth. "What a tyrant you are, Tabitha Fell."

"Can I watch?" The small Karl skimmed down the stairs.

"I don't think so." Robbie ran his elegant hand over his nephew's head, ruffling his hair and leaning down to confide, "Tabby will be giving me a good scold. I wouldn't want you to see me quaking in my boots."

"Aw, Uncle Robbie"—the small Karl leaned against his knee—"you aren't afraid of Tabby. She's just . . . just *Tabby*."

"You are wrong, nephew. Our Tabby isn't *just* anything."

His gaze climbed to meet Tabitha's, and she felt it like a touch. A tender, lover's touch that reached the farthest corners of her being, leaving light and laughter behind. In spite of her melting heart, her warming soul, she gave him a frosty look. "Thee will not come around me so easily, Friend Robert."

"Nothing worthwhile is ever easy, Friend Tabitha."

Would she never have the last word with the man? She moved past him, climbing the stairs. "Follow me."

"I leave you, Karl," he said, casting a glance at the militant Anne, "to your wife's . . . ah, tender mercies."

Tabitha struggled with a smile. He was like his nephews in more than appearance. Like them, if he saw the least chink in her armor, he would consider the war won.

At the turning of the stairs, out of sight of those below, she faced him. "Thou art a terrible influence on thy nephews."

"Only on my nephews?" He grinned, unrepentant.

"Did I forget to mention Friend Karl?" She turned away to hide her growing smile.

His fingers coasted down her arm, caressing the back of her hand. "Tell me, Tabby," he whispered with melodramatic emphasis. "Tell me I have not lost my meager talent to influence you."

Like Anne with her Karl, Tabitha found herself melting like hot wax before the potent power of Friend Robert's playful charm.

* * *

Milling-Jemmy Shadwell, his huge body rocking awkwardly in the saddle, rode out of London heading for Darenth Hall. His murky black eyes were red-rimmed with sleeplessness. His mind was in ferment. He suffered neither remorse nor regret. He was niggled by neither conscience nor fear. But he could not forget the woman's voice.

She had summoned the ghostly remembrance of another voice. One that spoke with the warmth of a spring breeze blowing down a back alley in Spitalfields. One that had said *thee* and *thou*. One that had spoken with the same gentle cadence, the same bell-like notes of concern.

He tried, as he had tried for days, to capture the memory, to give the voice a face, a time, a place. Sweat oozed down his temples in oily streams. His huge hands—hands that had snapped von Fersen's neck with a powerful twist—shook as if palsied.

He was afraid of the memory. Afraid it would reveal a horror that would destroy him. Yet he was driven against his will to learn what it was.

If the woman had summoned it, then she might be the key to full remembrance. He had to see her, to hear her speak.

Anne and Karl returned to London with the complete assurance that Tabitha would provide a check on Robbie's more rash pursuits and keep the boys out of trouble—which proved more difficult than either of them imagined, for in his nephews Robbie found soulmates. They were fearless daredevils who gave even him a twinge of worry. At last he understood the expression of mingled rage and pride his father had so often worn.

The boys were not content to ride over the rolling hills carpeted with wildflowers. They had to race at breakneck speed, tumbling off into a bed of bracken and leaping up, laughing, while Robbie's mouth dried to dust and his heart pummeled his ribs and he fought the twin urges to clasp them fiercely to his chest and find the nearest willow switch for a good hiding.

They were not content with jumping from the hayloft into the cushion of the rick below. They had to swing out on the pulley ropes and drop onto the hard wooden bed of the hay wain. Robbie, rounding the barn, didn't know whether to give them a tonguelashing for their recklessness or kiss them for their courage. He consoled himself with Cousin Knox's favorite proclamation: "Aye, a Ransome through and through. More mettle than sense!"

For his own peace of mind, he devised a pursuit that lacked the least mite of danger. He was sprawled on the floor, rolling the dice and teaching his rapt nephews the finer points of hazard, when Tabitha strolled in—and he realized he'd been wrong. There *was* a danger. To the music of her tapping toe, the boys assured her that they must, as gentlemen, know how to play this game of chance. She remained unimpressed, so they sneaked away—the three of them—and gathered armloads of bluebells and daffodils, stately tulips and sweetly perfumed wallflowers. She was, as Robbie expected, mightily impressed with their gift, but she did not reveal her hiding place for the dice.

Robbie quickly found Tabitha a refreshing and restful counterweight to the exhausting work of standing *in loco parentis* to his soul-mates.

Where his nerves began to fray around the edges, she remained serenely amused by his growing exasperation . . .

"I was never the rascal that these two are!" he said, while slumped in a dining room chair and watching her capture suicidal, flame-drawn moths to release outside the window.

"Were I thee"—her misty gray gaze danced with laughter—"I would not suggest that to Anne or thy father."

Where he found his manly spine turning to jelly when Franz's ear was impaled by the small Karl's hook—how could he ever have thought a day of fish-

ing was a good idea!—she remained calm and unruffled . . .

"Tabby, you are sure he won't . . . won't feel—"
Robbie's throat closed. His body shuddered. His eyes
slammed shut. The scissors clicked as she clipped the
point from the hook, preparing to pull it out.

"Thee may open thy eyes now, Friend Robert," she
said, her voice curiously unsteady.

After two weeks he began to think the boys had been
sent as divine retribution for his misspent youth. Then
a footman rode up the drive bringing news that Anne
and Karl, the earl and his countess, would be arriving
on the morrow. In a flood of relief, Robbie insisted they
celebrate "their heavenly release" with a picnic in the
home wood.

Its remains lay scattered about—a crust of bread, the
tooth-marked half of a pickled peach, the hind of a
roast—attesting to the appetites of one man and two
small boys. Robbie lay, his head in Tabitha's lap, his
ankles crossed, and his hands folded over his belly,
nearly giddy with the imminent restoration of his care-
free bachelor existence.

"I swear to you, Tabby, had I not been conscious of
my dignity I should have stooped to the revolting Gal-
lic custom of kissing the footman's cheeks!"

Tabitha's hand coasted over his brow, lifting the
tangle of black curls. "Come now," she coaxed. "Admit that thee will miss the boys when . . ." She
paused, her gaze lifting to the lacework of branches
overhead. "When thee leaves England on thy travels."

"Like an aching tooth," he said shortly, though his
voice was thick and his heart oddly panging. He would
miss the boys. Even more, he would miss their governess, their Tabby.

In the time they had spent together at Darenth Hall,
a strange and wonderful thing had happened. He had
begun to sleep, deeply and dreamlessly, his nights un-
broken by the familiar nightmares that usually jerked
him awake, sweating, panting, and trembling. He had

begun to feel his roots sinking deep into the soil, and it didn't give him the old, restless itch to move on. He had begun to wish that Tabitha were not bound to . . .

"I haven't liked to mention this before, but . . ." He looked up, at the tender line of her mouth, the long spiky black lashes framing her eyes. "I cannot believe that Abraham Leeds has approved your return to Anne's employ."

She gazed down at him, her gray gaze unreadable. "How delicate thee has become of a sudden," she murmured. "Surely thee means thee cannot believe that Friend Abraham has approved my return to *thy* presence."

"He hasn't, has he?" Why, he wondered, did he want to know?

Why was her answer so important to him?

"No, but it no longer matters." She smiled gently. "We have decided that we would not, as Anne says, suit."

The tension that had crawled through him instantly eased. The darkness that threatened to blight his lazily happy mood lifted, leaving an inner glow to warm his heart. Yet he felt compelled to say, "I'm . . . I'm sorry, Tabby."

A smile trembled over her mouth, setting the dimples in her cheeks to winking. "What a rogue thou art, no more sorry than Anne, and she said she didn't know when she had had such good news. Is it so hard for thee to be honest?"

"Is it important to you that I am?"

"It is the Lord's commandment that—"

"But is it yours?"

"I have no right to command thee."

Robbie found himself wishing she did. The past two weeks, in spite of the scares his nephews had given him, in spite of the constant need to be alert should Shadwell appear, in spite of the internal warning that constantly buzzed in his head, had been filled with contentment. The burden of his past seemed to have sloughed away like the molting feathers of his falcons.

The restless demand for action had died to an occasional, easily ignored pang. The tension that had kept his mind spinning, his belly churning, and his every nerve taut had slackened day by day, until he felt utterly at peace.

Tabitha had done that for him. With a gentle look she could calm a spurt of anger. With a gentle word she could quell his hasty speech. With a gentle touch she could warm the cold core of fear that claimed his heart. Almost he could believe that he could tame the beast if he kept her at his side, his talisman, his light against the darkness that overshadowed his soul.

She looked like a Botticelli madonna, her eyes shining with untainted innocence and worldly wisdom—a wisdom that seemed to recognize all that he was, all that he had been. Yet he saw neither censure nor revulsion. Only a deep understanding and acceptance of his all-too-human weakness. And it was the acceptance linked with understanding that he found irresistibly appealing. She saw him, knew what he was, and—

"Uncle Robbie! Uncle Robbie!"

The boys had vanished in the woodland to play. Now they came back, running, casting terrified glances over their shoulders.

"A man!" screamed the small Karl. "A man in the bushes!"

Robbie lurched to his feet, and the boys swarmed about his legs, tugging at his arms. "What did he look like?"

"You won't let him take Tabby, will you, Uncle Robbie?" cried Franz.

He cast a quick glance at her, standing now at his side.

"You don't think . . ." she began, her eyes wide and dark with a fear that did not seep through to her voice or her face.

"I don't know, but I will," he said grimly, fighting the rage that shattered the peace she had given him.

It was Shadwell. The boys' description of a giant with black hair had assured Robbie it could be no one else.

So now he knew. Shadwell would not vanish. He had ignored Anne and the earl, now in London, and had come instead to Darenth Hall. In search of Tabitha? Robbie could not doubt that any longer.

Though Robbie had rounded up the footmen and summoned his tenants and carefully planned the hunt, Shadwell had escaped without a further sighting. They had searched all night with baying hounds and torches, but they had failed. *He* had failed, Robbie thought as he marched into the cozy salon overlooking the topiary garden.

The contentment was gone, burned away by the restlessness that sent him striding to the mullioned window. His gaze rose above the brick wall encircling the garden below, seeking the blue sky, the far horizon.

What a fool he had been! He should have known there could be no rest for him, no peace. He had been a disappointment to his father, a trial to his mother, a threat to Anne—and now to Tabitha. He had brought danger to everyone who loved him.

The only decent thing he could do was to remove the threat of Shadwell and leave England . . . leave Tabitha. She needed a man who could preserve her tranquil spirit and her quiet enjoyment of life. That would, unfortunately, require a man of faith and hope, a man willing to settle down and take a wife.

"Friend Robert?"

He didn't turn, didn't want to see her, didn't want to be ensnared by the quietude that radiated from her like heat from the sun. "Yes?" he said sharply.

"Thee has a visitor. Abraham Leeds."

The Great Chamber was little changed from the days when the manor had been built, a gift from Elizabeth I to the first Earl of Darenth and so cherished by his descendants, who resisted any suggestion of modernization. The ceiling was decorated in an intricate plasterwork design. Tapestries and embroidered hangings splashed color over the oak-paneled walls. Aromatic orris root potpourri scented the chamber. Sunlight streamed through the mullioned windows in thick bars of gold.

Robbie paused in the doorway, watching Abraham Leeds drum his fingers on a chip-carved oak chest. Odd behavior for a man who prided himself on a calm demeanor that no trial could ruffle.

"You wished to see me?"

Leeds spun around, his expression shadowed by his hat brim. "Thee must send Friend Tabitha back to Fell Cottage."

Robbie hooked his thumbs beneath his belt and canted his shoulder against the doorjamb. His hard night and harrowing bout of soul-searching had left him in no mood to deal favorably with Abraham Leeds. "Must I?"

"Yes," Leeds shot back. "In honesty, I do not like thee. I have prayed to have my heart softened, but the Lord has not heeded those prayers. Thou art a wicked and godless man—"

"And you"—Robbie smiled frigidly—"take an odd approach if you want something from me."

" 'Tis the only . . . approach. The Lord commands honesty of His servants."

Honesty. Yes, Tabitha had told him. Another difference between them. She could not be dishonest; he could not be honest.

"However," Leeds continued, "wicked and godless as thou art, I cannot think that thee would wish to harm Friend Tabitha. She makes a man better than he was, simply because her faith in him is strong enough to make him believe it."

Makes a man better than he was. Yes, Robbie thought, she did that. She even made him believe it, too—for a while.

"And what does this have to do with—"

"Thee has not been in the village of late. Thee does not know that it is rife with iniquitous gossip. They slaver over Friend Tabitha's name, yoking it to thine in wanton speculation which grows worse by the day. If thee has any care of her, thee will send her back to Fell Cottage.''

''And if I choose not to?'' the devil prompted him to say.

''Thou art wicked and godless, Friend Robert, but not, I think, truly evil. Thee might hurt her through thoughtlessness and selfishness, but not with the intent to hurt. And keeping her here now would be by evil intent.''

He tugged at his drab coat and marched to the door, pausing. ''I regret being forced to leave thee to thy uncertain conscience, for Friend Tabitha would neither hear a word against thee nor heed my warnings.''

Robbie swung on him, his hands fisted, his eyes slitted. ''You spoke to her about this?''

''Yes,'' he said, a strange, almost savage note entering his voice. ''Hast thou heard the parable of the pearls cast before swine, Robert Ransome?''

Leeds left on that unmistakable suggestion that Tabitha was the pearl and he the swine, and Robbie could not naysay him. He strode to the window, standing in the bars of sunlight, lifting his face to the fiery ball high in the sky. How strange that Leeds could read him so well. It was never by evil intent that he wrecked the lives around him. Always it was by thoughtlessness and selfishness, like now.

The damage had been done. Tabitha had been ruined in the eyes of the villagers, in the eyes of the Friends. And when a man of Society ruined a woman, he was left no alternative. He had to marry her—and that Robbie could not do.

Chapter 8

The blue waters of the River Darent peeked through the screen of willows at the carriage slowly trundling down the river road. Anne sat arrow-straight on the azure-blue squabs, nibbling on a nail. It helped her to think.

If only she could know she had done the right thing.

"You are plotting, sweet Anne," said Karl, lounging in the corner, his long legs stretched out, his ankles crossed on the seat opposite. "I know that look."

She darted him a glance rife with loving exasperation. "What a suspicious mind you have."

With a swift, lithe move he tumbled her across the seat and set the tapered tip of his forefinger beneath her chin, tilting her face up. "Once upon a time I thought I had but to wed you, and my need for suspicion would be past. However, I find myself shackled, not to an innocent and submissive maid—"

"I should think not!"

He raised a tawny brow, his forefinger meandering down the tender curve of her neck to the voluptuous swell of her breasts, while his cornflower-blue eyes took on a slumberous aspect. "But," he continued, "to a lusty wench with a devious mind."

"Devious!"

The effect of his sensual smile had not diminished but had grown stronger with the years. It snatched her breath away. She strove mightily to ignore the elegant finger delicately exploring her low, square neckline. She did not go so far as to stop it, even when it discovered the pouting tip of her breast and sent her wits scattering.

"Ah," he said thickly, his voice rich with utterly masculine triumph, "I see you do not object to my calling you . . . lusty."

"And would you"—she leaned forward, her lips poising a taunting breath away from his—"prefer a cold fish?"

"I wouldn't know." He closed the distance between them, nibbling at her mouth, grazing the corner. "I've never had one."

"Wretch," she whispered throatily, leaning into the warm hand that had palmed her breast.

He captured her nipple with his hot, seeking mouth and tugged gently, sending molten flames leaping through Anne. "I fear your education in bedsport is sadly lacking, *liebchen*."

"A tragedy that we must remedy at once." She curled around him, her lips caressing the smooth, honey-gold flesh behind his ear, just as his caressed the aching peak of her breast. She nibbled the lobe of his ear, felt him tremble, and uttered a soft purr of utterly feminine satisfaction. "What must I yet learn?"

"How to make love in a carriage."

Her head climbed, her eyes alight and a smile hovering about her mouth. "We really shouldn't."

"But now that you've paid homage to the demands of modesty"—he shifted her onto the seat and pressed an ardent kiss to her mouth—"we will."

"Had you any doubt?" She watched with immodest interest as he fumbled with the buttons of his trousers, releasing the thick pulsating shaft of his manhood. There was much to be said for the passage of years together, the freedom to be shy or bold, hasty or slow.

"No doubt whatsoever." His hands encompassed the tiny span of her waist and set her astraddle his thighs.

"Fascinating." She wore the air of a bookish scholar,

one at odds with the flush of her cheeks, the sparkle of her eyes, and the pounding anticipation of her pulse. "Now what must I do?"

"Enjoy," he murmured, delving beneath her skirt, finding the slit in her lacy pantalettes, seeking the dewy folds of her femininity, the treasure that was his alone.

Her breath caught in her throat. She felt the sweet silken melting—so familiar, yet so wondrous that each time felt like the first—the aching emptiness that begged to be filled. "Karl," she said huskily, her hands braced on his broad chest, her lips seeking his.

A tinge of passionate red rode the golden arch of his cheekbones. Desire flaming a fiery blue in his eyes, he kissed her mouth, teasing the corners, sliding away to her ear, while his tempting, taunting fingers drove her to the edge of desperation.

The carriage rocked and swayed. Hoofbeats clippity-clopped. Birdsong trilled through the sun-dappled day, and the flower-scented breeze purled around her exposed nipple, while the man in her arms looked at her as he always had, as if she were the answer to his every prayer.

"Karl," she whimpered softly, trembling beneath his touch.

"Yes, love, yes."

He lifted her, sheathing himself within her, so slowly her heart threatened to burst with the exquisitely unbearable sensations. She rocked against him; his breath shattered in his throat. She rocked again; his head pressed back against the seat, his butter-gold hair clinging to the velvet, his dusky lashes clinging to his cheeks, and the tendons of his throat straining against his skin.

A sense of power stole over her, as it had the first time. Her potent, yet humbling, power to give him the pleasure he gave to her, to steal his strength as he stole hers, to banish thought for feeling as he did for her.

Then he began to move, retreating, advancing, stealing her sense of power, her strength, her capacity for thought with every silken glide of flesh to flesh. Her senses spiraled away, ravishingly aware of the intense pleasures of power and submission.

Ecstasy approached with a subliminal tautening, a growing tension. It arrived at last with rippling convulsions that left her weak and spent. And, as always, shudders racked him as he whispered in her ear, "I love you, Anne. Dear God, how I love you."

She lay against his chest and raised a lethargic hand to curl around his neck. With a supreme effort of will, she rolled her head to the side and raised her gaze to him. "Should you ever again find me lacking in my education, do not hesitate to suggest a new lesson."

His arms wrapped around her, and his laugh rumbled through his chest before it came spilling through his lips. Another joy that time and intimacy had given them—the freedom to laugh.

His kiss wafted across her temple with a hint of regret. "I fear we have entered the drive to Darenth Hall, love. Unless you wish to educate our sons in the delicate arts, I suggest—"

She whipped up off his lap, straightening her clothes, smoothing her hair, gasping for air, while he casually buttoned his trousers.

"How do I look?"

He skimmed his knuckle down her cheek. "As if you've been thoroughly loved."

"I shall have Tabby blushing to the roots of her hair."

"I doubt that," he said, grinning. "After two weeks with your brother, I suspect very little could make her blush."

"Do you really think so?" Anne said hopefully.

He leaned back, eyeing her with a frown. "God help us!" he said, his eyes widening with a look of dread. "You cannot be . . . you are! Anne, you are matchmaking!"

"Why do men always say the word 'matchmaking' as if it were an insect they are spitting out?" she said, knowing full well that an attack would blunt the force—

"Anne"—his heavy warning note said he would not,

this time, be put off the scent—"stirring this pie may well get your pretty little fingers scorched."

"I will have you know—"

"What have you done?" he asked ominously.

"Very little." She looked out at the chestnut trees lining the drive, aspiring to a casual note whose failure found voice in the nervous fingers pleating a fold in her skirt. "I simply told Father about the gossip in the village and . . . and that Abraham Leeds has broken off his engagement to Tabitha."

"You didn't!" He sank back on the seat as if—she thought resentfully—he had taken a blow to the heart. "Anne, your father will demand that Robbie do the honorable! He will insist that he wed Tabitha! You cannot have been unaware of that!"

Since she had reckoned on precisely that result, she could hardly deny it. "Now, Karl," she began in a wheedling tone.

"I am no boy to be struck witless by a melting gaze! You have meddled where you should not," he said with more force than she thought necessary. "Imagine the problems they would face. Tabitha is a Quaker! You cannot have forgotten that! She would never be happy in the Society to which Robbie is heir. Can you see her meeting your king and calling him Friend George?"

Their eyes met, the humor of that imagined meeting striking them both at the same moment. A reluctant smile tugged at Karl's mouth, a mischievous one at hers. "I only hope," she said, giggling, "that I am there to see it."

"Anne," he said, softening, capturing her hand between his, "they would not suit."

"But they would," she insisted. "Even you must have noted the difference in Robbie when Tabitha is nearby. There is a restfulness, a peace, a quiet about him that I have never seen, even when he was a boy."

But it seemed she was wrong, for when they arrived at Darenth Hall they found Abraham Leeds bowling away in his cabriolet and the boys weeping before the gate. Uncle Robbie was shouting at Tabby. He could be heard clearly the moment Anne stepped from the carriage.

"Was ever a woman born as stubborn as you?" Robbie paced the salon, raking his fingers through his hair, grasping the back of his neck to ease the tension. Guilt had joined a frustrating sense of helplessness to whip his anger to fever pitch. He could not find Shadwell. He could not stop the gossip. He could not help Tabitha. As always, he was safe and unharmed in the eye of the storm that savaged those around him.

He spun about, his violet eyes aflame. "I tell you, you will return to Fell Cottage!"

Tabitha stood in the full light of the mullioned windows, the diamond pattern striping her plain gray gown. "I would please thee if I could, Friend Robert," she said, her voice as gentle as the gaze that beheld him. "But I will not be hectored by unkind gossip."

"Unkind!" he snarled. "It's more than that. Had I that clutch of biddies here, I should ring their necks."

"Violence would gain thee nothing." She moved out of the light into the shadows, walking gracefully toward him.

For a fleeting moment his anger waned. He stoked the fires of fury anew. He had need of it.

"Thee must not keep this anger in thy heart. Think of how poor their lives are that they must waste—"

"Robbie," Anne said breathlessly, rushing into the salon, "I will not have you shouting at Tabby. It is cruel to her, and it frightens my sons."

"Cruel," he said coldly, casting her a furious glance. "If you want cruel, ask Abraham Leeds about the village gossip. If Tabitha does not return to Fell Cottage, her reputation will be beyond reclaim. She has, after all, been staying alone with so wicked and godless a man as myself," he added on a self-castigating note.

Tabitha moved quickly, placing her hand on his arm, raising her gaze to his. "Thou art the best of men," she said fiercely. ''I will not have thee think otherwise.''

''I should have known what would happen,'' he said angrily. ''Anne warned me, but I . . .''

Wouldn't listen, wouldn't hear, wouldn't believe that anyone could think Tabitha other than perfect. He had selfishly thought only of his desire to have her near.

''But I,'' Tabitha said, ''needed no warning. The gossip began before I came to Darenth Hall. I knew it would grow worse.''

His brow wrinkled in a frown. ''Then why did you come? Why did you risk your reputation, your future?''

She laid her hand on his cheek, caressing it with her thumb. ''Because I will yield nothing to evil.''

He covered her hand with his, his tortured gaze searching her face. ''And if it destroys you?''

''It cannot, for I will meet it with good. And good will always triumph.''

''Tabitha,'' he murmured, ''are you a saint or a fool?''

''Neither.'' She smiled up at him, as if she longed to ease the burden of his doubt. ''I am only a woman.''

''Only?'' he asked, the corner of his mouth tilting up in an attempt at a smile. ''I should say you are much more.''

''Then thee would be wrong. As thou art wrong to ask me to return to Fell Cottage.''

''Then I will leave, taking with me the spur that goads the gossipmongers.''

A stricken look darkened her eyes before her lashes fell to shield them from his view. She swallowed hard, sliding her hand from his, curling it into a small fist at her waist. ''Thee must do what thy heart tells thee is right.''

She moved away, her back straight, her pristine white cap gleaming in the shadows, and her skirt swirling gracefully around her feet. Yet Robbie sensed an aura of dejection about her.

"I must go to the boys." She paused in the doorway, looking back. "May I assure them that we are friends again?"

Soon he would leave Darenth Hall, leave England, and never see her again. His throat clenched tight. "We will always be friends," he said hoarsely.

"I know." She smiled sadly and was gone.

Anne, her toe tapping an irritated rhythm, folded her arms over her breast. "And what of Shadwell? The boys told me you have searched for him through the night."

"Father can hire men to find him, men more capable than I."

"So," she said shortly, her silvery gaze brittle, "you will run away again."

He stared through the doorway where Tabitha had vanished, holding in his mind's eye a vision of her. The tender curve of her cheek. The gentle light in her eyes. The dimples that winked when she laughed. "No, Anne," he said softly. "For once, I'm not running. I'm walking away quite deliberately, with full knowledge of what I'm doing."

But it wasn't with full knowledge, Anne suspected. If he knew . . .

"She loves you, you know."

"She loves everyone," he said firmly, "even the gossips who drag her name through the mire of their salacious mouthings."

Could he really be so blind? Anne wondered. Or was that blindness as deliberate as he thought his leaving was? Had he been more forthcoming, she might have enlightened him. But there were currents and undercurrents in Robbie that were new and strange to her. The man held complexities that the boy had not had, and she hesitated to trod amiss.

"Will you wait at least a day or two? You've had so little time to visit with Father and Mother, and she will need to prepare herself for your leaving."

He nodded. "I can spend the time searching for Shadwell."

Anne stared into his handsome face, seeing the shadows of pain. "When you leave us, where will you go?"

"Greece." He smiled, with a glint of the adventurous boy. "The Turks have landed Egyptians in the Morea—"

"And they cannot have a war without you." She tried to keep the fear from her voice, partially succeeding.

"It's an adventure, Anne."

"An adventure," she repeated. One, she determined, he would not have. If she trod amiss, it would be in a worthy cause.

But it seemed she needed only to wait for events to unfold, for her parents arrived at Darenth Hall one carriage length ahead of a delegation from the Society of Friends. They had come, a buxom matron told the frowning earl, to lead Sister Fell back to the paths of righteousness—and Robbie, unfortunately, overheard.

He had hurried down the forecourt walk to aid his father up the stairs, and the hiss of "righteousness" still lingered on the woman's lips when he yanked open the wooden door, slammed it against the wall, and tore through the brick archway.

"If there is any lack of righteousness here"—his burning eyes surveyed the dismayed delegation of four—"I am looking at it! How dare you darken this door seeking to smirch the name of a woman whose boots you are not fit to lick!"

The leader stepped forward, her bosom heaving beneath her elbow-length cape. "Friend, we come in peace to—"

"Peace? I doubt it! You come like jackals to pick over the bones! Hypocrites, the lot of you!"

"Robert," said the earl, "that is enough!"

"Enough? I am only getting started!" He scowled the women into a collective fit of trembling. "The only wrong has been done by your foul tongues! Tabitha Fell is innocent of—"

"Friend Robert!" The only voice that could calm him spoke at his back with a sharp note of alarm. "I pray thee, cease thy harangue of these good women."

"Good women!" He stared down into her flushed face, noting the trembling of her mouth, the suspicious shine of her eyes, and his anger flared higher, perilously close to ungovernable rage. "Gossipmongers, come to spread malice and pain. They are not worthy of your consideration."

"Say no more," she pleaded in a broken whisper, her hands clasping his upper arms. "Every child of God is worthy of my consideration . . . and thine."

"Even such as those." He jerked his head at them. Though he longed to take her into his arms and soothe the hurt he could see in her eyes, he dared not add that fuel to what had obviously become a scandal *extraordinaire*.

"Especially such as those," she said softly. "Thou art ignorant of the ways of the Friends."

He parted his lips, his expression as hot as the words that seared his tongue, but her small hand covered his mouth.

"My sisters have come, no doubt, at the request of the Meeting. It is their duty to warn those who err in the ways of the Truth, to pray with them, to guide them back into the Light."

He pulled her hand from his mouth, his expression stormy. "But you have not erred! You have done nothing wrong!"

"But I have," she said gently. "We believe that we are but pilgrims in this earthly life, our purpose to seek the Truth. We must, in order to do so, turn our back on worldly ways—and that is where I have failed."

"You are mad, Tabitha! A less worldly woman I have yet—" The look in her eyes stopped him cold, sent his tongue tripping over the last word and cleaving to the roof of his mouth. A look of torment and self-doubt that he recognized well. He had felt them often enough himself.

"Tabitha," said his father, his voice at a well-modulated and mollifying tone, "if you would like to take the ladies to the Great Chamber, where you might visit in privacy . . ."

They had come, Tabitha knew, in a spirit of love and charity. Little good did it do. As required, they sat together in silence, awaiting the inspiration of the Inner Light. But God's grace could find only those souls that were at peace, and hers was in tumult.

Had she come to Darenth Hall because Anne needed her? Because the boys needed her? Or because she would use any excuse to be near Friend Robert? Now they had all been tainted by the ugliness of the gossip, the suggestion of sin. She had with her willfulness—how right Abraham Leeds had been!—hurt everyone.

And yet she could not regret a moment. She would hug so many happy memories to her heart. Friend Robert, grumpy of a morn, his eyes still heavy with sleep as he slathered butter on his toast. Friend Robert, his manly spine turned to quivering jelly by the fish hook impaling Franz's ear. Friend Robert, taking her hand, looking deep into her eyes, smiling, laughing, frowning . . . alive. Always so alive. Vibrant, even at rest, the very air seeming to crackle around him. Immoderate in thought, action, and speech. Sinfully, passionately, fascinatingly so.

But beneath his lively surface dwelt pain and guilt and doubt of himself. Almost, in the fortnight past, she had seen the pain vanish, the doubt vanquished. He had been lulled by her presence, at peace with himself.

No, she could not regret a single moment.

The women of the Friends spoke with tender charity. They reminded her of the snares laid by the Devil, each obviously certain that Robert Ransome was Satan personified. They reminded her of the temptations awaiting her in worldly Darenth Hall, obviously certain that she had succumbed to them already. She didn't defend herself. There was no defense against the truth. She had succumbed, giving her heart to a man not of her faith, and it had led, as Friend Abraham had said, to doom and care.

The women left, as aware as Tabitha that they had failed. She had not seen the Light. She had not adjured her wicked ways.

After seeing them to the door and giving each a tender parting, she started up the stairs and heard raised voices: Friend Robert's, his father's, each with a temper at full boil.

"Robbie, we've run around the Maypole on this. I grow weary of your evasions, your shrinking from what is right. The girl has been ruined! I insist that you do the honorable."

"I am no boy to be ordered to the altar!" Robbie roared.

"No, you are a man. Act like one! Accept your responsibilities for once in your life!"

"And you think it my responsibility to cure the ruin of Tabitha's reputation by ruining the rest of her life? I have told you, Father, I am no suitable husband for her!"

"Not suitable! Don't be daft! You are from an old and honorable family, high in the *ton*, wealthy—"

"None of which matters a pin to Tabitha! Can't you see—"

"I see," said the earl hotly, "that you will marry the girl or I will disown you. At my death you will have of my estate only that which is entailed. I will claim no son who refuses to own up to his duty."

"And I will petition Parliament to remove me from the entail," Robbie raged. "Leave your title, your manor, your monies to Anne's sons. I neither need nor want them."

Tabitha, staring across the landing to the door of the parlor, listened to the swift march of his boots. Friend Robert appeared, his face flushed with rage, his eyes snapping. Eyes that met hers briefly with an angry apology before he turned and strode rapidly toward the Long Gallery.

She wavered and gripped the turnpost, her head

spinning and her heart pounding. How true that evil begets evil as good begets good. She could not allow this. She could not be the cause of father turning against son, son against father.

She burst into the parlor. The earl sat in a high-backed oak chair, his face white, his chest heaving, and Anne kneeling at his side.

"Friend John," Tabitha said, approaching with her hands outstretched, "thee must not do this cruel thing. Thee must not threaten Friend Robert with the loss of all he holds so dear."

His arctic-blue eyes held a sorrow that seeped deep into her own heart. "He was a wayward lad; now he is a wayward man, my child. I cannot allow him to make of our illustrious name a hissing and spitting that will spread throughout the land. He must, for his own sake, live up to his responsibilities. If he does not do that now, he might never find the spine for it."

She knelt beside Anne, capturing his cold hand. " 'Tis not courage he lacks, Friend John. 'Tis faith in himself."

"Then help him, my child. Help him to find that faith."

"He must find it for himself. I cannot help him."

"Can you not?" He leaned down, searching her face. "I have never seen Robbie so tender of a maid, so willing to do battle on one's behalf."

"Friend John," she said mournfully, " 'tis naught but liking thee sees. I cannot lead him where he will not go."

"Then," he said, his expression chilling, "I will disown him, and that step, once taken, will be irrevocable."

Chapter 9

The manor house was as quiet as a tomb. Even the boys were subdued, having sensed the tension and turmoil radiating from the adults. The earl, exhausted by the trip and the emotional argument with his son, took to his bed. The countess, terrified that she might lose Robbie forever, took to hers. Anne wept in Karl's arms, tearfully vowing that she would never—never!—set her hand to matchmaking again. Karl stroked her hair and held her close and knew that, should she again be confronted by a pair whom she thought perfect for each other, she would succumb to the temptation to nudge them in the "right direction." And while he had a man's full-bodied horror of a woman meddling in affairs of the heart, he viewed it with wary indulgence, for it was a testament to her happiness and to his.

The Elizabethan passion for symmetry extended from the architecture to the grounds. The manor house was encircled by six walled enclosures, each mathematically ordered. Marching across the back from west to east were the orchard, the maze, and the kitchen garden. It was to the latter that Tabitha repaired.

Unlike Anne, who thought better while nibbling on a nail, Tabitha thought better when her hands were busy. She wept over the lettuce, picking small green worms and dropping them into an empty flowerpot to

133

toss over the high mellowed brick wall. She sobbed over the tender shoots of the vegetables, pulling weeds, dusting the loamy soil from their roots, and filling the holes where they had been. She sniffled over the blooming rosemary, longing for the heat of summer and the pungent scents of mint, thyme, and basil. From the dovecote in the center of the garden, there came a cooing as soft as her own sighs of sorrow and discontent.

At length she moved to the arbor flanking the outer wall and sat on a bench enveloped in the heady fragrance of honeysuckle and eglantine, cocooned in shadows.

She had been selfish. Selfish to come here knowing of the gossip. Selfish to come only because she wanted so desperately to be near Friend Robert. Selfish to love him . . .

Was this a part of God's Plan? For her to love a man, and with that love to destroy him and his family?

She prayed for the illumination of the Inner Light, begged for the earl to soften toward his son, pleaded for Friend Robert to be given the heavenly peace of faith in himself, in his Lord.

She received no illumination. She knew the earl would not soften, for he was desperately seeking a last chance to save his son. And Friend Robert . . .

Had refused to wed her. Had been so violently opposed he was willing to give up his family, title, and inheritance. How that hurt. How richly she deserved it. This would not have happened had she been stronger in her faith, more willing to give him up.

But if she tried that now, he would lose everything: his father, whom he loved with the passion of a son who had always failed a man he admired; his title, which, strongly as he might deny it, meant much to him; Darenth Hall and the manor lands. In the past fortnight, she had seen him in the hop fields kneeling to examine the tender shoots, speaking to the tenants, running his beautiful hands down the foreleg of an injured draft horse. Though he made light of it, he loved the land, loved the men who tilled and sowed it, loved the animals that worked it. And when his time came, he would make a kind and caring manor lord.

He must have the future he should have, but that could happen only if they wed.

Could even her deep and abiding love overcome the religious differences that would reach into every part of their lives, affecting more than her service to God and her fellow man?

Faith was gained and maintained through quiet and retirement, but Friend Robert was a man of laughter and action, of consequence in a world that could never be truly hers. Even their language was different. His *Sunday* was her *First Day;* his *you* and *your* was her *thee* and *thine.* Her religion forbade the use of titles of respect; his Society demanded them. She was forbidden to take an oath; he was a man to whom an oath was sacred. Even their joining would create problems. The Church of England required an oath of marriage, which she could not take. The Society of Friends would refuse to allow them to *testify,* because they were out of unity—of different faiths. But worst of all, most frightening of all, he was a man of violence and she, a woman of peace.

She could neither ignore nor accept his seething rage. She had seen it when the boys had come screaming, when he had realized that Shadwell was lurking in the home wood, and she had been terrified that Friend Robert would find him. That prayer, at least, had been answered. His soul was not stained with the murder of Shadwell.

Yet to bind them together was her love, her belief in his innate goodness, her faith in the future, and . . . the need she saw all too clearly. The need for acceptance and love, which she, if only he would let her, could give him. Surely the love that burned as strong as her faith was strong enough to overcome their differences and to make him whole and them one in truth.

There was only one problem, and it loomed quite large. If his father's threat to disown him would not force his agreement to wed her, what could she do to gain his willing consent?

Scraps of blue sky peeked through the tangled vines overhead. How often Friend Robert's gaze had turned to the horizon as if he longed for the freedom of far-away places, the . . .

Was that the gift she must give him? Freedom. But it would be a perversion of God's commandment to be fruitful and multiply. Her normally clear, serene gaze clouded with doubt.

She rose, wandering the garden paths to the wooden gate, easing through it to the maze beyond. She had studied its circular layout from her window in the nursery wing, and now she walked quickly round and round, finding the center where a raised flower bed beckoned. She delved among the lilies of the valley, the sweet williams and candytuft, uprooting weeds, sniffing flowers, scouring the heretofore unrevealed regions of her heart.

She had always thought she knew herself well. She was finding that she didn't know herself at all. And now she was afraid she would err. In trying to help them all, would she precipitate the disaster she tried to avoid? Did she do the Lord's will, or did she merely justify what she wanted?

Did he do what he knew was right, or did he merely seek to thwart his father's will? He had done that so often as a boy, clinging with mad determination to his independence, that now Robbie was unsure. And it was important to him that he do the right thing for the right reason.

He had pounded out of the house, flying across the terrace and down the stone steps into the orchard garden, where he had thrown himself down on the green turf beneath an apple tree.

He scanned the brick wall hemming the orchard about, hemming him in. He'd seldom come here as a boy, preferring the open spaces of the fields and commons. Even the home wood had been too confining.

Now these walls seemed more liberating than confining, just as the thought of settling down and taking a wife—of taking Tabitha to wife—seemed more appealing than threatening.

Fearing he would succumb to that appeal, he had bitterly opposed his father's demand. Couldn't he see that Robbie would, in the end, do the more "honorable" by *not* marrying Tabitha?

There were so many reasons, he scarcely knew where to begin. They tumbled through his mind, end over end, like the boys somersaulting over the greensward.

He could not trust that marriage would, as Simon Crumpp had suggested, "nail his boots to the floor." The itch of restlessness still goaded him, weaker now to be sure, and why, he could not fathom. All he knew was that Tabitha deserved a till-death-us-do-part man, and that vow he could not take.

He did not love her. That tender emotion might be rare in Society's arranged marriages, but he had lived with his parents' nearly obsessive love of each other. He'd have that or nothing.

He had, however, fallen in "like" with Tabitha Fell. He liked her gentle humor, her stern sense of right and wrong, her belief in the goodness of man, her courage, her tenderness . . .

She was a saint. But what full-blooded man could abide for long in the presence of a saint? And what even-tempered, sweet-natured saint could abide for long in the presence of a devil?

She deserved better. A man of her own kind who would live the faith she believed, who would love and cherish her. She was too fine and good to be cast to the wolves of the *ton*. She'd be chewed up and spit out like an indigestible bone. And he was too—how it galled him!—"wicked and godless" for her. With his wild roaming ways and his vicious temper, he would make her thoroughly unhappy.

As if that were not enough, there was the matter of religion. Hers was as foreign to him as the Islamic faith of Araby, and it made her as exotically strange as the

belly dancers of those sun-baked desert lands. A swift
smile creased his cheeks. She would, no doubt, be horrified at the comparison.

Yet it was apt. In his milieu violence was an old and
honored method of settling an argument between gentlemen. In hers it was unthinkable under even life-
threatening circumstances. She believed in loving her
neighbor. He believed in watching his back. She believed in forgiveness. He believed in vengeance.

They would never suit. Never! His father must be
made to see that. It would be far better to leave her as
she was in the hope that someday she might find her
happiness. To wed her would be to ensure a life of
misery for her.

Marriage was out of the question.

He should have been satisfied with the exquisite logic
of his arguments but he wasn't. For one more came
creeping into his mind like the inchworm scaling his
trousers.

"Hell and damnation!" he cursed, pinching the tiny
green worm between his forefinger and thumb—but not
hard enough to crush it as he once would have done.
He couldn't, not with the memory of Tabitha capturing
moths that flew perilously close to the candles at table
and releasing them outside the dining room window.

He bent to the violets ringing the foot of the tree,
waiting impatiently while the inchworm step-folded,
step-folded off his finger onto a leaf. She would assuredly approve his care of the least of the Lord's creatures, and that approval was for whatever reason—God
only knew why!—important to him.

And that was the part of the argument that set his
satisfaction to flight: the woman scared him witless!

She made him uncomfortably aware of his shortcomings, made him yearn to be better than he was, made
him question his beliefs. All without scolding, nag-
ging, pleading prettily—using none of the wiles he had
seen practiced on men of his acquaintance, none of the
artful crafts he had had practiced on himself. She simply expected the best of him, and he found himself

striving to live up to her expectations. Unfortunately, he wasn't capable of the goodness she expected of him.

Robbie climbed to his feet and set off for the maze. A suitable place, he thought, for the snarl his life had become.

Tabitha was pinching dried blossoms from the sweet williams when she heard Friend Robert's unmistakable footsteps, the heels of his boots clicking on the flagstones, his strides long and sure. The soothing effects of her labor scuttled away before a rush of panic. She was not yet prepared to take the once unimaginable step of proposing marriage to him.

She sat on the brick rim of the raised flower bed, her apron dusty and her hands dirty. She rubbed them together, hastily cleaning them with a plain linen handkerchief. The day held the heat of early May, and her face was shiny and her eyes swollen by tears. She rubbed them with the backs of her hands and tucked wispy curls beneath her cap, freezing, her cheeks burning with shame.

How quickly vanity had overtaken her. She did not need to set her appearance aright, but her heart and her soul and her mind. Resisting the nearly overpowering urge to scrub her face with her handkerchief, removing any stray smudges of dirt, she settled her hands in her lap and struggled for composure.

She had almost found it when he appeared in the opening in the tall hedge. The light in his eyes sent it scattering like dandelion puffs on the wind. A light that said he did not welcome the sight of her. Her gaze dropped to her hands while the silence stretched, broken only by the whistle of a blackbird.

"You heard everything, didn't you?" he asked sharply.

Her gaze climbed, drawn irresistibly to him. He stood with his feet spread, his hands clasped behind his back, and his shoulders squared. Sunlight gilded his dark skin and lent its brilliance to his violet eyes. He was the most comely man she had ever seen, even when he frowned, as he did now.

"You understand that my father asks the impossible?"

Her gaze drifted away to the neatly trimmed wall of the hedge. Was this to be her punishment? Was she to discover that the son of the manor thought her unworthy of him? Quite suitable for idling away his time, but not suitable for a wife.

"You must see that we would not suit," he said forcefully. "I am no fit husband for you. I should make you miserably unhappy."

She looked at him quickly, searching his face, his eyes, seeking a betraying tremor, a shadow that might tell her if he was speaking the truth. She saw only his unhappiness, his belief that he was right, and not a hint at any disgust over taking her to wife. Relief flooded through her, breaking out in a smile.

"Any woman should be proud to be thy wife, Friend Robert."

"Proud in her misery, no doubt." His impatient look was softened by a wry smile. "Damn, Tabby. What a coil we are in."

She stood and walked toward him. "There is a remedy."

His vivid eyes searched her face. "Now why do I suspect it will be as unpalatable as Granny Goody's nostrums?"

"I hope thee will not think so."

"If you can convince my father—"

"I have tried and failed," she said softly.

"How fortunate that I gave that solution scant hope." He sighed heavily. "So tell me, what do you suggest?"

"Marriage," she said softly.

His eyes widened. "You cannot be serious!"

"Will thee hear me out?" He nodded reluctantly. "Thy father commands only that we wed. What we choose to do beyond that is of concern only to us.

Marry me, and thee may go thy way without let or hindrance. Thee will be as free as thou art now.''

A flush darkened his skin. ''A marriage of convenience! You cannot mean it!''

''But I do.''

''Why would you want this?'' Robbie asked sharply, antagonistically, disappointed, though he couldn't put his finger on exactly why.

''Thou art a good man, Friend Robert.''

She laid a small hand on his arm, and peace began stealing over him like mist across a meadow. He yearned for that peace and struggled against it, for that way lay danger. His very need of it made him prey to his own weakness.

''I would not be the cause of unhappiness for thee or thine,'' she continued. ''Thou art like thy father in thy pride and thy virtue—''

''Virtue?'' Robbie burst out. ''God, you cannot be so blind!''

''Do not take the name of the Lord in vain, Friend Robert,'' she said gently.

''And that is exactly what I mean!'' he said hotly. ''I take many more things than the Lord's name in vain, Tabitha. I am a violent man with an ugly temper and—''

''Do not try to convince me that thou art an evil man,'' she said firmly. ''I have looked into thy heart, and it is good.''

Oh, God! he thought, then flinched and tried to backtrack, replacing it with a strong, solid ''Hell and damnation!'' She was at it again, thinking him better than he was, making him wish she was right. Before he knew it, she'd have him replacing his powerfully satisfying curses with a lady's mealymouthed ''Stuff!''

The feeling of being wretchedly misused sent his temper soaring. ''If you expect to make a Quaker of me—''

''I do not.''

''If you expect me to give up swearing and dicing and gambling—''

"I do not."

It came to him suddenly that they were strange comments if he was not giving real consideration to marrying her. Hard on the heels of that realization came another that was painfully lowering: he *was* considering it. Considering marriage to beautiful, saintly, serene Tabitha, who would, by her very existence, forever remind him of his shortcomings.

Hastily, cruelly, thoughtlessly, he added, "And wenching."

Her gaze climbed slowly from his boots. Delicate color fanned over her cheekbones, while the hot red of shame flamed over Robbie's. "I expect nothing of thee that thou art not willing to do," she said, an eddy of sorrow in her translucent gray eyes.

His temper thoroughly quenched, Robbie stared woodenly over her head. "Forgive me. I should not have said—"

"Truth can never be ugly, Friend Robert."

"Can it not?" he asked with the lofty cynicism of age and experience. "And what do you, Friend Tabitha, gain from this marriage? Even you, Friend Tabitha, could not be so selfless as to wed me only for my own good."

It was a question she had prepared herself to answer, and the answer was the truth, if only a part of it. "I expect to have my reputation restored."

Deviled by the answer that pleased him not at all, Robbie folded his arms over his chest. "You don't trust to God for that?"

Color fled her cheeks. Hurt flared brightly in her clouding gaze. "I trust to God in all things," she said in the melodic cadence that fell on his ear like a gentle rain on thirsty earth.

Why was he driven by her to be cruel, when cruelty was not numbered among his many faults? Why was he considering this marriage, more and more as every second passed, as every question was asked and answered? "You believe this is God's will?"

Tabitha could not answer. The Inner Light had not

been her guide. She stared into the flower bed, where the glistening white bells of the lilies of the valley danced in the breeze that ruffled the hem of her prim cap and snared a loose ebony curl.

Robbie felt the painful breaking of her peace, the confusion that beset her as it beset him.

"I do not know if this be God's will, Friend Robert. I am afraid—"

"Don't be." He was unable to tolerate her suffering the least fear, unable to understand why it was so painful for him. He grasped her shoulders with his large, sun-browned hands. "We can only do the best we can, Tabitha, and hope it is good enough."

"Thou art wise, Friend Robert." Her eyes cleared, peace returning to dwell there once more, to envelop him in a perfume as sweet as that rising from the flowers behind her.

Her lips trembled lightly under his steady regard. Slowly, Robbie's head lowered, claiming her mouth as his own. She swayed against him, her hands rising, touching his chest, her fingers curling around the lapels of his coat. Sweetly, her breath sighed through, and he plummeted deep into the clear, tranquil pools of her eyes.

Why not? he wondered. After all, he would be leaving soon, and it was very likely she would be left a wealthy widow of high repute. He could help her, and for a while, a little while, he could absorb her peace and serenity.

"I am leaving for Greece . . ."

Her gaze fell to the buttons of his waistcoat, her long lashes shielding her eyes. "I will not hold thee."

Why did that pique him so?

"Wilt thou do me the honor to become my wife, Friend Tabitha?" His voice was low, rough, yearning.

Her gaze rose slowly, meeting his. "Yes," she said solemnly.

Robbie, of course, thought his problems were over. He quickly discovered they were just beginning.

First, there was the look of quiet pride in his father's eyes. How long he had waited for that look. How bitter that he received it now, when he planned to follow the letter of his father's command, but not its spirit.

Then there was the family Fell. Had he announced himself an atheist in the quiet of their unadorned parlor, he could not have been greeted with more stunned dismay.

"Let us pray," said Tabitha's brother Ezekiel, and every head bowed obediently—save Robbie's.

Tabitha's hand touched his, and his chin dropped to his chest. The air of mourning in the room scraped him on the raw. After all, he was Lord Langley, wealthy in his own right, heir to an earldom that would bring him an even greater fortune. He was respected by men, coveted by women, high in the annals of the *haut ton*. Dukes did not consider him beneath their touch or unsuitable for their daughters. Yet the gloom pervading the parlor said that these people thought him unworthy of Tabitha. It mattered not that he agreed, for his pride had been flayed.

When the silent prayer was done and every head raised as one, he leaned forward, speaking to Ezekiel. "Perhaps you do not understand what I can offer your sister. I am a wealthy man who can ensure that she will never want for anything. Additionally, I will be settling on her the sum of five hundred pounds per year pin money, which she will be free to spend as she wishes."

He leaned back, unsettlingly aware that his telling point had fallen flat. The Fells, far from impressed, were simply polite.

"Friend," said Ezekiel, "it is not Tabitha's physical needs which concern us, but the state of her soul."

Robbie's eyes narrowed dangerously. "Her soul is as pure as a swaddling babe's. I should have thought you, her brother, her family"—his burning gaze circled the gathered clan—"would have put no faith in the witless gossip of cackling hens."

"Friend Robert," Tabitha began on a gentle note of reproof.

"Friend," said Ezekiel, "we have heard this gossip, and we believe no word of it. We know our Tabby too well, just as we love her too well not to fear for her soul. If she marries thee, she will be subject to worldly temptations such as she has never faced before. In thy world thy women are expected to adorn themselves in fine raiment and jewels. Our Tabby must clothe herself soberly if she is to remain a Friend."

Ezekiel's gaze shifted to Tabitha, and Robbie saw her brother's very real fear, the love he had not, until now, revealed.

Tabitha straightened. "Thee must know I would not abandon my beliefs."

"Yet thee will abandon the Society of Friends if thee marries out of unity. Thee knows what that means. Hast thou prayed for the Inner Light?"

The pause lasted so long, Robbie turned to study Tabitha. He could see the darkness in her eyes, the fear on her face.

"I have prayed," she said, but her voice was choked.

"And the Lord's grace has descended upon thee?"

"No," she whispered, and Robbie felt the terror arcing from sister to brother to mother like lightning arcing from one cloud to another. It invaded each serene face with shattering force.

"Daughter," said her mother, "thee must not make this marriage. Thee must not without the blessing of the Lord."

"Oh, Mama," Tabitha began, and burst into tears.

Robbie swept an arm around her and drew her close, his hand cradling her cheek, her tears falling across his fingers. He had not the least understanding of what was happening. He only knew they had made his Tabby cry. Angry as he was, he bit back a hasty retort. "I swear she will be free to live her faith as she believes."

Ezekiel beheld him sadly. "In this house, Friend, in Tabitha's house, we do not swear. Can thee say the same for thine? Thy house where thee will take our Tabby to live.''

Robbie realized then that he had only the merest glimmering of the difference between them, how difficult it would be for her to enter his world, how difficult it would be for him to understand hers. He needed to hear no more to understand that, but . . .

''Thou art not the cause of our fear for our Tabby, for she would not have you were you not a good man. But we believe what Paul wrote to the church at Corinth, 'Be ye not unequally yoked together with unbelievers: for what fellowship hath righteousness with unrighteousness?' When a man and a woman are bound in holy wedlock, they become helpmates in matters of the world and the spirit. If they are of different faiths, they cannot help each other lead a Christian life. The demands of the Lord's Truth cannot be met halfway. Compromise is surrender, and surrender leads to everlasting perdition. If Tabitha weds thee, she will be disowned by the Society of Friends.''

''Disowned?'' Robbie said. ''Cast out of the church?''

''No, Friend,'' said Ezekiel. ''We cast out the sin, not the sinner. She may attend Meeting and regard herself as a Friend, but she can participate in none of the business or the tasks of the Meeting.''

Robbie felt her trembling in his arms and looked down at her bowed head. He tucked his finger beneath her chin, tilting her face up, seeing the wet tracks of tears on her cheeks.

''Tabitha?'' he questioned, wondering why he felt so cold in the heat of the day. A cold that reached into his very marrow to chill bone and sinew and rime his heart in ice. ''It would not work. Surely you can see that.''

Her small hand clutched at his lapel, crushing it. ''Dost thou forget what our marriage will be?'' she whispered.

A marriage of convenience. One where he would quickly leave her, never to return. He had forgotten. He had begun to see it as real, stretching through a lifetime. He grew colder still. How could he have done that?

"I but grieve for the pain I cause my family, for nothing more," she whispered.

"But this will cost more than I am willing for you to pay."

"Tabitha," said a new voice, the low, deep voice of Adam Fell, who had until now remained silent, "thee must tell me. Hast thou looked to thy heart?"

She turned to him, a tender smile curving her mouth. "Yes, Adam. And it has told me that this is right."

He stood slowly, crossing the parlor with his rolling gait, his hand outstretched. Robbie stood and shook it. "Our Tabby told me that I would like thee should I come to know thee, and I think I will have that chance. Tabby cannot wed thee in thy church; thee cannot wed her in hers. Thee could go to the magistrate, for they make provision for the wedding of Friends, but I think our Tabby would not be happy with that."

He took her hand. "The captain of the *North Star* is a Friend wed out of unity. He would find much sympathy with thy plight. If thee would be willing to leave on the voyage with us two days hence, thee could testify before us on the high seas."

Tabitha looked to Robbie. "If it would make you happy," he said, his heavy heart strangely lightened by the sweet smile that reached into her eyes, the soothing calm that radiated from her.

Chapter 10

If ever the Lord had sent a sign of His displeasure, this was it. Tabitha had been seasick from the moment she stepped in the longboat to be rowed out to the *North Star*. Now, on the North Sea with Adam assuring her it was as smooth and unruffled as their father's conscience had been, she knew she was dying.

"I doubt Papa's conscience pitched and rolled and wallowed," she responded testily, her eyes widening, her hand flying to her mouth. She flung herself over the side of the captain's narrow bunk, while Adam hastily procured the chamber pot from beneath.

Dry heaves shook her from the tips of her toes to the crown of her head. She fell back on the bed, gasping for air, her hair straggling from her cap and her face pallid and sweating.

Adam's callused hand gently smoothed damp tendrils away from her face. "Thee will sit up, Tabitha Fell," he said, sternly uncompromising. "I have here salt pork and biscuits—"

"S-s-salt p-p-pork!" She groaned and rolled toward the wall, but his determined hand pressed her back.

"Sit up," he said with the tone of command he used on deck. Like the sailors who "jumped to," she struggled up on the pillows he plumped at her back. "Eat. Thee will feel better."

Eyeing the pork as if it were hemlock, she stretched out her hand, pinched a square between forefinger and

148

thumb, brought it to her lips, closed her eyes, and nibbled. One bite, two, and a strange thing began to happen. Her stomach, rolling and pitching in tune with the ship, began to settle.

'' 'Tis a miracle,'' she said, smiling.

"Thee will feel even better when thee walks about the ship.''

"Walk! Adam, I can't! I stagger about as if bedeviled by strong drink!''

"If thee hopes to wed thy angry man when the sun sets this day, thee will rise from this bed and get thy sea legs.''

Confined to her bed and violently ill, she had not seen Friend Robert since they boarded. She had so longed to impress him with her sturdy adventurousness. She had, instead, been justly rewarded for that vanity. But ill as she had been, she had not stopped fearing that he would change his mind, that he would sacrifice himself for what he thought to be her good.

"How is he?'' she asked urgently.

"He'd make a sailor.'' Adam gave Friend Robert his highest accolade, then smiled his slow smile. "He was in the rigging of the tops'l when I came below.''

"A-above?'' Tabitha whispered with horror.

"Aloft, Tabby,'' he corrected. 'Aye, that he was.''

She thrust away a vision of Friend Robert clinging to rigging that looked as insubstantial as cobwebs when viewed from the deck. "I have not thanked thee. We should have been forced to wed before a magistrate, but for thee.''

He patted her hand. "It was little enough.''

"Thou art wrong. I should never have felt truly wed save by testifying.'' She paused a moment, searching his face. "Adam, why did thee take our part, when thee might be disciplined for simply attending our wedding? I fear to think what will be done when the elders learn that thee made the arrangements for it.''

His eyes narrowed thoughtfully. "Partly it was the way Friend Robert leapt to your defense. 'As pure as a swaddled babe.' '' He chuckled softly. ''The man thinks thee a saint.''

A smile toyed with Tabitha's mouth. ''I assure thee, he does not. My sharp tongue has nettled him beyond bearing.''

''It has obviously given him no desire to escape thee. He did, after all, ask thee to wed him.''

Tabitha's gaze dropped. To leave Adam thinking that Friend Robert had proposed to her was the next thing to a lie. Yet she could not bring herself to confess the truth of their marriage: that it, too, was a lie. She and Friend Robert had discussed it quite thoroughly, quite painfully before leaving Darenth Hall. They would live together, he had said, not as man and wife but as friends, and she, wanting to give him the gift of his freedom, agreed. She had no choice, but she did have hope. Hope that he could be held close, could be drawn closer, by letting him go.

''In the end,'' Adam added, ''it was the way he looked at thee.''

Her head raised, her eyes widening. ''Looked at me?''

''As if thee were the answer to a prayer he dared not pray, to a hope he dared not feel. Surely the Lord has sent thee to him.''

Was it true? Had he begun to care for her as more than a friend? The sick doubts of these long days lifted, leaving her feeling strong and sure and eager, so eager, to see him.

''I will leave thee. Wash thy face, garb thyself, and come above. A stroll from the bow to the taffrail will give thee thy sea legs.''

Unlike Tabitha, Robbie had his sea legs from the moment he climbed aboard, longing for the clear blue water and the salt tang of the briny deep. He balanced on the topgallant crosstree, his arm looped around the mast, the royal sail—fourth up from the deck at the very top of the brigantine—billowing and snapping at his back. He'd found a sailor of his height and size who had willingly raided his locker—for a goodly sum.

Now Robbie wore the unofficial uniform of the jack-tar: white duck trousers that pulled tight around his narrow hips and belled at his ankles, a checked shirt, and a black silk handkerchief with a creditable slip-knot.

The wind hummed a sea song through the rigging, whipped his hair and reddened his cheeks and put the sparkle of adventure in his eyes. How many trees had he climbed as a boy, standing straight and tall on a narrow branch while he pretended he was in a crow's nest watching for a Jolly Roger on the blue horizon. There was enough of the boy left in him to regret that the North Sea was as empty of pirates as the River Darent.

His smile spread, his teeth a blazing white against the skin that soaked up the sun and turned a rich brown. God! How he . . .

Do not take the name of the Lord in vain, Friend Robert.

Lud! How . . .

Damn! A frown whittled at the edges of his smile, but it could not be kept down for long. It spread wide once again. How he loved the sea. It seemed that the wind carried the smells of foreign lands. Cedar and spice and citrus. Smells that beckoned to him with the new and the exotic.

But he had, he thought, the most exotic of all in the Quakeress Tabitha Fell. And he viewed their swift-approaching marriage with the same feeling he had when sailing into the teeming port of a foreign land—with a mixture of apprehension and excitement.

With an ease he did not care to consider, he had put behind him the fear that this marriage was a mistake. He ignored the insistent warning that he should stop, think, and back away, as he should have once before. Had he considered the possible dangers then, he might not have been captured by Prince Friedrich, Anne might not have been forced to commit treason, and Tabitha might not have been abducted by von Fersen.

Instead, he looked only at the good this marriage could do, that it had done already. His father's anger was appeased. His mother was happy. Anne was delighted. Tabitha's good name would be protected. She would have wealth beyond her imaginings, and he would be free to do, to go, to stay at will. Could any man ask for a more complacent wife?

His only disappointment was Tabitha's failure to enjoy their short voyage. It seemed she would never peek a nose from the captain's cabin or appear at a meal. She huddled alone in the throes of *mal de mer*, something he had never suffered. Indeed, he thrived, his appetite hearty and his mood exultant. What more did a man need than the wind at his back and the mystery of foreign climes before him?

The whitecaps of the rolling waves curled like fingers, giving him silent come-hither messages. He thought of Greece and suffered the irresistible itch to be off to war.

But he had much yet to do. He had to see Tabitha accepted as his wife and settled in her new life, plans for which had already been put into action. After a short honeymoon in France, they were to return to Langleyholm, where his parents would be awaiting them. He hadn't, quite deliberately, warned his father that he had summoned the bane of his existence, Cousin Knox. Only she could teach Tabitha the ins and outs, the curious rules of the *ton*. What he wouldn't give to see the fireworks when the Dowager Duchess burst upon the sleepy Surrey countryside.

He also had to remove the threat of Shadwell, which he would do on their return to London. The City was Shadwell's haunt, but any man could be found with the will and the gold to do it. And he had both. He could not leave Tabitha until he knew she was safe.

Below, she emerged from the bowels of the ship and staggered to the railing like a sailor who had dipped deep into the grog cask. His mood soared higher. He didn't ask himself why. He simply accepted it.

"Weather abaft!" came a voice from the mainmast.

And there it was to the rear, a darkness on the horizon with flashes of lightning streaking through it.

A moment later, Adam shouted, "Lay aloft! All hands! Furl the royals and topgallants! Bear-a-hand!"

The sailors sprang into the rigging. Robbie longed to add his hands to theirs, to hang over the yardarm and haul up the sails, but he knew he would be in the way. He launched himself into the air, his hands closing around the twisting rope of a shroud that anchored the mast to the ship's railing.

Below, Tabitha, her eyes wide, her seasickness forgotten, watched him sliding down, dangling by his hands, so far aloft that he looked like a child. An illusion that was dispelled only by his size as he drew nearer. He dropped to the deck, spread his bare feet, and hooked his thumbs into the low-slung waist of his trousers.

"We're in for a storm," he said, his eyes sparkling, his smile widening.

He *was* a child! Tabitha decided with a touch of asperity. A boy delighting in the promise of raging elements, strutting his fearlessness before wind and rain and crashing wave. "I wish I could look forward to it with thy pleasure," she said stiffly.

He looked instantly contrite. "I'm sorry, Tabby."

He didn't mean it, though. She could tell by the eager look he cast at the rapidly darkening sky, by the way he turned his face into the rising wind.

The *North Star* nosed into a heavy swell and rocked back on her stern, pitching Tabitha forward and back. If only she could get the knack of balancing on a deck that was never still, then perhaps her stomach would not tumble and roll . . . as it was doing now. Desperately, she looked aloft, at the sailors clambering along the yardarms and furling the sails, but they swung to and fro against the clouds above, to and fro . . .

She closed her eyes and swallowed hard. Was this divine retribution for her sins?

"Here." Robbie pulled her back against him, his

hands on her waist. "Lean against me. Unlock your knees, and let only your feet move with the deck."

The vigorous heat of his body warmed her. His easy balance became hers and her queasy stomach began to settle. She watched the waves cresting, the spume flying over the bowsprit, and thought she might live after all, until she shifted her gaze to the stern and saw the approaching storm gobbling up the sky and sea.

"It's beautiful, isn't it?" Robbie whispered in her ear.

But it wasn't to her. She could never feel his fierce exultation. She was a woman of home, hearth, and pattering rains on the good earth, of family and friends and forever after. And he was a man of none of those things.

Suddenly she was afraid that she could not hold him close by letting him go free, that she would demand more than he could give. She turned in his arms, facing him, her fearful gaze searching his face for the look Adam had seen.

"We won't sink." He answered the fear he thought he saw. "It's only a squall. Hard while it lasts, but quickly gone."

Quickly gone. Like him.

"Does thee fear that we are doing wrong?" she asked urgently.

His gaze moved from her pale cheeks to her tremulous mouth to her overbright eyes. "No, Tabby," he said. "This may be the only right thing I've done in my life."

"I wish I could be sure," she said.

"Can we ever be in this life?"

She could be, if only the Inner Light would come to her.

"Don't be afraid." His lips grazed her temples, his arms molding her to the long, hard length of his body.

Tabitha's arms slipped around his neck and she strained against him, seeking the warmth, the solace that he offered.

And when the storm came lashing the ship with pellets of rain, they were locked together and unaware.

The squall passed quickly, leaving a trailing wind. The *North Star* ran before it, all sails flying.

The setting sun poured its liquid gold across the sea, spangles of light skipping over the waves toward the brigantine. Both watches were out, dressed in their best, the air thick with the scent of their freshly tarred queues. Robbie, dressed for his wedding, paced the quarterdeck under the amused gaze of Captain Josiah Smythe.

The gilded buttons of Robbie's waistcoat and the jeweled pin buried in his cravat glittered like his eyes. The frills of his shirtfront bounced with his every agitated step. He stroked his sweating palms down his black dress coat onto his pale buff-colored pantaloons and cast yet another anxious glance at the hatchway.

Smythe rocked on the balls of his feet, his hands clasped behind his back, as he broke into a rare smile. "Thee should not fear that Sister Fell will change her mind. 'Tis the rare woman who combines common sense and piety. Her decision to wed thee will not have been made lightly, nor will it be changed easily."

Robbie yanked at the fingers of one glove, jerking it off and dragging the back of his hand across his sweating brow.

The helmsman at the wheel exchanged a swift smile with his captain.

"I should think she would have second thoughts about this," Robbie said heavily. "She gives up much—"

"She gives up nothing," said the captain. "I, too, made this choice, for my wife and I are out of unity. Sister Fell follows her heart, as we of the Friends are taught to do. It won't be easy, for there are many differences between thee—many more than are between my wife and myself—but they may be overcome."

Perhaps, if it were a real marriage. Perhaps, if he were going to be a real husband and Tabitha a real wife. But this was a sham, a convenience that would be "convenient" only to him.

Was it, as he had told Tabitha, the only right thing he had done in his life? Or was it another in a long series of mistakes that those who loved him suffered for? Surely she wanted a man who would love her, cherish her, protect her. One who would sit by the fire in his slippers at night—every night.

Robbie's hand climbed to his cravat, one finger sliding beneath the starched linen that had begun to feel like a noose.

In the cabin below, Tabitha and Adam sat in the familiar, comforting silence of the Friends. Her seasickness was gone, vanished in Friend Robert's arms. Surely that was a sign of the Lord's pleasure, but she sought a further sign now—the Inner Light. She did not pray, but waited in stillness and quiet, watching the sunlight that fell across the Bible on the table.

A pale wraith of light, it seemed to tremble and strengthen, glowing a brilliant gold before her eyes. It expanded, reaching into the dark corners of the cabin, into the dark corners of her soul. As quickly as it had strengthened, it winked out, leaving darkness behind.

Her wondering gaze turned to the porthole where the sky beyond was a lush velvety blue inset with a single vibrating star. And like that pale wraith of light, her soul seemed to tremble, to strengthen, expanding with the saving Light, the grace she sought, the assurance she needed.

"Adam," she whispered, "I am ready."

Robbie stood at the rail, staring at the spot where the sun had vanished in a last blaze of light that stretched across the horizon, then winked out. It seemed to him that the blaze of light had illumined the murky regions of his heart, leaving behind the darkness of weakness and doubt.

Tabitha deserved better. An icy cold stiffened his every muscle as Robbie turned, watching her emerge from the hatch. She had her sea legs now, and she crossed the deck as gracefully as the swans gliding over the millpond at Darenth Hall. She wore a simple, unadorned gown, as blue as the English sky of a morning. Matching it was a capelet that hung to her waist. Framing her face were the white cap and a straw bonnet with a narrow brim.

She reached the stairs to the quarterdeck, lit by lanterns in honor of their wedding, and he hastened to her. Her face was luminous and her eyes incandescent. And for the first time he thought she was beautiful, for the first time in the full meaning of the word that she was a woman . . . and he, a man.

She had been angel, saint, savior, and innocent child, all rolled into one. Now there was added the awareness that she was a woman of flesh and blood; of earth, not of Heaven. And it seemed more imperative that she be freed—

She smiled, and every drop of happiness that could be found in the world seemed to have been distilled in that smile. How long would it last while he went his way, swearing, dicing, gambling . . . and wenching? The thought of which now filled him with shuddering distaste. Yet he knew what he was. No saint, to be sure. He was a full-blooded man with a man's needs and a devil's vices.

Her hand slid into his, confidingly, confidently, and he felt her serenity stealing through him like the mist crawling over the sides of the ship and gliding silently over the deck.

"I have been visited by the Inner Light," she said softly. "He has shown me His grace."

"Tabitha," Robbie murmured, fighting her serenity, "I must speak with you."

He led her to the railing and stared down into her face, lit by the lanterns swaying in the shrouds above. He sensed a vibrancy, an inner joy, that left him dazzled and unsure. How appealing it was. The sheen of her eyes. The flush of her cheeks. The tremulous corners of her mouth. The gaze that searched his face, as if he were a miracle happening before her eyes. It almost made him believe . . .

"Thou art afraid."

She placed her hands on his chest, and he felt them through the layers of linen shirt, white velvet waistcoat, and dress coat, as warm as her heart, as gentle as her smile. He felt the emanations of something new, something deeper than her usual serenity.

"I don't want to hurt you, Tabby."

"Thee cannot, for I have sought His grace and He has answered me. He has taken away my doubt and left in its place the knowledge that I am following His path for me."

Robbie's cursed humor tugged at his lips and set a twinkle in his eyes. "If you tell me that I am the path He means you to take, I shall be assured you are fit for Bedlam."

"Oh, ye of little faith." She smiled, and it seemed the stars had abandoned the sky to dwell in her eyes. "Can thee not see the many steps He has taken to bring me to thee?"

"And I had thought it all the Devil's work." Robbie could feel his concerns seeping away. He struggled to revive them, but found himself incapable of anything beyond a faint yet irresistible hope.

Her small hand in the crook of his elbow, she led him toward the front of the quarterdeck. Bemused, Robbie found himself standing above the gathered crew of the *North Star* and before Captain Smythe and Adam Fell—with none of his objections voiced.

"Let us pray in silence, each with our own heart," said the captain, his deep voice rolling over the deck, rising to the whipping sails above.

While heads bowed around him, Robbie stared at the restless waves crowned by creamy tongues of moonlight. He waited for the restlessness to return, but he was as becalmed as a ship in a windless sea. It was exhilarating to know that he could feel that calm, that sense of oneness with himself. Had that, too, come from Tabitha?

"When you are ready, Friend Robert," said Captain Smythe.

Would he ever be ready? Did he have nothing more than the doubts that every man faced before his wedding? Or were his deeper, more telling, more threatening to the hope of future happiness?

Tabitha's head rose, the brim of her bonnet tilting back, her small face shadowed. She took his hand and smiled up at him, and his doubts fled. But not the whispering remembrance of Abraham Leeds saying, *Thee might hurt her through thoughtlessness and selfishness, but not with the intent to hurt.*

"Tabby," he began, frantic with the need to convince her that this would be a mistake.

"Do not dwell on thy faults or fears, for thou art the best of men," she said softly, her voice mellow and low and stroking him like the hand that tenderly clasped his. "I take thee to husband by the Lord's will and my own. I give my heart into thy keeping without fear, for I have hope and faith enough for both of us."

The hard knot of tension unraveled and a smile rose to his lips. "I, Robert Bragg Ransome, take thee, Tabitha Fell, to my wedded wife, to have and to hold from this day forward, for better for worse"—*Was it so easy now because she had seen his worst, accepting it, accepting him?*—"for richer for poorer, in sickness and in health, to love and cherish"—*It wasn't a lie; he loved her already, not with passion but with friendship*—"till death us do part, according to God's holy ordinance, and thereto I plight thee my troth."

"Friends," began Tabitha in the manner of the Quakers, "I take this my friend, Robert Bragg Ransome, to be my husband, promising through divine assistance to be unto him a loving and faithful wife, until it shall please the Lord by death to separate us."

Robert Ransome, Viscount Langley, scion of the nobility, rakehell, sporting blood, and gentleman, confirmed bachelor committed to untrammeled freedom of thought and action, was now husband to Tabitha Fell—

and not loath to embark on the first of his duties, a kiss.

He sipped deep of the sweet nectar of her mouth, while the sailors cheered below. "I will try to be the man you think I am."

She cupped his cheeks in her palms, as she cupped his heart in her tender assurance. "There is no need to try, for thou art all I would have thee be."

And it was almost as if they were truly wed, truly united as one. It was only later, much later, that Robbie, remembering they were wed for convenience sake, stopped and thought and frowned.

But first there were the congratulations on their marriage and the crew's joyful thanks for the feast Robbie had boarded. And the signing of the certificate of their marriage, witnessed by Captain Smythe, Adam, and the second mate. And then the dinner on deck, filled with delicacies fit for an earl's table and taken—Robbie smiled—from his father's pantry.

In the dark of night, he strolled the deck, a cigar clamped between his teeth. Stars sparkled overhead. Water slapped against the hull. Sails flapped in the wind. But his heart was strangely still, and that summoned a frown.

This was no true marriage. He must remind himself of that yet again. His wife was below, changing into her night rail in privacy. Soon he would join her, but not to bed her. His frown deepened.

Tabitha left a single lantern blooming in the darkness and slipped between the covers of the narrow bunk. Soon he would join her, but not bed her. A tiny frown gathered above the bridge of her nose. It was a contravention of the Lord's commandment to be fruitful and multiply. And yet the peace of His grace remained with her, the certainty that she followed His Plan. The frown smoothed away. On the creaking of the door, it was replaced by a welcoming smile.

Friend Robert brought the faint scent of tobacco and the freshness of the sea air to the musty cabin. He paused by the door, his head bent beneath the low ceiling, his gaze skimming the cramped space as if he measured a coffin for himself. Even in the dim light she could see his skin paling, reminding her that Adam had said he had been slinging a hammock on the deck and sleeping there at night, rather than in the tiny closet of his cabin.

She sat up, stretching out her hand. "Come."

Her voice sang gently above the rhythmic wash of the waves against the hull, but for once it did not leave peace in its wake. It could not penetrate the vibration of Robbie's pulse, traveling along every nerve to set him atremble. He swallowed hard, hearing the suction of his dry throat. He rubbed his palms down his sides, the sticky dampness of sweat tugging at the fabric of his coat. He stared around the cabin, into the darkness at the corners. The familiar panic scurried through him, pushing the air from his lungs. He closed his eyes and struggled against the overpowering urge to fling about, to race to the deck, to breathe deep of the salt-sea air, to feel the infinite expanse of the sky overhead. He could not, would not, make such a fool of himself.

"Would thee prefer to return to thy hammock on the deck?"

He opened his eyes, and Tabitha stood before him. The lamplight shimmered through the thin linen of her night rail, leaving her body a luscious shadow framed in a halo of white. He dragged his gaze from the gentle bell of her hips, from the enticingly tiny span of her waist up to her serious heart-shaped face.

He struggled to smile. "And have every man aboard think me mad to leave my wife on my wedding night? I fear my pride could not stand the blow."

She stepped closer, rising on tiptoe, bracing her hands against his chest while she pressed a kiss to his cheek. "Then bring thy sinful pride to bed with thee," she said with a ripple of tender laughter. "But I warn thee, it will make for tight quarters in Friend Smythe's narrow bunk."

"No doubt," he said, his smile a genuine one. Suddenly he was aware of nothing but Tabitha, of the thin night rail, of the saucy thrust of her nipples against the daintily pleated yoke, of the fact that she was his wife—to have and to hold, if he could but reach out to take her, not for a night or a week or a month, but for the rest of his life.

She moved away, climbing into the bunk, leaving him with a last flash of slender leg before she slipped beneath the covers. Robbie ignored the heavy pounding of his heart, the surge of his pulse, the heaviness in his loins, as he moved to the lamp, reaching up to turn it off.

"No," Tabitha whispered. "I would have it light us through the night in memory and thanks of His holy Light."

He turned slowly. She knew. She knew he was afraid of the dark, afraid of the cramped and confined space of the cabin. How that stung his pride. Yet there was none of his own self-disgust in her steady gaze. She accepted his flaws as she accepted him, without judging, without finding him lessened by them. Now, as each time he discovered this anew, he felt a deeper ease, a greater comfort. He wanted to thank her, but the rigid wall of his pride was a barrier he could not cross.

The words he could not speak shone in his eyes, and that was enough for Tabitha. She smiled and nodded and turned to the wall, listening to the rustle of his clothing. She did not need to see him when she could remember the powerful muscles that capped his shoulders, the swath of crisp curls that covered his chest, the masculine beauty of his body—a body about which she had formed an unbecoming, unmaidenly, even shocking interest. She was fascinated by the smooth texture of his skin, the downy softness of his hair, the crisp prickle of his bearded cheeks. She loved his smile, his laugh, his voice—him. She wanted him as friend, husband . . . lover.

Would patience, time, and freedom be enough?

He slipped between the sheets beside her, and she scrunched up against the wall, trying to turn and give him more room. Her hand touched his bare hip, and a thrill scampered up her arm. She shifted quickly away, and her elbow sank into his ribs. He grunted softly, and her head snapped up, butting his chin.

"Forgive me," she whispered in mortification.

"If I am black-and-blue on the morrow," he warned, a thread of laughter winnowing through his voice, "the crew will assuredly think that you did not submit tamely to your wifely duties."

She laughed softly. "And thee, no doubt, will strut like a peacock to prove that thee was a worthy master."

"I hadn't thought on it, but now that you've suggested—"

"Thou art vile to tease me so," she said, laughing.

"Here, before you push me from this wretched bunk, shift this way . . ."

His hand touched her breast and he froze, his gaze falling and carrying Tabitha's with it to the tender swell captured in his dark hand. The soft rasp of the linen was like a scourge across her peaking nipple. The searing heat of his hand traversed the thin fabric, branding her with his touch. And that heat spun down through her, deeper and deeper, until she could feel it as a heavy waiting stillness in her womb.

Her gaze climbed slowly to the leaping pulse at his throat, to the dark desire in his eyes. Cautiously, he removed his hand, watching her all the while, his gaze tracing the trembling contours of her lips while his tongue slicked along his.

"If you will turn over," he said, his voice tight and dry, "we might make it through the night if we fit like spoons."

She did as he bade, as cautious as he, and felt him form to her back, carefully not touching her.

"The Lord bless thee, Friend Robert," she whispered, staring at the wall, achingly aware of his nearness, of the insistent heaviness in her loins.

"Good night," Robbie said, his nostrils flaring to

gather the sweet smell of her, his body achingly aware of her nearness, of the insistent heaviness in his loins.

He swallowed hard and wondered how he would survive the night. If ever a more exquisite torture had been planned, he could not imagine it. Could he really feel this—what he could only call *lust*—for the angel, the saint, the Quakeress Tabitha Fell? His wife . . . for convenience sake.

Chapter 11

Wed but a fortnight and Robert Bragg Ransome was in the devil of a pet. All because he got what he thought he wanted—a complacent wife. While he suffered a constant and uncomfortable state of semi-arousal, she smiled sweetly, spoke softly, and seemed utterly, infuriatingly unaware. After the enforced intimacy of their Parisian honeymoon, he looked forward to a se'ennight at Langleyholm like a prisoner to his release.

Arriving at noon, he found his family in residence at the small Georgian manor, all save Cousin Knox. The boys and baby Magda were in the attic nursery suite, while their parents and Robbie's own inhabited the two guest bedchambers. His first thought was one of relief: they could now have separate bedchambers, he installed in the master's, Tabitha in the mistress's with a sturdy door in between. Not that she would notice.

Just as she did not notice that they were separated throughout the day. She admired the frog Franz pulled from his pocket, the bird's nest young Karl brought for her inspection, and the fabrics his mother had ordered up from London. She studied the household accounts with Anne, and when Robbie suggested that could wait, Tabitha joined his sister in turning on him that especially irritating look women reserve for a man intruding on a feminine domain.

"We've but a week before we leave for London, and

Tabitha has much to learn.'' Anne dismissed him with a flutter of her hand and a "Run along, Robbie,'' as if he were a boy in leading strings.

He wandered the home farm, pausing at the mews to pensively study his falcons, Samson and Delilah, who summoned thoughts of the biblical Samson, shorn of his hair and his strength.

Once again, what Robbie thought he wanted was chafing him like a hair shirt. He caught no more than glimpses of Tabitha: a flick of her plain gray shirt vanishing around a corner; a wave of her hand from the bedchamber window as he played at bowls with the boys on the lawn; a tender inquiry as to his sullen mood before she was whisked above for fittings with the meek mouse of a dressmaker summoned from the City.

By evening his mood was as foul as the air of London's sewers. The bottle of port poured atop his untouched dinner and fully imbibed wine did little to alleviate his raw and rattling nerves. Negligently disposed against the fireplace mantel with his Wellingtons crossed at the ankles and blue smoke curling up from his cigar, Robbie wished his chattering family at the deuce, while he scowled across the width of the parlor at his oblivious wife.

The scruffy ruffian of a marmalade tomcat sleeping in her lap was indisputably aware of that unfriendly stare. The tip of his tail—curiously denuded of hair—began to quiver, then to tap, tap, tap his irritation. One yellow eye opened, then the other, and his fiendish gaze locked with Robbie's. The tom's battle-scarred head lifted, his single ear twitched back, and his upper lip purled away from his sharp white teeth in a growl.

Robbie, fingering the claw marks on the back of his hand, resisted the urge to snarl. Of all he might have thought to bring back from Paris, a vicious feline of neither birth nor breeding was not among their number. Particularly one who assumed that Tabitha was his personal property and her husband his deadliest enemy.

She leaned over the cat, candlelight casting her lashes in shadows across her peach-blushed cheeks. Her small finger stroked him between the ragged stub of one torn-off ear and the angry prick of the other. A painfully lowering pang of jealousy struck and quivered like an arrow in Robbie's ribs.

"Monsieur *le chat*," she murmured, and the lord of all he surveyed snuggled his chunky body to her generous breast, squirreled his nose beneath her chin, and mewed piteously. Her reproachful gaze climbed. "Thee should not provoke him, Friend Robert."

"I?" he said belligerently. "Provoke him?"

The arrogant feline turned a triumphant cat smile on Robbie, and Anne leapt into the threatening breach. "Tabby, you never told us how you found Monsieur."

"Friend Robert found him."

"And a blacker day I will never know!"

Monsieur ceased licking his paws to cast Robbie a malignant look.

"A group of boys," said Tabitha, "set fire to his tail, and he came streaking out of the alleyway—"

"Over my boots. Cheddar still swoons over the scratches."

"Friend Robert dunked him in a barrel of rainwater—"

"And had my hands shredded for the favor," he added dryly.

"Then we—"

"She," she amended.

"Brought him back to the inn—"

"Where he laid claim to Tabitha."

Anne scratched the cat's arching back and cast Robbie a quizzing glance. "He seems a perfectly amiable creature."

"He's possessed by the Devil," said Robbie repressively.

Monsieur hissed in his direction, then licked Anne's hand.

"I see that you share at least one thing," said the earl, a smile softening his austere mouth.

"If you mean by that a low opinion of each other," said Robbie, "then you are quite right."

"That, too," said the earl, clearing his throat of a sound suspiciously akin to laughter. "I thought, perhaps . . . Tabitha."

Yes, Tabitha. Robbie chewed viciously on the fine Havana cigar wedged into the corner of his mouth.

"Aside from wretched boys setting fire to cats' tails," began the earl, "how did you find Paris, my dear?"

The sights that Tabitha had seen were ones she was not loath to discuss. She spoke not about the dazzling sunlight that poured over the Pont Neuf, but about the legless veteran of Napoleon's army reduced to selling paper, nibs, and pens beside the bridge. Not about the statuary, the terraces, the stately avenues of the Tuileries, but about the scabrous orphaned child selling nosegays of violets on the Champs Élysées. Not about Bonaparte's Pillar in the Place Vêndome, but about the infant with a bloated belly squalling in its mother's arms.

She had an alarming penchant for ferreting out the dregs of society. As delicately as possible, Robbie had explained that a lady should ignore these unfortunates, but the look she had turned on him was filled with such disappointment, such gentle reproof, that he silently swore never to mention it to her again.

Now it seemed his father would take up the cudgels. The earl's interest in the lower orders was tenuous at best, and none rivaled him as a high stickler for the proprieties of his class. Robbie frowned, perversely deciding that Tabitha was as nearly perfect as a human could be. If Society could not appreciate her as she was, then be damned to it!

"Dear girl," said the earl, "your interest in unfortunates is admirable. However, should you bring this habit to London, you will not be accepted by the Society to which your husband is heir. I scruple to say you might drop a coin in a beggar's cup, but consorting with the poor in the streets is beyond the pale."

Her gaze of gentle reproof rested on his father with,

Robbie noted, the same effect it had on him. The rigidly correct and top-lofty Earl of Darenth squirmed.

"Friend John," she said gently, "I know thee means only the best for me, but I must live according to the Friends. It is a woman's duty to relieve the wants of the poor, to see the divine potential in every man. I cannot pass by any whom I might help."

His father's gaze shifted to Robbie with a silent question. He shrugged lightly. "The *ton* can take Tabby on her terms or none."

"Just as you have demanded to be taken on yours or none?" asked the earl, his thick black brows beetling over his eyes to cast them in shadow. "You forget that, as a man, you might dare what a woman cannot. I should think you would have more care of your wife."

"Is it care, Father," he asked meaningfully, "to try to change her, to mold her into something she was not meant to be?"

A quick cold silence fell over the parlor. The earl shifted on the settee, his pale thin hand gripping the rose-brocaded arm, his face set like iron. "As you think I," he began in frigid accents, "have done to you?"

Robbie removed the mangled cigar from his mouth, squinting against a curl of smoke as he tossed it into the cold hearth. "Haven't you?" he asked with a marked lack of concern.

"For your own good," said the earl, unflinching, "just as this will be for Tabitha's. Should you hope for her to be accepted, she must conform to the manners and modes of Society. That was, after all, why you asked us here, was it not? To train her for her introduction to the *haut ton?*"

That, of course, had been the plan. One Robbie had made, as he made so many others, without looking to see where it would lead. His violet gaze, dark with anger at himself, at his father, at the circumstances he could not change, moved slowly to Tabitha. The small heart of her face lifted to him, her misty gray gaze serenely reassuring. Oddly, its once soothing effect seemed to be a thing of the past.

"Thee must not concern thyself for what must be," she said, her voice the sweetest of music to his ear. "The Friends believe that we must participate in the world according to our station, whether high or low. I accepted the need for change when I married thee."

"And gave up your religion," he said bitterly.

"I may attend Meeting, as my brother told thee. And if I were willing to admit my error in wedding thee, I would be accepted back into the full fellowship of the Friends."

He went still for a moment, his eyes locked with hers and asking the question his lips could not form.

She smiled, her expression tender, her incandescent gaze radiating an inner light of joy and peace. "No," she said softly. "I cannot call my wedding thee an error when it was not."

He shouldn't have felt so free of a sudden, as if he had been divested of a wearisome burden. He shouldn't have felt so lighthearted and light-headed that he wanted to snatch her into his arms and laugh with her, to hold her, to caress her, to make her his own. She wasn't, nor would she ever be. He wasn't like his father and Karl, men content to sink deep and binding roots.

Even as he assured himself that he would be leaving her soon, he was beset by an irresistible impulse to whisk her upstairs for a few moments alone. "Tabitha," he began hastily, thoughtlessly.

The rattle of carriage wheels penetrated the parlor.

"Were you expecting someone?" his mother asked.

"As a matter of fact, I was. I had expected her to be here when we arrived." The promise of emotional fireworks consumed a swift spark of irritation at this untimely arrival. In high good humor, very like the boys awaiting the outcome of a prank, Robbie set his back to the marble mantel and crossed his arms over his chest, declining to enlighten them further.

A clatter and chatter burst from the entry chamber,

flowing into the parlor. Hard upon it came a deep-throated feminine bellow: "Announce me? Announce me indeed, nodcock! Step aside!"

The earl turned an expression of abject horror on his son, and Robbie laughed aloud, a merry lilt in the deep resonance of his voice. "Yes," he said, "that *nonpareil*, Cousin Knox."

A moment later the spider-shanked butler, Thistle-wood, scuttled past the entrance to the parlor, no doubt seeking safe harbor in the hinterlands of the manor. Hard on his heels came the Dowager Duchess of Worth. Squat and square as a box, she erupted through the portal, her flower-bedecked bonnet askew and her fur tippet sailing behind her.

"Where is that dratted boy?" she trumpeted, her lace-trimmed parasol, better suited to an ingenue, assuming the *en garde* position of a fencer.

The invalorous Monsieur, his marmalade fur standing on end, his hairless tail straight as a fireplace poker, sprang from Tabitha's lap to the windowsill and vanished into the dark of the night.

"Leg-shackled and none to see it!" Cousin Knox barked, her fine brown eyes snapping at Robbie. "You might as well have absconded to Gretna Green! Well, where is she?"

"Good God!" burst out the earl. "What are *you* doing here?"

"Good God, indeed! You provoking ninnyhammer!" She rounded on him in a drift of ruffles and laces. "I was summoned by your son, whom *you*, Coz, have once again allowed to rub against the grain of Society!"

"I?" roared the earl, his face an alarming shade of red. "As if you were unaware that he has been neither to have nor to hold since the cradle, Arabella!"

"Fustian!" She stabbed the tip of her parasol into the carpet with a resounding thump. "I have told you, Coz, since he was a babe at the breast, that he might be led where he will not be pushed! He's a Ransome through and through! Have no doubt of that!"

"As you yourself have noted, Arabella, he's a ramshackle, care-for-nobody hellhound," said the earl in a rage, his eyes chips of blue ice in the wine flush of his face.

"And thank God for that! He puts me in mind of the men of my day. Now, those were *men!* Not like these flummery, frippery sprigs of fashion! Not a dram of mettle in them!" She reached for the lorgnette dangling from a satin ribbon, raising it from her swelling bosom to her sparkling brown eyes. Perusing Robbie from his ebony curls to his mirror-shined boots, she heaved a gusting sigh. "Now *that* is a man to set a gel's heart to thumping!"

Robbie smiled quickly, vividly, his teeth flashing white against his sun-kissed face. "At last you've come, you delicious creature. I expected to find you awaiting our arrival."

"And so I should have, had I not been in the Highlands of Scotland when your billet found me." She tilted her head back, and the field of scarlet poppies surmounting the straw brim of her hat quivered as if in a high wind. "Where is the gel who can get the rascally Robbie Ransome to tie the parson's knot?"

He stretched out his hand, feeling Tabitha's rest in his palm as warm and soft, as gentle, as a dove. He'd wanted to touch her all day, and now he drew her to his side with an air of possessive pride. "Cousin Knox," he said, "my wife, Friend Tabitha Fell Ransome."

A bright, shrewd gaze surveyed Tabitha from her neat white cap to the toes peeking from her hem. "I needn't warn you that he's a town buck of the first cut, a very devil at every rig and row. He'll need a light rein."

"I'm not a hack to be broken to the saddle," Robbie protested a trifle uneasily. Should Cousin Knox begin to spin tales of his misspent youth—

"Humph! Every man chafes at the bit of his marriage vows." She dismissed him with a glance, her full and daunting attention returning to Tabitha. "Welcome to the family, gel. I've no doubt you'll grow accustomed to us in time. Now''—she twirled a stubby finger—"turn around. Let me see what we can make of you."

Robbie, with the growing certainty that Cousin Knox might well have been the worst of his ideas, shoved his hands in his pockets and scowled while Tabitha spun slowly about. The candlelight stroked her smooth, delicate skin, casting light and shadow in tempting patterns at her temples, at her lips, at her throat. He noted the slender stem of her neck, the fragile curve of her cheek, the innocent sweep of her long silky lashes, the lush inviting swell of her breasts, the waist that he could span with his hands. It seemed suddenly that he was throwing a lamb to the lion.

"Neat waist. Good shoulders," said Cousin Knox. "A fine, determined chin."

"She's not a blood mare set for sale at Tattersall's!" Robbie burst out.

"Is there a difference?" Cousin Knox asked in some amazement. "If she has no bloodlines to her favor, she'll need the wit and wind to see the race run."

He drew himself up to his full, imposing height and stared down the length of his boldly chiseled nose. "Tabitha need be nothing more than herself," he said. "I require you only to teach her what she must know. Should she not wish to follow your instruction in any matter, the choice is to remain hers."

"Fustian!" crowed Cousin Knox with a sprightly air. "You'd not have had the gel if she was witless and spitless, and I should have found you excessively tiresome if you had. Before the Season's entertainments are in full feather, we shall launch Friend Tabitha with fanfare, defying the censorious, balking the . . . good God!"

All gazes followed hers to the window. Monsieur perched on the sill, as if he were a Royal giving audience to his minions. His marmalade fur shining with dewdrops, his eyes gleamed triumphantly over the mouse trapped between his jaws. He leapt onto the carpet, his hairless tail waving as he padded to Tabitha, dropped the mouse at her hem, and sat back with an expectant "Meow!"

Tabitha dropped to her knees and scratched him beneath the chin, producing a quivering ecstasy that Robbie thought quite revolting.

"Good God!" repeated Cousin Knox, undaunted by the mouse, horrified by the cat. "Forbear to say that this creature is attached to the gel! It won't do. It won't do at all. A King Charles spaniel. An Irish wolfhound. Either would give her countenance and cachet, but . . . but . . ."

"It should be capital sport," Robbie said with a wicked smile, "to see if war-weary alley cats become all the kick among the delicate flowers of the *ton*."

"Good God!" said Cousin Knox, her dusty brown cheeks paling to a sallow yellow. "Lead me to my bed, where I might cherish my gloomy expectations of your wife's come-out."

Robbie's wicked smile dwindled. To make room for Cousin Knox, there being a shortage of guest rooms, Tabitha would be bumped from the mistress's chambers to the master's, from the mistress's bed to the master's. And he must suffer yet another se'ennight of temptation. He was beginning to understand why monks so often resorted to the scourge.

The soft fragrance of meadowsweet curled around Tabitha in the window seat, filtering through the breeze that played among her unbound curls. A pensive moon brooded over the scudding clouds, as Tabitha brooded over a life that had changed beyond recognition.

How much longer could she sustain the pretense that Friend Robert's presence left her unaffected? How much longer could she create emotional and physical distances between them? She should have begun to see his tension easing, his acceptance of her as casual as his acceptance of Anne. Instead, he seemed taut-strung and angry, his mood low, his temper high, his tongue sharp.

Did he, as Friend Arabella had said, chafe at the bit

of his marriage vows? Those loosest of all vows that left him free to follow his will, while she stood bound till death by her testimony and her heart.

She did not seek peace, for she knew it was not to be found. She had quiet, and it was abhorrent to her. She needed Friend Robert, but he was below, a dark shadow pacing beneath the oaks amidst the rustling night creatures and the whispering leaves. Was he, even now, pondering his plans to leave her?

Monsieur leapt onto the brown moiré silk window seat, stepped on the sill, and sat with his hairless tail wrapped over his paws. She nuzzled his neck. He licked her chin.

"What a rogue thou art," she said softly. He flicked his pink tongue over the tip of her nose. "Thee should not provoke Friend Robert."

He stared down into the shadows of the oaks and hissed.

Tabitha's light laugh rippled through the night. "Two of a kind," she whispered, stroking his furry back. "Pride is a sin, Monsieur *le chat*."

A sin of which she was guilty. She longed to throw herself into Friend Robert's arms, to plead with him to see her, to need her, to love her, but pride stilled her pleas. If only they were not here at Langleyholm, wedged into the small Georgian manor like herrings in a cask. There was no escape from him, from herself.

Monsieur, growling, bounded away, vanishing into a dark corner. The brass doorknob clicked. A step scraped at the portal. Friend Robert stood in the doorway, dimly lit by a flickering candle that molded his features into a demonic mask.

"You are not asleep?" he asked sharply.

"It . . . it was such a lovely night." How easily lies spilled from her lips. She would soon be lost to all grace and light.

Just as she was lost to all sense. Near or far, he was the focus of her world, her thoughts, her heart. Would he really sink into vice when they returned to London?

Swearing and dicing and gambling and . . . wenching. Her heart would break.

She studied him as if he were a stranger. Long, even strides carried him to the hearth, as they would soon carry him away from her. His warm, honey-sweet lips could so swiftly break into laughter or as swiftly thin in a frown, as they did now. He shed his frock coat, tossing it across a massive wing chair, as easily as he would shed her and toss her aside. She measured the broad width of his shoulders and the narrow span of his waist, her gaze lingering on the graceful hands tugging irritably at his cravat.

"Shall I summon Cheddar?"

He cast her an angry glance. "I am not yet a doddering antiquarian that I need to roust my valet from his bed."

"Of course not," she soothed.

"I'll not be patronized, Tabitha!" Robbie jerked at his cravat, snarling it into a hopeless knot. A knot as tight as the ties that bound him to his wife. Ties that he wanted, in spite of himself, to draw even tighter. He was mad! It was lust, pure and simple. Once it was assuaged the old itch would be upon him, the irresistible urge to wander footloose and free. Whatever he had become, he had not sunk so low that he would attach Tabitha to him and then abandon her. He should be glad that she was so complacent a wife, even-tempered, sweet-natured, and undemanding. But he wasn't. Dammit! And the hell of it was, he didn't know why.

She approached, her white night rail flowing around her bare feet, her black hair spilling in wanton disarray, curls adrift at her shoulders, at her waist, around her face. His fingers ached to bury themselves in the silken fall of her hair, to wind the alluring tresses around his hand, drawing her closer. As close as she came now, her eyes shining like moonstones in the exquisite setting of spiky black lashes.

She reached up and touched his hands, curled into

fists. "Let me do at least this for thee," she said on a low note of strain.

His fists dropping to his sides, he endured the torture of her nearness, the bewitching scent of woman, the tantalizing presence of her hands at his throat, gently tugging at the knot. He closed his eyes, but he could not escape the warm tendrils of yearning that twined around his heart or the passion that grew with each sigh of her breath, each feather-light caress of his hand by a fold of her linen night rail.

He found no peace, no serenity, no tranquility in her now. Only the need of a man for a woman, for the surcease of passion shared. But she was still angel, child, innocent. What would she think of the hot, desirous thoughts that set him to tossing through the night? Would she be shocked, dismayed, disgusted, afraid?

"There," she whispered, spreading the crinkled ends of the cravat and patting his chest as if, he thought with rising rage and thwarted passion, he were a moss-grown fossil too long in the tooth to be dangerous.

His fists unlocked. His hands clamped around her waist, sending instant messages of curves and hollows and unexplored secrets. She caught at his arms to brace herself, her head rising, her wide gaze questioning.

"Do not take me too lightly, Friend Tabitha. I am no Abraham Leeds to consider denial a path to Heaven."

Her hands tightened on his arms, and a shiver spread through him, half-delight, half-dread, and wholly unwelcome. She studied him, her eyes cloudy with doubt, her lips parted in an unconscious invitation.

"What have I denied thee?" she asked breathlessly.

"What have you not?" His voice was as rough as the storm of unfettered emotion that whipped through his chest.

He claimed her mouth, punishingly, possessively, passionately. Even as he told himself it was madness, her slight frame surged against him and her hands splayed urgently around his nape. He dove like a swimmer into a red-hot delirium, a drunken joy. Lost, and he didn't care. He cared only that the ache in his loins be eased and the emptiness in his heart be filled.

"Tabby," he whispered, his mouth gliding down her throat to the frenetic pulse at its base. Soaring on the glory of her eager trembling and her soft sighs, his hand climbed to worship the generous swell of her breast, his forefinger and thumb capturing the taut bud, rolling it gently through the smooth linen. It was not enough; never would it be enough. He wanted to suckle at her breast, to feel her flesh to flesh, to sheathe himself in the wet heat of her womb, to become one with her.

His seeking lips traversed the column of her neck, finding her chin, her tremulous mouth, while he tugged the bow from the thin ribbon at her throat, feeling when it opened like a conqueror at the gate of a vanquished city.

"Tabby," he whispered huskily, sliding the thin fabric aside, the heel of his hand gliding along her fragile collarbone to the delicate cap of her shoulder and down her arm, pushing the fabric before it. His thumb stretched out, gently stroking the satiny mound of her breast, climbing slowly to the engorged peak. He flicked it lightly, once, twice, and heard the thick hiss of her breath and felt the involuntary arching of her body against his.

His tongue replaced his thumb, swirling round and round, gently teasing her quivering nipple with the ridge of his teeth. Her fingers convulsed at his nape, rising to tunnel through his ebony curls, pulling him closer and closer.

"Fr . . . Friend . . . Rob . . ."

She sagged against his bracing arm, boneless and weak, her breath short and sharp. He swept her up, holding her high to nuzzle at her breast, to suckle the nectar of a passion that equaled his. She curled around him, her knees drawing against his arm, her hand curled around his nape, her lips pressing feverish kisses above the rim of his collar.

Arrayed on the bed in the frail moonlight, her hair

was a tempest-tossed sea lit by silvery spray. He followed her down, his lips melded with hers, his heart full and aching. His hand wandered down to the curve of her waist, explored the swell of her hips, glided down to her thigh, and began gathering the folds of her gown until he touched the scalding heat, the satiny texture, of the flesh beneath. Then a silken glide up and up, pausing at the juncture of hip and thigh, kneading lightly, shifting to the nest of curls and hearing her soft cry.

A cry that was answered by a yowl from a dark corner, by a scrabbling of claws across the oak floor, a rapid padding of paws across the carpet.

The cat! The damn cat! Robbie thought in the second before Monsieur launched through the air and landed on his back with an unearthly squall and a clenching of needle-sharp claws. As quickly as he landed he was gone, bounding from the bed, slipping and sliding over the polished oak planking, coming to a halt beneath the satinwood *bonheur du jour.*

Robbie forked up, glaring into the shadows lit by two unwinking yellow eyes. The deep gouges in his back stung like his conscience. How quickly his good intentions had been abandoned for the needs of his body.

"He is . . ." Tabitha began.

"A devil," Robbie snarled, his frustrated body burning, his mind cooling. "But a timely one."

He rose from the bed, catching a glimpse of her that he knew would linger through the nights, through the days. She had struggled up, leaning against the pillows, her hair in wild tangles that fell across her breast as if to shield her from view. But it was her face that stopped him and forced him to turn back. Her face, with its dazed expression and silvery-bright eyes and kiss-swollen mouth. She raised her trembling hand, pushing a froth of curls away from her eyes, and he wanted to take that hand, to hold it, to kiss it until the trembling stopped.

"I'm sorry . . . I'm so sorry," she whispered.

He hardened his melting heart and ignored the clamoring of his blood. "I'm not."

He strode rapidly to the door, closing it behind him so carefully that Tabitha knew he longed to slam it. She stumbled from the bed and tumbled onto the window seat, curling around the hot, heaving ache deep in her womb. He had awakened a thousand pulse points that throbbed throughout her, making her suddenly, strangely aware of her body in a way she had never been before. He had awakened her to the pleasures of the flesh, and then he had left her unfulfilled. Like their marriage, it was a beginning that would have no end; one that left her poised on the brink of an earthy, earthly paradise whose gates were forever barred to her.

She lifted her head. Her night rail rasped across her swollen breasts, sending flurries of sensation rising to her lips, coursing low in her belly. Friend Robert was in the yard below, staring up at her. The moonlight bathed his white shirt in a pale radiance. It danced across the tumble of his hair, leaving his eyes in shadow. It gleamed across the strong bone structure of his face, carving it like a stonecutter's chisel with light and dark, with hope and despair. He looked as alone as she felt, as if neither he nor she would ever again be touched by human hand or heart.

Why? her heart cried. Why did you leave me?

There was no need to hear an answer. She knew. She had seen it happening. His feelings for her were growing deeper, and he was afraid. Just as she was afraid that they would send him fleeing.

Her lashes sagged over her eyes.

Sometimes a man doesn't know what he really wants.
And always it is better to let him learn for himself.
Unless he is stubborn.
Especially if he is stubborn.

But was there any patience left in her to wait for him to discover himself, to find and renew his own strength? And when he did, would she have lost herself in the interim?

* * *

Tabitha spent the night alone in the broad empty bed in the master's chamber. She had never felt more alive, more aware of fragrances and textures and sounds. She longed for the intimacy, the privacy, of their fortnight in Paris. She longed to stroll in the park with Friend Robert, knowing that for a little while she would be the center of his world as he was the center of hers. She longed to lavish upon him all of the love that ached for release.

Slowly her despairs and her fears slipped away. Hope was too integral a part of her nature to be abandoned so quickly. After all, the Inner Light had been her guide. It would not lead her astray. Friend Robert might be stubborn and afraid, but she was not. She would become the wife he wanted and needed. She would weave a web of caring and concern that would gently ensnare him.

In the golden light of the morning she tripped down the stairs with Monsieur at her heels mewling for his breakfast—only to find that Friend Robert was gone. To London, Thistlewood said. He'd await her arrival there at the end of the week.

Then she knew that his fear was stronger than her love, that her hope might be in vain.

Chapter 12

The Lads of the Fancy gathered at Old Mother Damnable's, a brothel in a side street off Drury Lane. Peers of the realm rubbed shoulders with the lowest denizens of the backslums, every eye straining upward to the gallery to see if that hell-bent tempter of Providence, Langley—better known in this milieu by his sobriquet "the Falcon"—would, at last, break his neck.

Robert Ransome, Viscount Langley, balanced on the balcony rail like a ropewalker in Astley's Circus. He was beyond the blush of youth and in his prime, tall and lean and reckless to a fault. His hair gleamed in the candlelight, as black as a cutthroat's heart. As always, the twinkle in his violet eyes danced over the surface, leaving the depths dark and untouched.

He hooked an elegantly clad arm around a spindly column, flashed a smile that fluttered the hardened hearts of Mother's barques of frailty, and bowed low, teetering on his perch. "Drinks all around!" he shouted. "Tonight we toast that lover of liberty, Lord Byron, dead this year past in the struggle for Greek independence!"

A roar of approval rattled the rafters, and a whiff of cynicism hardened Robbie's smile. Not one of them understood the real meaning of liberty. The Pinks of the *ton* had never been without it. The dregs of London's rookeries, alumnae of Newgate, Bridewell, and

Coldbath Fields, were too brutalized to care. Only he understood what it was to crouch beneath a low stone ceiling, to shuffle in no direction more than six feet, to live with the stench of his unwashed body, to be helpless and at the mercy of a madman. And that would always set him apart. The knowledge that he had been tested . . . and broken.

The scar on his wrist burned as if it were newly cut. Would he ever forgive himself for turning his rage and his madness on himself? For trying to take the coward's way out. For running, always running away from himself.

And now running from his wife.

Tabby, with so much passion hidden behind her placid exterior. If once he succumbed to it, there would be no escape. He wanted her beneath him with her body bared to his touch and her lips at the hollow his throat. He wanted to rip away her serene facade, exposing the woman he had found waiting like a gift in a plain paper wrapping.

It wouldn't happen now. He had seen to that. He had maneuvered himself and manipulated his friends into a bet. If he could walk the railing they would join him on the voyage to Greece at summer's end. If he won, honor—honor! he thought bitterly—would hold him fast. By then the threat of Shadwell would be no more. He had spent his week wisely, spreading the news through every low haunt in the City and its environs that he would pay one hundred pounds to the man, woman, or child who turned Milling-Jemmy Shadwell in to the Bow Street Magistrates. He had no doubt that the man would soon be caught.

The swarthy Earl of Audley, known here as the Spaniard, leapt atop the table by the fire, raising his blackjack o' blood. "Walk, Falcon! Walk, and the Spaniard and Old Nick will fight at your side against the Turks!"

Robbie swung on the column, cantilevered over the sea of upturned faces. Though his head spun giddily, he flung out his arm in an expansive sweep. "And the Vicar? Will he join me?"

His defiant gaze found Brat Raeburn disgustingly sober. Though they had shared the adventures and dreams of boyhood, that time was long past. His friend had become the conscience Robbie could not tolerate. But then, Brat had nothing to prove. He had covered himself with glory in the late war, first losing an arm at Salamanca, then whipping the Frenchies at Waterloo.

"The Greeks have no need of me," Brat called out, his liquid brown gaze sadly disapproving.

Robbie pulled himself up, poising on the railing. "What a pleasant diversion you will miss."

"And what a hell you will find." Brat's riposte rang over the bets that flew through the long main room, being matched and raised in the inveterate gamester's point-counterpoint.

Robbie shot him a sharp glance. His foot slipped, and he went plunging down. The *filles de joie*, their eyes brilliant with belladonna, shrieked and buried rouged cheeks in their hands. Robbie caught the railing, jerking himself up short and wrenching his shoulder. In spite of the pain, exhilaration bubbled through him. This was what it was all about—grazing the sharp teeth of disaster and surviving. His hand slipped and gripped, every tendon straining against his sun-kissed skin. Slowly he pulled himself up and regained his footing atop the narrow, none-too-sturdy banister.

"Well done," came Old Nick's bored drawl.

Robbie smiled exultantly, a boyish curl dancing across his brow. "To Greece and liberty!"

"Walk! Walk! Walk!" chanted the crowd.

He began, his arms extended for balance. A faltering step, another, and he wobbled like a half-spun top. The faces of his audience blurred. From one of the private boudoirs lining the balcony he heard a feminine groan of, no doubt simulated, passion. Smiling wickedly, he focused on the turned column ahead and sped toward it in a flurry of steps.

Below, the Earl of Darenth entered, shaking the rain from his cloak. It was a foul night to be out on the Town. Had his quest been less important, he would have been warming his aged and aching bones at a cozy fire with his wife at his side. Instead, he had traveled from the elegant clubs of St. James's Street to the hells of Jermyn Street to the taverns and brothels of Covent Garden. He had observed the town bucks in full cry, which did not improve a mood that was as low as his opinion of the younger generation.

His gaze swung up to the focus of all eyes—his rackety, ramshackle son clinging to a column with the tips of his fingers and swinging out over the motley gathering like a hurdy-gurdy man's monkey.

Darenth snatched off his top hat, revealing a full head of steel gray hair, slipped his cloak from his shoulders, and tossed them to the waiting porter. His lowering brows promising a storm ahead, he followed Robbie's unsteady progress along the creaking banister.

Brat Raeburn joined him. "He has not been . . . himself tonight, my lord," he said softly, by way of explanation.

The earl cocked a brow, shooting Brat a glance of patent disbelief. "I should say he's being very much himself. He will sail too close to the wind one of these days."

"Sometimes, my lord, I think he wants to."

"So do I, Brat. So do I." His gaze rose to his son, now nearing the last column. He had been proud of him once long ago. He couldn't say it then. Later, Robbie hadn't wanted to hear it. Now . . . God, what now? His son was a stranger. He didn't know what Robbie thought, what he wanted, what he dreamed. And every attempt to learn ended in the disaster of angry accusations.

The crack of shattering wood sounded like a pistol shot.

Darenth's heart surged into his throat, thick with the

love he could not deny even at his son's most outrageous moments.

Robbie's heart sank to his toes, leaving him lightheaded on the railing. He hurled himself forward, reaching for the last column. If he could touch it, he would win the bet. He would leave for Greece at summer's end. There, he would prove his courage once again. How many times must he prove it, whispered an anguished voice, before he would believe it himself?

The railing fell away beneath him. A baluster struck his thigh an agonizing blow, but it held him that moment needed to thrust forward with a grunt of effort, to touch the smooth spindle of wood, to grasp it and victory. His legs swung down, slamming his hip into the ell-turn of the balcony, and a grimacing smile revealed the even row of his teeth, a startling white against his sun-darkened skin.

His collar *à la Byron* flapped up, brushing the crisply curling side whiskers neatly squared at his jaw. His French cuff inched down his arm, revealing the ridged scar that crossed his wrist in a jagged line. The visible mark of his unforgivable weakness, it shone in the candlelight, silvery with age.

His fingers slipped. He began to fall. A vertiginous swirl spun him back in time to a crypt, to darkness and despair. He had screamed then, an enraged animal in pain. Now he set his teeth against any sound. The top of his head grazed the edge of a Windsor chair, feeling as though it peeled away his scalp. He hit the floor with a thump that stole his breath. While he gasped for air, Audley came hovering, his onyx eyes revealing a rare worry.

"Are you hurt, Langley?"

He sucked in a long draught of air that carried the scents of roasting beef and cloying perfume and tobacco. His elbow felt as though it had been attacked by a hive of bees and his heel as though a Spanish Inquisitor had put him to the boot, but worst of all was the throb in the top of his skull. He reached up, gingerly probing a rising bump. A slow grin wound across his mouth, and the ever-present twinkle danced in his eyes. "Just the pate, old boy."

"Then we should have no concern, for that is the least likely part of you to take an injury," came the icy voice of the Earl of Darenth.

The chamber the earl engaged was dominated by a massive four-poster draped with sunset-colored gauze in the eastern style. Old Mother Damnable herself directed the housemaid to place a silver salver of Irish whiskey and glasses on the low papier-mâché table ringed about with pillows for lounging. Darenth waited by the only chair, a monstrosity of velvet squabs and swarming cupids. Robbie, his head still pounding, leaned against a bedpost, one knee bent, one hand jammed deep in his pocket.

"My lord," said Mother, a plump partridge with an arch expression, "I have a girl, tender and fresh. Perhaps you would like to share her with—"

"Madam," snapped the earl, his color rising intemperately, "the only thing I would like to share with my son is privacy."

The door closed on her hasty exit, and Robbie grinned. "It might have been capital sport, my lord."

"You brazen-faced coxcomb! I'm in no mood for your quizzing!" Darenth slammed his hand down on the intricately carved chair railing. "What was that all about below?"

"A bet, my lord," Robbie said stiffly. His father would have to be told, but he wished it did not have to be now.

"Pray be more forthcoming," said Darenth acidly.

"The Spaniard, Old Nick, and I will be leaving for Greece at summer's end. We will join their fight for liberty."

Darenth went still, his fingers biting into the back of the chair so hard his knuckles turned white. "You have a wife now."

Flinching inwardly, Robbie reached into his vest

pocket and withdrew a long, thin cigar, casually inhaling its aroma. "And we have an . . . understanding."

"And did she *understand* that she would be left at Langleyholm within a fortnight of her wedding?" the earl said furiously. "That you would not greet her on her arrival in London, leaving her to make her own introduction to your servants? That you would abandon her after a few months? What kind of marriage is this?"

"One that will return to Tabitha her good name. One that will leave me free—"

"To run away again! And this time you will leave a wife behind!" the earl burst out. "By God! I never thought a son of mine would be a coward!"

Though the blood fled his face, leaving it pasty white, Robbie cocked a gently inquiring brow. "Surely I am exactly as you expected, my lord."

Darenth stared at his son, seeing the tension behind the careless pose, the pain behind the smile. Must they always tear at each other? Though he ached to heal the breach between them, he found himself falling into the old and somehow comforting pattern of accusation.

"A coward fleeing his own shadow, fleeing his obligations and responsibilities! Do you think it gives me pleasure to admit it? I despair of the day you succeed to my title!"

"Then, my lord," said Robbie lightly, "let us hope that day is far away."

"Pray God! Let us hope!" said Darenth bitterly.

Robbie's smile wavered, then slipped firmly into place. He walked to the table, impressively graceful in spite of the tension that jerked every nerve taut. Swiveling away to hide the tremors racing through his hand, he raised a candle to his cigar. The light frolicked across his face, glittering in his violet eyes, gleaming across the fine arch of his jet-black brows, and shining over the sweat beading on his forehead.

"Why have you trailed me into the stews of Covent Garden, my lord?"

"Because your wife is home alone on her first night

in London. Your wife, whom you have so easily, so casually forgotten.''

But he hadn't forgotten her. He had known only too well that she was arriving in the afternoon. He stared at the glowing tip of his cigar. Facing her needed more courage than he could summon. His father was right. He was a coward. He could do nothing but try to escape Tabitha and the painful yearning to root himself so deeply in her heart that he could never be torn away.

He cleared his throat, raising his gaze to his father's reflection in the pier glass mirror. "I'm sure she was welcomed by the servants with all due ceremony, my lord. I doubt my presence was necessary.''

Utter fury engorged the earl's face, leaving his eyes white-hot with rage. "She is your wife! For that alone, she should be treated with respect and consideration. Good God! What a fool you are! Wed to a woman whom any man would consider himself blessed to have, and you do not grant her the most minimal of courtesy!''

He marched to the door with rigid rectitude and affronted pride. His hand on the ornate glass knob, he looked back. "I am done with threatening you, Robert, for you have at last proved to me that threats are useless. But for Tabitha, I should give you the cut direct at our every meeting henceforth. For her sake, and hers alone, I will continue to welcome you at Darenth House. But know this. I am ashamed to call you my son.''

It was said at last. Robbie was almost relieved. He had expected it since his earliest awareness that he could never please the earl. How quickly he had stopped trying. It was easier to be shocking and outrageous, for then he knew what the reaction would be. But he had never stopped hoping that he would someday see his father's face soften with pride, that he would someday hear from him a "Well done, my boy.''

The door slammed behind the earl, and Robbie poured a hefty glass of Irish whiskey and drained it dry. He added a generous dollop to the glass, raised it to his lips, and paused. "To Tabby," he said softly, and downed it in a gulp, reaching for the bottle once more.

In the tiny terrace house in Queen Anne's Gate the servants were asleep. Only the mistress remained awake, wandering the candlelit rooms like a ghost in her white *robe de chambre*. The storm raging outside matched the one in Tabitha's heart. Friend Robert's absence showed her quite painfully that he wanted no ensnaring of his heart. How quickly she had forgotten that she married him to give him his freedom. The freedom he would take, will she, nill she.

Her only welcome had come from the servants: a scullery maid, two chambermaids, two footmen, to whom had been added Thistlewood the butler and Mrs. Belcher the cook and the coachman brought from Langleyholm. More symbols of the changes in her life.

It had been so easy to tell Friend Robert that she had accepted the need for change when she married him. How little she, in her ignorance, had understood what those changes would be, how they would strike to the very core of all she was and believed.

She had not known then how her husband's touch would awaken a new awareness of herself as a woman, of her body as an instrument of intense pleasure. She had never felt more alive, more acutely in touch with her senses. The wet night wind screamed through the barely raised parlor windows, purling around her body, snatching at her hem, stroking her cheeks. The scent of lavender potpourri rose like a mist from a delicate chinoiserie vase. A handsome console table exuded the tart smell of lemon wax, and a vapor of pungent linseed oil wafted from the polished wainscoting. All blended to mingle with the sharp taste of the storm, saturating her every sense. The lightning came in successive strokes of blue-white brilliance and soul-deep darkness, leaving the single candle flickering with a light as wan as her hopes.

Allied to the new awareness of her body and its pleasures was a growing desperation.

How could she ignore the bitterly poor in the streets,
the wretched, the ill, the maimed, and worst of all, the
children with their hollow chests and swollen bellies
and huge, haunting eyes?

How could she spend her pilgrimage of life leaving
cartes de visite, drinking tea in elegant parlors, arranging routs and fêtes, and remembering the orders of
precedence Friend Arabella had so assiduously drilled
into her unwilling head? Baronets were ranked by the
dates of their patents. A lady's precedence was derived
from her father or her husband, unless she was a peeress in her own right. A Dowager Peeress took precedence before the wife of the incumbent of the title. The
children of a living peer took precedence over the children of the previous possessor of the title. Were they
not all God's children and equal before Him? What did
it matter who sat above the salt and who sat below if
they were all in charity with one another?

Which they very definitely were not.

George IV, king of the realm, was despised and rid-
iculed by his subjects high and low. What could one
expect of the man responsible for the renovations at
Brighton? Friend Arabella had asked, adding that they
were an insult to the delicate sensibilities of those with
a sense of style. Though what his architectural prefer-
ences had to do with his worth as a man, Tabitha was
at a loss to understand.

The Duke of Wellington, hero of Waterloo, "conqueror of the conqueror of the world," was a man of
inordinate courage and capacity, though he had a de-
plorable habit of mocking his own consequence. But
wasn't it admirable that a man of his standing placed
himself in perspective in the sight of man and God?

Princess Lieven, patroness of Almack's, had been so
servilely flattered by those in quest of a voucher to the
seventh heaven of the *ton*nish world that her penchant
for airs and graces had become quite shocking indeed.

And wasn't that to be expected when the focus of a life became the world rather than the soul?

And the Dowager Duchess of Lethbridge and the Duchess of Wrexham were never—never!—to be seated near each other, for they would launch into a shocking row. "Sisters, don't you know. Once upon a time the Misses Persia and Pegotta Ponsonby," Friend Arabella had said in a confiding tone that suggested Tabitha should instantly leap to some conclusion. Before she could question it, Friend Arabella had continued that their sons ignored their feud and became boon companions. For spite, she thought, and who could blame them, for two more shatterbrained moonlings were not to be found in the *ton*. Tabitha would be meeting them soon—the sons, that was—for they were part of the frippery set to which Robbie belonged. "Why, Lethbridge and Audley, gel, town bucks of the first cut, and you'll do well not to encourage them, for they thrive on riot and rumpus."

It seemed to Tabitha that she had been thrown bodily into a topsy-turvy world where all she esteemed was infamous and all she held low was admired. She desperately longed for the peace of the Meeting, for the fellowship of the Friends, for the serenity that had deserted her. And she would have it tomorrow, for it was First Day, the Lord's day of rest.

But there was still the night ahead, and her restlessness to assuage. It seemed there had never been a time when she sat in repose, her thoughts in order and her heart at peace.

The rattle of coach wheels over the cobblestones and the crack of a whip punctuated drum rolls of thunder. Monsieur at her feet, Tabitha stood at the window, moving aside the crimson curtains. A dagger of lightning froze an odd scene in her mind's eye. At the rim of the footway a hackney-coach ejected four heavy tipplers into the rain-swept night. One, tall and angular, with an empty sleeve flapping at his side, seemed to be more sober than the rest. The trio remaining were draped together, arms hooked over shoulders, legs wandering aimlessly. The wind snatched the topper from the man in the center, revealing the black hair, the face of Friend Robert—drunk as a lord. Was that the only way he could bring himself to face her?

Tabitha hurried to the door and flung it open. The uninvited rain splattered the Purbeck stone floor, and closely behind came the staggering trio. On Friend Robert's right was a bandbox dandy with a white-toothed smile, a roving eye, and a cluster of seals hanging from his waistcoat and jingling merrily.

"You sly devil!" He stumbled to a halt in the door, eyeing Tabitha from her mobcap to her bare toes and jabbing Friend Robert in the ribs with his elbow. "What'll your wife think of this tasty piece? And under her own roof."

"M'wife? Why, you sapskulled Tulip, thass her!" Friend Robert disentangled himself from his fellows and stepped forward as if climbing a stair. He removed his nonexistent topper, swept it to his breast, and bowed low, his wet curls spilling across his brow. Momentum carried him, head down, in a step-stutter, step-stutter to the wall. He thumped into the wainscoting, bouncing a Turner landscape off its hook. The heavy gilt frame cracked on the stone floor, while he slid in a boneless heap to a semi-sitting sprawl.

Tabitha leapt to his side, kneeling, and found the fourth of the quartet squatting opposite her.

"Lady Langley." His melting brown eyes darkened with sympathy.

"Friend Tabitha," she amended.

"Thass right," said her husband. "Friend Tabitha. She's a saint, don't ya know."

Robbie struggled up with their help, leaning against the wall, while he swept his arm out in an expansive sweep. "M'wife, Saint Tabitha. Old Nick, the Spaniard, and the Vicar. And, o' course, himself, yer husband. The Falcon. A grand and glorious bird, the falcon. Keen-eyed, long-winded, and courageous." He hiccuped.

The first of the men, slight and slender as a boy,

bowed, a wealth of burnished bronze hair falling in a curtain over his brow. "Nicholas Devereaux, Duke of Lethbridge, m'lady."

The swarthy-skinned Spaniard followed. "Edward March, Earl of Audley, m'lady."

And the last with his kind brown gaze and empty flapping sleeve. "Brat Raeburn, a mere honorable, m'lady."

"I pray thee, call me Friend Tabitha." Though she longed to fling herself away to some private spot and burst into bitter tears, she smiled. "Friend Robert's Cousin Knox has said that thee thrives on riot and rumpus. Perhaps"—she shepherded Lethbridge and Audley into the parlor and rang for the footman—"thee might like to meditate on the morning that awaits thee."

The footman appeared in his hastily donned knee breeches and tail coat, his coarse yellow hair standing on end.

"India tea, strong and hot." She waved a hand toward her guests and hurried into the hall passage, dreading the difficult task of getting Friend Robert upstairs and abed.

Brat Raeburn greeted her with a lopsided grin sandwiched between deep dimples. "We could have used you at Waterloo, Friend Tabitha. Such generalship shouldn't be wasted."

"But I am a woman of peace," she said, liking his straightforward smile, the lack of complexity in his direct gaze.

"Aye, Brat, peash," said Friend Robert, leaning against the wall and studying her with a puzzled expression. "Where did it go, Tabby?"

She touched his face. His head turned, his lips pressing a kiss into her palm, and all of her fears, her uncertainties, all of the hurt of being called Saint Tabitha, all of the despair that had been creeping over her dissipated like the alcoholic fumes surrounding him.

"Thee will find it again, Friend Robert. Together we will find it for thee."

Chapter 13

It was a hop, step, and jump from the Bank of England in the financial heart of the City to the seamy purlieus of Spitalfields, where even the air was tainted by vice and venality. Doss houses leaned haphazardly in the wind, stuffed from garret to cellar with the wretchedly poor, the dangerously mad, and the treacherously criminal, pallid men, gaunt women, and starving children lying shoulder to shoulder for a ha'penny a night. The maze of lanes and alleys and airless courts were deep in dirt and mud and ordure, all overhung by squalid tenements abuzz with squabbles and screams, with the whispering steps of silent theft, with the desperate noises of murder. For Milling-Jemmy Shadwell it was home, the only place he felt safe.

His flash ken—thieves' den—was a huge cellar beneath an abandoned brewery. The rough, unplaned planks of the ceiling were stained black with the soot of the center fire. The clay floor was hard packed by the tramp of cadgers and flatcatchers, cracksmen and dragsmen, footscampers and knucklers, sneaks and smashers, all members of a society as rigidly ordered as the peerage.

Milling-Jemmy's courtly chamber was a corner sickly lit by crusie lamps burning odoriferous fish oil. A threadbare Saracen carpet spread over straw provided his bed. A rickety table with a single chair was the throne room to which his subjects came for orders, for

195

praise, for punishment, for reports . . . like the one he awaited now.

He sat on the tottering chair, the great hams of his hands clamped over his knees, his black eyes unwinking in the round moon of his face. He had learned the habit of stillness as a youth starving in the streets, where the expenditure of unnecessary energy might mean an early death. That habit had followed him into the full flower of manhood and the success he had met; yet now that he had the blunt to live and feast like a king, his needs were few and his wants less. The cabbage soup cooling on the table and the crust of bread beside it were enough for him, but even that he did not touch. While his massive frame might have been carved of stone, his mind was bubbling like the cauldron over the fire.

He had caught but glimpses of the woman outside Darenth Hall. That great manor set in green fields and green hills and greener woods, all beneath a vaulting blue sky that made him feel as small and exposed as a rat fleeing a cat across Petticoat Lane. He hadn't liked it: the open spaces, the silence, the strangeness of it all. Even the air had been different, tasteless and scentless.

Set him down in London with eaves framing the sky and streets weaving madly about and his belly sloshing with Daffy or Ould Tom, and he could find his way with the unerring precision of a pigeon homing in to its roost. But in the country there were no markers, in the woods there were no lanes, and in the fields there were no sounds to lead him on his way.

That was how he had been so nearly caught. Only the habit of stillness had saved him. That and the reed bed rimming the River Darent. As he'd huddled in the chill water listening to the baying hounds, he'd known he was going about his search all wrong. He'd have to wait until she came to him. He'd have to wait like a spider in the center of his web. A web that was growing more dangerous by the minute.

First the Nob, the woman's man, had set the Bow

Street Runners on him. Now he was offering a one-hundred-pound reward. Milling-Jemmy's cold black eyes surveyed the cellar from the pickpocket and his ladybird coupling in a dark corner to the footpad plucking his humstrum before the fire. Not a one would cross him. They wouldn't dare. Better a ha'penny doss house here than a hundred pounds in hell. Still, he'd take no chances. He'd run to earth and wait till the time was right to find the woman again.

"Out o' me way, Rooster Annie!" intruded the shrill voice of a boy threading his way around the piles of straw, broken chairs, and stools, all inhabited by flash coves smacking over their peck and booze.

"I'll take no sass from the likes o' ye," cried Rooster Annie, cuffing his ear.

The boy kicked her in the shins and darted by, his thin legs pumping up to the rickety table. He tossed his head of matted, flame-red hair, set his hands to his hips, and cursed mightily. "She's enuf to make a saint swear at his liver!"

Milling-Jemmy spared a narrow glance for the ill-tempered Rooster Annie. He didn't hold with cuffing the urchins, an idiosyncrasy that was respected because it didn't extend to adults, whom he would beat to a pulp for an attack on a child. As a result his flash ken was overrun with sniveling, sniffling urchins who showed him more loyalty than the Nobs showed King George. No one questioned when one or more vanished on occasion, for they were always the sickliest and weakest of the lot, the signs of approaching death writ deep into their sunken eyes.

"I seen 'er," said the boy. "Got a 'ouse in Queen Anne's Gate wit' 'er gentry cove. Looked right in the winder and seen silver candlesticks and gold snuff-boxes and a sight o' gewgaws to make a fence sit up and pant. Cor, 'e could buy an abbey, 'e could."

"And the woman, Wild Jack?" asked Milling-Jemmy. "What o' the woman?"

The boy took a pinch of merry-go-up, sniffing the snuff from the back of his hand and sighing mightily, his green cat's eyes narrowing with delight. ''Followed 'er ter a Quakin' 'ouse and left 'er there. Cor, guv, she'll be at it fer the day.''

'' 'Ave yer peck and booze, Wild Jack Burdett. Then get back ter the woman. Lose 'er, and it'll be St. Geoffrey's Day ere ye see yer blunt.''

''Aye, guv. I'll stick like a nettle, I will, but I 'ad ter see ter Tansy and 'Enry 'Icks.'' The boy paused, a frown seaming cracks in his dirty face. ''Guv, I'm nippered, I am, and the blunt 'ull be Dutch comfort if it comes too late ter get 'Enry 'Icks ter the doctor.''

Milling-Jemmy's coal-black gaze rolled to a dark corner where Wild Jack's tiny sister and his friend Henry Hicks huddled together. Even as he watched, a deep rattling cough shook the boy's skeletal frame. The runt of the litter, too weak to survive. No use in letting him suffer.

''Don't fret yer noddle, Wild Jack. I'll see ter 'Enry 'Icks.'' And then he'd run to earth like a fox and wait.

While Wild Jack Burdett slurped his cabbage soup and danced a farthing piece across his knuckles, boasting to a wide-eyed Tansy and Henry Hicks that he'd someday lift the purse right from fat old George IV's pocket, Tabitha rose from the hard wooden bench at the Westminster Meeting House and slipped out while the Meeting was still in progress. Her mind and her heart were in such turmoil it seemed a blasphemy to sit among the Friends.

She stood on the plain wooden porch before the unadorned facade, tears stinging her eyes. The Meeting should have been a homecoming. Everything was familiar, from the dais with the bearded elders awaiting the Lord's inspiration to the plainly dressed Friends. Though she could sense the heavenly peace and order in those around her, she could not feel them within herself. Not when her thoughts swarmed and stung like bees.

She was a wife who was no wife, a Friend, and, according to Society, a lady. She was unaccustomed to idleness, but she had a houseful of servants who were not only appalled but also frightened by her need to work.

If Friend Robert had not been sunk so deep in the aftereffects of his night of vice, he would surely have been awakened by the furor raised by her simple effort to make her own bed. The chambermaid had shrieked and tossed her apron over her head, stumbling down the stairs to summon the butler. Soon Tabitha was sitting in the parlor with Thistlewood, Mrs. Belcher, and rotund Cheddar ranged round her with all guns, however politely expressed, firing. It simply wasn't done. She had servants to see to her needs. A lady was to be cosseted, protected, and waited on hand and foot. She was to order meals, arrange flowers, remember who was enemy to whom, who was connected to whom through family or marriage. But she wasn't a lady. She was a Friend, and idle hands were the devil's work. So what was she to do? Surely there was something of use and worth.

She studied the street. At the corner a crossing-sweeper waited for any passerby who might flip him a coin for clearing the cobblestones before his path with the broom clutched in his arthritic hands. Beneath the streetlamp stood a flower girl in her rags, a babe in one arm and a huge basket of spring delights dangling from her hand. Her cheeks were stained a hectic, unhealthy red, and her thick, deep cough set the babe to wailing. A chimney sweep trudged by, soot-blackened and scrawny, a vicious sore oozing on his cheek. A gang of boys ran like a pack of wolves, their thin faces cunning and wild, as they stole pewter pots and milk cans from the area railings before the houses lining the footways.

There were children everywhere. Small and large, thin and pale, unwatched and unwanted. Hungry. Tabitha thought of the masses of food Thistlewood had served up for her breakfast: a rasher of bacon, slices of ham, eggs, toast, jams and jellies. And most of it sent back to the kitchen. The waste of it made her ill.

The door behind her opened, and a woman, plump

as a pastry tart, stepped through. Alone, she and Tabitha had sat in the last row of the women's section, one on either end of the wooden bench, like two children on a merry-totter.

"Sister," the woman said gently, "pray forgive me if I intrude, but thee seems troubled."

She stood like a bird with her head cocked inquisitively, the look in her eye at once lively and kindly. Tabitha quenched the spurt of pride that urged denial of her concern. Her need for someone who spoke as she spoke, who thought as she thought, who believed as she believed was too strong.

"I am Tabitha Fell—" She paused, then added belatedly, "Ransome."

"Ah." The woman smiled, her eyes crinkling and sparkling. "A newlywed."

Tabitha's gaze dropped, her throat closing tight. "Wed out of unity."

"Oh," said the woman softly, reaching out to touch her arm and squeezing it lightly. "As am I, Sister Ransome. As am I."

Plump Mary Seymour was the wife of a banker as firmly attached to the Church of England as she was to the Society of Friends. It hadn't been easy to adjust to their differences, she told Tabitha as they took tea in the garden of her Berkeley Square mansion. She, too, had come from a large family and a small village. She, too, had wanted to take a feather duster to the classical statuary and a scrub brush to the fine marble floors.

"And what did thee do?"

"I was miserably unhappy for quite a long time, until my husband . . ." Her eyes brightened with laughter and love. "Sister Ransome, what a fine man he is. He said, 'Mary, my love, St. Peter won't have you scrubbing the steps at the Pearly Gates before he lets you in. There's more you can do, so climb out of the dismals and find what it is.' And I did." She leaned forward. "Hast thou heard of Elizabeth Fry?"

"The reformer of the women's prison in Newgate?" Tabitha asked.

Mary nodded. "I've joined the Ladies' Committee that carries on her work. Three days a week I teach knitting and needlework. Another day I hound friend and foe alike to let their pockets in the good cause of those poor, wretched women. Sister Ransome"—she leaned forward, quick as a pigeon—"thee would be welcome to join us."

Tabitha, considering it, watched a chambermaid hurrying down the flagstone walk, a small grimy boy's reed-slim arm grasped firmly in her hand. She was neat and clean, but her face was hard and seamed with a look of having lived and seen too much.

" 'Scuse me, Friend Mary," said the maid. "I'd've waited, but the lad's come ter say me brother's been took ter Newgate fer debts and his mam's dead, ye know. The parish churchwarden come ter take 'im ter the work'ouse, and Lemmy 'ere but a lad. Ye done a goodish lot fer me, ye 'ave, and 'tis obliged I am," she said in a rush, "but Lemmy's commencin' ter go bad, and I'm afeerd the work'ouse'll finish 'im. If times was tidy—"

"Thou has done right to bring him to me," said Mary Seymour. "Lemmy, hast thee a liking for horses?"

Tabitha, watching closely, saw the spark of interest flare on his face, saw it die quickly, deliberately pushed away. As if, she thought, he dared not hope. How well she knew that feeling.

"I might," he said sullenly.

His aunt cuffed his ear. "Ye'll keep a civil tongue in yer 'ead, Lemmy."

"We'll have none of that, Polly," Mary Seymour said softly. "Take him to the kitchens and feed him well, then to the stables. We've need of another good man to look after the coach and horses."

They left quickly, the boy struggling in his aunt's firm grip. Tabitha stared after them with the germ of an idea forming. "I've seen so many children like Lemmy roaming the streets alone."

"And thee will see more. We've foundling hospitals, orphan asylums, and charity schools, but still they roam unchecked, sinking into every form of vice and wickedness. And who is to blame them, for their lives are horrid beyond our imaginings. Take Polly there. She was born in the slums of St. Giles, her mother an orange seller and her father a bone-and-rag grubber. They died of the pox, leaving her and her brother alone. And she, not yet a woman, sold herself to a procuress. I found her in Newgate—"

"And brought her into thy home." Tabitha prepared to rise. "Thou hast given me much to think about, Sister Seymour. May I come again?"

"Thee will always find a welcome here, Sister."

It was nigh to noon when Robbie woke with his head pounding like a drum, his mouth tasting like a stable's sweepings, and his mood as dark and low as that subterranean world beneath the City of London. It was a moment before he realized that he had been awakened by an odd and subtle movement, a stroking of his rump through the bed linens. Not Tabitha, surely, he thought, torn between delight and dismay—until he remembered the words *Saint Tabitha*.

He clenched his teeth, his cheeks hot with shame. He might wonder how he could face her, but his pride would brook no delay. He shifted upwards to peer over his shoulder.

Monsieur *le chat* reclined on the satin coverlet, one thick back paw thrust in the air, while he performed the most intimate of ablutions in apparent preparation for a snooze. At Robbie's movement, he paused, turned his blocky head, narrowed his yellow eyes, and hissed.

Robbie, yielding to disappointment and temptation, hissed back.

Monsieur, unimpressed, rose slowly, flicked his hairless tail, leapt lightly to the floor, and strolled away, as if to say that he had decided after all that the bed was not big enough for both of them and he would not stoop to argue.

"Tabitha!" Robbie bounced from the bed with a roar. A mistake. He clutched his pounding head and cursed the silken glide, the fiery taste, the sweet forgetfulness of Irish whiskey.

Cheddar came in a puffing trot. "Milord, Friend Tabitha is not at home." He whisked the curtains wide, leaving only the lace undercurtains to bar the sun. "She left—"

"Left?" Had he driven her away? God, he was not only a coward, he was a fool! "How did she leave?"

"Afoot, milord. She refused the coach, quite insistently, if I may be so bold as to say."

"And when have you ever hesitated to 'be so bold as to say'?" he snarled, squinting against the sunlight that jabbed into his eyes and acted as a triphammer on his brain. "Did she take a portmanteau with her?"

"A portmanteau?" Cheddar, setting out shaving brush, soap mug, and razor, paused. "I shouldn't think she would need one at Meeting."

"Meeting?"

"Church, milord. She was walking to the Westminster Meeting House."

Robbie, sighing, sank into the canary-yellow chair before the hearth. Relief flooded through him, surging up, swirling around the quickly rising dam of a shocking realization. He went cold to his fingertips, to his toes, to his heart. How had she become so important to him that he could feel that sick fear at the thought of losing her? That soaring consolation on knowing she had not?

He was leaving soon. Leaving for Greece at summer's end with the Spaniard and Old Nick. Leaving behind Tabitha, the slip of a woman who had become more important to him than she should have. He felt like a man sinking in quicksand, a part of him wanting to reach out, a part of him wanting to sink beneath it and find surcease.

Just as he had tried to find it once before. Unconsciously, he rubbed the ugly, puckered scar on his wrist. *A coward fleeing his own shadow, fleeing his obligations and responsibilities!* his father had said. *I am ashamed to call you my son.*

If he faced those obligations and responsibilities, if he claimed Tabitha as his true wife, would his boots then be nailed to the floor? Or would he find that he had made promises he could not keep?

The tiny ell of Queen Anne's Gate was sandwiched between St. James's Park and Birdcage Walk on the north and the slums of Tothill Fields on the south, a rookery so vicious no Bow Street Runner would enter it for fear of his life. In Westminster, as all over London, exquisitely arranged squares inhabited by the wealth of Society and Trade abutted the tumbledown doss houses and dirt streets of abject poverty.

Tabitha returned from Berkeley Square in the Seymours' capacious barouche, requesting of the horrified coachman that he swing down Horseferry Road to Medway Street in the heart of Tothill Fields. They rode in splendor behind a herd of swine rooting in the refuse of the gutter, the object of catcalls and shouts and curses. The street was alive, writhing like maggots in putrid meat. Ladybirds cast shameless eyes on jacktars strutting up from the Thames' dockside. Troops of urchins fluttered and flew like a gathering of swallows. On one corner a filthy crone, bloated by gin, curled up in the mud, a stray piglet thrusting his snout into the palm of her hand. There were hawkers and peddlers of the lowest sort, and a groundsel seller dragging his useless legs behind makeshift crutches. Over all was the miasmic odor of fish heads and cabbage leaves and corruption. In every face there was despair and hopelessness.

The coachman returned to Horseferry Road by way of Holland Street at a racing clip that said he was glad to have escaped with his life. Tabitha sank back on the seat, the germ of an idea now broached and bearing fruit. She thought of her father: *No child went ragged in the environs of the village of Lamberhurst.* She thought of the pin money Friend Robert had settled on her. For the first time in days a smile touched her lips. For the first time since her marriage she felt at one with herself.

Children of her body would be denied her by Friend Robert, but children of the heart she could have in plenty.

Robbie was descending the stairs in full sartorial splendor when Tabitha burst through the front door, her color high, her lips curved in a smile that pleaded with his to join her. He resisted, facing her instead with an expression as forbidding as his father's at his worst. She was tempting, too tempting, but he would not succumb. Whatever his father said, he had courage enough for that.

Tabitha checked, her hands at the bow of her bonnet, her smile slowly dying. Angry tension radiated from him, interring her joy in ashes.

He tugged at his French cuffs, descending the stairs step by measured step. "You will not leave the house without escort again. It is neither safe nor in keeping with your position as my wife."

She removed her bonnet and set it on the console table, her hands trembling. Robbie, his throat tightening, forced himself to stroll negligently by, entering the parlor. He heard her step behind him, her light, quick step that seemed to pirouette into his heart.

It was Tabitha's nature to be yielding, to meet anger with sweet reason. But how hard it was when she wanted to weep, to scream. "It is a wife's duty to be subject to her husband in all things, but . . ."

Robbie turned, schooling his face, scouring away every betraying line of doubt and pain. How far away Greece seemed. How near she was. While she stared at her clasped hands, his hungry gaze roamed the contours of her face, the curve of her lashes, the tip-tilt of her nose, the lush promise of her mouth.

"But?" he questioned.

She stepped closer, touching his arm, her guileless gray gaze meeting his. "Thee wanted freedom from this marriage. Cannot I ask for the same? I shall feel a prisoner with an escort forever at my side."

He shrank from the touch of her hand, from the scalding awareness that she was his to take. Moving to a chair, he sat with a casual air. His gaze fled the hurt in her eyes, while the pad of his thumb stroked the bosom of a porcelain shepherdess on the tripod table at his side. "Have you forgotten Shadwell?"

"Surely he has forgotten me."

"Surely not." How could any man forget her? Robbie wondered.

Tabitha moved to the window, dejected and uncertain, lifting the crimson curtain aside. Across the cobbled street she saw a tattered boy kneeling on the footway, his matted hair rust-red in the sunlight, his filthy feet bare. "Has thee noted the children of London, Friend Robert? Those poor, hungry, lost little souls."

"Thieves and cutpurses."

"I saw Medway Street today."

"Lud!" He bolted up, careless unconcern forgotten. "Of all the hen-witted . . ." He caught his runaway breath. "I absolutely forbid you to enter that sink of vice and iniquity again!"

Tabitha turned slowly. He stood, his hands fisted at his sides, his face flushed and his eyes snapping. "Something should be done for the children," she said softly, testing him and fearing he would fail.

"There are charity schools and foundling hospitals and orphan asylums and the churchwardens to dispense poor relief," he said, unconsciously echoing Mary Seymour.

"Yet there is an unkempt and starving child at every turn."

"Do not think of them as children, Tabitha, for they are not. They are calloused and hardened criminals that would cut your throat for a copper."

"I see." She turned back to the window, watching

the boy dance a farthing piece across his knuckles. She had thought that, for all the differences between them, she could trust Friend Robert with anything. But she could not trust him with this. If she told him, he would stop her. If he stopped her, she would be left with nothing but the empty, meaningless life of a Viscount's wife. She would have to lie, transgressing with the worst of sins. Was it specious to reason that it was in a good cause?

"I met someone today," she said. "Friend Mary Seymour. Her husband is a banker in the City. She has asked me to join her in doing charitable work."

Robbie's tension began seeping away. Her talk of London's urchins had begun to worry him, but charitable works he understood. Both his mother and Anne had always involved themselves in various committees and societies devoted to improving the lot of the unfortunate, the ill, the maimed. How often as a youth he had dropped his hazard winnings into Anne's lap and said, smiling wickedly, "For the Forlorn Females' Fund of Mercy, Puss. Your favorite charity . . . and mine."

If Tabitha wanted to do this, he could not deny her. After all, the committees and societies to which the women he knew offered their monies and their time never came in touch with the vermin-ridden poor. Tabitha would be safe.

"You can, of course, join Mrs. Seymour," he said, feeling expansive in offering her this palliative—until she swiveled about, settling a gaze on him that said there was fire beneath the ice.

"I thank thee, husband," she said shortly. "Should I find myself incapable of making other decisions, I will surely bring them to thee, for thee—"

A sharp rapping of the brass doorknocker set her to biting her lip. "May I be assured that I will not need an escort to ride with me in Sister Seymour's carriage?"

"Of course not, though I do hope—"

"Pardon, milord," came Thistlewood's funereal intrusion. "The Earl of Audley for Friend Tabitha."

Audley swept the butler aside and appeared on the portal, seeming to be wearing, in place of a head, two dozen red roses. He leaned to the side, breaking into a grin that Robbie would have liked to wipe from his face with a fist. "Am I forgiven for mistaking you for a chambermaid, Friend Tabby?"

When had the Spaniard become so encroachingly familiar with his wife? Robbie wondered. Instead of the set-down he thought the bandbox creature richly deserved, Tabitha glided toward him with a warm welcome.

"Friend Edward," she said, smiling, "we settled that last night. Thee made a perfectly understandable mistake."

"Well, in case you cherish a grudge, I thought these might soften your heart." He pressed the roses upon her.

Roses! Robbie thought. How common and ordinary.

The Spaniard advanced on him and clapped him on the back. "Damn fine woman, you lucky devil!"

While Tabitha rang for the footman to bring a vase, the doorknocker rat-a-tat-tatted. Thistlewood gloomily announced, "The Duke of Lethbridge for Friend Tabitha."

It seemed no one was wearing a head. A bouquet of wallflowers sprouted from Old Nick's chest. Really! Robbie thought. It was disgusting! Lethbridge wasn't in his salad days any longer to be prinking about like a Pink.

Old Nick leaned to the side, something shockingly near a smile crossing his lazy mouth. "For one of the most pleasant nights I've spent in years, Friend Tabby."

Nights! Robbie scowled. What the hell had gone on while he was sleeping away his much-indulged whiskey?

Tabitha transferred the roses to the footman and skimmed across the parlor with a trill of happy laughter. "Friend Nicholas, how pleased I am to see thee. And wallflowers." She buried her nose in the bouquet, inhaling the sweet fragrance.

Old Nick slouched over to Robbie, his long hand sweeping back the spray of straight bronze hair that fell over his brow. "I shall have to amend my opinion of women. Both manner and sense, you lucky devil."

Robbie knew that was high praise indeed. He made what he hoped was an appropriate noise, while the doorknocker began rapping again.

Thistlewood appeared, and Robbie forestalled him with a raised hand. "No doubt the Honorable Brat Raeburn come bearing gifts. Send him away."

"Friend Robert," Tabitha chided, vanishing into the entry hall.

A mutter, a murmur, a trilling laugh, and she appeared in the door on Brat's only arm, a spray of daisies cradled like a babe in the crook of her elbow.

Robbie's headache returned, tiny hammermen scurrying around his skull with bone-cracking force. She invited the motley trio to stay for luncheon, and the hammermen went wild. He quickly discovered that while he had been arrayed on his bed in a drunken stupor, Tabitha had entertained his friends until dawn. They had sneaked down to the kitchen, where she had cooked ham and eggs, plied them with India tea, and read them a lesson on the evils of strong drink.

Robbie, on hearing of it, resorted to a brandy, while his thrice-curst friends, like choirboys, requested India tea.

Chapter 14

❦

Tabitha had a way of stripping away the surface to find the man beneath. While luncheon stretched into the afternoon with moves from the table to the parlor to the tiny garden in the back, Robbie learned more about his friends than he had ever known.

Audley lost his hale-fellow-well-met air, seriously discussing his desire—thwarted by his mother—to run the Wrexham Manor farms, talking of cattle and crops, fertilizers and corn, revealing that he had carefully studied the latest discoveries in scientific agriculture. Robbie was stunned. The dandified Audley with a yearning for dirt under his well-manicured nails!

Old Nick shed his lazy aura of ennui and launched into a spirited verbal treatise of what the coming railroads would do for the expansion of trade. More than that, he was fascinated by the steam engine. It seemed he had an idea for its improvement!

Tabitha, pouring tea in the sunny garden with the bees humming and flowers scenting the air, settled her gentle gray gaze upon him. "Friend Nicholas, thee has but one pilgrimage of life, and thee should make the best of it that thee can. If thee has a gift, thee should use if for the betterment of all men."

Lethbridge smiled, the first genuine smile, the first heart-deep smile, Robbie had ever seen from him. "Does your husband know, Friend Tabby, how fortunate he is?"

All eyes, save Tabitha's, turned to Robbie. Her gaze drifted away to the roses espaliered across the brick wall. His throat thick, his chest aching, he said, "Only a fool would not see what a treasure our Tabby is."

Tabitha allowed a new hope to creep into her heart, only to have it dashed when they left and Friend Robert reverted to the chilly mien of the morning. He remained cool through their dinner at Darenth House in the heat of the June evening, and with his father he was frigid. Something had happened between them, but she had no time to consider it, for Anne and her mother were busily plotting the week: Tabitha must visit the milliner, the glover, the seamstress, and the bootmaker in preparation for her introduction to Society at Darenth House on Friday eve. Tabitha nodded agreement while feverishly pursuing thoughts of her own. She could not resolve what Friend Robert had said with how he was acting toward her. Unless . . .

Her gaze streaked across the table, studying his languid pose, the elbow on the table, the glass of wine at his lips. A pose whose insouciant appearance was put to the lie by the expression in his eyes. He looked like a man trapped and desperate to escape. It was there in the taut line of his throat, in the tense line of his mouth, in the faint spray of lines etched at the corners of his eyes.

Though she tried to find another reason for it, there was only one. He had begun to feel the pinch of his marriage vows. He had begun to feel ensnared and smothered by the wife he did not want and had not chosen willingly.

If she cherished a last doubt, it was quickly wiped away. He left her at their door in the late-night hours with the briefest of partings and a scanty wish that she sleep well. Then he hailed a hackney cab and was off on his own business—dicing, gambling, and . . . wenching?

She tossed and turned and waited for the tromp of his boots on the stairs. By dawn she was up, sitting by her window and looking out over the garden. It was badly in need of trimming and pruning and weeding, which she was eager to start. It would respond to a nourishing and loving hand. Friend Robert would not. That would only drive him further away.

While a single spry robin fluttered his wings in the birdbath, she planned to turn her back on her nature, her hopes, and her dreams. She would not gaze upon him fondly, speak to him tenderly, or expect of him the small everyday intimacies of shared moments or shared lives. She would leave him free to go his way, and she would go hers. Like Friend Nicholas, she had but one pilgrimage of life. She had to make the best of it that she could, and she knew just who could help her.

Mary Seymour looked like a kindly grandmother whose most pressing concern was her knitting, but she proved to have a housekeeper's organizational skills, a general's grasp of strategy, and the energy of a two-year-old intent on exploration.

Tabitha, after explaining what she wanted, was swept away on the whirlwind of Sister Seymour's enthusiasm. The black-lacquered barouche zigzagged across London from Berkeley Square to the heart of the merchant City for a meeting with the banking Mr. Seymour, thence to Lincoln's Inn Fields to see his man of business. Dubious as that supreme pragmatist was, he summoned an agent who bowled away with them into the backslums of Tothill Fields.

A trifle breathless, Tabitha descended from the barouche into Medway Street's stagnant gutter. Before her there rose a narrow brick house, its shattered windows trimmed in blue stones, its link snuffers gone, and its patchy purple slate roof surely leaking.

"It's good and sound," said the agent, a well-fed man dressed to the nines. "You'll not find better at forty pounds the year."

"Forty pounds! Robbery!" said Mary Seymour, her eyes stretched wide. "Come, Sister Ransome, let us hie within."

A strong smell of toasted herring greeted them at the door. The narrow hall was covered with a cracked marble floor, with litter and refuse and splinters of wainscoting. Tabitha hurried into the parlor, where a rat scurried beneath a pile of rubbish. Her eagerness growing, she moved from room to room, blind to the bare lathing showing through the peeling plaster walls, oblivious of the dangerously creaking stairs, deaf to the scurrying of vermin. She saw not what it was but what it could be with curtains at the windows and flowers on the deal tables and toys strewn across the floor. Most of all she heard the happy laughter, the giggles, the soft chucklings of well-fed, well-loved children. And when she entered the extension at the back of the house, a fifty-by-thirty-foot room with two fireplaces—perfect for a dormitory—she knew that she had found the residence for Friend Ephraim Fell's House for Homeless Children.

She clapped her hands, saying, "This is it," caught Sister Seymour's frown, and waited patiently through the chaffering that the Friends abhorred, but which Sister Seymour obviously thrived on.

"Forty pounds the year," repeated the agent.

"Robbery!" said Sister Seymour. "Look at the roof!"

His gaze drifted up to the patch of sky shining through. "Thirty-five," he said flatly.

"It will never do, Friend. Look at the walls. Think of the repairs that Sister Ransome must do."

His gaze reluctantly scanned the exposed lathing. "Thirty, and I'll not go below it."

"Very well." She puffed up like a pouter pigeon. "Come, Sister Ransome. I see we shall reach no agreement here."

She caught Tabitha's arm and thrust her through the door into the narrow rectangle of the offal-strewn backyard with its single sickly apple tree. The agent lurched after them, his hat crushed in his hand. "Twenty-five," he said desperately.

Sister Seymour paused, bending a stern gaze on him. "Twenty, and a five-year lease."

He looked so hunted Tabitha was tempted to accept his offer of twenty-five.

"Agreed," he said abruptly, cramming his crumpled hat on his bald crown and extending his hand.

Sister Seymour shook it solemnly, though her eyes sparkled mischievously. "I knew we should reach an agreement."

By the end of the week Wild Jack Burdett was glad of any chance to rest his weary bones and rub his aching feet. Horny and hard-soled as they were, they had taken a beating while keeping up with the Quakin' Lady. Though he could run for miles at a breath-saving trot, he'd found her the very devil for never staying in one place.

She was up with the dawn and running down Queen Anne's Gate, sometimes taking a black-lacquered rattler, at other times a hackney coach. And there was no predicting where she'd be heading. One day to Newgate, coming away with a knobby, long-faced hedgebird that could have looked Milling-Jemmy straight in the eye. Another day to the workhouse, leaving there with seven women—he counted them on his fingers, inordinately proud that he could—scurrying after her as if they'd been told they could enter a pastry shop and eat till they dropped—Wild Jack's highest aspiration, his only vision of Heaven. But always she made it to Medway Street before the morning was over, to the tall, narrow house crawling with carpenters and plasterers and glazers, roofers and bricklayers. Day by day it looked more respectable. The slates patched and shining. The shattered window glazing replaced. And when Wild Jack chanced a peek inside, he saw the new wainscoting, the freshly plastered wall painted a creamy hue, and the floors scrubbed spotless.

Every afternoon she returned to her town house, hurrying from there to St. James's Square. It was queer, it was, Wild Jack thought as he followed her through the streets of the fashionable, where she was accompanied by two gentry morts and their footmen. Cor, if 'e could buy fine togs and pastries and live in a big 'ouse, 'e'd sure enough not be back in the rookeries.

Friday morning drays trundled to a halt before the house in Medway Street. Deal tables, chairs, rockers, and beds, beds, and more beds were carried in. At the windows, the women he had seen scurrying out of the workhouse, now garbed in simple gowns with pristine white aprons and mobcaps, scaled ladders to hang curtains.

In the curious, gathering crowd of grubbers and ladybirds, drunks and jack-tars, boys on the cross, scamps and spices and culls, Wild Jack waited, his belly rumbling with hunger—a condition so common he paid scant attention to it. He watched the Quakin' Lady pick a dainty path across the reeking roadway with her friend—Sister Seymour, he heard her called—at her side. She turned back to the house, her slender arms folded at her waist, a peculiar and exultant tension emanating from her as she watched the men hauling on the pulley ropes to heft a sign into place over the door.

For the moment, Wild Jack was less concerned with the sign than with the woman. He studied her with a cunning and critical eye, thinking she was none too bright. A proper flat, she was, and ready for the picking. If Milling-Jemmy hadn't told him to spread the word to every flash cove that the Quakin' Lady and all that was hers were untouchable, every slate, every board, every nail would have been scavenged from the site of her house. She hadn't even hired an Old Scout to watch through the night, not that it would have done any good.

He drew his tattered sleeve beneath his dripping nose. He owed a lot to Ole Jem—something he'd never have dared to call Shadwell face to face—and he'd run his legs down to nubs if need be, but there was something queer about this. What did Milling-Jemmy want with the Quakin' Lady?

Across the street the sign slipped into place, sliding down the runners attached to the bricks. Ropes untied, the laborers skimmed down the ladders. Wild Jack, self-

taught and poorly so, began to read: Fri-end Ep . . .
rum . . .

He frowned and elbowed a path to the front of the
crowd.

"We've done it, Sister Seymour," the Quakin' Lady
said. "Friend Ephraim Fell's House for Homeless Children."

'Ouse fer 'omeless children. The frown deepened on
Wild Jack's dirty brow. He'd seen too many who had
escaped from the workhouses, the orphanages, the
asylums with tales of hunger and beatings. That was
why he was raising Tansy on his own. With his da
dead of gin and his mam of the cough—and he fiercely
glad that both were gone—he would see that Tansy
was pulled out of the gutter, that she had everything
that had been denied her. She'd never again be rented
to a beggar, her legs deliberately scratched to make
sores. Someday she'd have meat—real meat—to eat,
cakes and puddings and pies to fill her.

"We'll begin tomorrow," said the Quakin' Lady,
"walking through Tothill Fields in search of children."

Walkin' through Tot'ill Fields! Wild Jack straightened with a snap, his rags fluttering. Aye, a flat! And
dicked in the nob! She'd 'ave 'er throat cut fer 'er trouble! He'd have to warn Milling-Jemmy.

Shadwell had vanished like a rat down a hole. Not
a single person had come forward to betray him and
take the offered reward.

"I'm afeerd, milord, it'll commence to rain cats afore
the peevy coves 'ull whiddle the scrap on Jemmy.
Should we miss 'im, it's fer sartain 'e'd tear out their
throats. And should we not, 'is flash cove culls would.
Ye see, wit' 'is own 'e does the pound dealin'—a 'onest
cutthroat, if ye get me meanin'."

Robbie did, to his dismay. He had been so sure he'd
have Shadwell put away before the week was out. He
canted back on the legs of his Windsor chair, his narrow gaze studying Stark of the Bow Street Patrol. He

had been recommended by Karl, who had met the man when he was spying for the Crown during the late war.

Stark wore the uniform of the Patrol: a double-breasted blue coat with yellow metal buttons, blue trousers, black hat, and scarlet waistcoat. He was, as they all were, armed to the teeth with pistols and cutlass and truncheon. He had a look in his eye of a merry and genial man, but a deeper probing found the marks of his profession: disillusionment with the whole of mankind wed to a rigid rectitude akin to the Earl of Darenth's. All in all, Robbie thought, a good man to have at his back.

They were in Cribb's Parlor with its catnach ballads and prints on the walls celebrating the owner's pugilistic career. The air was rich with the scents of smoke and sawdust, of ale and roasting beef, and the vinegary odor of pickled pig's feet. The approach of evening would see a seething mass of odd-sorted humanity from dukes to bootcatchers bulging against the wainscoted walls. Now, in the late afternoon, it was quiet with the odd ripple of laughter, the gurgle of ale into glasses.

Robbie's gaze shifted to Karl, whose broad shoulders were sheathed in a frock coat of Superfine, his collar points touching the golden line of his jaw, his cravat knotted in the precise Mathematical style. "What do you think?"

Karl shrugged, his cornflower-blue eyes dark. "You could wait until he shows himself and hope that someone will be more tempted by the money than frightened of him."

"I could grow old waiting for that," Robbie said, his frowning gaze shifting to Stark. "I would prefer to search the rookeries myself."

"Aye, milord, yer impatient, but it 'ud be as much as yer life's worth . . ."

Robbie waved a silencing hand. "I'll begin on the morrow, Stark. If you are with me, I'll make it well worth your while."

"Oh, I'll be wit' ye, milord, from Ratcliffe Highway

to the Holy Land, but it's doubtin' I am that we'll find Milling-Jemmy.''

Stark stood, tipped his hat, and began threading around the tables and chairs. Robbie watched him go, his eyes narrowed thoughtfully. ''Do you think he's right?''

The tapered tip of Karl's finger idled up and down the handle of his cup. ''I suspect so. The rookeries are a world apart. They have their own hierarchy of felons, their own rules, and their own customs. The man who betrays one of his own comes to a quick and vicious end. One not unlike our own cut direct that banishes a man to the netherworld of social ostracism.''

''Or a woman.'' The legs of Robbie's chair settled to the sawdust-covered floor with a dull thump. ''Do you think she will take with Society?''

He had no need to explain who ''she'' was, for Tabitha was to be introduced to a select portion of the *ton* at a soirée at Darenth House that evening.

Karl frowned. ''I don't know,'' he said softly.

In the lulling afternoon, balmy and bright, Robbie paced the drawing room in Queen Anne's Gate, awaiting Tabitha's descent. They were to dine at Darenth House before the arrival of the guests, and he had garbed himself as befitted a member of the august *haut ton*—for once aping the starched formality of his elders. He wore a stylish pair of waistcoats beneath his frock coat: a white piqué and, atop it, a black velvet. His cravat—Cheddar had nearly wept for joy—was tied *à la Orientale* beneath collar points that nipped at his jawline. He would give the old dragons no reason to suggest that Tabitha was responsible for any carelessness in his apparel.

But it was not he who would be on trial, for he was a member of the chosen few. Only a social solecism of the lowest degree would banish him from the elect, while Tabitha had neither birth nor wealth to recommend her. Worse, she was of a dissenting faith whose creed of equality before God was an affront to the titled aristocracy's assurance that its supremacy on earth would be repeated in Heaven.

Robbie paced to the window, lifting the curtain aside to stare out at the cobbled carriageway. Idly, he noted the scruffy boy dawdling along the footway, one of that breed that had so engaged Tabitha's tender heart. Something should be done for the children, she had said. And his response had disappointed her. He had seen it in her eyes, just as he had in Paris when he tried to explain that ladies did not acknowledge the unfortunates in the streets.

How many differences there were between them. How many more there would be between her and the people she would meet tonight. Some with a kindly disposition would accept her, but there would be others . . .

The soft rustle of fabric pulled him around. Tabitha stood in the doorway, her eyes shining and a gentle smile curving her lips. His gaze raced from the plain white cap tied beneath her chin to the plain gown of lilac silk taffeta to the toes of her black slippers, peeping from the bell of her skirt. She looked as fresh as spring with her cheeks blushing like a milkmaid's beneath his steady regard.

Her gaze dropped shyly, as if they were newly met and strangers to each other. And weren't they? he wondered. He knew so little of this woman who was his wife. What made her happy? What made her sad? What did she want from him, from life?

Children, surely. She could not show such concern for London's urchins and not want children of her own. For a moment he could see her with a babe at her breast, her lips brushing its delicate white brow, her melodic voice soothing and low. If he left and never returned, she would be denied a child—as he would be.

And he wanted a child. Not an heir, but a son to raise in love and affection with the only expectation that he be true to himself—whatever that self was.

Tabitha could give him that son, as she could give

him herself, her peace, her assurance, her surprising passion. A passion that was not in evidence now. She seemed muted and quiet, but she had seemed that way for days. Not that he had been much in her presence. He had seen to that, despite his longing to be with her.

"You look lovely," he said, his voice strumming low.

"I shall be the hen to thy peacock," she demurred, her gaze lingering on the cravat that tilted his chin at a haughty angle. "Friend Cheddar must be swooning with delight."

A smile nudged Robbie's mouth. "I left him in rapturous transports, quite certain that he had seen the last of my slovenly *à la Byron* bows."

"He simply wishes the best for thee, as we all do."

He paused, the incipient smile dwindling. "And what is best for me?"

She approached him, her taffeta gown whispering. "Only thee can know what will bring thee peace and joy."

But he didn't know. And it seemed that he had never known. Even as a boy he had searched and searched, seeking excitement, adventure, laughter, only to discover they were like mirages on the deserts of Araby—illusions without form or substance. Only with Tabitha had he felt that the illusion could become reality, that he might find at last the elusive answers he sought.

Wasn't it time for him to stop running? To turn and face what he was, to accept it, to live with it? To, as his father kept saying, accept his responsibilities, and among them, Tabitha as his wife, his life's mate, his heart's ease.

Friend Robert was different somehow. He seemed to have undergone a sea change, though Tabitha could not put her finger on exactly what the change was. She only knew that she needed to lend her full concentration to the evening, to the names, the faces, the people she would meet, but her concentration was proving to have as many holes as a sieve. He punctured it at will with his assiduous attention, the touch of his hand at

her waist, the twinkle in his eyes, the soft murmur of
his voice, the courtly manner of a man wooing a maid.
How easy it would be to succumb to his charm, to forget that he had quite definite plans to leave her soon.

After the dinner at Darenth House, after Friend Arabella's last booming admonitions, they formed a receiving line at the entry to the drawing room while the
tiny butler, Rumford, announced the first guests: the
Duchess of Wrexham and her son, the Earl of Audley.

"The devil take him!" Friend Robert leaned down to
whisper, his breath flowing warm and moist beneath
her ear, as distracting as the caressing hand at her
waist. "Should you doubt, my dear, that you are at
first oars with the Spaniard, this should prove that you
are. He takes to his mother like Monsieur to water. I
suspect he has not accompanied her to a soirée since
he moved into his own lodgings as a beardless boy."

Tabitha's gaze climbed to meet his, finding his eyes
sparkling and his mouth curving into the smile that she
had often imagined before she met him. Compounded
of equal parts of high good humor and wicked deviltry,
it set her heart to tumbling. He had shed his low mood
as if it had never been, but although he could forget it,
she could not. What did it mean? she wondered, refusing to entertain any capricious hopes.

While Tabitha basked in her husband's full atten-
tions, her Grace the Duchess of Wrexham appeared
before her. She was toweringly tall and as thin as the
silver-knobbed rosewood cane she leaned upon. She
was—how unkind of her to note it, Tabitha thought—
a Friday-faced creature who stared down the long narrow ridge of her nose with the expression she might
use on a street urchin running alongside her carriage
to beg a coin.

"Your Grace," said Friend Robert, "my wife, Friend
Tabitha."

She nodded stiffly, eyeing Tabitha up and down,
while Audley waited at her side with an encouraging
smile.

"Tabby, her Grace the Duchess of Wrexham." Friend

Robert paused, and she did not dare glance in his direction for fear she would discover his smile of wicked deviltry. "Friend Pegotta," he added, the smile in his voice.

Her Grace's eyes narrowing, she drew herself up to her full height, obviously incensed. Though Tabitha knew it was her first misstep of the evening, she could not be other than what she was.

"Friend Pegotta"—she extended her hand—"how pleased I am to meet thee. Thy son has—"

"Lady Langley," she said in frigid accents, ignoring Tabitha's hand and turning to stride away, apparently in no need of the cane whose use she affected.

"Drat the soul-pinched witch!" said Audley, staring after her, his swarthy face thunderous. "I thought I had her primed like a pump!"

"And, of course, you're a dab hand at handling her," said Friend Robert dryly. His watch fob and seals jangling, Audley rocked on his heels and gave Tabitha a shamefaced look. "What a devilish coil! I fear I set her back up."

"Do not concern thyself, Friend Edward."

He tugged at his ear, his onyx eyes frowning darkly. "I was at some pains to do you a good turn, Friend Tabby," he said, the beginnings of a smile banishing the frown. "You see, I took your advice and spoke to my father. Man to man like you said, I explained my plans. Damned if he isn't making me manager of Wrexham Manor when I return from . . . from . . ." He paused awkwardly, his curious gaze dancing from Friend Robert to Tabitha, while a ruddy flush scaled his cheeks. "From Greece, you see."

Greece. How abhorrent the word had become to her. "Art thou traveling with Friend Robert?" she asked, assured that was the only explanation for his squirming discomfort.

"Well, I . . . I—"

"Yes, Tabby," said Friend Robert, his hand tightening at her waist as if he wished it to say something he could not. However, she could not read that touch, as she could not read him. "It was a bet, a matter of honor. Old Nick will be accompanying us."

Tabitha, her heart in her throat, carefully avoided her husband's heavy gaze. "Then I shall pray for thee, each and every one."

"Devilish good of you, I'm sure," said Audley, backing away.

"Tabby," Friend Robert said, his voice thick and low.

"Do not concern thyself," she said softly, still unable to look at him. "All is as we knew it would be."

But it wasn't. Robbie gathered himself to greet the next guest, the stately Lord Liverpool. But while he made the introductions and approved his lordship's kindly condescension to Tabitha, his thoughts were leaping like a hare through summer hay. Be damned to Greece! Be damned to honor! Wasn't the greater honor found in abiding by his vows to cherish his wife?

It seemed the guests would never cease arriving. Impatient to whisk Tabitha away to the privacy of their own town house, to the pleasure of an intimate evening together, he realized only after some time that Tabitha was, as the Polite world phrased it, "not taking."

Lady Castlereagh's warmth served as a foil, casting in high relief the cool, even icy greetings of Society's best. But she had always been sweet-natured and warmhearted, and Lord Castlereagh's death had not changed that.

Her place was taken by the Dowager Duchess of Lethbridge, a woman whom the years had marked heavily, though apparently her mirror failed to tell her. She was dressed all in white, like a maiden at her comeout, drenched in ruffles and frills and laces and jewels. She fluttered her lashes and smiled flirtatiously at Robbie, raising her hand and giggling behind her fan while he kissed it.

"Your Grace," he said, gritting his teeth, "you look quite ravishingly lovely this evening."

"Naughty boy." She tapped him with her fan in the manner of her youth and simpered, "Were I younger

I should not have allowed you to marry beneath your station.''

Robbie stiffened, dropping her hand as if it were a hot coal. The veins in his temples throbbing, he gave her a quelling look that she failed to notice.

''So this is the little Quaker who has become the favorite *on-dit* of the *ton*.'' The faded blue eyes that had gazed so warmly at Robbie cooled as they raked Tabitha up and down.

''This 'little Quaker,' '' he began hotly, ''happens to be my wife—''

''And a lovely one,'' said Old Nick, insinuating himself into the receiving line behind the duchess. ''Behave yourself, Mama,'' he said softly but firmly.

Her pale raddled cheeks bloomed with color. ''You know how I detest being called—''

''Mama?'' he questioned, with a look of active dislike. ''Then I suggest you make no scenes, or I will whisper your age into every ear here, as if they did not know already.''

''You wretched, unnatural boy.''

''I'm a man, Mama, and don't you forget it,'' he said cuttingly, before turning to Tabitha.

''Friend Tabby, this''—he gestured—''is my mother. To you, Friend Persia.''

Tabitha, unsure whom she pitied more, stretched out her hand and found it once again ignored. ''Friend Persia, I—''

Her Grace spun away with an audible sniff and a hating glance at her son, one he returned with equal fervor.

''Thee should pity her,'' began Tabitha.

''Perhaps you can. I cannot,'' he said abruptly, then softened, a slow smile tugging at his mouth. ''What a tender heart you have, Friend Tabby. Your only problem is that you are real, where they, most of them, are shams, frightened and mean-spirited. You should not care what they think.''

But she did. Not for herself, but for Friend Robert, for his father and mother, for Anne. She was now a part of their world, and she must find a place for herself in it. But she, who had never hated anything, found that she hated this world. And as the night wore into the wee hours of the morning, that hatred grew.

It was, Friend Robert said, a fashionable squeeze, which meant every chair, every corner, every square foot of carpet, plus a few aching toes, was inhabited by the frail flowers, the aging roses, and overdressed Pinks, and the roving-eyed rouès of Society. The summer night was stifling, a smothering mix of the heavy fragrances of powders and perfumes and sweat. Laughter rose above the roar of voices, shrill sopranos and deep bassos all sharing the same empty lack of true humor.

Fragments of conversation spoke of the cut of a waistcoat, the shine of boots, the ribbons for a bonnet, the jewels for a smooth white throat. Tabitha studied the parure of diamonds gracing the Duchess of Lethbridge, dizzily contemplating how many of the starving poor they might feed, how many families they might keep for a year, how many babes they might save from a grave in potter's field.

Her head throbbed. Her throat ached. She longed for peace and solitude. Friend Robert had stayed at her side, attentively, surreptitiously moving her around the room, easing her into groupings of families and friends and, on occasion, enemies who delighted in verbal cut and thrust, their anger masked by rigid smiles. Did none speak the truth in their hearts? From every side she was beset by animosity, anger, and tension: the daggered glances between husbands and wives; the sarcastic exchanges between parents and children; the servile flattery of flowery compliments exchanged beneath covetous, grasping looks.

She felt like a castaway stumbling through the quicksand of a foreign land. Was this what marriage meant in the society to which Friend Robert was heir? No, she must not think that. There was love between his father and mother, between Anne and Karl. She saw it, too, between Brat Raeburn's parents. So few, they seemed the exception to prove the rule.

Her parents had shared everything: laughter and tears, work and pleasure. They spoke from the heart telling the truth of their feelings, their hopes, their dreams. Theirs was a partnership, not a battlefield where each must best the other.

She stood before the hearth, framed by the Grecian-draped caryatids supporting the mantel shelf. Friend Robert approached from across the room, a refreshing cup of punch in his hand. She watched as he turned a chilly nod to one, a cool glance on another, his violet eyes dark with fury. That fury was for her sake, but it did little to soothe her. There were few here whose good opinion she would treasure. Above all, his.

Yet she could not succumb to the need that fed upon itself day by day. The need to have him as a true husband, as the kind of husband her father was to her mother. She longed to be free to run her fingers through his hair, to ease his anger, to speak of the small events of her day and to hear of his. But theirs was no true marriage, and she must not forget that. However much he cared for her, he did not love her as she longed to be loved.

And it was too painful to hope, to pray that he would. She had never before needed to protect herself, her heart. Always she had been open and honest, as the Friends required. She had never understood why anyone would erect a shield around his heart—until now. She had never understood the need for dishonesty—until now.

He was, she thought, the handsomest man in the room, tall and lean and dark. His hair, damp with sweat, fell in loose curls across his brow. His eyes, as he approached her, lightened, brightened, softened. His smile came, cleaving creases in his cheeks, revealing the startling white of his teeth.

He offered the punch, his fingers caressing hers as she took it from him, lingering a moment to revel in his touch. But that way lay more pain. She sipped the drink slowly, her eyes downcast.

"It can't go on much longer," he said, moving so close she could feel the heat of his body, the vibrant energy that made her feel so alive. "Tabby, when we get home, I must speak with you."

Her gaze rose, touching his face and fleeing. What could he have to say that she had not heard? If it was more about Greece she could not bear it. "Perhaps another time," she said softly. "I fear I shall be too weary to climb the stairs when we arrive."

But she wasn't weary at all. Not now. Not when she knew he had something to say to her, something she was afraid to hear.

Was that how they had begun, she wondered, all of these husbands and wives who now exchanged daggered glances of dislike and distrust? Had one small lie led to another until they smothered all truth, all love?

Chapter 15

Tabitha's bedchamber was at the back, overlooking the garden. She flung up the window sash, her shining face raised to the early dawn light tiptoeing over the rooftops. Mist crept over the green lawn below, huddling in the corners where the hollyhocks grew. She sucked in a deep and bracing breath, her countrywoman's heart gladdened by the heady scents and glorious colors of roses and clove pinks, of buttercups and snapdragons, honeysuckle and ivy, all neatly weeded and thriving. She longed to scamper down the stairs and walk barefoot through the dew, but the freshness of the morning could not cleanse her of the lie she was living.

Her smile fading, she withdrew from the sunlight into the shadows of her chamber. Her bed was unmade. How unthinkable that once would have been. Tucked into the white coverlet was the marmalade mound of Monsieur, snoring softly with his long whiskers twitching. He'd had a hard night of hunting and wenching—nights like those Friend Robert had so often had during their short time in London. How painful it was to wonder what he had done. Almost as painful as contemplating her own additions to the distance yawning between them.

She moved quickly, her hands smoothing the skirt of her plain gray gown, rising to tuck a stray curl beneath her white linen cap. She could not become an ornament of Society. She had to be useful, and no better use could she put her life to than to the children of London, who were as unwanted and unloved as she felt.

Her low mood began to lift like the mist in the garden, rising to meet the burning rays of the sun. She slipped the capelet around her shoulders, tying it at the throat as she hurried into the hall. Today she would begin to gather her flock. Eager as she was, she could not resist a peek into Friend Robert's bedchamber. Like a mother with a newborn, she must see that he yet breathed and slept comfortably.

He lay sprawled over the bed, the white linen sheet and embroidered blue coverlet wildly tangled about him, his restless spirit untamed even by sleep. His arm was crooked over his head, muscular and dark and sprinkled with silky black hair as thick as the pelt that covered his bare chest. How she longed to touch him, to trail her fingers over his warm flesh, to have his hand at her waist, at her breast. She studied his mouth, parted so slightly, and remembered his lips claiming hers with a possessive fervor. Her gaze moved down his bare chest to the taut line of his belly and the embroidered coverlet draping his loins.

Her cheeks burning, her heart fluttering in her chest, she suffered a quick and chilling thought: if he claimed her as his wife and abandoned thoughts of Greece, what would happen to Friend Ephraim Fell's House in the forbidden precincts of Tothill Fields?

Robbie was drifting between dream and reality, imagining himself a country squire years hence, his lean body thickened and his hair threaded with gray and Langleyholm overrun with marmalade cats and fine, strong sons who bore a remarkable resemblance to Anne's sons. At the center of it all was Tabitha, smiling. That domestic scene was abruptly shattered by the click of the latch.

He lurched upright with a muttered ''What the hell?''

Muddled by the last vestiges of sleep, Robbie heard the light, fleet whisper of Tabitha's departing steps. She was leaving. No doubt to be about her charitable works. Obviously, he thought, disgruntled and surly, she did not believe that charity began at home.

The sound of a carriage stopping in the street below pulled him to the window. Tabitha, dressed in gray with her white cap hidden beneath a plain straw bonnet, paused for a word with the chambermaid scrubbing the front stoop. It seemed she had a kind and thoughtful word for everyone—except him.

He turned back into the room, naked as a babe, the muscular sweep of his back and his taut buttocks and well-shaped legs bronzed by the sunlight. At the hearth he stared at the painting of a peregrine falcon in flight. A grand and glorious bird, the falcon. Keen-eyed, long-winded, and courageous.

How, Robbie wondered, had he ever come by his sobriquet? He shared none of that noble bird's excellent qualities. If he'd been keener of eye, he would have foreseen the difficulties this marriage caused Tabitha. If he'd been longer of wind, he would have found a way to overcome them. If he'd been courageous, he would have insisted that she listen to him last night.

God, she had been so lovely. So restful to the eye and heart in that room full of overdressed, over-perfumed, over-jeweled women. Without a frill or a lace, a ruffle or a jewel, she had looked like a queen—and she had been given the cut by every whey-faced bitch there.

He had not been able to save her from that humiliation. How did he think he could do more for her? It was best that she had not spoken to him, that he had not professed undying loyalty and a desire to see if their marriage might work.

She'd be happier in her new life if he were out of it.

He strolled to the window, lifting the curtain aside, his gaze rising to the sky, seeking the far horizon. He tried to recapture the passion for change, for danger, for the allure of foreign lands, but they had all seeped away, leaving emptiness behind.

In the shank of the morning Milling-Jemmy Shadwell eased through the wicket gate in the narrow backyard of the house on Medway Street. His expressionless black eyes stared at the newly constructed privy where a chambermaid emptied the night's slops, then slewed to the spindly apple tree and beyond, to the kitchen door standing wide, as if issuing an invitation.

An invitation he intended to accept. The woman would never recognize him as the man she had seen in the sewer, for there he had merged with the darkness and the mist, always in the distance. And he had whispered, his voice echoing eerily from the rotting tunnel walls.

He hooked his thumbs into his broad leather belt, his mouth thinning in the black brush of a newly grown beard. He could hardly believe what Wild Jack had told him. The woman would be scouring the rookeries in search of unwanted and homeless children. Like the boy, he thought her a proper flat, ready for the picking. If she'd lose nothing more than her purse, he'd leave her to learn a lesson. But she'd more likely have her throat cut from ear to ear, and that he couldn't allow. Precisely why, he wasn't sure. But he hadn't been sure of many things since he'd met her.

His eyes were red-rimmed from sleeplessness, from a night spent moving through every low haunt inhabited by the dregs of society. Though he'd spread the word earlier through Wild Jack, he wouldn't leave anything to chance. He'd gone himself, demanding that the word be spread: the woman was under his protection. He needed to say no more. As a young man clawing his way out of the gutter, he'd shown no mercy to those who stood in his way. They had been murdered, openly, viciously, as a warning to any who dared try to thwart him. Now he had no doubt that the woman would be safe—as long as he was alive.

And that was the rub. There was the matter of a hundred pounds on his head, a princely sum for those who could barely scrape together a ha'penny for a doss house bed. The safe haven of his Spitalfields flash ken had become as dangerous as the filth-strewn alleys of the rookeries.

What better place to lie low, he had decided with the cunning of a fox, than the last place anyone would think of looking for him. In the woman's house. In Friend Ephraim Fell's House for Homeless Children.

In the neat parlor, with its rag rug on the floor, its newly wainscoted walls and simple deal tables shining with polish, Sister Seymour sat on an overstuffed sofa. She was resting, she said, for the journey through Tothill Fields.

"There's summat to see ye, Friend Tabitha," said the housekeeper, late of the workhouse. "A leary cull or me name's not Mrs. Plate. Give me the shivers, he did, with them black eyes of his. I'll send him packing if—"

"No, Mrs. Plate," said Tabitha gently. "We'll turn no one away from our door. Send him in."

He came up the stairs, every step heavy and slow, seeming to shake the narrow house from garret to cellar. Sister Seymour arched a brow, her head cocking inquisitively. "Perhaps he is not a man but a mountain," she said with a mischievous smile.

One that Tabitha answered until the man appeared in the doorway, filling it in breadth and height. He wore the uniform of the poor: heavy brogans, corduroy trousers, a coarse linen shirt, and a fustian coat. But he lacked the underfed and downtrodden appearance, the humbly beseeching look of the poor. Instead, there was arrogance in the tilt of his head, assurance in the square set of his feet, and blunt curiosity in his glittering black eyes.

A wave of familiarity crashed over Tabitha, but try as she might, she could not grasp the threatening memory that shimmered just beyond reach. Surely nothing more than his appearance aroused feelings of fear. His mammoth frame. His ham-sized hands. The satanic halo of wiry black hair standing out in stiff shocks around his head. His wet pink lips peeking through the brush of his whiskers. His eyes, empty of all but curiosity, peering out from beneath the jutting shelf of his curling eyebrows. An ill-favored man, but a man was not meant to be judged by his face or form. His heart and his soul were all that were important. Beneath his rough exterior he might have the soul of a saint.

Tabitha thrust away her foolish fears and summoned a welcoming smile. "How may I help thee, Friend?"

He blinked and shifted. Not uneasily, but as though his thick, hard-muscled legs needed relief from supporting his massive body. "Ye need a man about ter see ter the coal and such, fer liftin' and totin'," he said, his voice a low boom that seemed to set the walls to shivering, his tone telling, not asking. "I'll work fer bed and board."

He turned go, as if all had been settled. Tabitha exchanged a helpless glance with Sister Seymour, who called out, "Wait, Friend. Sister Ransome has not said she'd hire thee."

He angled his head on the thick column of his neck, and a strange dart of familiarity-fear robbed Tabitha of breath. "But I'm stayin', and that's a fact."

"My good man," began Sister Seymour.

"Wait," said Tabitha, approaching the man. "Have we met before, Friend?"

His round black eyes, so blank and cold, roamed her features, leaving Tabitha feeling as if she had been touched by a corpse-cold hand. He shook his head slowly, watching her all the while.

"Why dost thou wish to join us here?"

"Ye need a man about ter keep the little 'uns safe."

And they did. Trust in God she might, but He helped those who helped themselves. Perhaps He in His wisdom had sent them this man. "Welcome, Friend," she said softly. "What should we call thee?"

He studied her outstretched hand, his own rubbing up and down his stiff corduroy trousers before reaching out and taking hers, swallowing it in the hard-muscled reaches of his palm and fingers. "Jem," he said. "Call me Jem."

A short time later, all thoughts of Jem were banished. Tabitha and Sister Seymour began their circuit of Tothill Fields. The filth, the poverty, the cruel hunger that she had espied from the safety of the carriage became all too real. They entered a warren of alleys and courtyards where every living thing, save the stray scratching hen and the rooting swine and the swarming flies, vanished at their appearance. She caught the occasional flick of a skirt, the solitary toddler snatched indoors while eyes followed her passage through chinks and cracks.

The odor of urine, the stink of pig wallows, the smells of boiling cabbage and toasted herring and sweat and hopelessness—above all, hopelessness—pervaded the mean, crooked lanes overhung with ramshackle buildings that blotted out the sun, as if its clean and healing light must be shunned. The ragged clothes on the lines hung straight and dreary. The doors in the weatherbeaten walls sagged on cracked leather hinges. Over all hung the ghostly shade of a frequent visitor—death.

Tabitha entered a courtyard where the pigs rooted and spindly children played in the offal of man and swine. At every doorstep sat a straggle-haired and weary woman with a babe at her sagging breast. They rose as one, hissing at their offspring, who fled to the door that quickly slammed behind them.

Tabitha picked her way beyond the sagging gate, where Sister Seymour had paused. "My name is Friend Tabitha Fell . . . Ransome," she called out. "I come in peace to say that Friend Ephraim Fell's House for Homeless Children is now open. If thee knows of any child that needs us, please come forth."

She waited, refusing to lift her scented handkerchief

to her nose to stifle the stench. If these poor creatures could live here, she could tolerate it for this little while. Yet the urge to gag tickled her throat, just as horror scraped her tender soul. She longed for the clean cobbled street of Queen Anne's Gate, for the perfume of her garden, and for the strong arm, the protective stance of Friend Robert. But she feared she would never again be able to enjoy any of it for thinking of these unfortunates. How pale and lifeless a word to describe those so destitute of all, even faith and pride.

A door screeched open a crack. A bony boy, half-naked, slipped through, a woman's hand at his back urging him on. He looked like a wild creature, his eyes darting behind the greasy screen of his hair. He said not a word, rather hooking his finger and beckoning her to follow.

At the opposite end of the courtyard there was a narrow passageway. The boy scuttled like a crab, pausing at the entry to beckon once more. Tabitha lifted her skirts and ran across the mud and filth, Sister Seymour at her heels.

At the entry she stopped, the sickly-sweet stench of putrefaction thrusting her back like a fist to her midsection. "Sister . . . Sister Seymour?" she questioned, yielding, stuffing the scented handkerchief to her nose.

"Come, Sister, come." Mary Seymour, hopping like a sparrow, surged into the passageway, following the boy.

He stopped abruptly before a door, pointed with a dirty finger, and fled away into the darkness beyond. Wafting out from the cracks was the sickly-sweet smell, so strong now Tabitha gagged.

"Lord be with us," said Mary Seymour, pushing the door wide.

The smell came boiling out, thick as rancid butter. Tabitha swallowed again and again, longing for the sunshine that was no more than a wan strip of light far overhead, for the fresh, clean man-smell of Friend Robert, for the powders and perfumes that scented Society. She didn't think she could force herself to enter that room, to find what it held—until she heard the thin, feeble wail of a child.

She rushed through the door into the twilight of the hovel, seeing only the little girl naked on the dirt floor, staked by the rope around her ankle, her thin arm weakly flailing. Tabitha fell to her knees, reaching out. A host of flies rose from the raw sores ringing the child's tiny leg.

"Oh, God! Dear God!" said Mary Seymour, her voice shrill.

Tabitha paused in the act of reaching for the child, her gaze shifting slowly across the room. Sprawled on the floor was the body of a woman, hideously bloated and discolored, maggots . . .

She spun away, bending over, retching, retching until there was nothing left in her stomach. Nothing but sickness and sorrow and grief.

Outside in the relatively fresh air of the passageway, she hugged the child to her breast, shuddering and shuddering, until she thought her bones would splinter and disintegrate. And she swore to herself—Quaker though she was and swearing against her faith—that nothing and no one would stop her from saving children like this frail scrap of a girl. Not even her husband.

While Sister Seymour hurried to the Magistrate to report the woman's death and make arrangements for her burial, the women of Friend Ephraim Fell's House gathered around the child, flying away at Tabitha's orders for nappies, a tiny neatly stitched gown, medicines, and linen toweling. When Milling-Jemmy entered the kitchen with buckets of water to heat for its bath, he found Friend Tabitha feeding the child while the cook, Colleen O'Shea, a hedgebird from Newgate, slammed her pots and pans atop the iron oven. She was a tall and bony woman, bracket-faced and morose, and—until now—stingy of speech.

"Aye, yer a foine women, ye are, Friend Tabitha," she said in a voice as dry as burnt toast, "and 'tis a

foine thing yer doin', but ye'll niver know the way of
it. Ye've had tidy times, ye have. Ye haven't had to
earn a honest crust on the streets."

Milling-Jemmy poured the water into a great iron pot
suspended in the fireplace, his cold and curious gaze
on Tabitha. The child was in her lap. Where it was not
crusted with dirt, it was as white as the milk it slug-
gishly suckled from a nipple of linen cloth. His gaze
rose to Tabitha's face, to her white linen cap, while the
long-buried memory nudged at the door of conscious
thought. His pulse began to race. The memory was as
irresistibly compelling as it was dangerous. How could
he know that if he couldn't remember it?

"But, Friend Colleen," she protested, her slender
thumb stroking the child's fleshless cheek, "they left
her to starve, knowing her mother was dead! How
could they do that?"

Milling-Jemmy, dropping into a reed-bottomed chair
in the corner, heard the righteous indignation in her
voice but could not understand it. Things were as they
were, without rhyme or reason. Children died every
day from hunger or violence or disease. What was one
more or one less?

Mrs. O'Shea swiveled about, her long face frowning.
"To be sure, and I'd be knowin' the way of it. When
yer man's got no work and yer childer no food and the
rent's comin' due, ye've got to think of yer own by
hook or crook. When ye watch yer childer die one after
the other, took by hunger and scarlet fever and such,
ye don't go lookin' fer more to give ye a heartache."

"But they could have informed the Magistrate."

Milling-Jemmy shot her a contemptuous look. He
had a minimal amount of patience with her desire to
save the children of the rookeries, but none with her
ignorance.

"To be sure!" said Colleen O'Shea, clumping to the
deal table and viciously scrubbing carrots with a brush.
"And they'd have brought the law down on them, and
the parish churchwarden nosin' about."

"I don't understand," said Friend Tabitha.

"And, God be gracious, ye niver will. The law and the churchwarden mean nothin' but trouble fer the likes of us!" She whacked at the carrots with a wickedly sharp knife. "When yer belly's sunk to yer backbone and not a crumb fer the table and not a sixpence fer the rent and yer man's a hasty one fer trouble, ye might see then how high-minded ye'll be."

"But I'm only talking about simple human kindness."

"Kindness," said Colleen O'Shea grimly, "is fer them as can afford it."

In his corner, whittling on a stick, Milling-Jemmy nodded.

"Shadwell?" said Meg of the Cock and Roost in Spitalfields, a malodorous gin mill that Karl had suggested as one of Shadwell's haunts. "The name ain't familiar-like, dearie."

Which was the response in one form or another that Robbie had been getting all afternoon, each accompanied as this one was by an unmistakable spark of recognition followed by a visible shrinking caused by fear. Shadwell would elude him forever if his only hope was what he learned in the rookeries.

Stark of Bow Street, his gold buttons glittering in the dull light of an oil lamp, leaned across the greasy bar and pinned the doxy Meg with a threatening stare. "We've complaints o' the lace, Meggie me girl. The tars are sayin' the ladybirds are rollin' 'em for their purses. Ye wouldn't be knowin' about that, would ye?"

She puffed up, her once magnificent breasts sagging around her thickening waist. "I'm a 'onest doxy, I am. I keeps me tarts on a leash. If ye've 'ad complaints, they ain't about us."

Stark rolled his eyes in disbelief. "A 'onest doxy, like ninepence to nothing. Watch yerself, Meggie me girl, or I'll 'ave ye up before the beaks."

Robbie slapped a guinea on the greasy bar in payment for the ale he and Stark had not touched. Slowly,

he slid his hand away, watching the avaricious gleam
that lit Meg's eyes. "Keep the change," he said softly.
"There's more where that came from. A hundred
pounds if you lead me to Shadwell."

Mesmerized by the golden coin, Meg caught it with
her broken, black-rimmed nails and bit it to see if it
was real. "More, yer lordship?" she said softly, her
hard gaze suspiciously roaming to see if any were listening. "It'd be me skin to turn cat in the pan on
Milling-Jemmy."

"A hundred pounds, Meg."

Outside the Cock and Roost, Robbie paused for a
word with Stark. "What do you think?"

"She'd give ye 'er mother fer a shilling." Stark
smiled slowly, his rosy cheeks contrasting with the cold
blue of his eyes as he nodded across the street. "Blue
Ruin Alley, milord. I'll meet ye there at midnight, and
we'll 'ave us a go at Meggie me girl."

Kindness is fer them as can afford it. Was Colleen
O'Shea right? Tabitha wondered.

It was the footpad hour of dusk. She had arrived
home and plunged into a bath, scrubbing away the ac-
cumulated grime and smells of the day but not the uncertainties, the grief for the dead woman, the concern
for the child, and the heartrending realization that
whatever she did would never be enough. The problem of London's destitute and forsaken poor was over-
whelming and unsolvable. And she, who had always
believed that faith and hard work could perform miracles, had to accept that there were limits to what she
could do.

She sat in the garden, where all was fresh and green
and clean within the safe enclosure of the brick walls.
The scent of newly scythed grass permeated the air,
mingling with the fragrance of clove pinks and roses
and honeysuckle, but there seemed to hang about her
the foul odors of Tothill Fields. Had the dead woman
or her child ever known the pleasure of a garden, the
peace of green and growing things, the promise in a

tightly budded tea rose? Tabitha doubted it, and that multiplied the horror of the day.

If only Papa were here, he could help her to understand. She knew what the Friends believed: it hath pleased God to give to some men more and to some less for each to use accordingly; through hard work, honesty, and virtue, the poor might rise. But how could they when every effort must be expended on earning a crust of bread to survive through the day?

She felt like a ship cut loose from its moorings and adrift on a stormy sea. Doubt was a part of faith, Papa had said, but he'd had her mother to anchor him during his rare times of darkness. They'd been two halves of one whole, sharing everything. If only she could bring her questions to Friend Robert . . .

She heard his step on the dew-wet grass. If she told him what she was doing, explained to him why she must continue, would he understand? Or would he try to stop her?

You might drop a coin in a beggar's cup, his father had said, *but consorting with the poor in the streets is beyond the pale.*

And she was doing so much more than that. She dared not seek the comfort she needed.

Friend Robert approached with a lazy smile, as powerfully graceful as the high-steppers that drew his perch-phaeton. What simple joy it was to watch him, what pain to know that she was erecting a wall of lies between them. He set a foot beside her on the stone bench, his Wellingtons shining like the last of the sunlight catching the rooftop slates. Crossing his forearms over his knee, he leaned down, sending the faint aroma of bay rum wafting toward her.

"How fortunate I am to find an angel in my garden," he said, his voice a caress that seemed to stroke the length of her spine.

She straightened precipitately, his intense gaze pressing hers down to study the runner of honeysuckle she held in her lap. "I thought," she said softly, knowing she should not, "thee believed me a saint. Saint Tabitha, thee said."

There was a pause while the crickets sawed and a bird twittered nearby. "You will sink me below reproach should you censure me with that. It was, admittedly, in the poorest taste. Quite beneath one of my . . ." He stopped and sighed, as if he could not continue in that light vein. "I'm sorry, Tabby," he said softly. "I should not have said it."

"Only thought it?" She stared at the star twinkling on the horizon, remembering how it had stung. *Saint Tabitha.* She closed her eyes.

"I suppose I have thought it in a way." There was a tinge of melancholy in the low thrum of his voice, one that mated with the sorrow gathering in Tabitha's breast. "I cannot hope to match you for courage and honesty."

For courage and honesty. How quickly retribution came. Her gaze rose quickly, meeting his, shying away. How much she would like to tell him . . . to trust him with the secret of Friend Ephraim Fell's House.

"Thee . . . thee holds thyself too low," she whispered. "Thou hast been nothing but honest with me."

"Have I?" he responded thoughtfully. "I wonder."

How dangerous this was. Tabitha stood abruptly. "It grows late, and we must dress for the Raeburns' rout."

He fell into step beside her, his hands plunged into his pockets. "Mother sent a note around. She and Anne wish to have a word with us tonight."

"Is . . . is there a problem, dost thou think?"

"I may perhaps put the wrong construction on it, but I suspect they have been feverishly plotting your insinuation into Society."

From the street there came a song from a dustman making late rounds: "Dust-O! Dust-O! Bring it out today. I shan't be 'ere tomorrow."

Tabitha glanced toward the wicket gate, her expression pensive. "Hast thou ever wondered what thee would be had thy father been a dustman?"

"I confess I have not. Why do you ask?"

''No reason,'' she said.
Lies and more lies.

Robbie was right. His mother and Anne had hatched
a plan that was both brilliant and daring. He knew he
had not gotten his gambling blood from his father, who
was in every respect a careful and cautious man. His
mother's willingness to chance all on a single throw of
the dice convinced Robbie as nothing else had that his
bent for reckless adventure must be the heritage of his
Bragg family blood.

They were to take Tabitha over the heads of the
highest sticklers, straight to the king. In two weeks a
musical evening was planned at Darenth House, fea-
turing Prince Karl von Schattenburg at the piano presenting to Society his latest compositions, as yet
unpublished. George IV, fancying himself a great pa-
tron of the arts, would beyond any question be in at-
tendance—as would Tabitha. While the *ton* might
despise and revile their fat and pompous king, he was
their leader. His nod of approval would see her accepted, however grudging it might be.

The faintest of smiles etching Robbie's mouth, he
leaned against a crumbling brick wall in the black shadows of Blue Ruin Alley, awaiting Stark's arrival. He
had to give them credit. Tabitha meeting the king. Robbie only hoped he was nearby when she called him
Friend George.

''Milord?'' said Stark, sidling into the alley, stumbling over the midden heap and cursing foully. ''If ye'll
follow me and stay close. Damn the fog! A fair soup it
is! She left the Cock and Roost a mite ago.''

Robbie's cloak flowed around his ankles like an ill-
omened wraith. He could hear the slip and slide of
Meg's steps on the wet, muddy street. In the fog-
diffused light of a gin mill down the way, her shadow
passed at a rapid pace. Stark set out at a trot. She
paused, turning to look back, then wheeled around and
took flight. Stark put on a burst of speed, Robbie fol-

lowing. She ran as if the devil were after her, and no doubt she thought he was.

"Meggie me girl!" called Stark down the deserted street.

She slowed to a halt, turning to face them with a drawn knife. When they approached she sighed in relief. "If it ain't 'is nibs, come ter fright a girl ter death."

"One hundred pounds, Meg," Robbie said, inhaling the stench rising from the gutter. "Do you want it or not?"

She searched the folds of darkness as if Shadwell might be hiding there. "What use'll I 'ave fer it if Milling-Jemmy learns I grassed 'im?"

"He won't learn, if you're smart. And I think you're a very smart girl, Meg."

"'Course I am, dearie," she preened. "A 'undred pounds, ye say?"

He nodded. "When I have him."

She hugged the wall behind her, speaking low. "Milling-Jemmy's run ter ground. A smart 'un, 'e is. Ain't been in 'is flash ken fer days."

"Where would he hide?"

"Yer got yer pick, dearie. The 'Oly Land, Southwark, Bermondsey. Why, 'e could be right 'ere in Spitalfields, and ye'd not find 'im."

"But you could."

"Aye, I might."

She flashed Robbie a sly, seductive smile, winked, and sauntered off with her full hips swinging. Stark muttered darkly under his breath. "She's up to no good, yer lordship," he said. "Meggie me girl's too sassy by half."

"You think she's up to something?"

"Aye." Stark rocked on his heels, staring after her. "But the question, yer lordship, is, what?"

Chapter 16

Robbie should have been satisfied with the progression of events, but he fell into what Anne—crossing verbal swords with him at the opera—called angrily "a fit of the sullens." Even he was appalled by his foul mood, which helped not a whit to alleviate it. He felt like a man suspended over a vat of boiling oil by a rope that was slowly but surely unraveling. The plans that had once appeared so simple and easy to achieve—find Shadwell, leave Tabitha, go to Greece—now seemed impossible. And why they should seem precisely "impossible" he could neither understand nor accept.

While he awaited news from Meg of the Cock and Roost, he plunged into the mind-numbing round of the Season's frolics and succumbed to the siren song of his old bachelor haunts, like—his father said coldly—the merest fribble.

Though he escorted Tabitha to fêtes and soirées, to balls and assemblies, he returned her home in the wee hours of the night, leaving her at the door to be off on his drunken revels. Never a word of censure did she speak. Never once did she ask him not to leave her. Not by so much as a glance did she betray a desire to have him nearby—his oh-so-complacent wife.

With a cruel perversity that was not normally a part of his nature, he began to push the limits, to see how far he could go before she complained.

He made the Grand Strut in Hyde Park, an elegant

figure atop his spirited Sin as he doffed his top hat to ladies and gentlemen. It proved to be an excessively dull and tedious exercise. The diamonds of the Season were giggling peagooses with little more than dust in their attics. How restful Tabitha was in comparison, with her long, comfortable silences, her keen perceptions, her ability to actually say something when she spoke.

He secured a voucher to Almack's, attending with his boon companions, Old Nick and the Spaniard. In less than an hour he was yawning discreetly into his glove—until Anne ripped up at him: Why was he haring around Town and leaving his wife alone? He ventured to remind her that the Friends did not approve of dancing, to which she rudely snorted. He escaped that engagement unbloodied but not untouched.

Why? he asked himself. Because Tabitha didn't care. There were no limits to what he could do, and he was increasingly disgruntled by the freedom he thought he wanted.

Why didn't she care? He was as clean as the next man and handsomer than most, he admitted immodestly. Any number of frail flowers had tossed their handkerchiefs after him. What was wrong with her? And then, quite painfully, what was wrong with him? If she wanted a saint, she should have married a Friend!

He discovered Tabitha one afternoon sitting in the garden drying her hair in the sun. A shiny blue-black, it rippled down her back to hang in tantalizing curls below the stone bench. Drawn mesmerically by it, he silently took the comb from her hand and began to draw it through the silky tresses. After a single startled glance, she succumbed to his ministrations with a sigh. He longed to gather it up in his two hands, to raise it to his nose and breathe deep of its fresh, clean smell, to rub his cheek in its softness, to wind it around and around his palm, making of it a tender tether to bind them together . . .

He must be mad! Did he not know himself better, he would think he was lovesick . . .

Sweat broke out on his brow in fat beads that scudded into his eyes. He was surely ready for bedlam! It was nothing more than proximity to Tabitha added to his lately discovered and disturbing distaste for the barques of frailty served up for his choosing at the low haunts he had been frequenting. He'd have to seek something of a higher order. Perhaps a visit to the little pink room where the opera dancers practiced or to Madame Lescal's modish establishment in . . .

Ah! Just the thing! Madame Lescal's. It was frustrated lust, purely and simply. Fortunately, there were no *tonnish* parties to which he must escort his wife tonight. He'd take the cure and be his old self again.

At that moment, Tabitha turned with a smile, her gray gaze sparkling. "Should thee desire to seek honest work, Friend Robert, thee would make a tolerable lady's maid."

Visions of Madame Lescal and her delectable Cyprians evaporated. Tabitha had quite the most kissable mouth it had ever been Robbie's pleasure to notice. Even as he told himself he very definitely should not be noticing it, his gaze was sliding down the fine line of her throat and he was comparing her skin to the finely textured Damascus silks he had encountered on his travels.

"Only tolerable?" He sank onto the bench, as if it were a serpentine love seat, leaning over to brace his hand opposite her thighs and bring his face close to hers. "You will put me out of countenance should you suggest that I would be less than the best."

A faint tinge of red colored her cheeks, while the spiky sweep of her lashes shyly lowered. "I should think that thee would be the best at whatever thee chose to do."

Did he imagine the slight catch in her voice? He certainly wasn't imagining the hammering of his heart. "What a pretty speech, from such pretty lips."

He closed the narrow space between them, touching his mouth to hers, ardor sublimated by a deeper longing to find her willing and eager. Her mouth had the smooth texture of rose petals and the haunting sweetness of young love. He suckled gently at her lower lip and felt her melt against him, one hand gliding up his braced arm, the other capturing his shirt frills and pressing against his chest. His tongue flicked the corner of her mouth, and her breath seemed to hang suspended.

"Tabby," he said throatily, burying his hand in her hair, tilting her head to facilitate his tender invasion of her mouth. His tongue touched hers, swirling around the tip with a velvety embrace. She went still, and he stroked once more, feeling her tentative response as an explosion of heat that settled low in his loins with an insistent ache. He waited, breath bated, his pulse surging through his veins. Slowly, cautiously, her tongue touched his, pausing for a heart-stopping moment, then swirling around the tip and reaving from him every particle of sense.

He pulled her across his lap, cradling her close, his mind bombarded by sensations of sound and sight and touch and feeling: the rustle of her gown and the rush of her breath; the pulse frenetically throbbing at the base of her throat and the dazed expression in her eyes; the eager trembling of her body and the heat of her hand at his nape; and, above all, the storm that swept through him, the desire, the need, the dread, the fear.

His reeling thoughts lurched to a halt. For a moment, he was utterly blank, unsure of how she had come to be in his arms, unsure of how he had moved so swiftly from his "fit of the sullens" to mindless passion. It seemed, he thought, that the beast wore more than one face. Strange that it had taken so long to reveal its latest facet—blind lust.

His face warmed and burned with a flush of self-disgust. Tabitha had shown him very convincingly that she wanted no part of a true marriage. If she did, she would nag or scold or plead as a true wife would.

Yet she welcomed his touch. He could not mistake that.

Her head lay across his upper arm, her hair cascading to the lush turf. In her face he saw a dawning awareness, a burning blush. She scrambled up and away, tugging at her skirt, smoothing the feathering curls from her face. Something perilously near shame darkened the gaze that grazed Robbie's and fled, leaving in him an anger that spread like wildfire.

He surged to his feet, catching her arms in a viselike grip, jerking her to him. Her head fell back, her expression betraying her shock and fear. "I am your husband!" he said harshly. "There should be no shame in what passes between us!"

"Thou . . . thou art hurting me," she said softly, her lower lip quivering.

He released her precipitately, stepping back, raking his fingers through his hair and leaving the ebony curls atumble. God! What was happening to him? He was running as mad as a March hare!

He drew himself up, staring down at her. "Forgive me," he said stiffly, striding away with his back rigid.

"Friend Robert!"

He stopped, not turning back to look at her.

"Thee . . . thee will be away for the evening?"

"Yes," he said shortly, ruthlessly tamping down the hope that she would nag or scold or plead with him to stay.

"I would . . . would bid thee a pleasant night."

He did not respond, moving instead to the steps and climbing them heavily. Tabitha stared at his broad back through a shimmer of tears. Did she imagine the slight slump of his shoulders?

She sank onto the bench, cradling her face in her hands, fighting the tears that threatened to sluice down her cheeks. He had made it abundantly clear that he was satisfied with their arrangement. She could not fault him on any score. Unfailingly polite, he had made every effort to smooth her way into the *ton*, attending her assiduously at the many events of the Season. Only she and his boon companions knew that he dropped her at their door like an unwanted puppy, seeking his pleasure elsewhere. Only she knew the many anxious hours she spent awaiting his return home.

She had not been blind to the inviting glances cast him by the diamonds of the *ton*, married women and widows who were—according to the scandalmongers— no better than they should have been. And she, Tabitha thought, could hardly be classified "a diamond of the first water." Friend Robert would assuredly not lose his head over the curve of her cheek or the cast of her brow when he might choose from the fresh lovelies who surrounded him—lovelies whom he regarded with singular indifference.

And now he had kissed her. Why?

The question propelled her from the bench to pace the width of the garden from the brass sundial to the bed of clove pinks. Much as she might shrink from the answer, she was terribly afraid she knew what it was. There was between them an attraction that was purely physical, and rare though it might be, on occasion it overcame them both. No other explanation could there be. No worse one could there be.

She needed more than the desires of the flesh, however much pleasure there might be in them. She needed the attraction of hearts and minds and souls, the deep-rooted love that would remain in faith and truth long after fleshly desires had cooled.

A short time later, while Tabitha—disgusted with her own moping and megrims—was sneaking out of the town house like a thief, careful to make no sound that would alert Thistlewood to her departure for Friend Ephraim Fell's, Wild Jack Burdett was lying on a bed of straw in the Spitalfields flash ken with Tansy curled up beside him, one tiny hand tightly clutching his ragged coat.

He stared at the soot-blackened beams overhead through the haze of smoke from the center fireplace. Rooster Annie coupled with One-Eyed Will in a corner, each singing a chorus of grunts and groans. Sleepers snored, urchins whimpered, a babe screamed in its basket—sounds so familiar Wild Jack did not hear them. Nor did he notice the smells of urine and rotting straw and fish oil and boiling cabbage.

He was aware of nothing but Tansy at his side, her tiny lips pouted in sleep, the fragile fans of her lashes lying on her cheeks, and his love for her welling in his chest as a painful pressure against his rib cage and a thickening of his throat. He'd known early on that he had none to depend on but himself and that Tansy had none to depend on but him, and he was sure he could take care of them both. Now that assurance had been knocked to smithereens.

He'd taken the weak and sickly lad, Henry Hicks, under his wing. Now Henry was gone, vanished as if he had never existed. Wild Jack had made frantic and furious inquiries of every man, woman, and child in the flash ken. No one knew anything. He scoured Spitalfields up and down Ratcliffe Highway, into Petticoat Lane, back and forth through its squalid and vicious streets. He'd talked to butchers standing in their doors wearing dirty aprons and sharpening their knives. He asked watercress girls and staggering drunks and dirty children if they'd seen a lad of about ten years who looked like a fresh-plucked chicken.

Henry Hicks was not to be found. Wild Jack had failed to protect him, and that failure wore heavily on him. His quick and fertile mind spun like a top, sifting out incidents he had not before now given due notice. Henry Hicks was not the first to disappear.

Though the urchins of the backslums came and went with no regularity, once they found Milling-Jemmy's headquarters, they stayed. No one dared beat them or bed them against their will, for Ole Jem would not allow it. But from time to time, one or another simply vanished. Only now did Wild Jack begin to think that ominous. Henry Hicks would not willingly have abandoned his responsibility to watch over Tansy while Jack made their meager living. And if he had not done it willingly, then . . .

Their safe haven was safe no longer.

Wild Jack wasted no time on wondering who might be taking the urchins of the flash ken or what had happened to them. When Milling-Jemmy returned, as he surely would after his business at Friend Ephraim Fell's was done, Wild Jack would tell him what had happened and together they would find the culprit and mete out rude justice. For now the most important problem was Tansy.

He could not, knowing what he suspected, leave her here alone while he worked the streets. He could not take her with him, for he needed to be as swift as a swallow to escape the *blows* whose pockets he picked. Having Tansy hanging on his coattails was the surest path to the Nubbin' Cheat, the gallows, for him and to an orphan asylum for her.

Wild Jack gently detached her grubby hand from his coat, sitting up to watch her in the dim light. She was all he had in the world, all he wanted. He had to see her safe, and as much as he hated it, there seemed to be only one thing to do.

He watched the rise and fall of Tansy's chest, the greasy strings of hair that wanted to curl around her face. They'd never been separated before, and it seemed he could already feel the emptiness and loss. His eyes stung and prickled, and he blinked hard while he prodded Tansy awake.

"Up, girl," he said gruffly. "Ye can sleep all ye wants arterwards. Aye, an' eat too! I seen 'em, I 'as, scrubbed clean as a laundrywoman's kettle, eatin' tarts and pies and bread. Ain't like them other places. They won't skin ye, nor work ye. Up, girl!"

Dusk came and went in Medway Street. Word had spread quickly. Children had been left on the doorstep by twos and threes, babes and toddlers and older ones, scrawny-limbed, puff-bellied, vermin-infested, bruised and battered, and on occasion, as drunk as lords. But Tabitha's expectation of toys underfoot, of laughter and chatter and riotous play, had not come to pass. The children were abnormally quiet, unusually quick to obey, and sadly suspicious. They seemed to want above all things to escape notice—so unlike Anne's 'ons, who thrived on attention. Tabitha wished they had not been left at Darenth Hall for the summer. She longed to see them. Even more she longed to see how they might enliven the children of Friend Ephraim Fell's.

The children had been fed and readied for bed. Now they crowded into the parlor, listening to the house-keeper, Mrs. Plate, read a chapter from the Bible. She was a small and comfortable woman with an unfortu-nate monotone that infused the Sermon on the Mount with the drama and enthusiasm of a bored bailiff call-ing a court to order.

It was Tabitha's first opportunity to remain through the evening. The children, dressed in unadorned white night rails, sat cross-legged on the rag rug, silent, still, and unsmiling. There was no pinching or shoving or teasing. How strange and disconcerting.

The Friends taught subjugation of a child's will so that every perverse passion might be checked. Anger was rebuked, as was speaking loudly. Discipline, they believed, must be practiced for the achievement of peace and order. But there was peace and order here, and it was not natural. There was no rich inner life, no striving for the Truth, no joy in living—only indiffer-ence and disinterest and distrust.

The tiniest babes, like the one she held in her arms, were responsive to a smile or a caress, but the toddlers had quickly learned what a cruel and uncertain world they had been born into.

She watched solemn Eve, their first foundling child, cling to Colleen O'Shea's skirts, the only evidence of her inner turmoil. The morose cook complained of Eve always being underfoot, even as she was slipping her crusts of bread and pastries. Kindness and time, Tabi-tha thought. They all needed time to learn that they were safe and loved.

The Bible reading at an end, she laid the sleeping babe in a willow basket, preparing to follow the silent regiment of children to the dormitory and tuck them in.

The bell pealed a trio of urgent notes.

Hurrying to answer it, Tabitha swung the door wide, admitting into the quiet precincts of the hall a forlorn squall. Standing on the stoop was a snub-nosed waif of about three years, whose big blue eyes ejected impossibly fat tears. She was as scrawny and vermin-infested as the rest had been, but she showed some evidence of care. Her face and hands had been recently scrubbed. Her greasy cropped hair had been combed. Her rags had been crudely patched. Hanging around her neck was a sign, laboriously lettered in charcoal: *Mi nam b Tanzee.*

Tabitha knelt, holding out her arms. "Come, Tansy."

"Bubba! Bubba!" wailed the child, turning to the dark street and stretching out her arm, her tiny hand urgently opening and closing.

Tabitha studied the alley across the way, the loungers in front of the gin mill at the corner. "Tansy, listen to me." She pulled the little girl into the circle of her arm. "Bubba has left thee with us. He wouldn't want thee to cry, would he?"

Tansy, her sea-blue eyes huge in her pale, thin face, stared at Tabitha and shook her head. "Want Bubba," she said, and drew a shuddering breath while another fat tear scooted down her cheek.

"Does thee know why Bubba left thee with us?"

Tansy, her eyes riveted on Tabitha's face, shook her head. "Want Bubba."

Tabitha, her heart aching, lifted Tansy in her arms, settling the child on her hip while she closed the door.

"Bubba?" Tansy mewled softly, her voice breaking on a sob.

Tabitha cradled her close as she made her way downstairs, feeling the child's thin legs and smelling her unwashed body and thinking of the Dowager Duchess of Lethbridge's glittering diamonds. Did she know or care how many children like this one she could feed and clothe and save from despair?

Tabitha knocked on the door to the tiny closet that was Jem's sleeping chamber. However hesitant she had been about him at first, he had proved to be a godsend, quick and willing to do the heavy work of hauling water and coal, always there to lend an extra hand when needed. Yet neither she nor the women of Friend Ephraim Fell's felt comfortable with him. He seemed, without any effort on his part, to inspire fear. She thought it was his massive size, his unruly black hair, and his truly villainous-looking beard, none of which he could help.

His door screeched open, settling her teeth on edge. Silhouetted by the meager light of a candle, he filled the portal from sill to sill, his bare chest matted with coarse black hair and his huge feet set as square as the sturdy stone supports of London Bridge. Once again, Tabitha felt the ripple of uneasiness, the tantalizing sense of recognition.

"Another 'un," he said, studying the back of the child's head.

Tansy stirred, lifting her face, her blue eyes brightening. Suddenly she flung herself out of Tabitha's arms, reaching for Jem. He caught her, his thick, meaty hands covering her back.

"Bubba! Bubba go! Find Bubba!" she jabbered excitedly.

"Dub yer mummer, girl," he said, not unkindly, his rough voice like the distant quake of thunder.

Dub yer mummer. A chill scampered over Tabitha's skin, sending goose bumps scrabbling one over and over. It was a common expression among the poorer classes, shouted every day in Tothill Fields, spit low and cruelly in the Almonry. But she had first heard it from Milling-Jemmy Shadwell in the sewer beneath the City.

Tabitha scoured her mind for every memory of him, but they were as murky and somber as the sewer had been. She summoned a picture of a massive, faceless frame silhouetted by the curls of mist rising from the viscous black water; another, of a shadow darkening the tunnel, hovering beyond the light. Always he had been a featureless bulk hulking in the gloom. A man she would not know if she came face to face with him. Had she now?

Milling-Jemmy Shadwell. Jem. Her mouth dried to dust.

She studied his face, the thick shelf of his brows, his ruddy complexion, his glittering black eyes. Eyes that watched her now without expression.

"I . . . I need coals for the fireplace and water for her bath," Tabitha said quickly, amazed that she could speak at all when her heart was pummeling the air from her lungs.

He nodded, handing Tansy back to her with the strict admonition, when her small face screwed up to cry, "We'll 'ave none o' that, girl."

Tansy quieted immediately, drawing a shuddering breath that shook her thin frame, while she watched him heft the coal scuttle and vanish through the door.

Tabitha, atremble, hastily delved into a crockery pot on the shelf, withdrawing an apple tart that Tansy fell upon as if she were starving—which she surely was. All of the children were when they appeared at the door. Tabitha sank into the rocker with the child in her lap.

"Tansy," she asked urgently, "dost thou know Jem?"

The child nodded vigorously, flakes of pastry ringing her mouth. "Jem."

"Does he have another name? What dost thou call him?"

"Jem," she repeated, digging into the tart with her forefinger and thumb, finding a piece of soft, sweet apple, and insisting that Tabitha eat it. "Good."

While Tansy devoured the remainder of the tart, Tabitha awaited Jem's—Shadwell's?—return in turmoil. There were many large men. The names Jem and Jemmy were common ones. Shadwell had no reason to come here and perform the menial duties of lifting and carrying. Surely she allowed her imagination to run away with her.

Should she confront him or leave well enough alone?

He certainly was no threat. He could easily have harmed any of them before now, had he wished to do so. And she could not forget that Shadwell had saved both Friend Robert and her by leading them out of the maze of tunnels. Neither could she forget that he had murdered von Fersen with his bare hands.

Milling-Jemmy Shadwell shouldered the door open, a coal scuttle in one hand, a bucket of water in the other. He paused on the portal, the night breeze cool at his back. The woman, Friend Tabitha, sat in the rocker, the girl in her lap curled up and sleeping with her thumb tucked in her mouth. She was always one to be sucking her thumb. Times must be untidy indeed if Wild Jack let her out of his sight.

Shadwell's expressionless gaze went to the woman's face, which was as white as her cap. She knew. He could see it in her eyes, silvery bright and sharp with fear. Ah, well, he'd known the risk to himself and to her.

He moved ponderously to the fireplace, removing the grate and revealing the red coals he had earlier banked for the night. Hunkering down to his task, he wasted no movement, nor did he hurry. There was no need. Time was no enemy to him. Not any longer.

He'd known Meg of the Cock and Roost for many a long year. She'd been a spry one in her day, but her day was no longer. Once, her cunning would have warned her against any attempt to blackmail Milling-Jemmy Shadwell. But the years and the booze and the pox had been unkind to Meg, robbing her of her keen wits. He'd made his way to Spitalfields in the wee hours of last night, with none in Medway Street any the wiser. He'd met Meg and listened to her threats. Meg of the Cock and Roost would blackmail no one again, and once she was found, none would dare betray him.

It was only left to see if the woman would; he could not bring himself to call her Friend Tabitha. He paused for a moment to puzzle over that. Not finding the reason, he allowed the mild curiosity to slip away.

Water was heating in the cauldron and heat was spreading into the kitchen, stealing the chill from the air, when he stood slowly, stretching up like a great oak reaching for the sky, looming over Tabitha like a dark and brooding mountain.

Everything had been so simple before he heard her voice, the soft "thees" and "thous" that summoned a memory of comfort and well-being. While he'd been at Friend Ephraim Fell's the memory had grown stronger, though still out of reach. It was as if it were behind a curtain, its outlines blurred, its colors dimmed, its voices indistinct. He was afraid—he who feared nothing—to tear the curtain aside, for it came—how did he know?—from what he had long called the Before Time. It was as if he had been born a boy full grown with his beard just sprouting, but he must have had a childhood, parents, kin. If he had, they lived now behind the curtain he could not tear aside.

"You know who I am," he said flatly, his voice like a drum reverberating from the walls.

Tabitha's heart sank to her toes. She gave scant thought to denying it, but she was so sunk in lies and deceit with Friend Robert that she could not add another to the list of her sins. Frightened as she was, she did not think Jem would actually harm her. "Yes," she said softly. "Thou art Milling-Jemmy Shadwell."

He pulled up a reed-bottomed chair, swiveled it around, and spraddled it. His forearms folded atop the slat-back, he studied her, saying, "Aye. Yer eyes gi' ye away. Ye'd not last a day on the streets."

She heard the contempt in his voice and wondered at it. "It must be a hard life."

He nodded slowly.

"I have not thanked thee for saving my life and Friend Robert's," she said, wishing he would not stare at her so intently. She still sensed no threat from him, only a curiosity that seemed to equal her curiosity about him. "Why did you do it?"

"Bad fer business." His eyes narrowed in thought. "Kill a Nob an' every man jack 'ud be 'owlin' fer blood."

"And . . . and what business art thou in, Friend Jem?" she asked.

"Thievin' 'n' such."

"I . . . I see."

His expression turned wary, cunning, and dark. Tabitha's fear, having seeped away as they talked, now returned full force, as if the breeze whistling around the eaves were whispering a threat in her ear. Her arm tightened around Tansy, who whimpered in her sleep, murmuring, "Bubba, Bubba."

"Will ye tell yer man ye got me 'ere?" Milling-Jemmy asked.

Tabitha's gaze dropped to the child in her lap. There were so many reasons why she should tell Friend Robert, and few reasons for why she shouldn't. Yet, somehow, it seemed important that she not.

"Will thee first tell me why thee has come to Friend Ephraim Fell's House?"

"Yer man's got a 'undred pounds on me head," he said, his narrowed eyes seeming to weigh her.

"I . . . I didn't know."

"Aye, then yer the onliest 'un in Lunnon that don't." He paused, staring at her. "As a lad I learned the best place fer 'idin' 'uz under the Old Scouts' noses."

She didn't know whether to be appalled that she had been used so or impressed by his ingenuity. "If thou art caught, what will happen to thee?"

"I'll go up the ladder ter bed."

"I don't understand."

" 'Anged, woman. I'll be 'anged."

Hanged! The Quakeress, the woman of peace, shrank from the thought. Whatever happened, she could not have Milling-Jemmy Shadwell's death on her conscience, nor could she allow it to rest on Friend

Robert's. Shadwell's sins—and that he had many she did not doubt—should be left to God's justice or mercy. She would be no part of any earthly retribution.

"Rest assured, Friend Jem, that I will tell no one that thou art here, and thee may remain with us as long as thee chooses."

"Ye'll swear to it, then?"

"Swearing is against my faith, but thee may believe me when I say I will betray thee to no man."

He studied his thick, hairy wrists, flexing his meaty hands as if, Tabitha thought faintly, he imagined her throat between them.

"Yer a queer 'un, ye are, but ye got a mort o' mettle, and I'm believin' ye."

While Tabitha gave Tansy a thorough scrubbing, Stark of the Bow Street Patrol tracked Robbie to the Royal Saloon in Piccadilly, known for its bad company. Strolling through the long main room beneath the balcony decorated with trelliswork and palms, he slipped into a curtained recess where a private party was in progress—though it didn't appear to be a very happy one.

"Scotched it, she did!" said the Spaniard. "Said I'd ruin the Wrexham Manor lands, leaving us all on poor relief! To the Duchess of Wrexham!" He hefted his glass. "May her soul rot in hell!"

Stark found his lordship lazing in a chair, much the worse for the Irish whiskey he seemed to be drinking like watered wine. "Sir, if I might have a moment."

Robbie blinked, struggling to focus. Stark swam into view. "M-my good man"—he stood slowly, bracing his hands on the table—"have . . . have you news for me?"

"Out here, if ye please, milord."

"Of . . ." He hiccuped. "Of course."

The news Stark had proved to be an astonishing restorative for the effects of strong drink. "Milord," he said, ''Meg of the Cock and Roost is dead. She was found in Blue Ruin Alley with 'er tongue cut out and a placard with Shadwell's name printed on it stabbed into 'er chest.''

Chapter 17

The first streaks of dawn light were painting the night sky in broad brushstrokes when Robbie wheeled his perch-phaeton into the mews behind Queen Anne's Gate. He had a dull headache, a sharper fear. Stark was convinced that the murdered Meg had tried to blackmail Shadwell, and her body had been left as a warning to any who gave thought to "grassing" him. Another sign of how dangerous Shadwell was, how dangerous he might be to Tabitha. And Robbie was no closer to finding the man. He felt as helpless, frustrated, and angry as he had in the crypt in Schattenburg.

He climbed the back stairs, deep in thought of the evening spent at the Royal Saloon in the company of the Spaniard and Old Nick—two men who were, in their separate ways, just as scarred and scared and confused as he was. They, like him, were running away from themselves, from the pain of their past.

The Duchess of Wrexham, seen through her son's bitter and despairing eyes, was a tyrant who ruled those around her with an iron hand and an ungenerous heart. Even her husband, a meek and mild man who was mad for the hunt, shrank from her shrewish tongue. The swarthy Audley had rebelled as a youth, seeking every frivolous fashion that his mother abhorred and every low companion whom she despised. Could he spite her, there was no end to which he would not go. But he was tired of living in her angry shadow. He wanted to return to the soil he loved—and she had thrust yet another spoke in his wheel, browbeating his father into reneging on his promise to give the management of the Wrexham Manor farms into Audley's hands.

It had been Old Nick who, looking as if he might imminently expire of boredom—a condition common to him—set Audley a poseur. "What a crochet you've taken about Wrexham Manor, you would-be farmer. Devil take the woman, you've Audley Hall, haven't you?"

Audley studied his claret, as if it might, like an oracle, give him the answer. "Not large enough by half."

"What a blockhead," said Old Nick without heat. "What of the fair Miss Fasham?"

"That . . . that ape-leader! She's three-and-ten if she's a day!" protested Audley.

"And she looks half that, while being tender of heart, mild of manner, and blessedly quiet," added Old Nick.

"Are . . . are you suggesting that I m-m-marry? By gad! You must be mad!"

"Quite possibly," Old Nick admitted. "However, it is common knowledge that her portion will include the village of Fasham and a thousand acres of tenanted lands and commons—which, I believe, adjoin the lands of Audley Hall. Not, you understand, that I would be so crass as to suggest that you—"

"Wed her for her portion." Audley's onyx eyes took on a feverish light as he made to rise. "By gad! I think I'll leave a *carte de visite* . . ."

Robbie clapped a hand to Audley's arm. "It's rising two of the clock," he said, laughing. "Fasham Esquire might look on you with greater favor if you arrived at a more conventional hour."

"Ah, yes, esquire." Audley sank into his chair, curling his hands around his claret glass and turning a beatific smile from Robbie to Old Nick. "Won't that depress the duchess's pretensions! The daughter of a mere esquire, and one with a whiff of Trade about her. I begin to think I must have the fair Miss Fasham."

He clapped Old Nick on the back, sending him coughing over the table. "You'll stand my best man, won't you?"

Old Nick slithered back into his chair, casting a wry glance at Audley. "Wouldn't miss it, for it'll put the Graces"—as he referred to their mothers, once the Misses Pegotta and Persia Ponsonby, now the battling duchesses—"into a tweak from which they may never recover."

"By gad! I hadn't thought on it! How delightful!"

"And I," Robbie said, "will have my mother add the Fashams to the guest list for her musical evening."

"And delete my mother's name, if she would be so kind," said Old Nick. "Have you see her latest *parti*? The MacInerny lad."

Robbie's eyes widened. "Isn't he a trifle . . ."

"You were going to say 'young'?" said Old Nick with dripping sarcasm. "No need to be delicate. The whole of London cannot have failed to notice that my dear mama is a snatch-cradle."

He took a copious draught of hot gin, a drink he resorted to only when his spirits were at low ebb. Robbie, thinking to change the direction of his thoughts, asked, "Have you seen the new Darlington Railroad line?"

Old Nick shrugged, as if immeasurably weary of the subject. "What good would it do?"

"But I thought you were interested—"

"A passion of the moment, a passing fancy, nothing more."

But it was more, much more, and Robbie, entering his bedchamber in the pearly dawn light, knew it. While he and Audley had fought their personal demons by striking back in their own outrageous ways, Old Nick had chosen the path of least resistance—ennui, the pretense that nothing was worth caring about.

But there were things worth caring about, worth fighting for.

Robbie had used his fear of the beast to avoid confronting his own weakness and doubt, but he was no longer a youth, prey to every passion. He was a man, and he should begin acting like one. And weren't his first responsibilities, his first duties, to his wife?

His wife, who was in the adjoining bedchamber. He tossed his cravat aside, shrugged out of his coat, and strode to the connecting door.

Tabitha knew she was caught in the throes of a nightmare, but she could not break its hold. She was in the sewer with the filthy water dragging against her skirt and the rats bobbing around her, their beady eyes glistening like the water gathered on the brick walls. Though she told herself it was a dream and she would soon awake, she could feel her heart pounding as if it might burst with terror. Behind her, Milling-Jemmy Shadwell lumbered toward her. Ahead, von Fersen's body bobbed in the current.

"Friend Robert!" she screamed. "Friend Robert!"

"Tabitha!" His hands, warm and strong, clamped around her shoulders, shaking her out of her nightmare and into the dim light of the new day. She clutched at his arms, staring up into his face and seeing the darkling light of concern in his eyes.

She pitched into his embrace, holding him and trembling. "A—a bad dream," she whispered, her teeth chattering.

"You're safe now. I'm here," Robbie murmured against her ear, while he stroked her silken hair. How right she felt in his arms, as if like a ship, he had sailed into safe harbor after a storm. "Don't be afraid."

"I—I'm not."

Slowly her trembling subsided. She soaked in the heat of his skin and the faint fragrances of Irish whiskey and tobacco and man. And still he clasped her to him with his lips buried in the tumble of hair at her temple.

"Would you like to tell me about it?" Robbie asked

softly, longing to protect her from all harm, even from her own frightened thoughts.

"It was . . . was the sewer."

His embrace tightened. "Do you dream of it often?"

"Never," she whispered.

"Had something happened to remind you of it?"

Something had, but Tabitha shook her head quickly in spite of her longing to say, *Yes!* Guilt had driven her into the nightmare, and guilt would not release her from it. Milling-Jemmy Shadwell was at Friend Ephraim Fell's House. Would Friend Robert forgive her, should he ever learn how she had lied to him?

Robbie hooked his forefinger beneath her chin, tilting her head up. "Why do you cry?"

He kissed one eye, then the other, and her tears flowed in diamond drops across her smooth cheeks, the sight of them like acid on his heart. He studied her sleep-flushed cheeks and her tremulous mouth, as irresistible to him as the far horizons had once been. He wafted his lips across hers, in a downy touch of consolation that took fire like flame to tinder, burning away his doubts and fears and leaving only his suppressed longings, his unspoken needs.

He bore Tabitha down to the pillows, plundering her willing and eager mouth. She trembled beneath him, but hers was not the trembling of fear. Not when her small hands threaded through his hair, brushed at his temples, and held him close.

"Tabby, Tabby, I have so much I want to say," he whispered against the hollow of her throat, his lips pressed to her leaping pulse. He raised up, his hand fanning over the side of her face to push the wildly tangled curls back. "I want you as a man wants a woman, as a husband wants his wife. I want to stay with you, to live with you, to be with you. I want our vows to be real and lasting. Am I asking too much?"

Tabitha wondered at the yearning in the rough velvet of his voice. Her throat ached at the tenderness of his touch, the soft light in his eyes. She turned her face, rubbing her cheek in the palm of his hand. How gladly she would place her heart in his safekeeping.

Her eyes glistening and her heart brimming with the love she could only now give full rein, she smiled up at him. "Thee could never ask more of me than I wished to give, for I long to be one with thee in body and in spirit."

"Tabby," he said, his voice strumming low, his lips claiming hers.

And she gave herself up to the pleasures of the senses, to the glories of touch and taste and sound. He murmured her name, as if he were singing an angel's chorus. He touched her, as if he were blind and must see her through his fingertips. He tasted her mouth, her throat, as if she were the sustenance of his life. And she delighted in the prickle of his beard, in the moist heat of his mouth, in the delicacy of his touch.

"Husband," she whispered.

"Wife," he responded, tugging gently at the bow at her throat, pushing back the deep yoke of her night rail with his lips, nuzzling a path along her collarbone to her shoulder, gliding down and down to the swell of her breast.

His lips closed around the taut peak, and she gasped, arching against him. What sweet torment it was. The tender-rough rasp of his tongue, circling round and round in spirals that seeped through skin and flesh, spinning up to tingle inside her mouth, spinning out to tickle her palms, spinning down to ache in her womb. She rubbed her palms across his shoulders, thrust her fingers through his hair, deliciously uncertain as to whether she wanted to push him away or pull him closer.

He abandoned the throbbing peak, dipping into the valley between her breasts, rising to the opposite peak and teasing it with his teeth, while his black curls fell across her tender white flesh.

The morning sun piercing the sheer undercurtains came as a benediction, a gift of light to the lovers.

A light that poured across Tabitha's face as Robbie's

head rose, as his gaze sought hers. In her eyes, the translucent gray of mist, he saw the hazy light of passion. A smile wending across his mouth, he stretched up and kissed her, lightly, fleetingly. "What a treasure you are," he said softly.

She captured his side-whiskers, holding him fast, her eyes asparkle. "And what a nip-cheese thou art with thy kisses, Friend Robert."

She set a hand to his chest and rolled him flat and flowed against him, her mouth melting over his, sliding down beneath his chin to the strong sun-browned column of his throat.

He pulled her atop him full length, his arms linked around the slender span of her waist. "Will you ravish me now, Friend Tabby?" he asked, a low, amused chuckle escaping him.

"If need be." She toyed with a diamond stud and flicked it open, her fingers dancing across the exposed vee of his chest.

His hands splayed across her back, rising to her shoulders, sliding down, slowly, slowly, exploring the curve of her back, the hollow of her waist, the gentle swell of her buttocks. His eyes locking with hers, fiery violet to smoky gray, he pulled at her night rail, drawing it up inch by inch.

The cool morning breeze flowed across Tabitha's ankles, her calves, the backs of her thighs, until finally, the heat of his hands cupped her flesh to flesh. She tried to breathe, but there was no air in the chamber, only heat and need and a desire that made her shift restlessly.

He drew a sharp breath, arching his hips, and she felt the rigid shaft of his manhood pressing against her. "I want you, Tabby," he said breathlessly.

"And I you," she whispered, her lips playing over his chest, while she ignored the tiny insistent whisper that wondered why he did not speak of love, only of want.

"It'll be devilish hard with both of us dressed," he said with a thread of laughter.

Her head snapped up, her cheeks aflame in spite of the ripple of laughter that matched his. "What a wretched man thou art. Dost thou not know what a serious business this is?"

"I assure you," he said, rolling with her and rising on a elbow to gaze down at her, "I am approaching it with the utmost seriousness."

His hand slid like silk across Tabitha's belly, a gentle touch that leached from her all strength and will.

"The pleasure should not only be mine," he said, his voice low and smoothed and as entrancing as his violet gaze.

He found the crisp nest at the apex of her thighs and drew the tips of his fingers through it. Tabitha's eyes widened, her blood rushing through her veins, hot and heavy and aching. She could not think, could not absorb what he was saying. She had become a being inhabited only by feeling: the pressure building in her womb; the gathering moisture that prepared her for him; and the need that escalated, catapulting her into a strange and alien world where pleasure was so closely mated to pain that they were indistinguishable.

"The pleasure should be yours, too, especially this first time," he murmured.

The cool morning breeze flowed across her, as gentle as the hand nudging her willing thighs apart. His lips lowering to hers, he touched the very heart of her, sending tiny rippling convulsions through her womb. Wanting to be closer still, she slid her hand up his outstretched arm to his shoulder, tugging at him.

"Shh, Tabby, shh," he whispered against her mouth, pausing to nip at her lower lip, to flick the corners with his tongue. "I want your first time with me to be a memory of pleasure undiluted by pain. Please, Tabby, let me give this to you."

In his eyes, shining in the sunlight, were the feelings he had not expressed: the tender emotions, the love, the joy. Though Tabitha longed to join with him, to feel him fill the cradle of her womb, to hold his seed deep within her and pray that it took root, she reached up and brushed her mouth across his.

"I am thine to do with as thee will," she whispered.

In her eyes were love and trust and an immutable belief in him. Surely she could see his weakness, his self-doubt. How could she so easily, so completely put herself in his keeping? How could she trust him when he was afraid to trust himself?

He felt a painful stirring in his chest, a breaking free from old bonds, a gentling of the fiery urgings of his turgid manhood. Snared in the luminescent glow of Tabitha's loving gaze, he admitted that he had once again lied to himself. He had not come to her for duty or responsibility. He had come—could he say it?—because she had taken his heart, molding and shaping it to make it her own. He loved her. He loved her kind and caring heart, her quest for Truth, her gentleness, her strength. Most of all, he loved her for believing in him so strongly that he had, almost, begun believing in himself. Suddenly it seemed that all things were possible, that he could become all she thought he was.

He wanted to say, *I love you, Tabitha,* but the thought and the feelings were too new to him. He needed to explore them and savor them, and then he would tell her. For now, he would simply adore her and show her.

He kissed her, gently, tenderly, thoroughly, his mouth meshed with hers, his lips speaking with the motions of love, while his fingers delved among the hot, moist secrets of her femininity, finding and caressing the taut bud of passion.

Tabitha stirred against his hand, crying out when his lips moved to her breast, closing around her painfully sensitive nipple. Every feathering touch of his thumb, every flick of his tongue, propelled her deeper and deeper into the wine-dark sea of desire. She was lost, but not alone, for he was there, guiding her with consummate skill through the crashing waves and surging tides—until, at last, she poised, like a mermaid riding the sea foam, anticipating the dive into the dark unknown. She arched back, taut and trembling, her fingers clutching at his arm, her eyes wide and wondering, while the waves crashed over her in shudders and ripples, in spreading warmth and lassitude, in weakness and delight.

And in the sweet honeyed aftermath, he took her in his arms and held her molded against him and pressed a kiss against the curve of her neck. "Pleasure, Tabby. Only pleasure," he whispered.

"Yes," she murmured, her eyes aglow, "but what of thee?" Struggling back to stare up at him, she took his face between her palms and searched his eyes. "This is not the way of fornication, I know—"

"F-fornication!" Robbie's eyes danced with laughter. "What a thing to call—"

"So the Bible calls it, and this is not what my mother described to me."

She looked so earnest, so adorably confused. Would she never cease to delight him with her incomparable innocence and her worldly wisdom? "No doubt she did not, Tabby, but there are many ways for a man and woman to share themselves and their bodies with each other."

"But it is written that marriage is for procreation."

He lifted her hand to his lips, moving from knuckle to dainty knuckle, while his gaze roamed her flushed face. "Is it not also for sharing, for caring, for joy?"

She sat up, leaning toward him, her gaze as soft as his melting heart. "For joy," she whispered, her mouth grazing his, "and I would pleasure thee as thee has pleasured me."

"You are sure, Tabby?" Robbie asked, unable to believe his good fortune, unable to believe that she could want him as he wanted her, with the twin passions of body and soul.

"Shall I help thee with thy boots?"

The desire that had simmered now burst into flame. Grinning like a boy, he rolled from the bed, hastily discarding waistcoat and shirt as he hurried across the chamber to grasp the mantel and slip his heel into the jack.

"Not the bootjack!" She sat up, her hair cascading around her. "What will Cheddar say?"

"To hell with Cheddar and his passion for my boots. I have another passion that I must slake on your"—he waggled his brows suggestively—"fair white body."

"Thee will put me to the blush, Friend Robert," she said, slowly pulling her night rail over her head.

Within moments he joined her, waiting patiently while her curious gaze explored every inch of him, lingering over the proud jut of his manhood, rising to his taut belly, climbing to his chest, his eyes.

"Thou art so finely made," she whispered, her breath catching. Tentatively she reached out, touching his shoulder with her palm, rubbing down his chest, as if memorizing its every curve. Her thumb stroked the dark pap buried in a whorl of crisp hair and drove Robbie to the precipice.

He caught her hand, his voice strained, his eyes haunted. "I would give you every freedom of me that you desire, but . . . but . . ."

She studied him for a moment. "I pray thee will forgive me. My mother warned me that it is hard for a man to wait."

A smile nipped at his mouth. "She was right, but I would prefer that your mother not come to bed with us."

A gentle sparkle brightened her eyes like the smile that brightened her face. "Only thee and me," she whispered, lying back on the pillows, stretching out her arms to him. "Come to me."

Robbie covered her with his body, whispering against her mouth, "Only thee and me."

Braced on an elbow, he moved his hand between their bodies, lingering over one breast, then the other, until he saw the new rise of desire in Tabitha's face, in the way her lashes sagged over her eyes and her tongue slicked over her lips. He moved lower still, pausing at her navel, exploring it with a thumb, until her breath caught and she began to move restlessly beneath him. Down to the crisp, curling nest that tickled his fingers. Further, to the wet heat of her, his finger sliding between the dewy petals, seeking the sheath that awaited him.

Never before had it been so important, so necessary that he give as much pleasure as he gained. Never had he wanted to imprint himself so thoroughly on a woman that she would remain his through eternity. However painful the ache in his loins, however hot the blood that coursed through him like sheets of flame, he must wait until she was as ready as he was.

Her fingers bit into his back. Her foot shifted restlessly against his knee. Her mouth blindly sought his, opening, her teeth tugging at his lower lip, her tongue seeking entry, finding his and tangling with it.

He shifted his hips forward, seeking, finding, probing gently. She closed around him, so tight, so hot. ''God,'' he whispered.

''Yes, yes,'' she murmured, going still, waiting.

He gathered himself for a swift, clean thrust, feeling her virgin's veil tear, feeling Tabitha stiffen, covering his mouth with hers to stifle her cry. Buried deep inside her, throbbing with the need for his release, he waited until she relaxed, until she breathed softly, until her clenching fingers opened and began to move in comforting circles over his back.

''Tabby,'' he whispered.

''Shh,'' she murmured. ''Thee and me.''

Though he trembled with the effort, he held himself back, moving slowly, retreat, advance, retreat, until her eyes widened and her lips parted for a soft, startled cry, as if she had thought this glory could not be hers again. Only then did he allow his own release to overcome him. Shuddering, he poured his seed deep into her womb, ridding himself of the last of his doubts, the last of his fears.

In the days that followed, Tabitha thought she had surely stepped through the Pearly Gates and entered

Heaven. Her nights were filled with tender passion, her days with laughter and affection. Had there ever been a man more perfect than her husband? She was utterly convinced there had not been.

As if Friend Robert was not enough to overrun her cup of joy, in Friend Ephraim Fell's House there was Tansy. Though she would sometimes stand at the front window crying softly, "Bubba, Bubba," she was a child whose happiness no one seemed able to resist—least of all Tabitha.

Tansy waited for her every morning, clapping her hands and laughing, her eyes as bright as a sunlit sea and her hair a halo of golden curls. She became Tabitha's shadow, making every step her "Tabby" made, while outside, in the filthy gutters of Medway Street, another shadow dwelt—a boy of about twelve, scruffy, dirty, shoeless, hatless, almost naked in his rags. He lurked in the alley, hid behind casks, hung in doorways, always watching Friend Ephraim Fell's House.

He was not unfamiliar. Tabitha recognized from Queen Anne's Gate his matted rust-red hair and his habit of dancing a farthing piece across his knuckles. "Jem," she said quietly, calling Shadwell to the window, "Dost thou know that boy?"

He set aside the coal scuttle and lumbered toward her, his huge hands lax at his sides. "Aye," he said, his deep voice rumbling. "The girl's brother."

"Tansy's? Why doesn't he come to us here?"

"A wild 'un, 'e is, wit' the pride o' Lucifer. 'E'd starve first."

"But he's left Tansy with us."

"Fair knocked me on me pins, that did. Times must be untidy fer 'im."

"Will thee ask him to come in for a meal if he doesn't want to stay?"

"No," he said flatly.

Tabitha's gaze shifted from the boy hunched against the gin-shop wall to Shadwell. "But why?"

" 'E won't come."

And he proved to be right. Tabitha marched through

the door and across the street, and the boy took flight, his rags flapping and his heels slapping through the mud. It was hours before he returned, and Tabitha, wiser now, left a bowl of meat and bread and cheese on the lowest step. While she watched through the window, he approached it like an animal, nose up as if sniffing for danger. Suddenly he darted toward it, snatched the bowl with his grubby hands, and raced away, tearing at the meat with his teeth.

How painful it was to remember that sight when Tabitha moved from the ravenous hunger, the bitter poverty, the stench of hopelessness to the glittering elegance of a Society soirée, as she did each night. So often she wanted to tell Friend Robert about the house in Tothill Fields, about Tansy, who had won her heart as completely as he had.

But she could not forget how he had reacted to her simply driving in the Seymour barouche down Medway Street: *I absolutely forbid you to enter that sink of vice and iniquity again!*

If he wished to stop her, he could. She, by the laws of God and man, was subject to him in all ways. But if he stopped her, what would happen to the children, now beginning to smile and play? Their trust was so fragile. Their needs were so great.

And she, who gladly trusted her husband with her own heart, could not trust him with their lives.

Chapter 18

Darenth House was freshly furbished in garlands
of ivy and potted tea roses whose sweet perfume
vied with orris root potpourri. The rosewood piano,
centerpiece for the musical evening ahead, sat in a
bower of candlelight before the bank of windows curtained in white lace. The tiny butler, Rumford, and the
footmen were arrayed in the entry hall, flawlessly at-
tired in dazzling livery to await the arrival of the king,
sure to be fashionably, royally late.

In the lavender twilight the guests crowded in,
bringing an aura of excitement that Tabitha found op-
pressive. She sought a quiet corner, unable to join in
the chatter and laughter. A fever had come to Friend
Ephraim Fell's House, infecting the children one by
one. Though it seemed to last but a day or two, leaving
no ill effects, she should have been there to lighten the
burden of nursing and to help gloomy Friend Colleen
in the kitchen. She could only give thanks that, so far,
Tansy had been spared.

Friend Robert sauntered toward her, his hands thrust
in his pockets, a lazy smile curving his mouth as his
gaze rose admiringly from her satin slippers to her
gown of oyster-white silk to her plain white cap. Her
low mood began to lift like the ripe summer scents
wafting in from the garden and swirling on currents of
balmy air. How light-minded she was becoming that

she could take such vain pleasure in the if-only-we-were-alone look in his eyes.

"Are you aware," he began on a bright note of amusement, "that your curst cat is yowling in the garden?"

"Monsieur?" asked Tabitha.

"None other."

She listened to the unmistakable and forlorn meowing filtering through the babble of voices. "But what is he doing here?"

"I assume that he, no more than I, does not wish to be separated from you."

Before Tabitha could express her unseemly delight, Anne hurried up, her cheeks flushed and her eyes dancing with mischief. "Cousin Knox has arrived. She has bearded Father in his den—the library," she added in an aside to Tabitha, "and I vow he's in such a pelter he might very well bark at Old George when he enters the door."

She paused on the point of laughter, and Friend Robert grinned down at her. "Well, tell us what's thrust his lordship into the boughs before you pop your corset laces."

"Wretch!" She swatted him with her fan. "You know that not a word, even screamed, can be distinguished through the door. We tried it often enough when Mother was trying to soothe Father after one of your pranks."

"Be careful of what you say in front of my wife," he warned lightly, casting Tabitha a glance of commingled tenderness and amusement. "She thinks me perfect in every way."

"Tabby is not so hen-witted," Anne said, linking arms with them both and leading them toward the library. "You've been summoned to attend the fireworks. Cousin Knox has always had exquisite timing. Well, it won't be the first time our guests have seen them kick up a dust." She eyed the arrival of the fair Miss Fasham on Audley's arm. "And speaking of guests, Audley and Fasham? Robbie, you must tell me what you know of this."

"I?" he questioned with an innocence Tabitha found suspicious. "What should I know of the Spaniard's fits and starts?"

Anne cast him a glance rife with loving exasperation. "Very well," she said, laughing. "Leave me to perish of curiosity."

The library door vibrated with the raised voices beyond. While Anne left them, Friend Robert whispered, "Courage, Tabby, courage."

Opening the door, he ushered her in.

"Arabella," the earl was shouting, the veins in his neck distended, his face a mottled red, "you could try the patience of a saint!"

"And you, Coz, are no saint," Cousin Knox huffed on swelling notes that set her ostrich-feather aigrette to trembling. "I well remember the time you filled my bed with toads."

"Good God, Arabella! I was only nine"—he raised a hand—"and before you tell me what a wretched boy I was, as you have done for this half-century and more, let me say that you are the most disagreeable, the most shatterbrained, the most singularly irritating, the most . . . the most . . ." He paused to catch his breath. "You, Arabella," he began, like a magistrate passing last judgment on a felon, "are a bluestocking!"

Cousin Knox, aquiver with righteous indignation, reared her plump shoulders back. "To which I proudly plead guilty! And if you had the least particle of sensibility, the least mite of discrimination—"

"Children, children," said Robbie, advancing on the desk which separated the combatants, "lest you have forgotten, we have guests."

The earl swiveled on him a fulminating stare. "You arrogant young pup! I'll not—"

"And where does he get his arrogance, if not from you?" interrupted Cousin Knox. "Not, you delicious creature," she added turning to Robbie, "that arrogance does not become you. Indeed, it does, for you mate it with sensibility and discrimination—''

"You are coming it rather too strong, Arabella," complained the earl, turning to Tabitha and forcing a thin smile. "Come in, my dear. For all the sound and fury, we are dangerous only to each other. If we have not come to cuffs, after all these years—''

"You forget when you were ten—'' began Cousin Knox.

"Hardly," the earl retorted, his face suffused with ill humor, "for I've had a lifetime to regret that my father pulled me off you before I had the opportunity to throttle you for good!"

"Ah-ha! I knew it!" crowed Cousin Knox. "Your mind is going in your old age, Coz, for I remember quite distinctly that it was I who was—''

"Enough!" roared the earl, startling Tabitha, silencing Cousin Knox, sending Friend Robert strolling toward the window and stifling a smile. "You will all be seated," he said in a voice that shook with suppressed fury.

Tabitha slipped hastily into a wing chair before the desk, where she was joined by Friend Robert, who sat on the arm and winked at her, the corners of his mouth suspiciously unsteady. Shuddering to think what his father would do should he succumb to inappropriate humor, she tried to warn him with a glance that he quite deftly and deliberately avoided.

"I should prefer to stand," said Cousin Knox staunchly.

The earl braced his fists on the polished desk surface, leaning over it and eyeing her ominously. "I said, sit!"

She plumped into a chair, sniffing mightily. The earl tugged at his cuffs, stretched his neck in the confines of an intricately arranged cravat, and slowly sank into his chair with an air of satisfaction. His eyes, still snapping angrily, turned to Robbie.

"You will be wondering why you have been summoned here."

"Why so?" said Friend Robert, much too casually. "This is better than a Drury Lane farce."

Tabitha trod heavily on his toe, drawing a wounded look. "We know thee would not have summoned us if thee did not have something of importance to say, Friend John," she murmured soothingly.

The earl, leaving his son with a last glowering look, said pacifically, "Just so, though it is not I but this . . . this . . ." He gestured toward Cousin Knox, at a loss for the perfect pejorative adjective to describe her. "Well, get on with it, Arabella!"

She sat on the edge of her chair, dripping Chantilly lace over the squabs, her fine brown eyes wide with satisfaction. "I have decided, you delicious creature"—her gaze shifted from the earl to his son—"that it is time for you to stand for a seat in the Commons. It is expected of the first—in your case, the only—son of the great families, and I see no reason why you should be the exception. After all, you are wed now—"

"I tried to tell her," the earl interrupted, "that you will not be remaining in England."

"To which I replied, 'Fustian!'" bellowed Cousin Knox.

"As well you should have," said Friend Robert, studying his father with a narrow gaze that held no small amount of malice.

How had they come to such a pass? Tabitha wondered. How could father and son view each other with such enmity? She thought of her own father and brothers, who had never exchanged a cross or unkind word, who had always lived in love and charity with one another.

"I have decided to stay in England," Friend Robert continued, surprising Tabitha as much as he did his father. Though she had hoped, she had not dared to believe that his lust for adventure might be behind him. "It was you, my lord," he added, "who told me it was time I grew up and accepted my duties and responsibilities."

Duties and responsibilities. Was that what she was to

him? Tabitha's breath, her heart, her thoughts hung
suspended before an onrushing cloud of darkness and
pain. He had never yet spoken a word of love, only of
desire, and that was a fleeting need of the flesh. Only
love was eternal. What would happen when desire was
gone and there was no love to bind them together?

Friend Robert's face was burnished bronze by the
candlelight, his side-whiskers crisp and curly, black as
the swiftly falling night. He had shown her such tenderness, such passion. Surely he felt what he did not
say. Yet she had never known him to bite his tongue.
If he loved her, he would have told her.

"If you have decided to act the man," said the earl,
"none will be more glad than I."

"Or more surprised?" questioned Friend Robert.

Tabitha touched his hand, longing to linger over it,
to raise it to her cheek, to her lips, to beg him to tell
her she was not only a responsibility that he must assume. "I pray thee, do not dispute with thy father."

He cocked a brow, obviously displeased. "And what
of his disputing with me?"

Tabitha stood abruptly, gliding away from the chair,
her cheeks flushing with anger and chagrin. Partly it
was her own humiliation and hurt. Partly it was the
pain of seeing them at daggers drawn. Wholly, it was
her impatience with their refusal to speak the truths
that lay in their hearts. In that brief moment she recognized her fear of speaking her own truth—that she
loved him as woman, as wife, as friend, and that she
yearned to have his love. It seemed somehow even
more important that Friend Robert reach the understanding with his father that he could not with her.

"Can thee not see that thy father loves thee? Can
thee not say thee loves him? How much longer will
thee tear at him and he at thee like thy beloved falcons
after warm flesh?"

"Hear! Hear!" cried Cousin Knox, rising from her
chair and marching to Tabitha, just as if she were not
as culpable of twitting the earl to distraction. "Give
them a taste of their own, gel!"

"Tabitha!" said Friend Robert, rising and frowning down at her. "You don't know what there is between us."

"I know what is not between thee—honesty. See if thee can find it together." She turned blindly to the door, wrenching it open, finding Anne on the portal, her hand raised to knock.

"Mother sent me to tell Father he cannot neglect his guests much longer." Her gaze shifted from Tabitha's pale face to her father's rigid expression to Robbie's flushed cheeks. "What has happened?"

"The gel," boomed Cousin Knox, "has just ripped up at Coz and the boy, right proper, if I say so myself. Told them it was time they stopped tearing at each other."

Tabitha, her emotional storm spent, leaned weakly against the doorframe, little heartened by the bracing smile Anne turned on her. Friend Robert would never forgive her for this.

"It's time someone said it," Anne said firmly, looking into the library at her father with a meaningful expression. "Tell Robbie, Father. It's long past time he knew."

The click of the closing door sounded like a death knell in the silent library. Robbie stood awkwardly beside the wing chair, still stunned by Tabby's anger. She was usually so amenable and agreeable, he often forgot she was capable of kicking up a dust when she believed she was right. He could only wish she had chosen some other object for her fit of temper. The problem between his father and himself could not be solved so simply as she thought.

But what had Anne meant: *Tell Robbie, Father. It's long past time he knew.*

He turned slowly, finding the earl slumped in the chair behind the desk, his finger tips drumming a Devil's Tattoo on the red leather arms. He stared sightlessly before him. "Sit down," he said softly, adding a belated "Please."

Robbie sank into the wing chair, sitting stiffly erect.

"Did you mean it when you said you were staying in England? You have given up on Greece? Adventure?"

Robbie, ever ready with a sharp and prodding quip to use as a weapon against his father, remained silent. *I know what is not between thee—honesty*, Tabitha had said. Wasn't it time for it?

"Strangely," he said, the tenor of challenge gone from his voice, "I find that my wife brings me all the adventure I need."

"Remarkable woman," said the earl, "and one whom not every man could appreciate. I . . . I am proud to learn you can."

Robbie's startled gaze swept up from contemplation of the red Turkey carpet to meet his father's steady stare. *Proud.* How long he had waited to hear his father apply that word to him. His gaze angled off, unable to remain and betray the flurry of emotions that beset him: anger that his father had not said it when he needed it more; pleasure that his father had said it at last; discomfort with the knowledge that he needed so much to hear it.

The earl glanced at the door, as if he could still see Anne standing there. "Your sister is right. It is past time I told you why you and I rub together like cross sticks. I have no doubt that she would have told you long ago had I not demanded that I be allowed to tell you in my own time and in my own way. Unfortunately, I never could find that right time to do it."

He lifted a quill from the desk, running the feathered tip across the palm of his hand and smiling ruefully. "Perhaps there is never a right time for a father to confess his failings to his son."

"I should find it hard to believe you have failings, Father," Robbie said.

"Oh, I've been a paragon of virtue and temperance, dedicated to duty and honor, to king and country. Like all dull sticks, I'm intolerant of those who do not match my own high standards."

"What a disappointment I have been for you," Robbie said quietly.

"And I for you," said the earl.

Robbie could not deny it, though he knew his father was not completely at fault. As a child, as a man, he had always tested the limits of his father's patience.

"You never knew my father, Robert, but you are his image born again," the earl began with a hint of strain. "In looks and more. You have the same reckless and feckless ways. The same lust for adventure. You differ in only one aspect. My father was not an . . ." He paused, and Robbie's gaze lifted to meet his, seeing the dark shadows of shame and pain. "My father was not an honorable man. His only loyalty was to himself."

Robbie swallowed hard. "And you were afraid I would be like him in that, too?"

"Yes," said the earl. "You see, after my father died, I found in his papers proof that he had sold military secrets to the American colonists during their war for independence." He rose from the desk, hands thrust in his pockets as he paced to the bank of windows. "I have spent my life atoning for my father's sins and punishing you for them."

Robbie leaned back in the chair, breathless and stunned. He had learned early not to ask questions about his dead grandfather, for nothing would put his father in a temper faster. But never had he suspected such a stain on the family escutcheon, such an explanation for the differences between him and his father.

"Even as a babe you were willful and headstrong, determined to go no way but your own, and I," said the earl, "was equally determined that I would train you out of your willful ways, that I would ruthlessly rid you of any glimmerings of dishonor. So I saw your childish pranks as a lack of principles, your thirst for adventure as a shameful irresponsibility, and your stubborn pride as the besetting sin that would lead you down the same path my father followed. I saw only what I was afraid you would become, not what you were—and I will regret that to my last breath."

Robbie rose from the chair and studied his father's rigid figure. "I did not make it easy for you," he said, unsure just how he felt, what he wanted to say.

His father turned, the candlelight gleaming in his steel-gray hair, catching the soft light in his eyes. "You were not, nor are you now, an angel," he said with an austere smile. "You are a rackety, ramshackle ne'er-do-well, but you are a man of principle and of honor and I . . . I am proud to call you my son."

However much Robbie had wanted to hear that, however long he had waited for it, the pain and disappointment between them was too old to be banished so quickly. "Thank you, sir," he said stiffly.

An awkward silence fell, thick with the emotion of the moment, the suppressed longings to reach out one for the other. At length the earl strode to his desk. "So, will you consider that dratted Arabella's suggestion? The only good one, I might add, that I've ever known her to have."

"Standing for the Commons?" Robbie said. "I am no politician."

"And thank God for it! That's the last thing we need," he said heatedly. "Had you had political leanings, throughout your life you would have told me what I wanted to hear and then done what you wanted to do."

"Perhaps it would have been easier for us both if I had."

It seemed that peaceful Tabitha was destined to be embroiled in controversy for the whole of the evening. No sooner had she and Anne exited the library—Cousin Knox, sighting Miss Fasham and Audley, hurried off—than she was caught in a group discussing the poor. Her thoughts lingering with Friend Robert and his father, worrying over what was happening between them, Tabitha was not at first aware of what was being said.

"Leapt on my carriage," said the Dowager Duchess of Lethbridge, her voice as breathless and soft as a girl's. "Flourished a knife and demanded a coin, and he not above one-and-ten years! Spawn of the rookeries! An evil and vicious lot!"

"Perhaps," Tabitha said softly, "he was hungry."

"And what have we Poor Relief for? He had but to go to the parish churchwarden—"

"And be sent to a foundling home or the workhouse—"

"And where else," demanded the Dowager Duchess, "would he be sent? A pauper, a charge on the public treasury. He should be working, earning his way."

"And how would thee," Tabitha said, struggling against her rising temper, "suggest a boy do that?"

"Why, he could work in a boot-blacking factory, run errands for a merchant—"

"Work in thy stables?"

"Certainly not! Filthy, thieving urchin! I shouldn't trust him with my high-steppers!"

"Perhaps he would not be filthy had he the means to bathe," Tabitha said. "Perhaps he would not be a thief had he the means to earn his way."

"Obviously, you know nothing of the poor. They prefer destitution to honest work, and Poor Relief simply encourages them to be lazy and worthless."

Tabitha, eyeing the diamonds sparkling around the Dowager Duchess's raddled neck, took fire. "Thee should think of that when next thee sees a crossing-sweeper standing in the rain or a flower girl shivering in the cold or a bone-grubber haunting the gutters or a swollen-bellied child holding a gentleman's hack. All of them trying to earn an honest living—and starving because clutch-pursed Society will not offer them the charity they need to better themselves. It is not laziness thee sees in the faces of the poor, but hopelessness and hunger and defeat."

In the disapproving silence that fell, the Dowager Duchess gave Tabitha a look of spite and enmity, swiveled on her heel, and marched off. With her went the gathered crowd, melting away by ones and twos.

"Oh, Tabby," whispered Anne, "she is the most selfish and disobliging creature, but I fear she represents the feelings of Society for the poor. You have not done yourself any good here."

"I could not stand silent," she murmured, her head aching and weariness sweeping over her as it always did when she allowed her temper to get the best of her. "For myself I cannot regret it, but for thee and thy family—"

"Then don't regret it at all." Anne slipped her arm around Tabitha's waist, hugging her lightly. "We shall make it through this rough patch, and someday Society will cherish you as we do."

Tabitha doubted it sincerely. The feeling of oppression would not leave her. The aching of her head became a full-fledged throbbing. A few minutes later, she slipped away, seeking the privacy of an anteroom to soothe and calm herself. But a gentleman was there, enormously fat, filling the small sofa, his swollen foot propped on a stool.

"Forgive me, I would not intrude on thee." She paused, studying his face with its pale and sweating skin, its cheeks hanging in dewlaps, its mouth thin-lipped and blunt at the corners. "Art thou ill, Friend? The physician, Friend Kennon, is—"

"We pray you, my dear, do not summon another physician to torment us." He shifted on the sofa, smiling with a singular sweetness, while Tabitha pondered the royal "we" used only by the king. Cousin Knox had warned her that he was an impulsive man, quick to take offense at any threat to his vanity, equally quick to be generous and kindhearted. She could only hope that his inclination now leaned toward the latter.

"Forgive our not rising to pay fair Beauty proper homage, but we are, as you can see"—he waved a chubby, beringed hand toward his foot—"felled by the curst gout."

"How painful for thee." She moved into the antechamber. "My father had a remedy that gave him some relief. If thee would give me thy direction, I should be happy to send it to thee."

He eyed her with a touch of malicious mischief. "The Royal Lodge."

While he waited in apparent anticipation of confusion and awkwardness, a series of shrieks and screams rose to a crescendo in the adjoining drawing room. The door flew open, and Robbie appeared, his complexion high and his eyes dancing with hilarity.

"Tabitha, your curst cat—" Robbie's gaze alighted on the king, and he bowed deeply. "I pray your pardon for this interruption, your Majesty," he said over the shrill cries, bumps, and stumblings issuing through the door.

"We grant it," said George IV, waving a hand. "Pray tell us, what is the cause of this riotous behavior?"

The cause, Tabitha noted with a sinking heart, slithered around Friend Robert's ankle, tail flying like a flag, bright yellow eyes searching for her. "Monsieur," she said with a whisper of a sigh as he dropped a dead mouse at the hem of her skirt.

"What is that?" asked his Majesty.

"A cat, sir," said Robbie with exquisite if unfortunate logic.

"We are not addlepated," said the king with a sniff. "We can see that it is a cat. What is it doing here?"

"It is bringing my wife a gift." Robbie gestured to the dead mouse.

"A gift? A gift!" he spluttered, his eyes crinkling with an amusement that quickly escalated to laughter.

Robbie, knowing that the king was a devotee of the lowest sort of gossip, a lover of all that put his subjects out of countenance, grinned wickedly. "First it leapt onto the windowsill with its gift, so startling Princess Lieven that she trod on Lord Liverpool's toe, causing him to step back into a footman carrying a tray of claret and brandy. He spun about, dashing into Lady Jersey—"

"Silence herself," said the king, erupting into a deep

belly laugh. He wiped his tearing eyes with an ornately embroidered handkerchief, then fluttered it at Robbie. "Pray tell, what happened to her?"

"She fell into a chair atop the Duke of Lethbridge, who was at that moment taking a pinch of snuff. He sneezed so heartily, he knocked her to the floor, where she tangled with Canning, bringing him down. It was all around a mad scramble to escape this vicious creature."

His Majesty turned a sparkling gaze on the "vicious creature," now emitting a low, deep rumble of utter bliss while Tabitha scratched between his ears.

"I am afraid, sir," Robbie said, his voice unsteady, "that he lacks both manner and sense, and should, of course, be kept from the drawing room."

"In no way," said the king, still chuckling. "I have not had so hearty a laugh in many a day. Lady Langley—"

"It would please me greatly if thee would call me Friend Tabitha," she said softly, staring up at him from her kneeling position on the floor.

"Humph!" he said, mumbling and grumbling into the handkerchief, drawing it back and forth across the florid tip of his nose. "So you are the little Quakeress who captured our Lord Langley's heart and set the *ton* abuzz." He paused, as if unsure whether to take offense; then his gaze alighted on Monsieur, now licking his paws with a lordly disdain. "It shall be our pleasure to give you the nod."

He struggled to rise, his face flushing with effort. "Langley, a hand here."

Robbie leapt to his side, finding Tabitha opposite. "Take care with Friend George's foot," she said softly, and Robbie held his breath, awaiting the king's unpredictable reaction.

"Friend . . . Friend George?" said his Majesty, eyeing her up and down. "Does she have as little concern for your consequence as she does for mine, Langley?"

"Less, your majesty," said Robbie carefully. "Tabby has a way of keeping me humble."

"Humble." The king surveyed him with a royal gaze and a low chuckle. "The day you learn to be humble, you young rapscallion, I shall toss my crown into the Thames. I suspect your Tabby has other charms to recommend her."

Moments later, Tabitha exited the anteroom on George IV's arm. In the disorderly drawing room, the Dowager Duchess of Lethbridge, a claret stain splotching her gown, hastened to curtsy.

"It would please us," said the king, "to make you known to our Friend Tabitha."

Chapter 19

By all reckonings, the evening was a rousing success. Karl's lively mazurkas, romantic waltzes, and fiery sonatas received thunderous accolades. Yet even as Tabitha was moved to smiles and tears, she knew why the Friends opposed music, for it captured the imagination and the mind, drawing them away from contemplation of the Lord's goodness and Light.

Life had been so much simpler in her family's bosom where there was time to meditate upon the Light, to await the illumination of Truth. As the chaise pulled away from Darenth House, she thought that her life had become like the night streets of the Town, full of fluster and ferment and strident discord.

"Why so solemn?" Friend Robert opened her fingers like the petals of a flower and pressed a kiss into the sensitive hollow of her palm. "You were the toast of the evening, the cherished companion of the king."

"Who is an old and lonely man, bitter and spiteful. Had he not wished to put his subjects out of countenance, he would have shared their disapproval of me."

"You have been accepted now, your path smoothed by the royal nod. Does it matter why he did it?"

"Thee knows that it does." She studied the gleam of his eyes in the murky darkness of the carriage. Did she dare hope he had forgiven her for thrusting him into a confrontation with his father? "I cannot be pleased that I am accepted not for what I am but because an old man desired to use his power. However much I believe in the divine potential of every man, all I see of Society is enmity and avarice and jealousy."

His lips glided over her knuckles, offering tender solace. "Would you like to retreat from it?"

"Thee knows that I cannot."

"I know no such thing." His voice drifted like velvet on the night air. "What you have seen is a small part of the *ton*. There are many who do not feel compelled to attend the Season's frolics. They are content on their country estates."

"Art thou suggesting," she began with a quiver of unease, "that I remove to Langleyholm?"

"Only if you want to and only, my dear, with me."

She sighed softly, the tension leaving her limp and spent. "Then thou hast forgiven me for . . . for ripping up at thee and thy father?"

He pulled her into the circle of his arms, leaning down to nuzzle beneath her ear. "Foolish Tabby, you must know that I would forgive you anything."

How quickly he stirred the banked embers of passion. She leaned her head back against his arm, accommodating the supple lips that followed the arch of her throat, the teasing nip of his teeth, and the low growl that was answered by a hiss from the opposite seat.

Friend Robert raised his head, staring at Monsieur. "Devil-possessed creature," he said without heat. "Expect no thanks from me for your night's work."

Tabitha touched his cheek, turning his face toward her, staring up into the dark eyes that watched her intently. "Hast thou reached an understanding with thy father?"

"Of a sort."

"He loves thee," she whispered.

He caught her hand, her fingers curling around his thumb as he rubbed it against his cheek. "Don't expect too much too quickly, Tabby. I know now why he has acted as he has, but it doesn't change the fact that we are as different as . . ."

"As thee and me?" she murmured.

"Are we so different?" he asked gently. "Sometimes I think there is a bit of the rebel in you, too."

"How so?"

He smiled the slow smile that made her heart tremble with delight. "Anne told me that I was not the only one to feel the rough side of your tongue tonight. I should like to have seen her Grace's face when you suggested she hire a street urchin for her treasured stables."

Tabitha's smile faded. "It was wicked of me to allow my anger—"

He pressed a finger to her lips. "Never could you be wicked, but neither, my dear, can you cure the sins of the world."

"But each of us must try to leave it better than we entered it."

The carriage wheeled into Queen Anne's Gate, thrusting Tabitha against Friend Robert's chest. His arms swept around her, holding her close to his beating heart. "And I have no doubt that you will leave it as you leave me, better than I was."

"Thou hast never believed in thy goodness—"

"Because there is so little of it to believe in," he murmured against her brow. "Forgive me, Tabby, but I must once more leave you at our door."

The carriage lurched to a halt. She searched his eyes in the light of the flambeaux burning outside their door. He had not left for a night's excursion since they had first made love, and now—

"I would not," he said hastily, "but I am engaged to meet the Spaniard and Old Nick for the purpose of wriggling out of the bet to leave for Greece with them. It is a touchy point of honor."

Hope surged in her breast. "Thee will remain in England as thee said?"

His hands cupped her cheeks, his mouth drifting over hers like swansdown. "I find the idea of leaving you insupportable."

"Then I am not simply a duty or a responsibility that thee must assume?"

"What a moonling you are," he murmured against her lips. "When have I ever chosen duty or responsibility over my own pleasure?"

"Am I only a pleasure to thee?" she asked softly, praying that he would at last say the words she longed to hear.

"Only," he whispered.

Only. What a whisker that had been, Robbie thought in the steamy heat of dawn as his chaise threaded the crowds of costermongers trundling laden carts away from the Covent Garden market. Had he not lied to Tabitha, he would never have left her. He'd have spent the night telling her—ah, better, showing her—all that she was to him, and he would not have gained his release from the bet to accompany the Spaniard and Old Nick to Greece.

After all of his concern, it had proved to be remarkably easy. The Spaniard had developed a *tendre* of fearsome proportions for the fair Miss Fasham, who was as quiet as his mother was loud, as amenable as she was disagreeable, as adoring as she was hostile. At tedious length, he had expounded on Miss Fasham's virtues, while Robbie and Old Nick dipped deep into their cups, dulling the edge of a growing amusement.

"Lovely girl, lovely. Tenderhearted and kind," prosed on the Spaniard, utterly blinded by Cupid's dart. "Langley," he added with some anxiety, "about Greece . . ."

Robbie waved a negligent hand. "If you will release me from our bet, I will be more than happy to release you."

"You will be," Old Nick said to Robbie with a lazy smile, "quite deliriously relieved, unless I miss my guess. Had you, Audley, let him have a word, he should have bent your ear about the inexpressible charms of our Tabby."

The Spaniard straightened, his onyx eyes hard. "Are you suggesting that I—"

"I am suggesting simply that I smell a wedding in

the air. Fall, I should think. The Greeks will have to make war without us.''

Robbie shifted his gaze to the tankard of hot gin that Old Nick hefted. ''You are sure?''

''Really, my dear boy, I grow weary at the very thought of the energy required to keep my hide in one piece.'' Old Nick stood, raising his tankard. ''To the ladies, who have saved me''—he paused, a playfully malicious look lighting his eyes—''and snared you.''

''To the ladies,'' they responded, quaffing Irish whiskey and claret and hot gin.

It was the beginning of a wild and tumultuous evening, which marked the end of youthful rebellion—at least for Audley and Robbie. He was the worse for a bottle of Irish whiskey or two or three—he had long since lost count—when he arrived home while the church bells chimed the hour of six, heralding the beginning of a new day, a new life.

He could hardly wait to see Tabitha, to tell her he was free of the old fears of confinement and commitment, of the pain of the past. Free, gloriously free, of everything but her. She had severed his chains with her trust in him.

He stumbled up the steps, and the door swung open. Thistlewood stood on the portal, looking anxiously behind him, as if he expected to see him accompanied by someone. ''Milord, a billet of some urgency arrived for Friend Tabitha last evening.''

Robbie halted and wavered, trying to decide which of his butler's three floating bodies he should focus on. ''Yes,'' he said with studied gravity. ''I assume you delivered it to her.''

''Why, no, milord,'' said the butler. ''I sent it around to Darenth House, only to be told that you and she had departed.''

Robbie set a hand to the doorframe to anchor his reeling world. ''Then you delivered it when she arrived home?''

''But she never arrived, milord. I assumed she was with you, and though I had the City searched far and wide, neither of you was to be found.'' Thistlewood's eyes widened. ''Are you saying, milord, that Friend Tabitha is not with you?''

Robbie's head miraculously cleared of its alcoholic daze. ''It was rising midnight when I left her at the door. Do you mean to say she never entered the house?''

''Not a step, milord.'' Thistlewood, pinned by his master's deadly and penetrating stare, shifted his feet. ''I was waiting up with the billet—''

''Where is it?'' And why did he think of Meg of the Cock and Roost now? Meg, with her tongue cut out. Dear God, had Shadwell been lurking in the darkness while he left Tabitha at the door? If not, where could she have gone?

Thistlewood whipped out the missive. ''I heard the carriage,'' he continued, ''but when she did not enter, I assumed it was a neighbor—''

''Of course,'' Robbie said, his burning gaze flying over the neatly scripted billet: *I would not concern thee, but Tansy has come down with the fever and she is crying piteously for thee. I shall remain here until thee comes, though I am a poor substitute for our little mite. Sister Seymour.*

''Who the hell is Sister Seymour?'' he demanded savagely.

''The Quakeress, milord, wife of the banking Mr. Seymour. She and Friend Tabitha are joined in some charitable—''

''Yes, yes, I remember now.'' Robbie struggled to catch his breath, to still the quaking of every muscle. He must believe that she had not been taken by Shadwell, that her disappearance had something to do with this billet. But who was Tansy? And where was ''here''? And why did he not know more of his wife, of whom she saw and what she did?

''This Seymour—''

''Berkeley Square, milord,'' said Thistlewood hastily.

Within minutes, Robbie was flying around St.

James's Park in his high-perch phaeton, his groom clinging to the seat with one hand and to his hat with the other. A few minutes more and the Seymours' breakfast was rudely interrupted.

"Forgive me." Robbie shouldered past the sputtering butler into the tiny morning room swathed in sunshine. "I am Lord Langley. My wife—"

"Friend Tabitha, of course." Plump Sister Seymour rose from her chair, extending a welcoming hand. "Thou art welcome, Friend."

"Madam, I am here on an urgent mission. My wife is missing, and I—"

"Missing?" She cocked her head like a sparrow. "I shouldn't think so. Why, I saw her—"

"Where? When?" he asked roughly.

"Oh, dear." She turned to her husband, a tall and spare man with a fringe of curling hair around a shiny pate. "I fear she could not bring herself to leave Tansy, and now . . . now . . ."

"The fat's in the fire," said Mr. Seymour. "Tell him, Mary."

"Oh, dear," she said again.

"For God's sake! Someone tell me!" Robbie burst out.

"Thee must understand that she was very unhappy," she began, and Robbie's heart sank. "To marry out of unity, especially to one of your station in life, means many changes that are—"

"I know," he gritted out. "Can you simply tell me where she is?"

"Oh," she said, smiling. "At Friend Ephraim Fell's House for Homeless Children, of course."

While the chaise had carried Friend Robert away from Queen Anne's Gate in the dark of night, its wheels rushing over the cobblestones in harmony with the ringing church bells, Tabitha had stood on the steps beneath the dancing flambeaux.

Only, Friend Robert had said. Only for fleeting pleasure, but there was so much more to life: love and laughter, faith and pride—and hers had been stung. Much as she loved him, she could not exist only for his pleasure. She had a need and duty to give of herself to the fullest measure, and she was needed now at Friend Ephraim Fell's.

She quickly discarded the idea of changing from her plain silk gown. Should she enter the house, she might not escape it. She set off down the footway, dreading the unlit streets of Tothill Fields. On her arrival at the turning of Cockpit Steps, a figure of Herculean proportions detached itself from a wall.

Her heart surged into her throat, choking off the air. "Who . . . who art thou?"

"Milling-Jemmy," rumbled his voice, coursing through the hot night like the last echoes of the bells.

"What art thou doing here?" Her pulse clamored at her throat, at her temples, even as she chided herself for her unreasoning fear. He'd never given any suggestion that he might harm her.

"I knew ye'd come when ye got the message. Ye've got no sense." He raised his huge hand. "Watch yer step."

She hesitated, then put her hand in his. "What message?"

"The girl's come down wit' the fever."

"Tansy? We must hurry."

He caught her arm, holding her to a steady pace. "Ye'll do 'er no good if ye break yer neck."

A cushion of heat lay over the night, heavy and stifling and somehow frightful. How strange that she should be hurrying through the dusty streets with Milling-Jemmy Shadwell acting as guardian angel. One she welcomed, for the darkness was alive with stumbling drunks and furtive steps, with shouts and screams and the barking of hounds.

"Why do ye do it?" Milling-Jemmy asked, having long wondered why she spent her blunt and her time on the foundlings of the rookery. She could be sitting in her fine house, eating her fine food, riding in her fine carriage. It made no sense.

''Do what?'' She dodged a prone and snoring body.

''The 'ouse, the brats.''

''Dost thou know the beliefs of the Friends?''

He hooked his thumbs into his broad leather belt, his long strides eating up the street. ''No, but if they're like ye, they're naught but flats waitin' ter be took.''

''Flats?'' she questioned.

''A cove what don't know nothin'.''

''Is that why thee said I don't have any sense?''

''I seen headless hens wit' more.''

''Then why did thee come to me tonight? Why has thee offered me thy protection?''

''Don't know,'' he said, but he did. It was the memory that grew stronger by the day, so close now he could almost grasp it. He could see the hazy outline of a dark and fetid room, of weak sunlight slipping through the chinks in a boarded-up window. He could feel the hollow ache in his empty belly, the pain of the rope tied around his ankle, the itch of the stale urine that had scalded his privates. He had been waiting, anticipating the arrival of food and comfort. And with every soft ''thee'' and ''thou'' that the woman Tabitha spoke, he grew nearer to learning who was to bring it.

It was almost a sickness, the way the memory had taken him over, the growing need to see it, to measure it, to learn what it meant. It was a weakness, and weakness was a danger. Yet he couldn't let it go.

He turned into Medway Street, listening to the soft rustle of her gown, the light pad of her steps. He believed in what he could touch and taste and feel and see, not in ghosts or God or goodness. Yet, he thought, if goodness existed it lived in the woman Tabitha. But goodness was another name for weakness, and she was a fool.

She sprinted ahead, climbing the steps, bursting through the door of Friend Ephraim Fell's. He followed at a slower pace, drawn by her as a knuckler—a pickpocket—was to a green 'un from the country.

By the time he climbed the stairs to the bedchamber where the feverish little ones lay, she was kneeling at

Tansy's side. He stared at Tabitha's face, framed by the white cap, her eyes as bright as shiny silver coins. She brushed a hand across Tansy's golden curls, touched her cheek, and smiled. "I'm here," she whispered. "Thou art safe now."

I'm here. Thou art safe now. An echo from the past, it thrust aside the concealing curtain, baring the long-suppressed memory in all its horror. Milling-Jemmy flinched back, his face pouring sweat as he stumbled against the door.

Sister Seymour rose from the rocker, a babe in her arms. "Jem," she said quickly, "art thou ill?"

He shook his head, flinging shocks of black hair into his eyes; then he spun about, thundering down the stairs, racing from the house. But he couldn't leave the memory behind. It chased him into the gin mill across the street. It slid down his gullet with his blackjack o' blood and bubbled like lye in the pit of his belly.

He remembered his father. He'd driven a mail coach on the Dover Road. The scent of fresh, damp air had hidden in the multitude of capes ringing the shoulders of his box coat. A giant of a man, his laughter shook the walls of their tiny, neat cottage—until his death in a coaching accident when he, then Jemmy-boy, was four.

He remembered the lost look on his mother's face when they lowered his father's broken body into a rain-flooded grave. That day began a rapid descent into a gin-soaked poverty that saw them starving in Seven Dials by the time he was six.

There comfort, safety, security reentered his life in the form of a Quaker woman performing good works. She, like Friend Tabitha, had worn simple gowns and clean white caps. She, too, had been soft of voice, tender of heart. She, too, had said "thee" and "thou." She, too, had tried to save the vermin-ridden urchins of the stews.

He could see the dark and fetid room clearly now, a rickety table in one corner, a straw bed in the other, the sunlight slipping through the chinks in a boarded-up window. His mother had left him tied with a rope around his ankle . . .

Mam had been gone so long. His belly hurt and his mouth was dry and his fingers were bleeding and swollen, but he couldn't get the knot out of the rope. And all he had to do was watch the sunlight move up the wall and the bedbugs crawl through the straw.

Were bedbugs good ter eat? He were fair starvin', he were.

The stairs began to creak. Not Mam's step. She was a rare one for gin, she was. But it seemed he could remember a distant time when she was light-footed and pretty. A time when his da was alive and there was food in plenty. He didn't know which he missed more: his da tossing him in the air and laughing, or having a full belly.

He listened to the steps. Aye, it were her, the Quaker woman what come to feed him and bathe him and clothe him. She wanted to take him to the foundling home, but his mom wouldn't have it. She loved him, she did, his mam. Said he was all she had of his da. She wouldn't let nobody take him, nor nobody hurt him. And she meant it, when she wasn't gin-swilled.

He strained against the rope binding him to the wall. She were coming, the Quaker woman. He smiled, as eager for her gentle touch and tender comfort as for the food his empty belly craved.

The door scraped across the floor. The gray hem of her skirt swirled in, and she appeared, smiling, with a basket on her arm. His dry mouth began to water. He could almost taste the meat and bread and apple tarts. "Jemmy-boy," she said, "I'm here. Thou art safe now."

She knelt to work at the knot of the rope, massaging his ankle and talking softly. It felt so good. The touch of her hands. The sound of her voice. The promise of the food in her basket.

"Leave the lad be."

It was the harsh, flat voice of his mother's latest light-o'-love, Oates. He stood in the doorway, tall and thin, as spindly as the handle of the shovel he used in his trade. He was a sack-'em-up-man, about the illegal business of digging up fresh corpses for sale to anatomical schools.

"She's sold 'im ter Barker," Oates said.

"No!" The Quaker woman swept Jemmy-boy into her arms, holding him so tightly he couldn't breathe. "Thee will not take this child for Barker's evil purposes. Step aside and let us pass."

Oates leapt at them, wrenching Jemmy-boy from her arms and tossing him into a corner with stunning force. He then turned on the Quaker woman, swinging his bony fist, catching her beneath the chin. The blow lifted her up and slammed her into the wall, and Jemmy-boy came up fighting. He jumped on Oates' back, pummeling him with his fists, screaming, "Don't 'urt 'er!" But he was plucked off and tossed away as easily as a bedbug from straw. He careened into the table, jarring his head against the leg, sliding slowly to the floor with his ears ringing.

Oates grabbed the rope, winding it around the Quaker woman's throat . . .

Milling-Jemmy Shadwell could see her as clearly as he had seen her that day: her hazel eyes wide with terror, her mouth gaping, her fingers clawing at Oates' arm. It hadn't saved her, and with her had died the last peace, the last comfort, the last hope he was ever to know.

He didn't want to remember the rest, but it was there in his mind, like a boil under the skin, and not to be rooted out.

Oates had taken him to Barker, a procurer of children. Mam had sold him into a very specialized brothel. There he had learned not to think, not to feel, not to remember the past. He had learned to exist from minute to minute, never hoping, never planning. He was ten when he killed the last man who used him, escaping to Spitalfields, where he survived day to day, by whatever means it took, foul or fair. He had been without a conscience, without a soul, without memory of the past—until he heard the gentle notes, the soft "thees" and "thous" of Tabitha Fell's voice echoing in the miasmic darkness of the sewer.

Shadwell captured his head between his great hands, squeezing his skull, as if he might pop the boil of the memory out.

Medway Street was alive with human traffic when Robbie pulled his high-steppers to a neighing halt and leaped from the perch-phaeton into the stagnant gutter. Cracksmen and their molls, drunk and reeling, returned to their hovels after a night of thieving and rabble-rousing. Squads of beggars left doss houses to prey upon the wealthy of the West End. Costermongers huckstered produce from trundling carts, fending off sniffing hounds and curious swine. This was where Tabitha came every day.

His gaze lifted to the sign: *Friend Ephraim Fell's House for Homeless Children.* Tabitha's secret. The one she had not trusted him enough to tell him. He had thought he could forgive her anything, but now . . . now he didn't know.

He climbed the steps with lithe, rapid strides, rapping impatiently at the door. It was answered by a small, neat woman, garbed in a simple gown, a white apron, and a mobcap.

"Lord Langley," he said. "I am here to see my wife."

"Yer wife?" the woman asked. "I'm afeerd ye must be—"

"Friend Tabitha," he said shortly. Even his name was unknown here.

"Of course, yer lordship," she said hastily, her eyes widening with curiosity. "She's above, first door, yer lordship."

The smells of frying ham and boiling porridge, the muted sounds of clanging pots, followed Robbie up the stairs to the tiny bedchamber. Sunlight, lemon-bright, poured through the window, bathing Tabitha and the child cradled to her breast in the luminous color of the day. The rocker was still, and Tabitha was sleeping, her cheek resting atop the tiny girl's cloud of guinea-gold curls.

Tabitha, safe, whole, untouched by Shadwell. The vision of Meg of the Cock and Roost, bloodless and white and cold in death, faded slowly. Relief poured through Robbie, stealing the disappointment that Tabitha had not trusted him enough, stealing the anger that was a natural part of his fear. He sank onto the narrow bed, his hands limp on his thighs, his heart beating sluggish and slow.

"Tabby," he whispered.

Compelling and low, his voice penetrated Tabitha's exhaustion. She opened her eyes, absorbing the sight of him with his wind-ruffled hair and brilliant violet eyes and high color. A smile began in her heart, but never reached her lips. Friend Robert was here. In Ephraim Fell's House. She had known the danger of staying through the night, but—she cradled Tansy's small, warm body close to her breast—she could not leave the loving child who had burrowed as deeply into her heart as her husband had.

"How did thee find me?" she asked.

"Sister Seymour," he said. "What are you doing here?"

"She must have told thee," she responded. "Work that must be done."

"Must it be done by you?"

"If not by me, then who?"

"Yes, who," Robbie said hollowly, watching the way she held the child, as if she thought he might snatch it away from her. "Dammit, Tabitha! How could you risk yourself going into the stews of the Town? Anything could have happened to you!"

"But it didn't."

Which mollified him not a whit. His trembling relief fled before an onrush of anger, which even he could not precisely define. It was directed at himself, at her, at the circumstances he could not change. "Why didn't you tell me about"—he jabbed a fist in the air, encompassing the bedchamber—"this?"

"Because I was afraid thee would forbid me."

"Would it have done me any good?" he asked, knowing the answer. How could she look so innocent, so loving, when she had lied to him, when she had not trusted him? God, how that hurt!

"Thou art my husband, Friend Robert," she said gently. "I would like to please thee in all ways, but . . ."

"There are limits," he supplied.

"No," she whispered, looking down at the sleeping child. "It is God's will that my good fortune be shared with others, and all made richer by it. Can thee understand that?"

"*Thee* understands only that you could have been killed or . . . or worse, and none by to protect you!"

"God was by, as He ever is."

"Tabitha"—he sprang up, standing over her—"this is the real world you live in. London. Riddled with every vice known to man. The only protection is a strong right arm and a cudgel!"

"Violence solves nothing."

"It may solve nothing, but it will protect you from being beaten or ravished or sold into the nearest bordello to service all comers," he said viciously, driven by the fear that quivered through his middle. The fear that any of those things might have happened to her, and he would not have been by to save her. "I forbid you—"

Her lowered gaze swept up, meeting his, and Robbie saw a resolve as great as his. She might be tender and loving and yielding, but when she thought she was right, she would stand as fast and enduring as the beliefs she lived by. It would do him no good to forbid her to return to the precincts of Tothill Fields, so he hastily amended what he had meant to say.

"I forbid you to leave Queen Anne's Gate without two stout, well-armed footmen to attend you!"

Her steady gaze lightened, as if she inwardly smiled.

"I would not allow them to commit violence on my behalf."

"I am well aware of that, *Friend Tabitha*," he said hotly, as frustrated by her as his father must have been with him in his reckless youth. "They will take their orders from me. If you ever fail to return home again or to send a message in your absence, you will long rue the day. I may be tempted to take up the old and honored custom of wife-beating. Do I make myself clear?"

"Thy speech is wonderfully precise," she said, a twinkle in her eye. "I am sorry that thou hast been worried. I should have sent a message, but I was so fearful for Tansy that I gave it no thought."

"Tansy?"

She beckoned him near, her small, capable hand brushing the bright gold curls away from the child's sleep-flushed face. "Is she not a comely child?"

"Handsome," he agreed cautiously.

Tabitha's gaze lifted to his, clear and pure and shining with hope. "I have asked nothing of thee since we wed."

She could not possibly mean . . .

"Thee and I have so much, and this child, so little."

She did. He shuddered. He was not yet accustomed to or comfortable with loving Tabitha and feeling responsible for her. He was certainly not ready to assume the care of another, to open his house to the castoffs of the rookeries. But that look was back in Tabitha's eyes. The one that said she expected only the best of him.

"She is a child of the streets, Tabitha," he parried.

"She is a child of God, Friend Robert."

While he tried to form an objection, Tabitha reached out and stroked his thumb with the back of her finger. In her gaze was the trust he needed so much to see, the shining innocence that he could not betray. "Please, Robbie," she murmured.

Not *Friend Robert*. Simply *Robbie*.

He felt his head nodding and heard himself saying, "Very well."

"Now?" she questioned.

"Now, if it pleases you, but don't, my dear, make a habit of this. I'd prefer to fill my house with children of my . . ."

Own, moaned the hot dusty wind, as if Robbie had spoken the word aloud. Her gaze met his, fled, and danced around the room.

"The, uh, the phaeton . . ." Robbie coughed and busied himself with his gloves. "The phaeton waits below. I will carry the . . . the child for you."

"Tansy," Tabitha said softly.

"Tansy," he repeated.

Soon they were driving away from Friend Ephraim Fell's, the blooded horses stepping high, the whip cracking, and golden-haired Tansy sleeping in Tabitha's arms. Behind them, Wild Jack Burdett slipped out of the odorous alley and began a breath-saving trot in pursuit.

Chapter 20

Robbie assumed that Tabitha would follow the *ton*-nish manner of child rearing by hiring a nursemaid and tucking Tansy away in an attic chamber converted for her use. She'd then be brought out like a doll for display. But Tabitha had been raised differently, and she kept Tansy with her, sleeping on the trundle bed in her chamber, eating meals with them, and going back and forth to Friend Ephraim Fell's with the escort of two sturdy, well-armed footmen.

Within the week, Tansy, dimples winking, laughter belling, golden curls bouncing, contrived to reorder the Langley town house to her taste. Thistlewood, the impeccably correct butler, had been seen to smile, a feat his underlings considered little short of miraculous. Mrs. Belcher, the cook, busy with Tansy's gooseberry tarts, burned milord's rasher of bacon and was late with his breakfast. From the coachman's postilions to the upstairs maid, Tansy ruled the roost—all but milord himself.

Robbie didn't deliberately withhold his attention or his heart. He simply didn't know how to give either. If she'd been a boy he would have known what to do, but there could be no rough-and-tumble with a fairy sprite that was as delicately boned as a fledgling robin. She seemed to him to be all shimmer and air, color and light, like a rainbow spinning through a mountain cascade. And he, brooding in the dark disappointment of

Tabitha's lack of trust, was terrified that he might cast a gloomy shadow over the brilliant, laughing child.

One by one, his family was toppled by her smile. Even his father, the top-lofty Earl of Darenth, succumbed to Tansy's charm, allowing her to crawl onto his lap and explore the exquisite folds of his cravat and his waistcoat pocket with her dainty, inquisitive fingers. In his eyes, plain to see, was amazement that this elfin child with magic in her smile was a product of the rookeries.

The earl took the news of Friend Ephraim Fell's House with surprising equanimity. "Tabitha has a mind of her own," he said. "I should not think she would be content with Society's strictures. I begin to believe"—he cast Robbie a neutral glance—"that none of us should be. Had I not been so intent on molding you into something you were not, perhaps you would not have suffered as you did in Schattenburg."

"And perhaps," Robbie said, "I would have suffered worse. We cannot predict what might have been."

"Or change what we are?" questioned the earl.

"Tabitha would tell you it was all a part of His Plan."

"And what of your plans?" asked the earl. "Have you considered standing for a seat in the Commons?"

"Yes," said Robbie, "but I've made no decision."

He'd made enough of those without thought of the future, and this one should not be taken lightly. If he went to the Commons, there must be something he hoped to accomplish by it. But he had no political ambitions, no lust for power, no need to thrust his own beliefs on others. For now, he was content with the house in Queen Anne's Gate, the wife who brought him peace, and the sprite who brought him secret joy.

Robbie woke of a morning late in the week and discovered that a small finger was exploring his ear. He opened one eye and rolled it to the side, and the small finger tried to close it.

"Ouch!" said he.

"Oh!" said Tansy. "Hu't? Kiss hu't." She proceeded to salve the hu't with an exceedingly wet kiss.

"Zounds! I'm being drowned!" Robbie gifted her with the wide, reckless smile that had melted many a heart older and wiser than hers.

Tansy put a dainty hand to her mouth, scrunched up her shoulders, and giggled. And it seemed to Robbie, laughing with her, that the air around her held the glimmer of light and the sparkle of joy.

"Tansy! Tansy!" Tabitha whispered frantically in the hall.

"She's in here," Robbie called out.

Tabitha peeked around the door and saw a sight that set her heart to fluttering. Robbie, drawn up on the pillows, leaning back against the headboard, the sheet wrinkling around his hips, and all bare above—muscled and browned and whorled with blue-black hair. Her gaze dropped dutifully, then willfully rose once more, gliding over the sleek planes of his chest, sliding over the muscular swell of his arm, seeking the strong column of his neck and the firm line of his jaw.

He'd been so distant with her, so withdrawn since his discovery of Friend Ephraim Fell's, as if he blamed her for something, though what she did not know. She was afraid now to trust the new and tender light in his eyes.

"She woke thee," she whispered.

"Without a doubt."

"Tansy," she chided, easing gingerly into the bedchamber that held such powerful memories of passion shared. "Come here. We must let Friend Robert—"

"No!" Tansy plumped down on Robbie's lap, leaned back against his chest, and put her thumb in her mouth, and he lost the last remnant of his heart that he held from her.

"Tansy!" Tabitha said, torn between laughter and frustration.

"Let her stay." Robbie hooked a gentle arm around the little girl's waist, resting his cheek atop the silky cloud of her hair. "Join us."

He patted the bed and raised a shiny black brow, and Tabitha's feet moved against her will. She sat on the edge, primly folding her hands in her lap.

"You smell of roses." His voice, still husky with sleep, stroked her with a touch as gentle as the long sun-browned finger idling up and down her arm.

"I—I've been in the garden," she said, her voice squeaking like an ungreased wheel.

He hooked a finger beneath the hem of her neat white cap and tugged it back to reveal the glossy waves of her ebony hair, the heavy bun resting on her nape. "I'd like to see it down," he said softly.

Tabitha ducked her head without answer, thrills and chills stealing her breath.

His knuckle grazed her cheek.

Her breath stopped altogether.

"Tabby p'utty," said Tansy around her thumb.

"Tabby p'utty," whispered Robbie, his brilliant violet eyes snaring her widening gaze, holding it until she thought she might literally die of the pounding, washing waves of hope.

She stood abruptly, switching back the curtains, pulling up her cap to cover her hair. She stood in the sun's golden rays, a woman of moonlight and mist and, Robbie saw with a sinking heart, stubborn determination.

"Thou art unhappy," she said.

"No."

"I pray thee, let us have truth between us."

"And was it truth for you to keep the existence of Friend Ephraim Fell's from me?" he asked.

She bowed her head, as if she gathered her strength. When her chin lifted and her gaze rose, he saw the pain in her eyes and the refusal to be cowed by it, and he wondered where her strength came from, why he had never had that kind of courage himself.

"I did it for Tansy, and for all the children like her. Look at her, Robbie." Not *Friend Robert*, but *Robbie*. Would his name on her lips ever fail to make his head and heart spin? "Look at her," she commanded.

Tansy turned in his lap and stared up at him, her tender pink lips curled around the heel of her thumb, her long lashes—the brown of autumn leaves— shadowing her eyes, her hair falling in corkscrewed curls around her small rosy face.

"Neither thee nor I can imagine the life she has led. The days she's gone hungry. The nights she's been cold. The danger she's faced. I've been into the warrens of Tothill Fields. I've seen the children nearly naked in their rags, their bellies swollen with hunger, their bodies covered with sores. I've seen what they become, not from desire but from necessity. The boys thieving and the girls selling themselves when they are little more than children. That's what would have happened to Tansy had she not been brought to me."

He knew she was right. He'd seen enough young girls haunting Covent Garden, climbing into gentlemen's carriages, working in the brothels. He'd seen the destitute poor, huddling in doorways in winter, sleeping in the parks at night. He'd smelled the stench of Spitalfields and tasted the hopelessness that permeated the air. And that was the life that Tansy had had until now, the life she would have continued to have without Friend Ephraim Fell's.

A hollow space expanded beneath his rib cage, a sick dark howling place that sent the bile churning up to sting the back of his tongue. He ran a finger over the downy curve of Tansy's cheek. Her smile arched away from the impediment of her thumb, and she reached up with her tiny hand to pat his cheek, as if she could sense the sickness in him and sought to soothe it. He thought of all the horrors she might have met and swore to himself that she would never be hungry or cold or unhappy again.

"Dost thou remember what thee said about the children of London? They are thieves and cutpurses, you said. That was the day I decided to lease a house in Medway Street, and I wanted so much to tell thee. That was also the day thee forbade me to enter 'that sink of vice and iniquity again.' But I couldn't stop. Can thee understand?"

"If I had known—"

"No," she said softly. "Thee would have seen only the danger to me. Thee would not have seen the salvation of children like Tansy."

Much as he hated to admit it, she was right. He did not have her capacity for goodness and compassion. His loves were particular ones: Tabitha, and now Tansy. He had never stopped to think that a Tansy, all shimmer and air, might exist under the grime and rags of a street child. But now he wondered how many there were.

It was not that Tabitha had not trusted him. It was that she had known him through and through. He remembered how quickly and accurately she had assessed him on their first meeting, this discerning, loving wife of his.

"Do you never weary of being wise, Tabby?" he asked.

She smiled sadly. "Anne has asked the same thing of me, but if I were wise I should have found a way to explain to thee—"

"You have now," he said softly. "That's all that matters. Come." He patted the bed once more. "Join us. I have something to discuss with you."

She came, as tentative as a doe emerging from the woods.

"I have been considering standing for a seat in the House of Commons, as Cousin Knox suggested," he began. "However, I hesitated because there was no issue that was of importance to me. Now I think there is. Tansy and all the children like her, who must be given a chance. The poor who need—"

"Dost thou mean it?" Tabitha's eyes shone as if the stars had been pulled from the sky and set deep in her soul.

"Will you help me?" he asked.

"Yes, yes," she cried.

"The life of a politician's wife is not an easy one. I warn you that you must be willing—"

"Anything! I will do anything for thy cause," she said, and softer, "For thee." She took his hand and held it to her cheek, and Robbie felt the cool caress of a single tear. "Thou art truly the best of men."

"Bes'," echoed Tansy around her thumb.

Tabitha laughed, leaning down to kiss her cheek. "The very best."

And Robbie felt the last of the shackles to his past breaking away, leaving him feeling young and free, as bold and courageous as the falcon he was named for. Adventure was not behind him, it was ahead. The adventure of living with a wife who expected his best and a tiny girl of dazzle and glitter who needed his protection. He sat, one arm around Tansy, one hand holding Tabitha's, and he knew that his life was as nearly perfect as a life could be.

"I love you, Tabby," he whispered.

Her eyes widened. Her lips rounded in a soft "Oh."

"I love you," he repeated.

She touched him, her hand trembling against his cheek, and he felt the peace come stealing over him, washing away all pain and doubt. "I love thee," she murmured.

"Tonight," he promised.

"Tonight," she agreed.

Tabitha, too, thought her life was as nearly perfect as it could be. She had heard "I love you," words of sweetness and magic from Robbie. She could think of him that way now. Robbie, her beloved, her lover, her husband. She thrummed with joy and pride. He would enter the Commons and change the world. Then on a less exalted note, he would enter the Commons and *try* to change the world.

She stepped through the front door of Friend Ephraim Fell's with Tansy clinging to her skirt and happiness clinging to her heart. A soft ripple of child's laughter came from the parlor. The clatter of Friend

Colleen's pots ascended the stairs from the kitchen. In the narrow hallway, tiny Eve toddled toward her.

She had gained weight, this first homeless, mother- less child. Her thin brown hair hung straight about her ears, as wispy as the smile she turned up to Tabitha. "Dog," she said in her tiny, tinny voice. "Dog."

She turned, toddling away with her unsteady gate, her skirt swaying to and fro. Tabitha swept her up and hugged her close. "Where is the dog, Eve?"

The child pointed down the stairs, and Tabitha reached out a hand to Tansy. "Let's go see it."

A scrawny bitch whose ribs could be counted had whelped a litter in the shelter of the backyard. She turned a listless, helpless stare on Tabitha, who knelt at her side with Eve and Tansy. The two girls squatted on their heels, jabbering and pointing at the five blind pups. Four rooted busily at a nipple, their minuscule paws kneading vigorously. The fifth, the runt, its ribs heaving with exhaustion, lay a tantalizing inch away from the nipple it struggled toward.

Tabitha was reaching for it when she heard, "I'll drown 'em in the Thames afore the day's out."

She looked up at Milling-Jemmy Shadwell, ap- proaching on his long thick legs, his bearded face as expressionless as his eyes. "No," she said quickly, "I won't have them drowned."

Beside her, Tansy and Eve rose as one, racing away to the swing beneath the apple tree.

Shadwell knelt where they had been, staring at the runt. A frail scrap of a puppy, lightly fuzzed with speckled hair, it struggled to push itself toward the nipple. Before Tabitha could reach out once again to help it, Shadwell scooped it into the hollow of his palm, clamped his forefinger and thumb on either side of its perfectly formed head, and twisted.

It happened so quickly Tabitha's faint smile of plea- sure lingered for a moment. Even when the smile trem- bled away she could not believe what she had seen. He had killed the puppy, almost delicately, assuredly quickly, but it was dead all the same. She was too stunned for anger, too shocked for tears. Her darkening gaze rose to meet his and found his black eyes as expressionless as ever.

"Why did you do that?" she asked, her throat so dry every word rasped out without force or feeling.

"It 'uz the runt," he said, his deep voice rumbling out of the barrel of his chest and carrying with it neither regret nor triumph. "No use in lettin' it suffer."

She stared at the pup, limp in the palm of his hand, the tip of its pink tongue showing through its muzzle. Swallowing hard, Tabitha forced back the clot of tears forming in her throat, then reached out and plucked the pup from his hand.

"It might have lived," she said, tenderly stroking its frail body, running her thumb over its perfect head.

"Likely not."

Why had he killed the pup? It hadn't been done with malice or viciousness or a desire to hurt. She could almost have understood that. "I pray thee, do not harm the others."

"They're strong. They'll live," he said, studying her as curiously as he had on his first day in Medway Street. "He 'uz just a runt. No use in lettin' 'im suffer," he repeated.

"Jem, has no one ever taught thee that the strong must protect the weak? The Lord has given thee a great gift of strength. He expects thee to use it in service to Him."

Milling-Jemmy Shadwell clearly saw the grief in her eyes, the tender, mournful stroking of her hand over the pup's cooling body—so like the tender, mournful stroking of the Quaker woman's hand over his brow when he was a child in Seven Dials. She had been weak, so easily killed by the sack-'em-up-man. She had needed a strong protector, but he'd been a boy, small and thin and helpless. He remembered the emotions that had torn at him, the terror, the grief, the painful sensation of being alone and lost. He couldn't feel them now; he could only see them, as if they were sharply limned etchings on a catnach ballad.

His curious gaze rose from Tabitha's stroking hand to her face. Her eyes were spangled with tears. Her mouth trembled at the corners. Her cheeks were flushed with the rosy-red bloom of a ripe peach. She, like the Quaker woman, was weak. She, like the Quaker woman, offered comfort to the children who came into her care. She, like the Quaker woman, gave no heed to her own safety or welfare while she went about her work in the dangerous streets of the rookery. She, like the Quaker woman, needed protection—and he was strong now, strong enough to protect her.

"Jem," she said, her voice sweet and low and thickened by the tears that clung to the rims of her lashes, "hast thou heard of the Inner Light?"

She explained the powers of God's grace, but God was an abstraction that he couldn't touch or feel or see. The light, though, he could understand. He could see it burning in the fireball of the sun, piercing the leaves of the apple tree to dapple the green turf, falling over Friend Tabitha's face to shimmer on the tips of her wet lashes and shine in her eyes.

"He has a Plan for each of us," she said.

A plan he could understand, too. Didn't he send out the urchins to scout the Nobs' houses? Didn't he plan how they'd *slum a ken*, whether the *cracksmen* would *jump the place* by going through a window or *do the rush* by knocking at the door and rushing in to steal what they could?

Yes, he understood the need for a plan, and one began to form slowly and carefully. He had been too young, too weak himself to save the Quaker woman. But he was no longer young, no longer weak, and Tabitha he could protect. The light. She needed the light.

Late in the afternoon Robbie returned to Queen Anne's Gate with a spring in his step. He'd been rootless and restless for so long he'd forgotten how good it could feel to have a purpose in life. He and his father had spent the day in meetings with the great men of the political world: Lord Liverpool, Lord Melbourne, and Canning. Arrangements for his standing for a seat in the House of Commons had begun and would assuredly move forward with alacrity.

He had just ousted Monsieur from his favorite seat in the parlor when Tabitha arrived carrying a large woven basket emitting whimpers and whines that raised the marmalade scruff of Monsieur's neck and sent a thrill of warning prickling across Robbie's scalp. Tansy followed, her white apron smudged with dirt, her small face alight. "Dog," she said, giggling as she tugged at a leash. "Dog."

The ugliest hound Robbie had ever seen poked a nose around the door, surveying him with sad, liver-brown eyes that matched the liverish spots and speckles dotting its white coat. Monsieur, every hair standing on end, arched his back and squalled. The hound, a rank coward, jerked back around the corner, pulling Tansy behind. The marmalade tom bounded across the parlor, hit the Purbeck stone floor of the entryway, and skidded around the door.

Tansy shrieked. The cat yowled. The dog barked. A vicious snarling battle ensued. By the time Robbie leapt into the fray, plucking Tansy out of harm's way, the combatants were squared off in preparation for round two. He stuck a leg between them, nudging Monsieur away with a mirror-shined Wellington. The cat swiped his boot with unsheathed claws, leaving deep furrows in the leather, spun about, and dashed up the stairs. At the landing he swung around to hiss his declaration of relentless enmity for the canine intruder.

Robbie caught the hound's leash, but she had no desire to enter this dangerous house. Like a mule, she sat on her haunches, refusing to move a step farther. Cursing mightily, he dragged her around the corner into the parlor, where Tabitha waited looking as cool and fresh as spring, as innocent as an angel.

"I assume," he said with what he considered to be amazing fortitude, "that we are adding this . . . this . . ."

"Dog," said Tansy helpfully.

"Thank you, my dear." He knelt, putting her down, before he looked once again at Tabitha. "I assume that we are adding this . . . dog to our happy little household."

"And her pups"—she paused, a glint of humor in her gaze—"if thee would not object."

"Ah"—his eyes sparkled—"I am to be given a choice?"

Tansy stepped close, winding her soft white arms around his neck and pressing a wet kiss to his cheek. "Dog stay," she said.

And what was he to do with Tabitha smiling and Tansy leaning against him, so vibrant and loving? "Dog stay," he repeated, grinning up at Tabitha. "But I warn you, we have only so much room for the castoffs of the Town."

"We'll take them out to the stables and make them a bed of hay." Tabitha stretched out a hand to Tansy.

He watched them move into the hall, hand in hand, the woman and child who had banished his shadows. They looked so much alike, each dressed in a plain gown, each wearing an apron and a smile. His own mouth titled up, as sunny as his heart.

"Milord," announced Thistlewood, his long nose twitching, "the boy still lurks across the way."

Robbie moved to the window, lifting the curtain aside. The boy hunkered down against the area railing, as he had for days, scrawny and ragged, his hair matted and red. "Is Friend Tabitha still putting food out for him?"

Thistlewood eyed him gravely, and Robbie laughed.

"Of course. She'd feed the whole of London if her pin money and my fortune would bear it." So why did he feel that strange pride in his wife? "Well, we can't have him lurking any longer. The neighbors will set the Runners on him. We'll have to catch him, find out who he is and why he watches this house."

Chapter 21

Catching the boy proved easier said than done. It took two burly footmen, two fleet postilions, and one brawny coachman—and they, not he, were much the worse for wear. He fought like a wildcat, and they soon found his name was Wild Jack, which they, even Robbie, thought exquisitely appropriate. A mop of lice-infested hair crowned a bony, pinched face liberally powdered with dirt from which vivid green cat's eyes spit defiance.

"Bugger off, ye blimey cove! Ye might be a Knight o' the Whip"—he directed a well-placed kick at the coachman's shin—"but ye'll not snabble me! I'll plump ye in the peepers, I will!"

"Why, ye little footscamper!" growled the abused coachman, undaunted by the boy's grimy, threatening fist. "Ye'll not slumguzzle—"

"Enough!" roared Robbie in a stentorian bellow that gave pause even to the boy.

A short pause, for he quickly drew a rag-clad forearm beneath his runny nose, eyeing Robbie over it. "Cor! If it ain't a Mister Nibcover!"

Tabitha, drawn by the uproar, entered with her shadow Tansy, who screamed, "Bubba! Bubba!" as she raced across the parlor to fling herself into the boy's arms.

"Tansy!" Robbie admonished her, moving toward them. "He's filthy!"

319

Tabitha caught his arm. "Let them be, Robbie. Thee sees his dirt, but Tansy sees his love."

And love was there, that even Robbie could see. The boy's defiant eyes softened and his hard mouth curved in a smile as he whispered to Tansy and she whispered back. Robbie slanted a glance at Tabitha and saw an expression that raised the warning hairs on the back of his neck. First Monsieur, then Tansy, then a scrawny hound and a litter of pups. She couldn't possibly . . .

But she turned a shining gaze from the children to him, a question dwelling in her clear and trusting gray eyes.

"No," he said firmly, flatly. "I am not running a home for the dregs of the streets."

"He is Tansy's brother," she said patiently.

"Tansy," he muttered, "is different."

"Only because thee loves her."

"It would not work," he said mulishly.

"Love, Friend Robert, can make anything work."

And hadn't love returned to him his life, his hope of the future? But this! His gaze scaled the boy's skinny frame from his filthy bare feet to his lice-infested head.

"Soap and water can work miracles," Tabitha said, as if she had read his mind.

The boy set Tansy on the floor, his filthy hand clinging tightly to hers. He hooked a thumb in his rope belt, canted his head at a cocky angle, and settled a remarkably adult gaze on Robbie. "Ye've took good care o' me Tansy, and I'm thankin' ye fer it, but I'm cur'ous, I am, as ter why ye snabbled me."

Robbie had the oddest sensation that he was being measured and found lacking. He stiffened his spine and canted his own head at a cocky angle. "I harbored a strong suspicion that you might be scouting for a cracksman."

The suggestion that he was in league with house thieves, far from offending the boy, seemed to please him. He nodded as if he had decided, Robbie thought, that the Nob was not quite a flat. "I weren't," he said.

"I were watchin' me Tansy, makin' sure ye were good ter 'er."

Highly offended, Robbie scowled at the boy. "And why would we not be?" he asked coldly.

The boy shrugged. "I seen the Quakin' Lady in Medway Street. She's a good 'un, but yer naught but a Nob, and who can say—"

"N-naught but a Nob!" Robbie stuttered in his ire. "Why, you young beggar—"

"I ain't never begged fer as much as a ha'penny." The boy drew himself up to his full height, his thin chest jutting proudly. "I'll 'ave ye to know I'm a knuckler, I am—"

"A pickpocket!" Robbie interjected.

"I'm a honest thief, I am, and proud of it."

Tansy, who had been anxiously looking from her brother to Robbie and back again, broke Wild Jack's hold on her hand and ran to Robbie, tugging at the skirt of his frock coat. "Bubba stay!" she cried. "Bubba stay!"

Robbie, his seething temper cooling precipitately, stared down into her small face, seeing the tears in her sea-blue eyes and the quivering of her rosy lips. He cast a helpless glance at Tabitha but found no help there, for her gaze was as beseeching as Tansy's.

Lud! What a coil! He simply could not open his house to that . . . that filthy, vermin-ridden thief! By God, he'd already taken in a cat, a dog and her litter, and Tansy. What more could Tabitha expect?

A great deal, if her steady, hopeful gaze told the tale. And he, who had treasured her soft-voiced "Thou art the best of men," who had melted when Tansy echoed with "Bes'," found that he could not diminish himself in their eyes. Was that how the best of men were made? Not because they were born with a saintly bent, but because they were living up to the expectations of their women?

He lifted Tansy, settling her on one forearm, while he scooped a tear from her cheek. "Now, now, heartling," he murmured. "Of course"—he must be mad!—"your brother can stay with us."

"Stay with ye!" said the boy, as if he had been insulted. "I can make me own way. Ain't needin' no charity from the like o' ye."

Milling-Jemmy Shadwell had been right; the boy had the pride of Lucifer. While Tabitha could not appreciate the description, even she could see that he would rather starve than accept charity. But he might accept work that would keep him near Tansy. If he did, he could be eased into the household with no threat to his pride.

His matted hair was rusty-red and his green eyes were cunning and his body was so bony and thin her heart ached with thoughts of how much hunger and want he had surely suffered. "What is thy name, child?"

"Wild Jack Burdett," he said.

"Jack, would thee like to work for my husband? He has need of a tiger—"

"Tabitha," began Robbie on a cautionary note, losing the obvious relief that had infused him when the boy had refused to stay, "I don't think—"

"But surely"—she gazed up at him, seeing the startled look in his eyes, the rejection of her plan—"a tiger would give thee added consequence among thy fellows."

His eyes widened the least bit, his lashes gleaming in the sunlight, his expression saying clearly, *As if you cared for that!*

"Tiger," said Tansy, the tiny star of her hand patting his cheek.

Robbie's gaze roamed her rosy and hopeful face, then shifted to Tabitha's with a look of helplessness she had often seen her father wear when he was beset by his wife and daughters. And like her father before him, he frowned and smiled at the same time, shaking his head even as he yielded. "Very well, I must have a tiger," he said, looking to the boy. "You do know what a tiger is?"

"I ain't a flat." Jack reared his head back, boldly challenging. "Ye need a lad ter dress in yer livery, to ride in yer rattler, and ter hold yer bloods when yer about yer business."

"It's honest work, Jack," Tabitha said, "and it will keep thee near Tansy. Art thou . . ."

In the entryway the coachman had remained on guard. Now the footmen returned and held an angry, hissing conference with him. He began running his hands through his pockets and scowling mightily.

"Is there a problem, John?" Robbie asked.

"Aye, yer lordship," said the coachman, stepping forward. "The young footscamper's picked pockets all around."

Robbie's air of indulgence vanished in an instant, replaced by a cold disapproval that narrowed the boy's eyes to a haughty cat's slant. "Whatever has been taken will be returned," Robbie said icily. "You are dismissed."

"I pray thee—" Tabitha began, worried that his temper might flare.

"To have patience, my dear?" he asked. "I will not open my door to a thief."

Tansy began to weep softly, fat tears forming on her lashes and dripping down her cheeks. "Bubba stay," she wailed. "Bubba stay."

In the midst of the sudden turmoil, Wild Jack Burdett stood foursquare on the lush carpet, his mouth watering with the smell of roasting beef rising from the kitchen below and his pockets sagging with his gleanings from the coachman and the footmen: a pipe and a bag of tobacco, a lean purse and two farthing pieces, and a Belcher neckerchief. Even in the midst of his struggles to escape them, his nimble fingers had been at work, as his nimble mind was at work now.

The survival instinct that had served him so well said he should escape this house and the angry Mister Nibcover, but a stronger instinct prevailed—his love of Tansy. He couldn't leave until he knew she was safe. And it looked like she would be, for the Nob held her close and stroked her back and murmured soothing words in her ear. Soon her tears subsided, and she drew a sobbing breath, wrapping her dimpled arms around the Nob's neck.

The man's cold eyes then turned to Wild Jack, who met his disapproving stare unflinchingly. He was naught but a highty-tighty Nob. Wild Jack Burdett could do without the likes of him, but oh, how he would like to wear shiny Hussar boots and ride atop a perch-phaeton and hold the heads of glossy high-steppers—the envy of every boy on the streets of the Town.

"Tell me, Jack," said the Nob, his voice surprisingly mild, "why did you leave Tansy at Friend Ephraim Fell's?"

He had not expected that. "I ain't left 'er there fer good, ye ken," he said, frowning, "nor 'ere neither. When times be tidy, I'll come fer 'er."

The Nob's eyes grew colder still, as hard and chilling as the hoar frost of deep winter. "And what will you offer her, Jack?"

"I'll do my best by 'er, I will," he blustered, feeling the full power of the man before him. A power that came not only from his age and size but also from his wealth and position. For the first time Wild Jack felt the sting of fear. If the Nob decided to keep Tansy, he'd have no way of getting her back. The beaks—the Magistrates—would never side with a boy from the streets.

"I'm sure you will." The Nob stood there in all his finery, his Wellingtons gleaming, the jewel in his cravat winking, the hand covering Tansy's back manicured and clean. Wild Jack tucked his grubby hands behind him, painfully aware of his filth and his growing sense of helplessness. "But we both know that the life of a knuckler can be a very short one," continued the Nob in that mild and inexorable voice that pried open Wild Jack's every fear, like the succulent flesh of an oyster exposed by the knife. "If you are caught, you will be jailed or hanged or transported. What will happen to Tansy then?"

To that Wild Jack had no answer, for it was his worst fear.

"What of your parents, Jack?"

"Dead, and thanks be fer it," he said sullenly. "They were a devilish pair."

"So there's no one to protect Tansy if anything happens to you."

Wild Jack ducked his head and stared at his bare toes, resentment scalding him.

"Robbie, I pray thee, don't hurt the boy," said the Quakin' Lady, and Wild Jack's resentment spilled over onto her. He didn't need her to be standing up for him. He could stand up for himself. Hadn't he been doing it since his earliest memory?

Watching the dull flush creeping up the boy's dirty neck, Robbie regretted the need to strip away his pride and expose his weakness. But he'd do far worse if it was needed to keep Tansy safe.

"I can give her a future of comfort and security, Jack. She will never again be hungry or wear rags or be cold."

The boy's head rose, his eyes darkly suspicious. "Why would ye do it? She ain't nothin' but gutter scum ter yer kind."

"Because she deserves to have a chance in life."

Wild Jack straightened, his heart panging heavily. Everything the Nob said was right. Tansy would be better off with him. She already was. Her cloud of guinea-gold curls was soft and clean and shining. Her small body was filling out, her arms dimpling, her temples and cheeks no longer sunken and gaunt. She wore a fine linen dress and a white apron and had shoes on her feet. The Nob had given her more than Wild Jack had ever dared to dream for her. His highest hope had been to have her hired on as a scullery maid in a Society mansion, but now he could see new dreams for her. Why, she might even wed a Nob, have a housekeeper and butler and lady's maid to curl her hair. He couldn't take that chance from her, no matter how lonely it would be to sleep in the straw of a night without her at his side.

He thrust his hands into his pockets, curling them into fists. "If ye 'urt 'er or fail 'er, ye'll be answerin' ter me."

Robbie stared at the boy's hard green eyes, repelled by his filth but strangely drawn by his pride. Tabitha had once asked if he'd ever wondered what he might have become had his father been a dustman. Perhaps, he thought now, a boy like this, full of cunning and suspicion. "And how will you know if Tansy is ill-treated if you are in the rookeries or transported to Botany Bay?" he asked. "You owe it to her to stay here with us."

"Ain't wantin' no charity. Ain't needin' it."

"And you won't get it," Robbie said flatly. "I'll expect a lot of my tiger—above all, that he be honest. I'll not have a light-fingered man about me. So what do you say?"

The smell of roasting beef was stronger now. It filtered through Wild Jack's nostrils, making his mouth water and his stomach growl. He swallowed hard, nodding reluctantly, "I'm yer man."

"Empty your pockets, Wild Jack Burdett."

Wild Jack quickly found that yielding up the treasures of a thin purse and tobacco was not the worst that would befall him in Queen Anne's Gate. "Water ain't good fer a body!" he protested, hanging back from the steaming bathing tub as if it were a cannibal's stewpot. "Gives 'em the ague and the plague!"

Blue smoke curling from the glowing tip of his cigar, the Nob sat in a slat-back chair, one ankle squared over the opposite knee and Tansy curled up on his lap with her thumb in her mouth. The kitchen had been deemed the safest place for him to scrub clean with its roaring hearth fire to burn his vermin-infested clothes.

"Cleanliness is next to godliness, Jack," the Quakin' Lady said, with a stern if gently voiced command. "If thee wishes to see how thy sister fares with Friend Robert and me, then thee will abide by the rules of this house. If thee refuses to do so, then thee must leave. Thee must never watch this house. Thee must never try to see thy sister again, for this door will be closed to thee. Thee must make thy choice."

And a cruel choice it was: banishment from Tansy or water.

He bathed, scrubbing his skin raw before the Quakin' Lady was satisfied. Cor, she even looked in his ears! Then she scrubbed his head with turpentine, not once but twice, to rid him of lice. He'd have died before admitting how good it felt to be so clean and to smell of fragrant Castile soap. His hair dried so soft it seemed to float around his head, and the clothes borrowed from the postilion felt like silk against his skin.

He quickly discovered there were other rules of the house: Thee must eat thy soup with a spoon, Jack; Thee must eat thy food with a fork, Jack; Thee must not spit on the carpet, Jack; Thee must not take the Lord's name in vain, Jack.

Heavy-eyed and sleepy, he climbed the stairs to the attic chamber, Tabitha rushing ahead to put all to rights and the Nob at his side. "Cor, yer Honor," he whispered, "the Quakin' Lady's a gentry mort, but me noddle's a-spinnin' with all these musts and mustn'ts. Never knew the Nobs 'ad it so 'ard."

Robbie, hiding a smile behind a cough, found both sympathy for and kinship with Wild Jack. It wasn't easy living with saintly serene Tabitha. It wasn't easy loving her—a woman who longed to tuck all of the poor souls of the world under her sheltering wing.

It was late in the evening before the morning's promise was kept: *tonight*, each had murmured before the day's full events. Under the twinkling of the stars, Monsieur padded around the garden, sniffing at the wicket gate where the noisome odor of the hound lingered to threaten his peace. In the mews the high-steppers snuffled, and the hound licked her sleeping pups. In the attic chamber Wild Jack ran wondering fingers through his soft, clean hair, snuggled between the crisp linen sheets, and summoned up a croaking belch to celebrate the rare joy of a full belly. In the mistress's bedchamber Tansy sprawled on the trundle bed, deep in soundless sleep. It seemed that only the silvery moon was wakeful in the night, watching over the lovers entwined in the master's bed.

Robbie's hand rode the curve of Tabitha's hip, his sensitive palm ghosting over the soft silk of her flesh. "I thank thee for opening thy house to Jack," she whispered, her lips gliding along the strong column of his neck.

"You understand there is a limit to the number of children we can take into our household," he murmured, his pulse pounding in his throat where her lips nestled with a moist, heated pressure.

She raised her head, her hair spilling around her shoulders in lunar-glided waves, her eyes shining with a pale translucence. "Most men of thy station would not do so much as thou hast done. I will not ask more of thee."

He smiled lazily in the darkness. "Do you think I know you so little?"

She laughed quietly. "It may not be a good thing to be known so well."

"And it may be the best thing of all," he said huskily, his heart full to overflowing. Tabitha had seen his worst weaknesses and loved him in spite of them. Had any man ever been so blessed?

He lingered over her mouth, savoring its taste and texture, its sweetness and delight, while passion began building like blue flames licking around a Yule log. His fingers winnowed through the blue-black mass of her hair, and his lips moved along the curve of her cheek, touching her eyes, her brow. She stirred in his arms, pressing her body the length of his, dainty-limbed and eager. What a treasure she was, this wife of his.

He thought long ago that he had seen love in all of its guises, but it seemed to him they had been pale imitations, like sparkling glass *brilliants* set as diamonds. He had only found love here in the slight and slender frame of his wife, in the tender heart that encompassed all she met, yet made him feel as though he was the very core of her life.

"I love you, Tabitha," he whispered, nuzzling aside the tumbling black tresses to press a kiss beneath her ear.

"Thou," she began, cheek to cheek with him, "art my one true, my only, love."

The eternal pledge of lover to lover, it was for Robbie as fresh and clean and unsmirched by use as a newly fallen snow. How empty his life had been, how joyless and dark, until Tabitha came like the silver streams of moonlight brightening the bedchamber.

He smelled the fragrance of her skin and felt the silken waves of her hair and thanked her with his worshiping hands.

Tabitha stirred restlessly beneath his touch, feeling the magic of their night as a throat-catching wonder that made her long to weep for pure pleasure. She threaded her fingers through his soft black curls and tugged his head down to mate her mouth to his, tasting the intoxicating flavor of brandy.

He cupped the generous swell of her breast, and her heart tripped over a beat. He laved the rose-tipped peak with his tongue and lips, and her hand moved feverishly over the muscled expanse of his back, feeling the ripples and rills of movement, the flushed heat of passion.

"Robbie," she whispered, and his lips rose to meet hers, while his hand gently explored the indentation of her waist and the swell of her hip. "I love thee," she murmured, her hand splayed against his chest with the crisp, curling hair tickling her fingers and the beat of his heart drumming against her palm. "Thou art so finely made—"

"But not so finely as you," he said with a low laugh that drew a smile from her. How she loved his laugh, his smile, his eyes. Even now they glimmered in the darkness like the stars hanging in the sky.

She longed to see him more clearly. "I wish thee had not blown out the candle," she said softly.

He paused at that, his lips wafting over the gleaming ivory of her shoulder. "I no longer need a candle in the night," he said, his voice low and velvety, "for I have you, Tabitha, to light my way through the darkness."

Her throat thickened with unshed tears. How long she had waited for him to cherish her as she cherished him, and how worthwhile the wait had been. She touched his arm, running her fingers lightly over the ridged scar on his wrist, lowering her lips to press against it, feeling the sprint of his pulse. "Art thou free now of the past, of the pain thee suffered?"

Robbie closed his eyes. Never would he forget Schattenburg and its hard-won lessons, but neither would he be haunted by it as he had been. It was over, at last, seeming now so dim and distant a memory it might have happened to another. And hadn't it? he wondered. Surely he was not the same man who had raged and despaired, who had carried that rage and despair into the flower of his manhood, clinging to it like a petulant child.

"Yes," he said softly, "I am free of it, free of all but you and Tansy and a pickpocket named Wild Jack."

Tabitha's fingertips fluttered against his neck, her smile wide and happy. "Dost thou forget Monsieur and Dog and her pups?"

"Heaven forfend that I should forget the wretched creatures," he said, growling and laughing and rolling atop her. "I cannot wait to hear what Cousin Know has to say about Dog."

"I doubt not that she will be suitably impressed."

"And I suspect she will have the blue megrims for a month at least." He buried his lips in the curve of her neck, nipping gently. "I should not like to catechize you for your faults, wife," he murmured, "but . . ."

A thrill sped at the light rasp of his beard, the gentle caress of his lips. "But?"

"You are a chatterer abed. Perhaps you are unaware that a man has his mind elsewhere when he is presented with such a tempting morsel as yourself?"

"I fear my education has been sadly lacking. Perhaps thee would like to show me what thy mind dwells on?"

"I thought you would never ask."

While his words were light, his mood was not. He lay heart to heart with her, his beating wildly and fiercely, hers throbbing with anticipation. His mouth claimed hers, possessing it fully, branding her with his taste, his texture, his very soul. She matched him touch for touch, kiss for kiss, sigh for sigh. Her body was no longer hers but his. He joined himself with her, and she moaned softly, running her hands down his ribs, across his hard flanks. When her release came, she cried out his name and heard him cry out hers. And she knew that faith and hope, peace and joy, had come to dwell in his heart as they had in hers.

On the far side of London in Spitalfields, Milling-Jemmy Shadwell stared through a dirty window at the pale sickle moon. He was in the old silk weavers' district, where the upper stories of the houses—now fallen into disrepair and disrepute—were lined with large windows that had once invited the sunlight to brighten the Huguenot refugees' looms. It would be bright in the day with the sun streaming in. The light. She needed the light, and he would see that she had it.

He turned to study the room, ill-lit by the taper in his hand. It was high-ceilinged, broad, and deep, with a fireplace at either end. He'd have to clean the windows, scrub the walls and floor, paint and wax. And he'd have to do it quickly. The strong must protect the weak, she had said. And none were weaker—or more foolish, to his way of thinking—than the Quaker woman. She had not the wit to keep herself safe, but must instead thrust herself into danger. He'd been too young to protect the first one, but he could protect this one from her own heedlessness.

He turned to the windows. She'd have the light when he brought her here to keep her safe.

In the gray mist of morning, while Shadwell slipped into the house on Medway Street, a stolen Bible clasped under his arm, Wild Jack asked the wide-eyed chambermaid what the Nob, the master's, name was. Though he'd watched the house and listened to passersby, he'd never learned it.

"His lordship?" said the girl, a frizz of straw-colored hair peeping from her mobcap. "Yer not after knowin' who his lordship is? And ye taken into his house?"

Wild Jack thrust his head back belligerently. "I'd not be askin' if I knew," he said, glaring at her.

"He's Lord Langley, he is, son of the Earl of Darenth," she said, tossing her head and sniffing. "Ye'd better hurry now. Friend Tabitha's askin' after ye."

Tugging on his borrowed coat, Wild Jack hurried down the stairs, pausing at the landing to sink onto the top step. Langley! Cor, who'd 'ave believed it! The very one what put up the reward for Milling-Jemmy. And there Ole Jem was, snug as a bedbug in the Quakin' Lady's house!

He scowled down the dark well of the stairway, listening to the industrious chambermaid cleaning above and the clink of cutlery rising from below. It put him in a rare spot, it did. He owed Ole Jem. The flash ken wasn't much, but it was warm and there was always a spot of peck and booze. He didn't know what would have happened to him and Tansy and Henry Hicks without it.

He paused at that, briefly wondering what had happened to Henry, but that was a problem to be chewed over later. He had another now. Did the Quakin' Lady know that her man-of-all-work was the Milling-Jemmy Shadwell that his Honor, the Nob, was trying to catch? If she did, why was she keeping him safe? If she didn't, why was Ole Jem there? Why had he insisted Wild Jack watch the Quakin' Lady?

Aye, it was a rare spot. He owed Ole Jem, but he owed the Nob, too. Should he tell him where Milling-Jemmy was?

Wild Jack's stomach rolled and tumbled queasily. No one was lower than the man who snitched on his mates. He'd not be the one to whiddle the scrap on Ole Jem. He'd stand blum, he would. Ole Jem had taught him the value of patience, of waiting and watching before he made any move.

Yet, as he rose slowly and began trudging down the stairs, he felt like a traitor to the man who had taken Tansy in and treated her like a daughter of the house. Wild Jack entered the dining room and found his honor with Tansy on his lap, her hands and mouth smeared with jam and both of them laughing as she fed him a liberally coated bit of toast. The game had obviously gone on for some time, because there was a smear of raspberry on his Honor's chin and a dollop on his cravat.

Wild Jack watched the way he held Tansy, a careful arm around her back, one hand bracing her knee. He'd seen men who were gentle with children before, but not so often that he ever failed to mark it. He should tell his Honor about Milling-Jemmy, and he should do it now before he lost his nerve.

"Jack," said the Quakin' Lady, "fill your plate at the sideboard, then come and sit by me."

He swung a hard gaze in her direction, noting the smile that curved her lips, the sparkle of laughter in her eyes. He wanted to join in that laughter, to be as easy as Tansy was, but he felt gawky and awkward in the room with its gleaming furnishings and shining silver. And as much as he wanted to trust his Honor and the Quakin' Lady, mistrust was bred in his bones and scoured into his skin like the creases of dirt in his knuckles that all of his scrubbing could not get out. Why would they want the likes of Tansy, the likes of him?

He shoved his hands in his pockets, frowning. "Ain't never 'eard of no tiger eatin' at table with 'is master nor sleepin' in 'is 'ouse," he said gruffly.

The Quakin' Lady rose from her chair, graceful and light, with the sun shining on her white cap and her gray skirt swirling around her ankles. "We do not do things here as others do, Jack. Come"—she draped an arm around his shoulders and urged him to the sideboard—"eat hearty, for thee will have a full day. Friend Robert will be taking thee to Bond Street to have thee garbed as befits his tiger."

"Tiger," said Tansy, giggling, thrusting her thumb in her mouth and leaning against his Honor's crumb- and jam-strewn chest.

Wild Jack heaped a Spode plate with sausages and ham and toast and jam, watching from the corner of his eye as the Quakin' Lady stood at his Honor's back. She touched him gently, leaning down to press a kiss atop his head, and he reached up to press her hand against his shoulder. She moved to his side, exchanging an intimate, loving look with him, and Wild Jack wondered if this was the way of the Nobs. The tender smiles, the tender touches, the loving words. All he had seen between man and wife had been the exchange of angry blows and flying fists.

The Quakin' Lady returned to her seat at the end of the table, beckoning Wild Jack to sit at the corner beside her. The smell of the sausage was making his insides tremble with hunger and his stomach ache with the need to be filled as it had been the night before. He reached for a sausage . . .

"Thee must not eat with thy fingers, Jack. Cut thy sausage with a knife and spear it with thy fork."

He cut with a knife and speared with a fork and found that he was holding the fork wrong. How he longed to be in the flash ken slurping his peck and swilling his booze—and what he couldn't do with those sausages, if only he could eat them!

The butler, Thistlewood, came treading into the dining room, a silver salver in his hand. "Milord, this was just delivered by a king's messenger."

Wild Jack's green eyes stretched wide. His Honor took the billet and cracked the seal with a nonchalant air—as if he received messages from the king every day! He scanned it at a leisured pace, his lean face smiling with a touch of wry humor.

"I am requested to convey his Majesty's thanks to Friend Tabitha. His gout is much improved," he said. "I fear I had not been aware you were interested in our illustrious Friend George's health."

"I sent him a remedy my father used," the Quakin' Lady said, as if she were much accustomed to dosing the king of the realm. "Wormwood blossoms steeped in brandy."

"I should say it has been so efficacious that you, my dear, are now at first oars with him. He hints rather broadly that he would not take an invitation to dine here amiss." His Honor tossed the missive aside and slanted a glance at Wild Jack. "What do you say to that, Jack? Would you like to meet your king?"

Aye, that he would. The spurt of excitement died aborning. He'd promised his Honor he'd pick no more pockets. But surely he'd understand if the purse was returned. If only he could boast that he'd picked the pocket of the king, he'd be the envy of every boy on the cross.

Chapter 22

The last week of July was oppressively hot. Slate roofs and copper church spires reflected blinding spears of light. In Hyde Park the turf dried to a sere brown and the trees hung limp in the still, breathless air. A pall of dust hung over the Town as thick as a winter fog, billowing clouds following the carriages that took the less hardy members of the *ton* to cool watering spas in Brighton and Bath and Tunbridge Wells. There was no escape, however, for the poor in the back-slums, where every winding alley and tiny courtyard was like an oven.

In the Holy Land of Seven Dials, Henry Hicks found a hiding place in an empty shed behind a gin mill. It wasn't as comfortable as Milling-Jemmy's flash ken. There was no straw to soften the hard, packed earth. There was no aroma of boiling soup to make his mouth water with the hope of finding a shred of meat hiding beneath a cabbage leaf. Worst of all, there was no Wild Jack dancing a farthing piece across his knuckles, and no Tansy to thump him on the back when he coughed and to cuddle up close when he slept. He would never have left them, but—he could hardly believe it, even now—Milling-Jemmy had tried to kill him.

He'd been so proud when Ole Jem had singled him out, asking for his help. He'd tried so hard to walk tall, to stifle his coughs, while he took the long walk to the banks of the Thames with Ole Jem's huge hand resting heavily on his shoulder. With the muddy water of the rising tide swirling at his feet, Henry had learned it was not his help but his life that Milling-Jemmy wanted.

Even now he didn't know where he'd found the strength to tear himself away from that death-grip around his throat. Even now he could hear the shout that followed his flight: ''Yer the runt o' the litter, boy. Yer sick, boy, sick. Why do ye want ter suffer?''

Aye, he'd run like a rabbit that day, and he'd not stopped running since: Bethnal Green, Bermondsey, the Almonry, and now, the Holy Land. But never, never to Tothill Fields, where, rumor had it, Ole Jem was hiding in an orfling home.

Henry didn't know if Milling-Jemmy was still after him, but he took no chances. He had run and run, until he could go no farther. He was tired and sick and afraid, so afraid that he'd die without help.

He lay in the shade, gasping for air and coughing until his lungs and throat burned. His stomach cramped with hunger. His mouth was dry as the dust swirling in the sunlight. His hands were skeletally thin with translucent skin. He closed his eyes and thought of boiled cabbage and bread. No dreams of currant tarts and apple pastries for a boy like him.

Henry propped his head on a rotting board and stared dully at the ceiling, speckled with sunlight where the shingles were missing. It was better to suffer than to be dead, and weak as he was, the life force in him was strong, much stronger than his frail and sickly body would make it seem.

Could he betray Milling-Jemmy? Aye, that he could. With a hundred pounds he could find Wild Jack and Tansy. He could help them as they had helped him. Tears rose in his eyes, stinging and hot. How he missed them, tiny Tansy and Wild Jack, the only family he had.

Wild Jack sweltered in his new clothes, but he was too proud of his frock coat and pantaloons, his Hussar

boots and stockings, and his snowy cravat to complain.
He spent much time before the mirror in his attic chamber, brushing his flame-red hair with his new ebony
brush, arranging the folds of his cravat with persnick-
ety care. It would have done Cheddar's heart good had
he only known how carefully the boy had listened
while he explained the intricacies of a gentleman's toi-
lette to a yawning Thistlewood.

The first time Wild Jack had come down fully dressed
for the day, his Honor had grinned and winked and
said, ''We're a fair way toward having a dandy in the
house. What do you think of him, Tabby?'' And the
Quakin' Lady had risen from her chair, cupped Wild
Jack's cheeks between her smooth, soft palms, and
pressed a kiss to his brow. He wasn't sure he liked the
kiss, but he did like the gentle caress of her hands, and
what she said filled him with an unbearable excitement: ''Our Jack is a fine boy, no matter what he wears,
but we must also think of his mind. When we settle at
Langleyholm in the fall, I should like to bring my
brother Matthew from Fell Cottage to tutor him. Would
thee like that, Jack?''

He'd dropped his eyes to the floor, to the hem of her
skirt, to the shiny tops of his Honor's Wellingtons,
afraid that he would reveal the hope that came full
blown. If he learned to read and write he could be anything, do anything! ''Aye, mum,'' he said, his heart
hammering.

His Honor was a right one, he was. A fine upstand-
ing man, tall and strong, and not above tossing the
pieman for a pie or stopping at a saloop stall to quench
his thirst. He was no pinch-penny either. Wild Jack's
pockets jingled with coins. The only blight on his blissful mood was the jingling that seemed to say, *Tell his
Honor about Milling-Jemmy.*

It was a busy week. His Honor had got a maggot in
his head about giving the Quakin' Lady a special gift
for their anniversary. The Nobs were queer ones, and
that was for certain. In Spitalfields neither man nor
woman remembered the day they were wed, much less

celebrated it with gift-giving—and certainly not after only two months!

And the gift! Wild Jack was mightily disappointed, but his Honor assured him the Quakin' Lady had no interest in jewels or carriages or shiny high-steppers.

Mrs. Belcher, the cook, was usually the most calm and amenable of women. But today wasn't a usual day. She had not heretofore displayed her culinary expertise for so exalted a guest as the King of England. A mere duke, even a marquis, she could take in stride, but the king was famed for giving the closest attention to his plate. She bordered on hysteria all through the morning, inspecting every freshly shelled pea before committing it to the pot, examining every lettuce leaf, and insisting that every slice of cucumber be cut with mathematical precision. It was the river trout that sent her over the edge.

Tabitha, hastily summoned by a harried footman, hurried to the kitchen where a roast turned on the spit, a goose baked in the oven, and steam boiled out of copper pots. A scullery maid slumped on a stool, her apron over her head and her shoulders shaking. Another huddled in a corner, a carrot in one hand, a knife in the other, and tears dripping from her chin. Mrs. Belcher, her hair straggling from her mobcap, her face flushed as red as the beets on the table, advanced on her mistress, waving a limp trout.

"It smells of fish!" she cried. "I cannot serve his Majesty a trout that smells of fish!"

What it should have smelled like, Tabitha could not imagine.

"I ordered fresh trout! Fresh!" Mrs. Belcher pointed a shaking finger at the fishmonger standing in the shadows near the door, his hat crushed in his hands, a rim of pinched white ringing his lips. "He delivered this!"

The fish was thrust under Tabitha's nose, leaving her little choice but to sniff. She expected a rank odor, but found instead the clean, crisp smell of the trout her brothers had often caught in the little brook behind their cottage in Lamberhurst. Mrs. Belcher's wild look said she would not appreciate hearing that. "Perhaps," Tabitha said soothingly, "we could do with one fish dish. The poached turbot with lobster sauce should be enough."

"One fish dish! One! For his Majesty?" shrilled Mrs. Belcher, a hand over her heart. "It would not do! It simply would not do! I should be the laughingstock of every kitchen in the Town!"

Tabitha bit her lip to still her impatience with this tempest in the teapot of her kitchen. Though she, no less than Mrs. Belcher, was concerned that the evening be pleasant for her guests, she could not summon a flutter and ferment to match the cook's. She had more to worry about.

The fame of Friend Ephraim Fell's House for Homeless Children had spread deep into the rookeries. So many children had been left on the doorstep that extra beds were wedged into the dormitory and cradles were jammed into the bedchambers. Now the children were sleeping two to a bed, and there was room for no more. Nor was there enough of her pin money to establish a second Friend Ephraim Fell's. She must feed and clothe the children she had, hire a tutor, apprentice the eldest, pay the wages of her help. Though she had spent hours pouring over the figures, the money would not stretch, and she could not ask Robbie for more. He'd been generous enough as it was. But that was a worry for tomorrow. Now there was Mrs. Belcher to soothe.

"Forgive me," she said softly, "I was not thinking. Of course thee must serve two fish dishes. I have no doubt that Friend George will be delighted with thy stuffed trout. Let me speak to the fishmonger, and we will have fresh fish delivered within the hour."

Mrs. Belcher sniffed, casting the man a malevolent look. "We should have had fresh—"

"Aye, and ye had it," said the man, his face ruddy

and angry. "Brought straight from the boat and still flippin' when I got it."

"My good man—" began Mrs. Belcher.

Tabitha hurried across the kitchen, touching the man's arm and guiding him through the back door into the garden. "I pray thee will take no offense. The king dines with us tonight, and we are more anxious than we should be."

"I tell ye, mum, the fish were fresh."

"Of course it was. Thee will be paid for it, and extra for thy trouble. If thee could deliver more—"

"Aye, I'll do it." He crammed his hat on his head. "And these 'ull be swimmin' in river water!"

He stomped off to the wicket gate, trailed by Monsieur, who detected a fascinating odor wafting from him.

Tabitha lingered in the garden, dreading her return to the house. She was not insensible to the honor of having the king to dine, but she was impatient with the dither and tension roused in the household.

She looked around her garden. Even the heat-loving marigolds drooped, their colors muted by the ubiquitous dust. How much worse it was in Tothill Fields, where no faint fragrance of roses perfumed the stench of the gutters. Sighing softly, she hurried back into the kitchen.

Tabitha wished she might remain there. Could she stir in the pots and lend a hand, she might sweeten the sour atmosphere and ease the lot of the scullery maids. But that, of course, was unthinkable. She was the mistress of a great house, a wife of Society. Sometimes she longed for the simple cottage, the simple life she had been born to.

In the dining room Thistlewood was running the footmen, both those of Queen Anne's Gate and those borrowed from Darenth House, through their paces. The meal was to be served à la Française, which required the footmen to hand around the dishes, a style that became the mode following the late war. Tabitha thought it a shame, for the old style à la Anglaise—all

the dishes on the table and every man for himself—
was more conducive to informality and pleasantry.

The door burst open and Robbie flew in, slapping
his dusty hat against his thigh. He'd hurried away in
the cool of the morning, taking Tansy and Wild Jack
with him—to escape the furor, he'd said. Tabitha
paused, as she often did, simply to look at him. Buck-
skin breeches and Hussar boots sheathed his long legs.
A form-fitting buff waistcoat molded the narrow span
of his waist. A blue frock coat with brass buttons
hugged his shoulders. He looked like what he was, a
man of the world. A quick smile flashed across his
mouth and sparkled in his eyes. Would she never cease
to feel a thrill of excitement when that bright, laughing
gaze met hers?

"Your carriage awaits, my lady," he said, sweeping
his hat back toward the door, a curly black lock falling
across his brow. He wore the expectant look of a man
with a secret he was eager to tell.

"I ordered no carriage," she said, laughing. "What
art thou about, Robert Ransome?"

"Do you know what today is?"

"I should hardly forget. It is the day Friend George
is coming to dinner, and our household is turning end
over end."

"That, too." He advanced on her with a playfully
lecherous look in his eyes. "I am disappointed, Tabby.
Have you forgotten that today is our anniversary? Two
months."

His hand whipped out, catching her wrist and pulling her to him. He smelled of heat and dust, of clean
sweat and man, an intoxicating blend that made her
head spin. Wrapped tightly in his arms, she submitted
to a kiss that weakened her knees. "How strange thy
mood is," she murmured, while he nibbled on her
chin.

"Strange?" he asked, smiling down at her. "Come
away with me, Tabby. I have a surprise for you."

"I cannot," she whispered. "I fear the scullery
maids—"

"Forget the scullery maids. Forget Friend George. Get your bonnet and come with me."

"Thee would not say that so lightly if thee had seen thy cook waving a perfectly fresh trout and claiming—"

He swept her off her feet and into his arms.

"What . . . what art thou—"

He began striding to the door.

"Where are we—"

"Hold your tongue, woman. I'm kidnaping you."

"In broad daylight with thy servants looking on?" she asked.

"I like to live dangerously."

In the sunny street Wild Jack, looking self-important and self-conscious in his biscuit-colored trousers and rich brown frock coat, stood at the head of the shiny bay bloods drawing the perch-phaeton. Tansy bounced atop the high seat, her golden curls flying, her small feet swinging.

Robbie lifted Tabitha onto the seat and leapt up beside her, lithe as a youth. "Up, Jack," he said, lifting the ribbons while the boy scrambled onto the rumble.

Tabitha pulled Tansy onto her lap, cuddling her small body close and whispering, "Where are we going?"

"'Prise," said Tansy, giggling at Robbie.

"So," she said, running a gentle finger down Tansy's cheek, "thou art in this together, one and all."

"One, all," said her little echo.

Robbie winked at Tansy, grinned at Tabitha, and set the bloods to a trot.

How good the wind felt on her face. Almost as good as the air of excitement that even involved that youthful curmudgeon, Jack. He stood on the rumble, hanging onto the back of the seat. When she chanced a glance back, his face was as solemn as ever but there was an unmistakable glow in his green eyes, a look of anticipation she had not seen there before.

"I suppose thee will not tell me either?" she asked.

"His Honor 'ud 'ave"—he paused, frowning—"hh-ave me . . . my head, 'e . . . hh-e would."

"A smart lad, that Jack," said Robbie, exchanging a conspiratorial look with the boy that Tabitha would not have exchanged for any gift he might give her. Another man might have resented Jack and Tansy. He might have thought them beneath his concern. But Robbie had not only accepted but welcomed them both. And she loved him even more for that.

They flew down Birdcage Walk, around the Royal Mews into Parliament Street, passing Westminster Hall and Westminster Abbey. Tabitha could not imagine where they might be going, but that they were close was obvious. Jack leaned over the seat. Tansy sat forward, watching eagerly for the turning—into the filthy, crooked lanes of the Almonry!

"Robbie . . ." Tabitha began as they turned into a narrow lane. Then she saw it. A tall and narrow house, freshly painted, its window glazing reflecting the sunlight, and over its porch a neatly lettered sign: *Friend Ephraim Fell's House for Homeless Children: The Almonry.*

She could only stare, transfixed by the sign, while Robbie pulled up the horses and Jack ran to their heads. She had been so afraid she would have to turn children away or transfer them to other orphanages in the Town. It was no conceit that she took the best care of them. Sister Seymour and she had made the rounds one day, and she had been horrified by the watery soup and crust of bread that made their meal. But now . . . now . . .

She turned quickly to Robbie, who had descended and lifted Tansy from her lap. He grinned, that slow, playful grin that reached right into her heart. "Happy anniversary, Tabby."

No words could express her joy and thanks as his strong, loving hands clasped her waist and lifted her as if she weighed no more than thistledown. How light and free she felt in his arms, as if nothing was impossible for her.

The pad of his thumb pressed lightly above the bridge of her nose. "Never again do I want to see a

frown gathered there," he said. "If you are worried
you will come to me."

"But how did you know—"

"Sister Seymour," he said, his smile wide. "She is
not loath to share your concerns with me."

She touched his cheek, her hand trembling with eagerness and happiness and pleasure. "Thou hast given
me so much. I hated to ask for more."

"You could never ask for more than I wish to give,"
he said, his smile vanishing, his eyes shining with dark
solemnity. "Don't you know how much you have
given me, Tabby? Life and hope and faith. Let me help
you, as you have helped me. Let me share not only
your happiness but also your worries and fears."

Like her parents, who had shared everything. How
blessed she was.

It was neither politic nor polite to ignore guests, but
the guests were family and Robbie was unwilling to
abandon his daydreaming. Where once—and very recently at that—he would rather have been hung,
drawn, and quartered than entertain serious thoughts
of marriage, now he could not imagine a more appealing state of being. The thought of footloose wandering,
of being empty and alone, made him shudder in his
patent leather pumps. He had been freed of the desire
for incessant, unremitting, and dangerous change just
as surely as he'd once been freed from the dark, dank
crypt in Schattenburg. Where Anne had been the key
to his freedom then, Tabitha was the key now. Freedom, real freedom, was being wrapped in tender bonds
of love.

"Robbie"—Anne slipped an arm around his waist,
tilted her chin, and smiled indulgently—"you are looking at Tabitha as if you'd like to begin nibbling at her
fingers and work your way up."

He grinned, a lopsided, devil-if-you're-not-right grin.
"I would."

"Then you are happy?" she asked, searching his
eyes. "Really happy?"

Happy. He tasted the flavor and lingered over the texture of the word, while his gaze sought Tabitha. She wore a plain silk gown in a shade of blue-gray that lent a subtle hint of sky blue to the misty hue of her eyes. Eyes that sought his with a look that touched and caressed and blazed with an incandescent light. He had not thought in terms of happiness, only of passion and love, of contentment and peace, of finding at long last the end of his lonely road. Happy? He smiled. "Yes," he said.

"I'm so glad," whispered Anne, "though I'm not surprised. I must confess that I have known all along—"

"Known, sweet Anne?" said Karl, approaching with her thimble-glass of sherry. "I should not be surprised to learn that you had been planning this outcome while still in Schattenburg."

She flowed from Robbie's embrace to Karl's, hugging him tightly and laughing up at him. "How well you know me, my love."

Karl slanted a glance at Robbie. Wry and humorous, it seemed to say, man to man, *Women!* "She'll be neither to have nor to hold now. One successful effort at matchmaking and no cheerful bachelor will be safe in her company."

Karl's warming gaze lowered to Anne's laughing face, and the smile they exchanged was that of man and wife, hinting of the intimacy of years that brought knowledge and understanding. "Tell me, sweet Anne, what would you have done had not von Fersen thrust them together?"

"I should have thought of something—"

"Devious?" he asked, his mouth quirking.

A faint blush warmed Anne's cheeks. "What else?"

Karl, his graceful musician's hand cupping Anne's waist as if she were the most fragile of crystal, looked at Robbie, his smile fading. "Have you heard nothing about Shadwell?"

"Nothing."

"Perhaps it is a good sign." But the look in Karl's

eyes said he did not believe that any more than Robbie did.

"Perhaps," he said, looking at Tabitha, who had at that moment settled a bewildered glance on Cousin Knox.

"Good God!" said the bane of the Ransome family. "You have taken children off the street . . . into your house! What do you plan to do with them?"

"Do with them?" Tabitha asked faintly, her gaze shifting to Robbie.

He strode forward, coming to stand by her chair, touching her shoulder. "We plan to raise them," he said.

"No, no, dear boy," said Cousin Knox, the pheasant feathers sprouting from the tiny bowl of her hat atremble, her fine brown eyes stretched wide. "I mean do you plan to train them as footmen, lady's maids, what?"

It was, Robbie thought, a good question. Once again, he had failed to look ahead. He thought of Tansy as a lady's maid at the beck and call of an imperious dowager or a thoughtless marchioness, her fingers pricked from darning milady's lacy chemises, her eyes ringed with fatigue. His quicksilver, laughing Tansy. Never. Her tried to imagine Jack as a footman, a silent servitor. Proud and intelligent Jack. Wild Jack. Never.

He gazed down at Tabitha, seeing the tiny frown gathering between her brows, the frown that he had never wanted to see again. He smiled and, still looking into her eyes, said, "We will raise them as our own children."

Tabitha's frown disappeared, vanishing like the darkness at the rising of the sun. Her rosy mouth widened in a smile. Her eyes brightened with a dazzling light. Her love reached out, enfolding Robbie in vibrance and warmth.

"As your own?" asked Cousin Knox. "Have you any idea what will be said by Society?"

"We are not concerned with what Society thinks or says." He tore his gaze from Tabitha's beaming face to study Cousin Knox. "I am surprised that you would ask that, since you have never given a pin for Society's approval or disapproval."

"I should say not!" she huffed, turning to the earl. "A Ransome through and through. More mettle than sense, I am proud to say. Well!" she boomed. "Bring them out. I should like to see those added to the Ransome brood. And pray calm my fears that they are like Anne's rascals."

"I assure you they are not," Robbie said, moving to her side, leaning down to press a kiss to her cheek. "What a delightful sham you are."

"Humph!" She snorted, blushing with pleasure.

Wild Jack was above, sprawled on the floor of the Quakin' Lady's chamber, painfully spelling out the headlines of the *Times*, while Tansy rocked the china doll his Honor had found in a tiny toy shop off Bond Street. They were, he decided, propping his head on his hand and watching Tansy croon a low dissonant melody, the luckiest children in all of London. Why, they'd had roast goose and barley soup, peas and cucumbers and potatoes, bread and currant jelly, apple tarts and plum pudding for supper. He rolled on his back, pooching his belly out, closing his eyes the better to feel how good and full it felt. Aye, he were . . . was the luckiest boy in the Town.

Yet he was afraid it wouldn't last. His Honor and the Quakin' Lady were gents, and that was a fact. But they were Nobs, too, and Nobs were notorious for their fits and starts. No matter how well he and Tansy were treated today, there was no saying what would happen tomorrow.

He slipped a hand in his pocket, pulling out a farthing piece and dancing it across his knuckles. His Honor would be in a rare taking, he would, but Wild Jack had long ago promised himself he'd lift the king's own purse. He wouldn't keep it, but he would do it, simply to prove he could. And if he and Tansy were put out on the streets again, he'd be the boy who picked Old George's pocket. That would open the door of any flash ken.

"Jack, Tansy," called the chambermaid—Jane the Plain, he called her, for she, poor thing, wasn't much to look at—who was acting as Tansy's nursemaid, "up quick. His lordship wants ye downstairs." She flew in like the dust devils spinning over the streets, scooped Tansy up, and stood her on the bed, tugging at her dress and apron, combing her flyaway curls. "Get yer frock coat, Jack, and comb yer hair," she said, tossing him the brush.

"Is it the king, then?" he asked, buttoning his waistcoat.

"Worse," said Jane, her homely, freckled face expressing abject terror. "It's his lordship's cousin, the Dowager Duchess of Worth."

Jane, panting and flushed, bundled them down the stairs, infecting Wild Jack with the terror she felt. Not that he would stoop to outright terror, but his knees were curiously weak and his stomach was fluttery and he wondered who the *aitch* the Dowager Duchess was to inspire such fear. He'd heard tales in the rookery about devilish Nobs who ate the babies of the poor—and he'd not believed a word of them. Still . . .

He stood in the entryway, Tansy's hand clasped in his, a sea of faces arrayed before him, His Honor beckoned, and Wild Jack moved slowly forward, somehow comforted by the strong, masculine hand that settled so gently on his shoulder.

"Cousin Knox," said his Honor, "I would like to present to you Jack Burdett and his sister, Tansy. Jack, Tansy, this is her Grace, the Dowager Duchess of Worth."

Why, she weren't . . . wasn't as big as a mite! Hardly bigger than him, and round as a cushion, all ruffles and ribbons and bows. The pomaded brown curls dangling over her brow were just like those on Tansy's china doll. And she had big, curious eyes the color of his brown frock coat. And she had dainty little hands, every finger with a ring. Cor, if One-Eyed Will could see 'em, he'd do the rush fer sure. He were ever the one fer sparklers.

"Well, boy," she said in a voice that boomed like a drum, widening his eyes.

His Honor would have bowed to her, but the Quakin' Lady didn't believe in bowing, which left Wild Jack in a painful quandary. He glanced her way with a questioning look.

"Thee must choose thy own way, Jack," she said softly. "Thee will find it only in thy heart."

And his heart said he wanted to be like his Honor. He lurched into an awkward bow, stuttering, "Yer w-worship."

"Your Grace," his Honor murmured.

"Your G-Grace," Wild Jack said, searching frantically for the expression the Polite world would use. "It . . . it's a . . . an 'onor . . . hh-onor to meet ye . . . "

She sat back in her chair, eyeing him up and down, as stiff and lofty as the duchess she was. And it came to Jack that she was the spit of Tanner the butcher's wife, and that grand dame prized honesty almost as highly as the Quakin' Lady.

"Is it an honor, Jack?" said her Grace the Duchess with a challenging look in her eye.

He tilted his chin, giving her a look as haughty as her own. "As ter that," he said, making no effort to speak like his Honor, "I couldn't be sayin'. It's what I 'eard the Nobs say."

"The Nobs?" she asked, her small mouth twitching. "Is that what I am?"

"Aye." He nodded. "A gentry mort, to be sure."

"Good God!" she said, her dancing gaze rising to his Honor. "What language is he speaking?"

"Thieves' cant."

"I should never have guessed," she said. "Jack, I can see that we have much to learn from each other. I shall insist that Robbie and Tabitha bring you and the gel to my seat in Surrey for a visit." She leaned forward, imperiously beckoning Tansy. "And what a lovely child it is."

Tansy, fairy-frail and light, leaned against her knee and giggled. "Funny lady."

"At last," her Grace boomed, "someone who will say it to my face! I predict a sterling future for you, child."

Thistlewood entered with a lugubrious air. "His Majesty's carriage approaches, my lord."

Wild Jack's heart began to race, excitement flushing his cheeks as it did when he was in the streets preparing to fleece a green 'un. He tamped it down ruthlessly. Neither then nor now was picking a pocket a game. It was business, serious business.

He watched his Honor offer the Quakin' Lady his arm, so gracious and graceful. "Come Tabby. We must greet . . . Friend George. You remember what we must do?"

"Of course the gel does," blared Cousin Knox. "She has been schooled in the proper protocol by no less a personage than the . . . funny lady."

Robbie, grinning, tipped his nonexistent hat and swept Tabitha into the entry hall. "Wait," he said urgently, "there is something that cannot wait."

She raised a horrified gaze. "Thee cannot tell me now that I have forgotten something."

"But I can, and I will," he said, spinning her gently into his arms. "Your husband," he whispered, and lowered his mouth to capture the soft sigh of relief that escaped her parted lips. He tasted the lingering essence of sherry and the potent essence of woman and silently cursed the long evening that stretched before him. Reluctantly, his mouth released hers, and she smiled and laughed softly, while her dazzling gaze ensnared his.

"Should thee always chastise me so," she murmured in bell-like tones, "I shall become very forgetful of thee."

Behind them, Thistlewood cleared his throat. "His Majesty's carriage is pulling up before the door, milord."

"We must not keep his Majesty waiting," said Robbie, dropping a light, swift kiss on Tabitha's waiting mouth, murmuring a soft promise of "Tonight" against her lips.

While she waited in the entry, he hurried down the steps between the footmen posted with flambeaux and approached the carriage as the royal pages flung open the door. George IV, fat and puffing on his swollen legs, descended with some effort. "Langley," he said with kindly condescension, "we must thank you for inviting us for this evening. We have awaited another meeting with your exquisite lady with the utmost pleasure. Her remedy for our gout has proved so efficacious we wanted to assure her of our gratitude."

"You are too kind, your Majesty," said Robbie with proper decorum. "We are honored to welcome you."

Wild Jack had hung about the streets, watching Society through the windows of its town houses. He had seen the ladies dip and sway into deep curtsies, just as his Honor's mother and sister did now. He'd seen the gents bow deeply, just as the prince and the earl did now. He watched them carefully, the placing of their feet, the fold of the forearm across their waist, mimicking each motion. Cor, it were queer, it were, bowing to the king.

To Wild Jack's way of thinking, George IV looked exactly as a king should. In the rookeries only a man of substance could afford the food that fattened him up, and if the king was not a man of substance, who was? Jack studied his waxlike complexion, the luxuriant brown whiskers adorning his cheeks, happily unaware that the complexion was the result of the creams and pastes supplied by his perfumers, that the luxuriance of the whiskers was due to artificial swatches of hair.

While the king made graceful greeting to the gathered Ransome family, Wild Jack studied him with a well-schooled eye that roamed from the triple chins folded over his high neckcloth to the straining buttons of his waistcoat to his tightly corseted pantaloons. He was an old gent, he was, and they did not usually take to the new styles. No, his purse would be in a pocket in the tail of his frock coat—the very easiest to pick. The only problem was, how to get close enough.

The king, a passionate lover of beauty, spied Tansy leaning against the earl's knee, his graceful hand cupped around her curls. Tottering on his swollen legs, his Majesty brushed by Jack, whose hand darted into the fluttering tail of his frock coat. In an instant, Jack palmed not a purse but a small metal object with one cold and nubby surface. His innocent gaze following the king's broad swaying backside, Jack slipped the object into his pocket. He had no need to look and see what it was. No gentleman would be without his snuffbox. Barely containing his triumphant glee, Jack watched the king sink heavily into a chair and summon Tansy.

Panting for breath and mopping his face with a huge lace handkerchief, George IV stared at her. "A lovely creature," he said, shifting to look at Anne. "Yours, madam?"

"I fear not, sir," she said, "though she and her brother, Jack, have been gladly welcomed into our family."

Wild Jack frowned slightly. *Welcomed into our family.* What did she mean? A moment later his Honor moved to stand behind him, placing his hands on Jack's shoulders and squeezing lightly.

"Tabitha and I are raising Tansy and Jack as our own, sir," said his Honor, explaining about Friend Ephraim Fell's, telling his Majesty how the Burdett children had come to them.

As our own. Like a son? Like a daughter? Never to be put back on the streets? Never to be hungry or scared or cold again? The snuffbox hung like a lead ingot in Wild Jack's pocket, dragging his sudden hopes into the nadir of despair. His Honor had said he'd have no light-fingered man about him.

"Commendable," said his Majesty, dipping a gracious nod to the Quakin' Lady, "but we should have expected nothing less from our Friend Tabitha."

He turned his watery gray eyes on Wild Jack, who trembled, but not with fear or awe. Had he ruined it all? Not just for himself, but for Tansy, too?

"Yer . . . yer Majesty, sir," he said, squaring his shoulders, digging into his pocket, "I'd like to return this to ye." The snuffbox, a gleaming gold rectangle whose lid was inset with sparkling diamonds, lay atop Wild Jack's steady hand.

"Oh, Jack," whispered the Quakin' Lady.

His Majesty weighed it in his plump, beringed hand, his expression unreadable. "We were not aware that we had dropped it."

"Ye didn't, sir," said Wild Jack, stiffening his spine. "I'm a knuckler, ye see. I picked it from yer pocket." He leaned forward to confide, "Ye shouldn't use yer tail pocket, sir. 'Tis the easiest to pick."

His Majesty blinked, wearing a curious expression poised between amusement and anger. "I shall inform my tailor at once."

"Sir, I never meant ter keep it," said Wild Jack, feeling as awkward as the fresh-from-the-shell chicks hatched in the back alleys and struggling to find their feet. "Ye see, sir, I've boasted ter the boys on the cross that I'd pick the king's pocket one day, and, sir, that was me word I was givin'. Like . . . like 'is 'Onor—"

"His Honor?"

"Lord Langley, sir."

"Ah, of course," said the king, flashing " 'is 'Onor" an enigmatic look. "We pray you, continue."

"Well, sir, it's like 'is 'Onor givin' 'is word to ye. Ye couldn't expect 'im to break it, could ye, sir?"

"Assuredly not," said his Majesty, sitting back in his chair, his finely garbed stomach mounding out before him. "We are to understand that this was a point of honor."

"Aye, sir, it was me word."

"And it had to be our pocket that you picked?"

"Cor, sir, yer the first gent o' the land!" said Wild Jack, innocently unaware that he was pandering to the king's greatest weakness—his overweening vanity.

''Pickin' yer pocket 'ud make me the first knuckler o' the land!''

''As well it should,'' said his Majesty, stuffing his lacy handkerchief to his nose. His stomach began to jump up and down, as jiggly as Mrs. Belcher's aspic. Then his shoulders began to shake and his small eyes to narrow. Soon, his deep belly laugh came spilling out, breaking the tension in the parlor, rousing smiles all around, except on Wild Jack's taut mouth.

He cast a worried glance at his Honor, who seemed to be chewing viciously on his lip. Would it be all right? Would he at least keep Tansy to raise as his own?

''Friend Tabitha,'' said his Majesty, gasping for air, a last chuckle bouncing in the air, ''first a cat bearing a gift of a dead mouse, now a knuckler whose highest aspiration is to pick our pocket. What, pray tell, will you do to amuse us when next you are graced with our presence?''

''I fear thee will be disappointed,'' said the Quakin' Lady. ''I cannot imagine what I might find to top this, Friend George.''

''Humph!'' he said, obviously still unsure whether he liked that familiarity, but too amused to condemn it. ''Master Jack''—a smile lingered in his eyes—''you'll need this to prove that you have indeed picked our pocket.''

Jack stared at the snuffbox, extended in the king's chubby hand. ''Cor, sir, I couldn't—''

''Ah, but you can,'' said George IV with a royal flourish. He settled his thick forearms on the brocaded armrests of the chair and studied Wild Jack up and down. ''England needs men with a sense of honor, Master Jack. Langley, I shall send around the papers presenting the boy with a cornetcy in my own regiment, the Tenth Hussars, when he reaches his sixteenth birthday.''

''Cor, sir!'' said Wild Jack, his green eyes as bright as the diamonds winking on the snuffbox in his hand. Everyone knew that the king's own regiment wore the best uniforms, dripping with decorations, designed by the king himself. And they rode the very best bloods. And had swords and . . .

"Jack?" said his Honor. "Is this what you want?"

How could he not want it! "Aye."

"He would be honored to accept your gracious offer, your Majesty," said his Honor. "I shall have him presented to yourself and the regiment when he comes of age."

Which meant that he expected Wild Jack to be with him, that he would not be sending either him or Tansy away. They'd live with his Honor and the Quakin' Lady. They'd have food in plenty. They'd have . . . a future. Wild Jack had never had a future before. If it had been thought of at all, it had ended on the Nubbin' Cheat—the gallows. Now he could see a dizzying vista spreading before him. Why, someday he might have his very own perch-phaeton and pair of high-steppers.

And he'd owe it all to his Honor. He'd have to give him something, something he wanted as much as Wild Jack wanted that future. And the only thing he knew his Honor wanted was Milling-Jemmy Shadwell.

Chapter 23

While his Majesty consumed prodigious amounts of Mrs. Belcher's fine cookery, Monsieur hunted in the walled garden, detecting a scent that set his nostrils to twitching. His belly skimming the ground, he stalked around the musty-smelling martagon lilies and poised, quivering, beneath the love-in-a-mist, its lacy green leaves crowning his blocky head. A fish. A fish that moved, gliding over the turf. His nose to the ground, his end in the air, Monsieur wiggled his rump, digging his claws into the earth, then leapt in a single bound, pouncing on his prey. A rough sack fell over him, rougher hands bundled him up, yowling and whipping back and forth in the confines of his prison.

By the time the ladies of Queen Anne's Gate had removed to the parlor for tea, leaving the men behind to indulge in more potent libations—his Majesty sipping deep of his favorite marischino—Monsieur was being released in a strange room. He sped away from the sack, scaling a bed, scrambling up its velvet curtains, to perch on the canopy with his marmalade fur standing on end.

Below, Milling-Jemmy Shadwell nodded in satisfaction and turned to survey the chamber that had once housed silk weavers' looms. He'd sent his cracksmen out to break into the great mansions and smaller town houses, standing empty now that the *ton* was leaving for the cool places of the country. Arranged before one

357

fireplace was a conversation area brought *in toto* from Berkeley Square: an Aubusson rug; two comfortable chairs; a small piecrust table with Jane Austen's *Emma* and Walter Scott's *Waverly* atop it. From Grosvenor Square there was a Chippendale mirror, an exquisite creation of gilt and mahogany with a swan's neck pediment and a center urn raised on a plinth. The four-poster bed with its molded cornice and reeded posts and heavy draperies of wine-red velvet and Brussels lace had been found in Hanover Square, along with the bonnet-topped chest-on-chest and the slant-fronted desk.

He'd sent the quickest and wiliest of his *hoists* into the best areas of Pall Mall to shoplift: linens; paper and pens and ink; books; handkerchiefs; needles, threads, and canvas for stitchery.

The only items he'd bought with blunt from his own pocket was the gilded cage in the corner and the linnet stirring sleepily on its perch.

But his deepest satisfaction came from the bank of windows, tall and wide, stretching from wall to wall. They'd been cleaned inside and out, polished to a high gloss. Not a single beam of sunlight would be dulled or lost as it pierced the clear, clean glazing of glass. And the night light of stars and moon would be so close she could reach up to touch them.

Here the Quaker woman would be safe from herself and others. Here she would have the light she craved, the Bible she read, the cat she loved, and a silver-songed, caged linnet to brighten her days. And here he would come to listen to her soft, soothing voice. Here he would recapture the sense of well-being another Quaker woman had given him long ago.

In the wee hours of the morning a knock came at the door of Queen Anne's Gate. Soon Thistlewood, a candle in his hand and a disreputably ancient but blissfully comfortable dressing gown over his nightshirt, tiptoed into the master's chamber. ''Milord, a man is below, demanding to see you.''

Robbie raised on an elbow, easing his arm from beneath Tabitha's head, her hair sliding sinuously, erotically over his hand. She was spooned into the curve of his body, warm and inviting. He could have stayed there forever, remembering the tender passion, the soft whispers in the night. But here was his butler—he opened his eyes. Lud! It was night!

"What time is it?" he asked softly.

"After five, milord. I should not have disturbed you, but Mr. Stark said it was urgent."

"Stark!" Robbie sat up, the sheet falling away from his chest, spilling in folds over his lap. Stark would not have come at this time of day unless he had learned where Shadwell was. "Tell him I'll be right down."

Tabitha shifted restlessly. "Robbie?"

"Shh, my dear." He leaned over her, dropping a light kiss on her parted lips. "I may have to go out for a while. It is nothing to concern yourself with."

And she, only half awake, murmured incoherently, curled up around the pillow, and slept deeply. He waited a moment, gazing down at her by the dim and flickering light of the candle Thistlewood had left on the bedside table. It seemed to Robbie that the cool line of her cheek and the innocent brush of her lashes contrasting to the Gypsy-black tangle of her hair told him all he needed to know of the angel-temptress who was his wife. He begrudged not a minute of his pain and despair if it was the price of the treasure he had found, a woman who fit him like a diamond in its setting.

"I love you," he whispered, and slipped from the bed, drawing up the sheet to cover her bare shoulder.

Within minutes he had dressed and hurried down the stairs. Stark, his eyes red-rimmed with sleeplessness, a day's growth of beard prickling his chin, levered himself out of a chair where he had been napping.

"We've almost got him, milord. I've received word to meet a Henry Hicks in the Holy Land."

North of Long Acre, bordering Covent Garden, was a knot of streets laid out by Sir Thomas Neale in 1693.

They formed a star in whose center sat a column with seven faces, each bearing a sundial, hence the name Seven Dials. It had quickly become a vice-ridden haunt of the lowest sort, a place of such wretchedness it was called, ironically, the Holy Land. Here pseudonymous poets with names like Tottenham Court Meg and Slender Ben wrote cheap Horribles, catnach ballads, and the "Last Dying Speech and Confession"—much embroidered upon—of the hangman's quarry. Here Robbie and Stark were met on a dark street corner by the boy who had delivered the message to Bow Street. He directed them down the alley and toward the rotting shed, bit the shilling Robbie tossed him, and disappeared.

The lantern Stark carried seemed to be the only light, far less bright than the Star of Bethlehem that once lit another Holy Land. He paused in the reeking alley, taking a painful grip on Robbie's arm. "It could be a trap set by Shadwell, your lordship. Keep an eye peeled."

He pulled a pistol from his belt and moved with the silent grace, Robbie thought, of Monsieur stalking a mouse in the garden. The night seemed alive with whisperings and skitterings, with howlings and distant screams. A bead of sweat purled on his brow and slid down his temple.

Shoulder to shoulder with Stark, he approached the door of the shed, slipping and sliding over the noisome refuse underfoot. From inside came a thick, congested cough. Stark peeked around the door, raising the lantern high. Its light fell over a ragged boy, curled up on the dirt floor, coughing and choking.

Robbie hurried to his side, dropping to his knees. He lifted the boy and held him over one arm, pounding his back. He was as light as a bird, all bones and skin, his ribs as clearly defined as the undulate metal of a washboard. As the spasm of coughing ended and he gasped for air, Robbie laid the boy back, bracing his head in the crook of his arm.

"Is he alive?" said Stark, holding the lantern close.

"Yes, but not for long without help." He stared at the boy's face, whose every bone seemed to be trying to jut through his thin, fever-flushed skin.

"Here, give him this." Stark proffered a flask.

Robbie held the brandy to the boy's lips, seeing his eyes open and focus slowly with a start of fear. "You'll come to no harm, lad. Drink."

The boy took a long gulp, wheezed, and coughed.

"Boy," said Stark, "we're looking for Henry Hicks."

He struggled in Robbie's arms, but his strength gave out. "I'm 'Icks," he whispered, his lashes sliding down, his body going limp.

"Damn!" said Stark.

Robbie lifted the boy in his arms and carried him out into the alley, less concerned with finding Shadwell than with getting Henry Hicks to a doctor. The boy stank of old sweat and filth and sickness and fear, and Robbie felt a tremulous pity welling in his chest. Was this what Tabitha felt for the children of the streets? Not the intellectual pity of the wealthy for the poor, but this heart-wrenching kinship of human for human.

How long had it been since the boy had eaten a good meal? Or slept in a bed? Or felt safe and secure? How long had it been since he had dared to hope for the future? What desperate straits had driven him to risk betraying Shadwell?

While Robbie roused Dr. Kennon's household in Grosvenor Square, Wild Jack woke with a start, leaping from his bed and throwing on his clothes. The sky outside his window was salmon pink and gray, the lip of the sun hanging tantalizingly on a rooftop gable. He'd tried to stay awake in the night, hoping to speak to his Honor after the dinner had ended. But he'd been so full from the pastries and cakes Mrs. Belcher had sent up from the kitchen that he'd nodded off and slept dreamlessly.

He scampered down the stairs, finding Tansy at the table, her mouth ringed with jam. "Friend Tabby"—

he stood in the doorway, looking around—"is 'is Honor still above?"

"He was called out early this morning," she said, looking as fresh as the dew-speckled roses artfully arranged in a vase on the table. "If thee needs to speak to him, thee will have to wait until he comes in."

Now that Jack had decided to tell his Honor about Milling-Jemmy, he was in a hurry to have it done. He picked over his breakfast so lightly the Quakin' Lady thought he was sick. A hand at his brow assured her he had no fever, but still his mood was low. It was no easy thing to contemplate betraying a man who had been naught but good to him.

"Jack, would thee like to accompany Tansy and me to Friend Ephraim Fell's this morning?"

Jack scowled at his scrambled eggs and kidneys, trying to decide whether it would be better to wait for his Honor or to follow the Quakin' Lady. If only he knew why Milling-Jemmy had set him to watching her, why he had chosen to hide in her house on Medway Street. He should have asked him, Jack thought, but it was too late now.

His gaze rose to the Quakin' Lady's face. She was as innocent as a lamb. The saints be sweared! Tansy had more sense! He'd better go with her, just in case, though he was damned if he knew why he felt such a sense of urgency. He'd not have a moment's peace until he'd told his Honor all he knew.

Milling-Jemmy Shadwell hunkered down in the alley across from Friend Ephraim Fell's. On one side was an empty keg smelling of yeasty beer and on the other was the brick wall of the gin mill, reflecting the heat of the sun. He wasn't given to reflection or introspection. He lived on instinct, and instinct said there was danger.

He'd gone from Spitalfields to the Cockpit Steps, there to watch the Quaker woman's house. What he'd seen was the Nob and Stark of Bow Street—famed as the most relentless and cunning of the Patrol's men—leaving before dawn. Since they shared only one common goal—his capture—he deemed that least seen was safest.

Still, he'd take the Quaker woman today. He'd close her up in the big furnished room in Spitalfields like the linnet in its gilded cage. He'd feed her and clothe her and keep her safe, as someone should have done for that other Quaker woman long ago.

He waited, so still the swarming flies settled on his hair and face, crawling through his beard and over his brow. A brow that crinkled and creased in a frown as he watched a man he knew, a man who had no business in Friend Ephraim Fell's, climb its steps and ring its bell.

Wild Jack slid into the parlor, melting around the walls, watching Stork of Blue Ruin Alley with patent distrust. His name came from his excessively long and knobby-kneed legs. He had a face that was all nose and a gimlet-eyed gaze that scurried around the salon, as if totting up the price of its furnishings. He wasn't Milling-Jemmy's man, and Jack could not decide whether that was cause for relief or greater distrust. But why should he want "ter see 'er what's called Friend Tabitha"?

"Yes, Friend," she said, apparently unconcerned by the shive in its sheath at Stork's waist or the pistol thrust into his belt, which only confirmed Wild Jack's opinion that she was as simpleminded as she was simplehearted. "May I help thee?"

"Aye, that ye can," said Stork in a voice as taut and thin and sharp as the blade of his knife. "Not me, ye see. 'Tis Billy Buck's doxy. Billy's a hedgebird, ye see—"

"Just out of prison," Wild Jack interpreted.

"Aye, that 'e is, and now Billy's in Blue Ruin Alley in 'is flash ken—"

"Thieves' den," said Wild Jack.

"Aye, and a honest trade it is!" said the gimlet-eyed man, flaring up like the stork he'd been named for. "She's got a mort o' mettle, 'is doxy does, but she's sufferin' fearful and Billy Buck's got dicked in the nob—''

''Crazy, Friend Tabby,'' Wild Jack whispered.

''Got 'er a midwife, but she sluiced her gob on gin, so Billy snabbled a gentry cove, a doctor, and brung 'im ter the flash ken, but 'e shot the cat—''

''Fainted,'' said Wild Jack.

''Aye, that 'e did. The 'en-'earted cove woke gabblin' worse'n them in Bedlam, so Billy Buck says to me, 'Stork, ain't nothin' fer it but ter get that Quakin' Lady or me Nance 'ull be 'oppin' the twig and the babe, too.' ''

''If thee will wait a moment, I will get—''

''Friend Tabby!'' burst out Wild Jack. ''Ye can't be goin' with this cull!''

''Dub yer mummer, boy! Billy Buck won't turn cat in the pan on you, lady.''

''Huh!'' snorted Wild Jack, well versed in the ways of Billy Buck of Blue Ruin Alley, who'd set himself up in opposition to Milling-Jemmy Shadwell. ''He'd betray 'is own mam if there was a bob in it!'' Though he'd obviously not had the courage to betray Ole Jem to his Honor, reward or no.

''Friend Jack,'' chided the Quakin' Lady, ''thee must learn to trust in God, for He is ever with thee.''

''But ye—''

''Shh, now, Jack,'' she said gently, running a knuckle down his cheek. ''Thee must take Tansy home and tell Friend Robert that I may be late.''

''But I'm going' with ye!''

''I will be perfectly safe. This good man''—*good man!* Wild Jack gaped—''will see that no harm comes to me.''

She was as stubborn as a mule, Wild Jack impotently fumed, frantically trying to decide whether to ignore her and follow or return to Queen Anne's Gate and enlist his Honor in seeing her out of Blue Ruin Alley. At least he knew where she was going. Cor, his Honor would be in a rare taking!

Helplessly he watched her climb into a shabby hackney cab with Stork, as unconcerned as if she were jaunting away with his Honor for a day in the country. Wild Jack's hands curled into fists. It wasn't safe to let her loose, and he'd tell his Honor so when he found him!

He turned back into the house, calling for Tansy, and Milling-Jemmy Shadwell slipped out of the alley, lumbering into the cloud of dust raised by the hackney's wheels.

"Bow Street!" Wild Jack Burdett shivered in his boots. No boy on the cross ever heard the name with any semblance of pleasure. It was for many the beginning of the end, a first step to Botany Bay or a hangman's noose. "Are ye sure it were Stark what come fer his Honor?"

"Quite sure," said Thistlewood.

" 'Ave Jane watch after Tansy," said Wild Jack, sprinting for the door. Cor, if it weren't the outside of enough! He'd have to go to Bow Street, where the Magistrates sat and the Runners congregated and the Patrol—

He shuddered once more. It was almost enough to make him wish he were back in the flash ken!

He set off at a breath-saving trot, too accustomed to making his way on foot to remember that he had the blunt to hire a hackney cab. The sun was high overhead, a blistering white that shed burning rays. Soon sweat was pouring from his face, wilting his collar and soaking the cravat whose folds he had so artfully arranged. And the boots that were his pride and joy were rubbing the skin from his toes, though he'd gladly sacrifice a little flesh for the envious looks of the boys he passed.

Bow Street Court in Covent Garden was a squalid place. Jack paused outside the door beneath the traditional blue lamp, wiped the sweat from his brow with his sleeve, thrust his hands in his pockets, and ignored the quivering of his belly. After all, he'd done nothing wrong. There was nothing to fear.

He strolled in as if he were in truth the son of a lord,

his shoulders back, his chin high, and his hat tilted at a cocky angle that was the perfect match of his Honor's. Bedlam seemed to be the order of the day. Frowsy women complained of the heat and the wait. Prisoners stood in the dock. The Magistrate reigned behind a railed dais. Runners slouched against the walls, their ebony tipstaffs in hand. Patrolmen, dressed in uniform, wandered about.

Wild Jack stepped up to one. "Sir," he said staunchly, "I'm lookin' fer Stark."

"Ain't here, boy."

"Can ye give me 'is direction?"

"Pringle!" the man shouted across the court. "Have ye got Stark's direction?"

Pringle shrugged narrow shoulders, and the man cocked a brow at Wild Jack. "Ye can wait, if ye've got a mind to."

Wild Jack shook his head, making his escape, trudging down the bow-shaped curve of Bow Street and kicking his toes against the uneven flagstones. He considered returning to Queen Anne's Gate to wait for his Honor, but Jack still had that itch between his shoulder blades. Something was wrong.

He set out again heading toward the City. The news of Shadwell would wait. The Quakin' Lady could not. He'd hide in Blue Ruin Alley until she came out.

Billy Buck's flash ken, opulently spacious for a thieves' den in Spitalfields, was a pockmarked brick house that leaned to one side, every opening of its door like the sign of a toothless old mouth. Milling-Jemmy Shadwell shambled up to that door, listening to the whistle of the boy on the roof, acting as a lookout. He lifted a meaty fist and pounded on the scarred wood, shouldering his way through the crack that opened.

Billy Buck was in the parlor, much the worse for gin, his eyes red-veined beneath a thatch of cornsilk hair. "If it ain't Milling-Jemmy," he said, stumbling up from a settee whose velvet upholstery had worn through to the horsehair stuffing. "Ter what do I owe the displeasure?"

Shadwell set his feet wide and folded his hands over his chest. "Where's the Quaker woman?"

A shrill scream echoed down the stairs, and Billy Buck's pale blue eyes rolled to the ceiling. "Me Nance's droppin' a babe, and the woman's with 'er."

"Humph," said Shadwell, falling into a chair.

Billy tilted his blackjack high, draining the hot gin to the dregs of the cup. "Stork! Gin!"

His man appeared, casting a fearful glance Shadwell's way, one Milling-Jemmy noted without impressing it with undue significance. He neither needed the bolstering confidence that being feared gave some men nor cared what any man thought of him. While the minutes slipped into hours and the screams rose to a crescendo above, he waited, utterly still, utterly silent, utterly thoughtless—unaware that he was infecting the inhabitants of the flash ken with the most dire expectations.

The Quaker woman's light, quick steps—imprinted on Shadwell's mind during the weeks of his stay in Medway Street—wakened him to the silence, to the quiveringly erect Billy Buck.

"Thou hast a son," she said, entering the parlor with a squalling babe in her arms.

"And me Nance?"

"Sleeping."

Billy Buck approached on tiptoe and peered at the infant, his face falling in ludicrous lines of dismay. "The poor little tyke's ugly as sin. Me darlin' Nance must 'ave been in a fair takin' when she seen 'im."

Shadwell watched the slow smile that curved her mouth, the twinkling of a dimple in her cheek. "I assure thee," she said, laughing softly, "she was as proud as any mother could be. He's a strong, healthy boy, and in a few days he'll be a handsome one. It isn't easy coming into the world."

"Aye, or livin' in it," Billy said.

She folded back the blanket, revealing the babe's tiny

red face, screwed up in a fierce expression of outright rage. Though it screamed with a volume that seemed little short of miraculous, she coasted a finger over its brow and laid her palm gently over the fuzz-topped crown of its head. Shadwell closed his eyes, remembering that other Quaker woman, the gentleness of her hands, the soothing tone of her voice, the tenderness and care he had never found after her—until now.

He rose from his chair. "Friend Tabitha," he said, her name tolling like a deep bell.

"Jem! What art thou doing here?"

"There's summat else what needs yer 'elp."

She took him at his word, without question, without hesitation, just as he had known she would. Aye, he thought, she was as witless as a headless hen, but she'd said the strong must protect the weak and he'd do it.

Billy Buck, the babe in his arms, accompanied them to the door. "Mum, there's not many Nobs what would 'elp me Nance. If ye ever need anything, just send word to Blue Ruin Alley and it's yers."

He watched them walk away into the deepening dusk, then motioned to Stork. "I want 'er followed till she's safe 'ome."

In Grosvenor Square, Dr. Kennon had put Henry Hicks in a sunny bedchamber, sparsely but elegantly furnished in bright primrose and green that would, at another time, have been cheerful. His wife at his side, he'd stripped the boy to his pitiful bluish skin, revealing pelvic bones that jutted out from his sunken belly. "Poor mite," murmured the doctor's wife. "Poor little mite," she said over and over. He'd been wrapped in an onion plaster that brought tears to Robbie's eyes. He'd been force fed hoarhound syrup and rich brown broth, and then he slept, breathing like a winded nag.

Now the dusk was gathering outside. Stark of Bow Street slept in a chair, his snores rattling through the chamber. Robbie, longing for Tabitha, had stayed awake through the day, waiting for some hopeful sign that the boy would recover. Since she could do little good here, he hadn't sent word for her to come. But oh, how much he needed her.

The heat of the day lingered in the chamber, bringing a fine sheen of sweat to Robbie's brow. He sat beside the bed, thinking of Tansy and Jack and Henry Hicks and the problems of children like them all over the Town. How often had he thoughtlessly tossed a shilling at a guttersnipe, blind to the huge eyes in the shrunken face, the hunger betold by the rags flapping in the wind?

The boy stirred on the bed, his frail body barely rippling the covers. Robbie stepped to his side and touched his hand, feeling the heat of the fever drying the skin. "Henry," he said softly, and the boy opened his eyes.

A tender blue as pale as the heat-washed sky, they looked around, studying the canopy, the coverlet, Robbie's dark hand. "Am . . . am I in 'eaven, sir?" he asked, each word rustling like the seared brown leaves on the tree outside.

"No, lad," Robbie said, smiling. "You're sick. This is Dr. Kennon's house."

The boy frowned lightly. "I . . . I 'aven't a ha'penny to me name, sir. I . . . I can't—"

"Don't worry about that, lad. I'll take care of Dr. Kennon's bill." And more, Robbie thought with a sigh. He'd been considering it throughout the day while he'd listened to the boy's stertorous breathing and thought of his thin, undernourished body. Since he already had Tansy and Jack, what could one more child of the street matter? One more—he smiled, thinking of Tabitha—child of God. She would no doubt be delighted. Equally without doubt she would, in a woman's inimitable fashion, remind him that he was the one who'd said there was a limit to the number of children they could bring into their home. He could hardly wait to see the look on her face when he carried Henry Hicks into their parlor.

"Sir," said Henry, "who are ye?"

"Lord Langley," Robbie said.

" 'Im what's lookin' fer Milling-Jemmy?"

"Yes, lad. You'll have much more than a ha'penny if you can tell me where he is."

"Aye, that I can, sir. Tothill Fields, 'idin' out in a place called Friend Ephraim Fell's 'Ouse fer 'Omeless Children."

Chapter 24

Puffs of dust rose from Tabitha's every footstep through the narrow lanes of Spitalfields. Dusk fell quickly between the tall, narrow houses, as if the sun were eager to escape this shabby and miserable quarter of the city. At every turn she saw the hunger, despair, and listlessness of poverty, but her pity was ameliorated by the birth of the child. Rosy-fleshed and innocent, he was a living miracle that had refreshed her heart and soul. She could hardly wait to share her joy with Robbie, but that, of course, must wait.

"Jem," she said, "who is it that needs me?"

He stepped up the pace, checking behind, almost as if he expected to be followed. "Ye must 'urry. It's just ahead."

The narrow street was flanked by decrepit houses lacking a flake of paint. Jem paused at a set of rickety steps, clasping Tabitha's elbow to help her over a missing tread. Inside the tomb of the entryway a single lamp burned, reeking of fish oil. Voices hummed in the distance with the sounds of life. How comforting they were. Until then, she had not noted the apprehension that curled in the pit of her stomach. Though why, she could not imagine. Jem had never by word or deed offered a threat to her.

Yet once she admitted to that faint alarm, a deep foreboding overtook her. "Jem," Tabitha said softly, "won't thee tell me who needs my care?"

He paused at the foot of the steep stairs, his huge head swinging around, his black eyes narrowed. "A boy," he said. "A boy alone."

"Thee could have brought him to Friend Ephraim Fell's."

"Nay," he said heavily, "that I could not."

Without further word or gesture, he began climbing the stairs, and she followed as if pulled by a leash. She could not abandon a boy alone, a boy in need. Yet she was afraid.

Up and up, she climbed to the top floor, winded and spent at the landing before the door. Jem produced a key and motioned for her to enter.

There was no boy, only a linnet singing in its cage and Monsieur loping across a deep-piled carpet to curl around her ankles and, behind Tabitha . . . the key turning in the lock.

Her foreboding turned into outright fear. She had been lured with a lie, by a man who could twist her head from her neck with his hamlike hands. She tried to take comfort in Monsieur. Jem had no reason to bring the cat here, unless it was to comfort her. If that was the case, she was in no physical danger. But if not, what other danger was she in?

How Tabitha wished she, like some, could vent her fear in hysteria or tears. Though her stomach fluttered like a cloud of sulphur-yellow butterflies and her hands grew as cold as her heart, she maintained a surface calm.

Jem strode to the fireplace, kneeling to strike flint to the waiting tinder. He fanned the tiny flame until it licked at the logs, then set a kettle on the hob in a frighteningly domestic and suggestively permanent scene.

She lifted Monsieur, cradling his warm body close, feeling the rapid beat of his heart, the vibration of a purr. "Jem," she said, her voice reed-thin, "what is this place?"

He stood slowly, his booted feet set wide apart to brace his massive body, his shocks of black hair glossed by the firelight, his hands behind his back. No emotion, no expression was betrayed by the pink line of his mouth or the glittering black of his eyes. '' 'Tis yours. It has all ye need. The light,'' he added, jerking his head at the bank of windows that looked like a mural of night, blue-black and dotted with stars, ''ye'll 'ave it 'ere.''

Tabitha frowned. ''The light?''

''Aye,'' he said, his broad, fleshy cheeks rose-red above the line of his beard. ''Ye said ye needed the light.''

Suddenly she saw his error and confusion. ''Jem, the light I spoke of was the Inner Light of the Lord, the illumination of knowledge that comes with the visitation of His saving Grace on the human heart.''

''The light, it'll come with the dawn,'' he said, utterly uncomprehending.

He did not, could not, understand. Had it not been so dangerous, it would have been sad. Tabitha moved into the room, gazing at the four-poster, the mirror on the wall, the costly furnishings and bric-a-brac on the tables. There were even embroidery threads in a willow basket by a chair. He meant to keep her here like the linnet in its gilded cage. A feathering of panic brushed through her mind. She must stay calm. She must test him and reason with him, but how to reason with a man who saw but one path, and that, his own?

''How . . . how kind of thee to do this for me.'' Tabitha turned slowly, her silvery-bright eyes watching his face. ''I shall enjoy coming here when I need the peace of the Light.''

He frowned, the thick shelf of his brow ominously lowering over his eyes. ''Ye shan't be leavin'. Ye 'ave 'ere all ye need. The light, the cat. I'll see to all else.''

Tabitha's mouth went dry. Her heart began to pound. ''I cannot stay here, Jem. I have a husband and a household that need me. And the children of Friend Ephraim Fell's depend on me. Children like you once were, going hungry and cold and friendless in the rookeries.''

Though his eyes flickered with dim recognition, he folded his arms over his chest. "Ye shan't be leavin'," he said implacably.

"But why?" she asked, her voice thin and high. "Why would thee keep me here?"

"Ye said the strong must protect the weak. Ye said it yerself."

And she had, after he had killed the pup. Tabitha shuddered uncontrollably, wishing she had not been reminded of his casual indifference to life. "I don't understand. Why am I here? Why won't thee let me go?"

"Ye 'aven't the sense of the youngest whelp in the rookery, and I've seen another like ye. She was murdered. Ye won't be."

Gaining time to think, she lowered Monsieur to the floor, then moved to the nearby chair, clenching its curved back with trembling fingers. She breathed deeply, again and again, aware that she, too, might be driven to hysteria and tears if the fear were strong enough. And the panic was growing, scurrying through her. "Thou . . . thou hast done this to protect me?"

He nodded, his beard brushing the yellowing cravat that was knotted and folded as carefully as any Cheddar might arrange. Cheddar and Queen Anne's Gate. Tansy and Jack and Robbie. How Tabitha longed for each of them, but most of all for Robbie. If she should not return, what would happen to him? Would the man of rage find new release? Would he sink deep into despair and hopelessness again? Worse, would he try to rescue her?

Of course he would. If he would go to such lengths as he had to rescue the unknown governess of Anne's sons, how much farther would he go to rescue his wife?

"Thee must know that my husband will try to find me."

He nodded. "If 'e does, 'e'll find me men armed and ready."

Wild Jack Burdett, whose ear had been pressed to the door, sprang back as if it had been thoroughly

boxed. Ole Jem's men were on armed guard. Cor! He
were in the devil of a spot. He'd followed Ole Jem and
the Quakin' Lady from Blue Ruin Alley and never no-
ticed those men about. That was what easy living did
to a man. Made him soft as the pillows he slept on!
And here the Quakin' Lady was took, and only him to
tell his Honor where she was. He spun like a top,
charging for the stairs and hugging the wall to lessen
the creaking of the worn steps.

One-Eyed Will appeared on the landing, two pistols
stuck in his belt, his single eye bright with suspicion.
"What are ye after, lad?"

Wild Jack's cunning mind whipped into gear. Will
was unaware that Jack was no longer a part of the flash
ken. Boys disappeared and reappeared regularly. No
doubt that was why they'd let him pass going up the
stairs. "Milling-Jemmy says the lady's peckish. 'E's
sent me ter market."

"Well, get along with ye." He turned to shout down
the stairs. "Ben, leave the lad go."

Wild Jack sped out into the night, mapping the
placement of each of the men. In the street, he ran, his
heart pumping like his legs—until a hand whipped out
of an alleyway and clamped onto his collar, jerking him
up short.

"Lemme go, ye scurvy cove! Lemme go!" He lashed
out with fists and feet, until the point of a knife dug
beneath his chin. He went still, his breath scraping in
and out of his throat, urgency pressing him to look for
any opening to escape.

"Stubble it!" said Stork of Blue Ruin Alley. "Billy
Buck's sent me ter watch after the lady."

"Why?" asked Jack suspiciously.

"She midwifed 'is babe. Reckons 'e owes 'er fer 'is
Nance's life." Stork spit into the gutter and nodded
up the street. "What's 'appenin'?"

"Lemme go," said Wild Jack, shrugging from his
grasp. "Can ye bring men ter watch that none come
or go? Milling-Jemmy's snabbled the lady, and I've got
ter tell his Honor."

Stork motioned a man out of the depths of the alley. "Ye 'eard? Tell Billy Buck." Stork clapped Jack on the back. "Get on with ye, boy. We'll not let a flea through."

Aye, thought Wild Jack, racing away. Billy Buck would be glad to do himself a favor while helping the Quakin' Lady. If he could rid himself of Milling-Jemmy, he'd be cock o' the walk in Spitalfields.

"Thistlewood! Damn you, man! Where—" Robbie, white to the lips, his eyes burning with violet fire, leapt at his startled butler the moment he appeared from belowstairs. Robbie had been driven by fear from Grosvenor Square by Henry Hick's solemn statement that Milling-Jemmy Shadwell was hiding out in Friend Ephraim Fell's. He tried to tell himself that if Tabitha had not yet come to harm, it was unlikely she would. Shadwell had had opportunities enough before now. But he could not rest until he had seen her, touched her, assured himself that she was safe. "Is Tabitha here?"

"No, milord," said Thistlewood, and Robbie's hope vanished like a dust plume in the wind. "She left early this morning for Medway Street, though the children did return later . . ."

"Then is Jack here?" Robbie asked urgently.

"No, milord. He seemed in some anxiety to see you, and when he learned you were not to home, he left again."

"Damn! Send footmen to the Seymours in Berkeley Square and to Darenth House inquiring after Tabitha. Tell them to make all haste." Robbie spun for the door. "I shall return and expect word from them."

He leapt onto his high-perch phaeton, shaking his head at Stark. "She's not there."

Nor was she in Medway Street, though the housekeeper, Mrs. Plate, had much to say that pushed Robbie over the line from quivering apprehension to outright terror.

"He came in the mornin', yer lordship, he did. Wouldn't give his name to me, but Friend Tabby will turn none from the door. She saw him, she did, then left with him. And he was a fearful mean-lookin' man, yer lordship. Skinny as a fence paling and tall as the door, with gimlet eyes what could chill a body to the bone. But she don't listen to me, yer lordship. I told her not to go."

"Go where?" Robbie asked impatiently.

"Why, to Blue Ruin Alley, yer lordship. Billy Buck's doxy was droppin' a babe."

Robbie's breath left him in a huff, as if he had been kicked in the belly. "Stark," he said to the fully armed man at his side, "who the hell is Billy Buck?"

"A hedgebird, yer lordship, what has his own gang in Spitalfields. He'd like nothin' better than to see our man laid low." Stark looked at Mrs. Plate. "Ye have a man here by the name of Milling-Jemmy Shadwell?"

"No, sir, we don't. We've only Jem to fetch and tote."

"Big as a mountain, coal-black hair?"

"That's him, sir."

"Is he here now?"

"Odd you should ask, sir. Jem's been a blessing, never drunk on gin and always dependable-like. But we haven't seen him since yesterday."

Robbie lashed his high-steppers into the Almonry. No Tabby.

God! He had to find her soon. He had to know that she was safe. He couldn't, wouldn't, lose her now.

The tiny parlor in Queen Anne's Gate was stuffed to bursting when Robbie and Stark strode in, planning to make one last check there before heading for Blue Ruin Alley. The Seymours had arrived, she as plump as a dumpling and he with his fringe of hair standing straight out around his long, lugubrious face. The earl and the countess were there, Anne and Karl, even Cousin Knox, who had been visiting when the footman had arrived to inquire after Tabitha.

They were all huddled around a chair in the parlor,

making such a din that Robbie's arrival went unnoticed until his mother looked around. "My dear, my dear, the news is dreadful."

They parted, leaving a path for him to approach the chair. Jack lay back, panting and sweating, his face flushed red and his clothes brown with dust. "Yer Honor—" He struggled up, wavering on his feet, gasping for air. "Milling-Jemmy's got the Quakin' Lady."

He'd been after her all along, just as Robbie had suspected. Though Jack assured him that Shadwell meant her no harm, it was little comfort. Robbie was too sick at heart and afraid for Tabitha. But beneath the sickness and fear lay a strength that had been tempered to steel. Though the rage spread like fire through his veins, it was neither ungovernable nor mindless, as it once would have been. Tabitha had done that for him, leeching away the formless anger against fate, rooting him firmly in the world, in her heart.

"Yer Honor"—Jack stood arrow-straight, his thin shoulders squared in a military stance—"I've known all along about Milling-Jemmy bein' at Friend Ephraim Fell's. Ye see, yer Honor, it were Ole Jem what set me ter watchin' the Quakin' Lady till 'e took 'isself off ter Medway Street ter 'ide from ye. I wanted ter tell ye, sir, but Ole Jem . . ." Jack paused, his green gaze beseeching Robbie. "Ole Jem, sir, 'e were good ter me and Tansy. 'E give us a place ter lay our 'eads of a night and kept us in peck and booze when me purse were thin. I wanted ter tell ye, yer Honor, but I . . . I couldn't turn cat in the pan on Milling-Jemmy."

Robbie knelt to the boy, his big sun-browned hands clasping Jack's shoulders. "It isn't easy to serve two masters, Jack. You did the best you could. That's all I could ask, but I must ask you now to help me in this."

"Aye, sir," said Jack.

Robbie stood in the dim, smoky light of the Spital-fields gin mill, where they had all gathered to plan their attack. Every man looked to him, for he wore a new authority, a ruthlessness born of necessity. The hedgebird Billy Buck rubbed shoulders with Stark of Bow Street, implacable enemies in uneasy harness. The Earl of Darenth, tall and spare, leaned on his cane, watching his son with a reawakening of his old pride. Karl, a lock of butter-yellow hair curling over his brow, checked the prime of his pistol with a cold blue gaze, reassuming the crisp and deadly mantle of the soldier-spy that he had once been. Robbie's hands rested on Jack's shoulders, where the whole of the plan would rest. Jack was the key to Tabitha's escape—as he never could have been had he not known Milling-Jemmy.

"Then it's set," Robbie said. "Karl, with five of Buck's men, will cover the back. Stark and Buck and the rest of the men will storm the front door. You will all wait ten minutes after Jack and I have entered, leaving us time to reach the top floor before warning can be given."

The men melted into the night, padding quietly into the back alleys to reach their positions unseen. Only the earl remained behind, too old for combat. His arctic-blue gaze met Robbie's with approval and the least darkening of fear. "Watch yourself, Robbie," he said, the closest he could come to saying, *I love you, my son.*

Minutes later Wild Jack Burdett, a sack over his shoulder, trotted down the street. Behind him came Robbie, garbed as a costermonger in stout boots, cable-cord trousers, and a corduroy jacket, with a gaudy silk *kingsman* tied at his throat. He pushed a handbarrow holding two small kegs of ale.

"Will!" Jack hailed his old mate, who slouched on the rickety steps. "Milling-Jemmy said ye might like a pottle o' ale to sluice yer gobs. I've me man 'ere ter take t'other keg up."

"Aye, lad," said One-Eyed Will, mopping his sweating face with his sleeve, "and 'twill be welcome. 'Tis a fair scorcher, the night."

Robbie hefted a keg onto his shoulder, pulling his cloth cap low over his brow and trudging slowly up the steps, in the manner of a weary costermonger.

"We 'aven't the night, mate," said Jack, nudging

Will in the ribs. "Aye, and if we 'ad to push a barrow, wouldn't we be quicker about it, Will? I've 'ad ter keep me eye on 'im from the market. I tell ye, Will, the costers ain't what they used ter be."

"Get on with ye, lad," said One-Eyed Will. "Milling-Jemmy don't take ter waitin'."

Jack slipped into the entryway and hurried ahead of Robbie, leading the way up the steep-turning stairs. The surreptitious signal of a finger pointing down his leg marked the placement of each of Milling-Jemmy's men.

At the top landing, Jack set a finger to his lips and pointed to the door. Robbie lowered the keg, careful to make no sound. He pulled the pistol from his waistband and the watch from his pocket, mouthing "Wait."

Sweat beaded on his brow, and his heart thudded against his ribs. Yes, now Karl should be at the back and Stark should be beginning his rush of the front. In moments Tabby would be out, and then he would never let her go. Robbie flattened himself against the wall, his pistol held up, and nodded at Jack, who hammered on the door.

"Milling-Jemmy," the boy called out, " 'tis me, Wild Jack."

"What are ye after, boy?" Shadwell's voice came like thunder through the door.

"The mates sent me up with a keg o' ale fer ye."

The key scraped in the lock, and Jack stepped away. On cue, shouts and curses rose from below. The door creaked open, Shadwell filling the portal, a giant of a man. Robbie swung around, his pistol pointing. "Make a move, and it will be your last."

Shadwell's pink mouth parted in a snarl that raised the hairs on Robbie's arms and vibrated through flesh and bone. The man's great paw swatted at the pistol. Robbie pulled the trigger. The gun exploded in a burst of flame and smoke, and a blossom of blood bloomed in the thick meat of Shadwell's shoulder. He caught Robbie's wrist and gave it a twist that set the bones to cracking and snapping, sending a fireball of pain shooting up his arm. The pistol hit the wooden floor with a loud crack, and Robbie dropped to his knees, his free hand scrabbling for his knife.

Wild Jack shrieked and fell on the thick trunk of Shadwell's leg, wrapping himself around it and biting with his teeth. Shadwell plucked him off like a feather from a goose and tossed him onto the landing—gently, it seemed—but Jack hit the wall shaking the old timbers and crumpling into a heap.

Robbie fought to get the knife free. Shadwell kicked it from his hand, numbing his fingers. David and Goliath meeting. Goliath winning. Robbie saw the thick knee coming at his chin, tried to dodge it, and failed. He caught a single glimpse of Tabitha, her skirts hiked to her knees, her mouth rounded in a long, shrill "Nooo," before his teeth clacked together and pain crackled through his jaw and darkness swooped down like a falcon from the sky.

Tabitha, forgetting the teachings of her faith, hurtled across the chamber and beat her small fists against the broad, hard-muscled sweep of Jem's back. He had hurt her beloved Robbie. He had hurt her proud Jack. He had roused in her the deepest instinct a woman possesses, one that responds to neither reason nor rule: the instinct to protect her mate and her nurslings—the same instinct that was driving Milling-Jemmy.

He spun her around, catching her wrists. Gently, so gently, he reined in the strength that could have crushed her every fragile bone. It weren't going like 'e'd planned. Not at all like 'e'd planned. She should have been happy. She should have welcomed the light. But she didn't understand what he was doing for her. She wasn't glad. Instead, she was afraid. Afraid of him.

"Enough, woman!" he roared, giving her a little shake that snapped her head and whipped the breath from her lungs.

Tabitha hung from his hands, her eyes starred with tears, her heartbeat wild and unsteady. She blinked, slowly returning from the mad and mindless rage that had consumed her. "I pray thee," she pleaded, "let me go. Let me see to my husband and the boy."

His grip tightened the least bit, and she winced under the pressure of bone grating against bone. He couldn't let her go. She must see that. "Ye'll come with me, for I'll give ye the light. I'll keep ye safe, as he"—Milling-Jemmy threw a hard look over his shoulder at the Nob's sprawling body—"has not. I've got ter do for ye what I could not for her."

He dragged Tabitha through the door, across Robbie's body. She hung back, watching for some sign that he still lived, but Jem tugged her along, heading for the old servant's stair in the back. Rising from below, up the front stairwell, came the sounds of a pitched battle, the coarse shouts of men, the popping of pistol shots. Pray God, Robbie's men would win the day and save him, she thought, stumbling down the narrow stairs behind Jem.

She lost her balance and tumbled down a trio of steps to the landing. Milling-Jemmy cursed vilely and hefted her beneath an arm, carrying her like an empty sack. She should have been glad. She would have had the light and her Bible. What more could she need? But she was kicking and squirming and trying to escape him. Why would she do that?

He raced down the stairs, reaching the ground floor, heading along the narrow hall toward the back door.

At the top of the house, Robbie was rudely jolted into consciousness by a weight that landed heavily on his chest, by the clenching of claws that dug into his ribs, by a yowl that was the unmistakable hallmark of that fiendish feline whose sole mission seemed to be to make his life hell. He sat up with a start, hearing Monsieur's claws scrabbling across the wooden floor, catching a glimpse of marmalade fur vanishing down the stairwell at the far end of the hall.

His wrist felt as it were on fire, every move seeming to send shards of bone like knives through his flesh.

His teeth hurt, his jaw ached, and his head throbbed. He must have been hit with an anvil! He rolled to the side, climbing up the wall, stumbling across to Jack, and prodding him with a toe. He didn't dare bend over with his head spinning.

"Jack, lad, Jack."

The boy stirred, moaning softly. He was alive, and help should be coming soon. Robbie could hear Stark shouting below. He turned and stumbled toward the back stairs. How long had he been unconscious? Where was Tabby now? Tabby, who had launched herself at Shadwell's back like a maddened Fury. That unbelievable sight seemed of a piece with the nightmare of this night.

Gritting his teeth, Robbie bounded down the stairs two at a time, every footfall sending agonizing bolts of pain like lightning from his shattered wrist, from his bruised but—thank God!—not broken jaw.

He reached the ground floor. Ahead he saw Monsieur, his back arched, his hair at attention, his hisses and howls echoing eerily from floor to wall.

A moment later Milling-Jemmy appeared, backing out of a side hall with Tabitha tucked under his arm. Robbie leapt ahead, but Shadwell sidestepped to a door and passed through, closing it behind him.

Karl came charging out of the side hall, his pistol cocked and pointing. "Where the hell did he go? I couldn't shoot for fear of hitting Tabitha."

"Here." Robbie wrenched at the door, which would not open, He slammed a shoulder into it and went white with pain.

"Here." Karl thrust him aside and rammed his shoulder against it. Again and again, until it cracked and splintered, releasing into the hall a foul and fetid stench, the familiar odor of the sewer that ran below, beneath the cellar floor.

Karl looked to Robbie, his eyes diamond-bright and hard. "Do you think he'll take her—"

"There's nowhere else to go."

* * *

"No! No! Not there!" Tabitha cried out, clinging desperately to the flimsy stair railing leading down into the black, malodorous bowels of the cellar. She'd kicked and writhed and twisted, trying to break his hold, succeeding only in exhausting herself. But now, with the putrid odor summoning slithering memories, beady-eyed memories, terrifying memories of the sewer, she found new strength. Splinters dug into her palms, but she held on while Jem yanked at her. A crack, a split, and the railing screamed away from the posts.

Milling-Jemmy rushed down the stairs toward the dim and ghoulish light of a crusie lamp. He had prepared his escape route in case of a rescue attempt, but it was dangerous one, for the sewers running beneath Spitalfields were ancient and crumbling relics. He scooped up a waiting torch, set it to the flame, and waited for it to catch, then slammed it into a waiting bracket.

"I pray thee," Tabitha whispered, unable to do more, "let me go. Thee will not be harmed. I will see to that. Let me go."

He grunted for answer, digging the heavy toe of his boot beneath the trapdoor, sending it flying back and thudding against the floor. In dark corners the screechings and scurryings of unseen creatures began, sending horrified chills scrambling over Tabitha's skin.

He lowered her to the floor, capturing her wrists in his hands. She pulled back, dragging with all her strength. "I pray thee," she begged, "don't do this. I am afraid, so afraid."

He paused for a moment, a hesitant light in his eyes, a dull curiosity carving the creases of a frown into his brow. "Yer a witless woman, a flat," he said. "Can't ye see I'm doin' this for ye? Ye told me yerself that I've got the gift of strength."

"But I meant that thee should use it for the children, for the weak . . ." She began, desperate to make him understand.

He swung her up, dangling her over the opening, lowering her to the sluggish stream below. "Get yer

feet under ye, woman," he said. "I'm goin' ter drop
ye now."

Above, footsteps pounded down the stairs.

"Robbie! Robbie!" Tabitha screamed as Shadwell released her. Her feet settled into the muck, the water
soaking through her skirts, clinging clammily to her
legs. The hot, turbid mist closed around her, like the
claustrophobic brick-walled tunnel, five feet tall,
shaped like an egg, its walls slick and slimy. Something slithered around her foot, and she stumbled to
the side, her arm swinging out, her hand banging into
the arching wall. The mortar had long since been eaten
away. Now the ancient brick, rotted by the acidic mist,
disintegrated before her eyes, crumbling and pouring
into the gray sludge of the stream.

Jem dropped down beside her, the torch in his hand,
Robbie's bellow following him down: "Shadwell, you
can't get away with her! Let her go!"

Jem scooped her up under his arm like a mother with
a toddler and splashed away in the knee-deep water,
parting the thick, swirling mist. Tabitha trembled uncontrollably, splattered and splashed as she was carried speedily past the moldy, slick walls. The bricks
had in places crumbled away to the dark earth and
clay, leaving ragged-edged holes like gaping mouths.

"Shadwell!" Robbie's voice came full-bodied and
strong, echoing down the tunnel. "Shadwell!" he repeated, seeing his quarry turn, seeing more that made
his blood run cold—Shadwell's torch brushed a colony
of rats living in a collapsed niche in the tunnel wall.

Skittering and squealing, they attacked Milling-
Jemmy's back. Needle-sharp teeth bit through his thick
coat and shirt, tearing at his flesh. He lurched away
with a masculine roar of pain and rage, and the torch
hit the low ceiling like a bludgeon. It began to crumble,
slowly, ominously, the trickles of rotten brick and mortar quickly becoming streams.

He couldn't escape the rats; he couldn't protect the
woman. He stumbled and fell, and the torch dug into
the rotten brick of the opposite wall. Wet, sandy gran-

ules sifted down, faster and faster, eating away the footing of the brick above. It fell with a splash, then another and another. Still he grasped the woman, whose screams echoed from the walls, battering at his ears, while he struggled up, blundering into the wall, setting up another rain of sodden brick dust. He started to run but realized with a start that he was facing in the wrong direction, facing the Nob—who was running, running toward him.

"Shadwell! Let her go! My God, man! Let her go!" Robbie struggled against the current, hunched beneath the low ceiling, his eyes not on Shadwell, not on Tabitha, but on the fissures forming in the ceiling above them, on the surface that was flaking away in a steady and pitiless shower of grit and sand. He was unaware of the darkness, of the fears that had once beset him. His every thought, his every fear, was for Tabitha. He'd never reach her in time!

Shadwell paused in the mist, the torch clasped in one hand, the woman hanging from his arm, while the rats swarmed around his knees and the brick dust continued to rain down around him. The woman was screaming, writhing, twisting, kicking at the wall—and the wall, like the ceiling, was breaking away.

A brick fell from the ceiling, grazing his cheek. Another hit his shoulder, followed by a clump of sodden clay. He twisted around and saw the bricks shuddering above, as if the pressure of the earth was at last winning the battle of centuries. A rupture appeared, the mortar giving way, the bricks gaping like teeth, and he raised himself up, bowing his back, setting it to the ceiling as a brace.

Still he could not let the woman go, even when she arched around, her eyes meeting his. The weight above bore down on his back. Sweat formed on his brow. There was no escape. When he moved, the ceiling would come tumbling down. But he had sworn to protect the woman. Why, he couldn't remember. He only knew she must come to no harm. Her eyes staring into his, glittering in the torchlight, must never wear the expression of terror that filled them now.

He released her and pushed her away, his hamlike hand on the small of her back. Pushed her toward the Nob, saying, "Run, woman, run!"

Tabitha splashed through the water, uncaring of the sleek-skinned rats, long-tailed and swimming in beady-eyed hordes. She ran toward Robbie, her arms outstretched, meeting him, melting into his welcoming arms, trembling against his warm body, protected from the rats by the torch Karl held out in front of them.

"Tabby, Tabby," Robbie whispered brokenly, lifting her up and thrusting her at Karl. "Take her above. Take her above now. We can't leave him here—"

Behind him the tunnel groaned, as if it were a living being whose flesh was tearing away. Single bricks plopped into the gray sludge. Whole sections dropped with a splash. Clots of clay fell with a sucking sound. A seam appeared in the ceiling. A seam that groaned and spread, moving up the tunnel toward them.

"Run, Tabby, Karl. Run!" Robbie shouted, but he couldn't leave the man.

Shadwell, his back still arched against the ceiling, had fallen to his knees. But he continued to watch, his eyes black and glittering—whether with hate or something else, Robbie couldn't tell.

"Go!" bellowed Shadwell. "Go to the woman!"

Still Robbie hesitated. Why? Why had he kidnapped Tabitha, then saved her? Saved her at the expense of his own life.

"Go!" Milling-Jemmy, his teeth gritted against the strain, the sweat pouring from him in rivers, watched the Nob hesitate, while the bricks fell around him. "Go," Milling-Jemmy whispered, the pressure tearing at the muscles of his back, of his thighs.

At last the Nob turned and blended with the mist.

Milling-Jemmy was alone, his head pressed down to his knees, the earth exerting its deadly and inexorable weight. He wasn't afraid. He'd never suffered the fears of other men. She was safe. The woman was safe. His mission was done.

It seemed he could feel a gentle hand at his brow, a gentle voice whispering in his ear. "Jemmy-boy," the voice said, softly, sweetly, "it's time for thee to come home. Reach out thy hand and come with me into the Light."

Karl hoisted Tabitha up through the trapdoor and climbed after her, reaching back to pull Robbie up. Below, the tunnel shivered and shook, the cave-in rumbling through the foundations of the house.

Tabitha threw herself into Robbie's arms, shivering and weeping softly. "Love," he murmured, "why? Why did he do it?"

"He . . . he wanted to protect me. To protect me," she whispered wildly. "Dear Lord and Saviour, take him to thy bosom."

Robbie's gaze drifted to the trapdoor, to the crumbled mass of bricks and earth below. To protect her. Had Shadwell, too, recognized the treasure that Tabitha was?

He held her away to study her face in the dim light of the crusie lamp: the dirt-smudged curve of her cheek, the long sweep of her lashes, the silvery mist of her eyes, the tremulous curve of her mouth. "I love you, Tabby," he whispered, soft and low.

She smiled, her hand touching his face, her fingers trembling against his cheek, her thumb coasting over his lips. "I love thee, Robbie," she murmured, sliding into his arms.

He cradled her close and peace stole through him, as serene as moonlight, as gentle and gentling as his Tabby, as tranquil as the Light that welcomed Milling-Jemmy Shadwell.

Epilogue

May 1826
Schattenburg

Teams of straining horses towed the barge up the winding Neckar on a journey Robbie had never expected to make again. But he owed Tabitha a second honeymoon—the first had hardly deserved the name—and she wanted to visit Anne, while he needed to prove something to himself. He wanted to see Schattenburg, to summon the memories, to ensure that the last of the ghosts had been laid to rest. He wanted to test his hard-won peace.

Hour after hour they moved against the sluggish current through sinuous walls of red sandstone crowned by a dark and brooding primeval forest. On occasion a hamlet drifted by, the window boxes of its half-timbered houses sporting gay arrangements of geraniums, lobelias, and marigold. Stilt-legged herons stood on gravel shoals. Ducks feasted on the waterweeds, sailing through the reeds and the water forget-me-nots. The very air breathed of unspoken mysteries, but it was the mystery of his wife that held Robbie enthralled.

There was a fresh bloom to her cheeks, a secret in her eyes, a glow that emanated from deep within, as if from a closely held joy. She seemed different somehow, still complacent and serene but with a new and shimmering excitement. He watched her and smiled, for he could do little else. Her mood was infectious.

He closed his eyes, listening to the tromp of the horses, the ripple of the water, the distant scream of a falcon on the wing. A grand and glorious bird, keen-eyed, long-winded, courageous—and untamable. He would have to give up his sobriquet, for he had been thoroughly—Old Nick would say disgustingly—tamed. He'd found his greatest pleasure in rusticating at Langleyholm with a growing brood of Tabitha's adopted strays.

Dog and her whelps, having long since discovered his tenants' chickens, were want to embark on an orgy of barking and chasing that roused the mild-mannered Surrey farmers to near revolt. Robbie always assumed his severest manner with a flop-eared pup, but found it hard to maintain his gravity when it frisked around his boots, assuming an innocent air with a betraying feather sticking to its lolling tongue. Dog and her whelps had been removed from temptation. Full-grown now, they were being outrageously spoiled by the tiny tots in Medway Street and the Almonry.

Monsieur—Robbie's gaze rolled to the side, narrowly eyeing the ball of marmalade fur curled up in Tabitha's lap—had expended every effort to impregnate every tabby in the environs of Queen Anne's Gate and Langleyholm. Little Monsieurs seemed to be tumbling and hissing everywhere Robbie went—a lowering prospect.

He'd looked forward to his travels *sans* the irritating, aggravating feline, but no sooner had their ship sailed out of Dover than Tabitha had discovered Monsieur—stowed away in her willow embroidery basket. Heartlessly giggling over Robbie's chagrin, she had assured him that the cat was a small cross to bear in a life that was so full. Robbie thought that a matter of perspective, and hers was skewed.

They had sailed first to Italy, where Cousin Knox had taken Henry Hicks to recover from his lung ailment. She'd always wanted to see the country, she said, and the cold winters of England gave her rheu-

matic complaints. They were an unlikely pair, but surprisingly well matched. She bullied him mercilessly,
and he adored her.

"Thou art smiling," Tabitha said, reaching out to
touch Robbie's hand.

"I was thinking of Henry and Cousin Knox."

She smiled, her eyes sparkling. "He is so good for
her."

"I should have said that she was good for him."

"She is lonely, Robbie, and childless. He is the answer to her prayers, a child whom she can love."

"And bully," he said, grinning.

"But that is how Friend Arabella shows her love."

Robbie raised Tabitha's hand to his lips, caressing it
with a kiss. "I shall have to inform Father. He's spent
the last half-century and more thinking she despised
him."

"What a wretched man thou art," she said, laughing
softly. "Thee knows very well that they have an understanding. They enjoy their verbal fisticuffs too much
to ever give them up."

"Let me say, my love, that I give thanks every day
that you are cast in a gentler mold."

The dimples quivered in her cheeks. "Every day?"

He eyed her askance, admitting to himself that there
had been occasions when he did not give thanks. When
he'd returned her to Queen Anne's Gate from the
sewer in Spitalfields, when he'd found relief replaced
by a towering rage, he had demanded her reason for
hiding Shadwell's presence at Friend Ephraim Fell's.
He had been afraid that, once again, she had not
trusted him enough; he'd learned instead that she
loved him too well. Had Shadwell been hung by
the authorities, she had said, it would have been at the
direction of Robbie's hand. She didn't want that resting on his conscience—as if it would have. Another
reminder, and not the last, that his wife's *gentler mold*
was foreign to him.

"Ah, yes. I'm trying to be brutally honest. I forgot."

He cast her a wicked look, suppressing his smile. "Perhaps not *every* day."

"I remember quite well the day I brought Baby Belle home. Thee was—"

"Writing my first speech for the House of Commons. I ask you, my love, if any but a saint could maintain his equanimity when his brilliant introductory passage had been torn to shreds and eaten—"

"She didn't eat it. She simply chewed it up and spit it out."

"I rest my case."

"She said it was good," Tabitha coaxed.

"No doubt, had she been able to say the word, she would have said it was brilliant, too," he added wryly.

"Of course," Tabitha touched his cravat, running her finger along his chin. "Thee cannot convince me that thee regrets my bringing Baby Belle home."

Belle with her big brown spaniel eyes, sturdy and shy, so unlike Tansy, so needful of love. How could he regret it when she pressed a wet kiss to his cheek and ran her tiny fingers through his side-whiskers and fell asleep in his lap with her hand tightly grasping is lapel, as if she were afraid he wouldn't be there when she awoke.

Tabitha sighed softly, looking away to the green and fertile banks sliding past. "I wonder how the children are doing at Darenth Hall."

"Jack has a tutor and a horse, which is all he needs to be happy. Tansy has my father wrapped around her least finger. I vow the man is besotted with her. And Belle has captured my mother's heart so thoroughly, she might not give her back to us. Then, of course, there is the family Fell—"

"I know," she said, looping her arm through his and smiling up with that inner glow that radiated warmth like the sun. "They are in the best of hands, but I miss them."

"We shan't be here long—"

At a shout from the deckhand, Robbie looked ahead. The village of Schattenhausen huddled on a crescent

of land at the foot of the precipitous slopes of the Reisenberg, a pine and beech-clad mountain. Curling
around a loop of the river was a single row of triple-
storied half-timbered houses, whitewashed and decorated with pale ocher beams and stays. Old men
gathered around doorways. Old women plucked chickens. Children played in the long street.

Far above, on the lush green cast of the Reisenberg,
stood the ancient castle called Schattenburg, wreathed
in evening mist. A series of curtain walls snaked down
the mountainside, each of a brighter red sandstone,
each more recently constructed. In a dim and dank cy-
lindrical tower of the lowest wall, Robbie had been enclosed in a crypt for more than a year.

He stood on the barge, moving to the prow, staring
up at the steep slopes studying the turreted castle
where he had suffered so much pain and despair. So
little did the memory touch him, it might have happened to another man.

Tabitha rested her hand on his arm, her serene gaze
searching his. He covered her hand with his palm,
smiling gently while his violet gaze returned to the curtain walls. "Yes," he said softly, answering her unspoken question, "the ghosts are laid to rest."

The silence and peace of sweet contentment flowed
around him like the fog gathering on the river's surface. He breathed deep of the resinous fragrance of the
forest and the fishy odor of the lazy Neckar, and he
knew he could not ask more of life than he had already
received.

"Robbie," said Tabitha, a quivering excitement in her
voice, "I have something to tell thee. Something I have
waited to tell thee here, because I wanted to give thee
a happy memory of Schattenburg."

The smile that she turned up to him was one he had
seen before, one that looked as if every drop of happiness that could be found in the world had been distilled for her alone.

"I am expecting a child, our child," she said.

Robbie stared at her sparkling eyes and her smiling

mouth, remembering the time when he would rather have been hung drawn and quartered than to take a wife and sire an heir. What a fool he had been! Slowly, the stunned spaces of his mind filled with the knowledge that he was to be a father. It was, surprisingly, an intoxicating thought.

He caught Tabitha around the waist and held her high in the air, swirling around the flat deck of the barge, his ebony curls flying and his violet eyes shining and his hearty laugh sending the moorhens scurrying along the riverbank. At length he set her down and clasped her to his pounding heart. He'd received all he thought he could ask for of life, but now he was to be given still more.

"Thou art happy," Tabitha whispered.

"I am blessed beyond anything I deserve," he said, wondering at the excitement glowing in her eyes, as if she yet held a secret she was eager to share.

"Perhaps doubly blessed." She gazed up at him, a smile trembling on her mouth. "Did I forget to mention to thee that twins run in my family?"